CRISIS IN BIG-G CITY

(Book Four in the Small-g City series)
S. D. Matley

WolfSinger Publications ⸹ Brackettville, Texas

ackNOWLeOGemeNTS

It takes many people to write a novel, and I've had plenty of help along the way.

For technical matters I turned to Vic Vanderbilt (thanks for cluing me in on Sabrett hot dogs!) and Cheryl Richmond-Witwer (cherry crop harvest expert).

Thanks to Jannelle and Ben and all the wonderful folks at Book & Game, Walla Walla, WA, for encouraging my literary efforts, carrying my books, and hosting me and many local authors at book signing events. Likewise, to David at Earthlight Books in Walla Walla whose labyrinth of new and used books has stirred the heart of many a bibliophile. Thanks also to the Walla Walla Country Rural Library District for acquiring the "G" series for their collection, and for including me in their 50th anniversary speaker series to present "Myth-Taken Identities: Using the Greek Pantheon in Fiction."

Eternal thanks to my critique partner and friend, Martin McCaw, aka the Line Editor from Hell. His influence on my writing is incalculable, his patience is boundless, and I'm pretty sure he's starting to actually enjoy the fantasy genre.

Undying thanks to Carol Hightshoe, Editor and Publisher at WolfSinger Publications, for having faith in me, and in *Small-g City*, and never looking back.

DEDICATION

To everyone who enjoys reading. Read this!

FRIDAY, DECEMBER 12, 2025

City of Mount Olympus

Hermes leaned against the elevator wall, his drooping shoulders and dark-circled eyes reflected in polished metal. He looked like goat droppings, no wonder after days of nonstop pleading with Monique. Late last night, probably just to get rid of him, she'd at last agreed to stay in Mount Olympus through the winter holidays before spiriting P. B. off to her new post—WomanFront's Beta Village in the mortal desert. Hermes hadn't slept well for days, wracked with worry about how she'd manage to take care of a baby—their baby—while running a brand new microlending bank.

Fifth floor, sixth floor. His eyes blinked closed. Hermes shook himself awake. Why, after fathering dozens of children over dozens of centuries, had he been hooked by this one? P. B. wasn't even half his, only a quarter. The baby had a second biological father, an evil force known as The Power, who'd recently been absorbed into the Chair of Forgetfulness in the Underworld.

Seventh floor, eighth floor. Must be a sign of age. Always before he'd flitted from lover to lover, from invention to invention, perpetually liberated from the present and driven by the urge to see what came next. Now he rose early every morning (if he slept at all) to receive a chilly reception from Monique and spend an hour with their son before work.

The thought of P. B.'s baby eyes, fixed on his, was the only thing that kept Hermes going. It was as if his son knew Hermes and all of Olympus, Inc., was mobilizing to defeat climate change. If mortals ceased to exist, so would the gods who served them. If they didn't succeed and the mortals drove themselves extinct, P. B. might never see his five-hundredth birthday.

Ninth floor. Continental Managers, also the Director of Armed Forces: Athena, the bane of his existence. The elevator doors parted. The receptionist, in deep conversation on her digital device, nodded and waved him through. He could walk blindfolded to Athena's private office; he'd been there so many times. Veronica, the Olympus, Inc., CEO, had assigned Athena the strategic piece of the War Against Climate Change. Summoned to daily meetings, Hermes felt like her lackey.

A wall covered with masks, Nyctimene (aka Tim) the owl opposite on his perch, the Goddess of War and Wisdom at her desk in between.

"Good morning, Hermes," Athena said in a flat tone that made him feel like she was describing a specimen under a microscope. "You look whipped."

"All in the name of progress," he bluffed. "Waller has so many new initiatives going it takes half a day to sign authorizations. Green World Works has as many heads as the Hydra."

Actually, that wasn't true. The Hydra, a gigantic water snake, only had nine heads.

"And your own projects regarding the fossil fuel industry on top of that," Athena added. The owl muttered a drowsy hoot from his perch.

Hermes had made several trips to the mortal world lately, working alongside inventors as an invisible muse, people who pursued carbon sequestration, more safe and efficient nuclear power plants, biofuels, wind, solar. A promising new technology, Living Breakwaters, was being implemented by the mortal landscape architect Kate Orff. All of these could help reverse climate change, but as far as being scalable in a short time frame? Even in combination they were far from all that was needed. What was needed was—

"Take a look at this dossier, Hermes, from our Secret Ops department."

Athena slid a digital tablet across the desk. A file named east.cyril. and.edwin was on the screen.

"East Fossil Fuels?" Hermes shook his head. He'd haunted their massive R & D department just last week. "Those guys are impenetrable."

In addition to his on-site visit, Hermes had read everything he could find online about the East brothers, the biggest oil magnates in North America. Not only were they reported as major grantors to carbon sequestration science, their personal lives were squeaky-clean. No marriages, divorces, children or affairs. No gambling or boozing or recreational drugs. One of them had been Secretary of Energy under an American president.

The corners of Athena's eyes crinkled. "Not completely, as it turns out. Reconnaissance picked up something we can run with. If we can infiltrate their operation with someone highly intelligent, naturally inquisitive, and skilled in both business and scientific method, someone who inspires confidence and trust in an employer, we might find a means to disrupt their exorbitant levels of fossil fuel extraction." She raised an eyebrow. "Does anyone come to mind?"

Someone did, but Hermes wasn't going to name her. He needed her in the Digital Devices and Robotics Department, running experiments in the lab and, he admitted to himself, lending moral support. Her six-month leave of absence should have been over by now, but it had been extended, with CEO Veronica Zeta's approval, by two weeks so she could spend some idiotic mortal holiday with the Bernstein twerp.

Athena snapped her fingers, summoning the owl to her shoulder. She stroked the bird's feathers. Her silver eyes plunged deep into Hermes'.

"Hermes," Athena said against his tight-lipped silence, "I'm sending in Cleo Petra."

SUNDAY, DECEMBER 14, 2025

Seattle, Washington, USA

Cleo Petra and David Bernstein stood hand in hand on the sidewalk in front of the Parthenon Building, waiting for a taxi. Their Seattle hosts, Jim and Candy Smith, lived in the building's penthouse, with a panoramic view of Elliott Bay.

Cleo's cell phone vibrated in her windbreaker pocket.

A text from Hermes, cc: Veronica.

Extended leave cancelled. Return to Mt. Oly ASAP. Critical climate work requires your personal skills.

For David's benefit Cleo said, "Shit."

What she actually felt was relief. David had sweetly invited her to spend Chanukah with him and Saul Crispin, his recently discovered father. Her gut told her she should have declined, that after two thousand years of separation the men needed time alone to get to know each other. But the visceral and emotional thrill of romantic love, what she and David had danced around for months and at last confessed to each other the morning after Saul was found, tugged her toward Saul's studio apartment in New York City to celebrate the Jewish festival of lights.

David set his suitcase on the pavement and slipped his arms around her waist. The newness of his embrace sent a tingle through her body. "Bad news?"

"Bad enough. Looks like I need to change my flight." Her backpack was heavy with Seattle souvenirs she'd purchased as holiday gifts—a small bronze statue of Clifford's former haunt, the Space Needle, for Veronica; a Starbuck's mug for Hermes; Fran's Gold Bars for Roderick Waller, who had a sweet tooth and had subbed for her at Olympus, Inc., during her leave of absence.

"Not your folks?" David said.

"No, thank goodness." Peter and Titania Petra both enjoyed vibrant good health. "Work."

David withdrew his arms, the silence between them cold. Her shoulders tensed under the tug of backpack straps. He'd confessed his jealousy of Cleo's boss, Hermes. She'd tried to reassure him there was not and had never been anything romantic between her and the brilliant bad boy of Olympus, Inc. It rankled that David didn't quite believe her. She took a breath to ease her frustration and searched for diplomatic words.

"Hermes cc'd Veronica on the text. It must be something crucial to the climate change initiative."

Honestly, she was grateful to be called back. Her employment following her six-month leave was guaranteed but there'd been no promise she would return to her same beloved job, or even to the same department.

"Doesn't he have enough to do, looking after the baby?" David said.

"Like you have room to talk! *You* could just as easily have been its father."

It flew from her mouth without thought, her jealousy of Monique, the mirror of David's hatred for Hermes.

David spun toward her, head tilted defiantly up, their faces nose to nose. "It was one night!"

They'd promised each other not to bring up his one-night-stand with Monique Reynard, the baby's mother. Or any previous romantic encounters for either of them. Even after blissful weeks together in romantic Seattle, the wounds of not being the first remained illogically deep. But how could she help it, by Zeus? The thought of David with that Monique creature, even though it happened before she, herself, had become his lover, made her roil inside.

"You don't trust me," she fired at him before she had time to regret it. He didn't answer.

Cleo turned toward Third Avenue. She shivered, the bracing December damp penetrating her windbreaker. It was going to be a long taxi ride to Seattle-Tacoma International Airport.

MONDAY, DECEMBER 15, 2025

City of Mount Olympus

Eighteen hours after takeoff Cleo deplaned at Athens International. Thank Heaven and Earth her flight had routed through Atlanta, Georgia, and Amsterdam instead of New York City. Not having to endure David's chilly silence (he'd broken it once, a terse goodbye when they'd arrived at the Sea-Tac ticketing area) made even an epic day of travel desirable.

I don't need this and I don't need him!

Maybe. Tears choked her throat with the silent declaration.

And now she was nearly home. Cleo followed purple-tinted signage only the gods could see to their exclusive waiting room, what looked like a broom closet to mortal eyes. When her suitcase arrived, she shouldered her backpack and caught the next available high-speed chariot to the behind-the-scenes City of Mount Olympus.

The sun was setting as she turned the key in her apartment door. Low pink light flooded her west-facing studio in the fashionable New Mycenae district, a place she could have afforded when she'd first arrived in the city as a college student but had opted for dormitories to conceal her considerable family wealth. Dad was a son of Poseidon (one of thousands, if you believed the rumors) and Mother was of central European royalty. None of her immortal friends, bosses or co-workers knew this. Except for David.

Zeus on a crutch! She'd almost stopped thinking about him. Him! How dare he doubt her faithfulness? If he were here right now she'd… she'd…

Cleo dropped her suitcase and threw herself face down on the natural-fiber upholstered beige sofa, her backpack sliding perilously sideways, and sobbed until she felt hollow inside. They'd both been asses, she knew it. She knew it! But…

She rolled to a sitting position, wrestled her way out of the backpack straps, and wiped her face with the back of her hand. It was past quitting time at Olympus, Inc., but Hermes might still be there. She powered up her cell phone, having turned it off for landing, and selected his work number. It was picked up in three rings.

"Department of Digital Devices and Robotics, Hermes' office. Roderick Waller speaking."

"Oh." She took a few seconds to pivot. "Hi, Roderick. It's Cleo Petra. I'm back."

"Already?" His voice indicated surprise.

"Y-es. I…there was a text from Hermes yesterday, instructing me to come back as soon as possible."

"Interesting," Waller said. "We just confirmed next week's plan for the Green World Works campaign—"

"That's *you?*" The online platform had been absolutely everywhere the past few months. She'd never imagined it came from Olympus, Inc.

"It is." He laughed—nerves or confidence? "Perhaps there's been a misunderstanding. Have you checked your email recently?"

She noticed the envelope icon at the bottom of the screen, a 3 superimposed on top.

"I'll stop by tomorrow, Roderick, so we can sort this out." Was there an email from David? "See you in the morning." She ended the call before he could say goodbye.

The first email was Veronica, the second from Hermes, the third Veronica again. Hermes left instructions to meet him at Athena's office tomorrow morning, 8am. Was she being transferred? It made no sense, since she had no background in war or diplomacy.

Veronica's first email was an invitation to dinner for this evening, acknowledging she knew Cleo must be exhausted but…her other email said to meet her at Club Dionysus, 7pm. Cleo rubbed her hands over her face and let out a huge sigh. She was physically and emotionally exhausted, and baffled by what her return to Olympus, Inc., would bring. Veronica, as her dear friend, would understand if she begged off, but Veronica was also the CEO.

Clifford's working late so it'll be just the two of us.

That cinched it. Veronica had gone to bat with Hermes to get Cleo her leave of absence in the first place, and again for the two-week extension. Numb with uncertainty about her future with David and her work in Digital Devices and Robotics, she dug the toiletries kit out of her backpack and trudged to the bathroom, praying to Heaven and Earth a shower and fresh makeup would restore her balance.

Cleo, groggy though she'd risen at 6am to be at Olympus, Inc., a few minutes early, was transfixed by the owl perched behind Athena's desk. His name was Tim, and Tim was staring at her. Could the owl, with its avian senses, detect her dry mouth, the mild pounding in her head?

It had proven surprisingly easy to sip three glasses of wine while dining with Veronica last night, a purely social occasion between friends with no pressure or agenda or trying to guess what the other one was thinking. The well of intimacy between them had run dry while she'd been away, Cleo realized. In moments her breathing slowed, her smile warmed, and her heart perked with the joy of sharing confidences. It was past midnight when Ganymede looked pointedly at the clock above the bar and said, "Last call."

Her attention shifted to a tapping sound: Athena's fingers drumming on her desk.

"Thank you for being punctual, Cleo. I wish I could say as much for your boss."

As if on cue, Hermes rushed in.

"Sorry I'm late, Athena. Ruffled feathers with Waller I had to pat down."

In the years Cleo had worked for him she had never heard Hermes apologize. He was thinner than when she'd last seen him, with bruise-dark crescents under his eyes. "Welcome back, Cleo." He sat next to her.

His impersonal greeting left Cleo nonplussed. True, he'd been pissed about her leave of absence, but she'd thought they were still friends. The Starbuck's mug in her shoulder bag, the one she'd brought back for him, seemed trite and silly now.

Athena cleared her throat. "You must be wondering why we're meeting with you today."

The silver-eyed Goddess of War and Wisdom gazed steadily at her, waiting.

"Ma'am?"

"It concerns War and Diplomacy's contribution to the climate change initiative," Athena said. "We're targeting mortals engaged in the fossil fuel industry. Our effort is coordinated through Olympus, Inc., Intelligence, Secret Ops."

Cleo had studied the Olympus, Inc., organizational chart when she'd worked as Veronica's executive assistant but didn't recall seeing an intelligence department. Athena stared at her. Was she waiting for a reply? Tim hooted, as if to prompt her.

"I don't understand, Ma'am."

Hermes touched Cleo's shoulder. She turned toward him. His expression was solemn.

"Cleo," he said, "we're going to make you a spy."

The transition happened immediately. Her cover inside Olympus, Inc.: during her leave of absence Roderick Waller had performed so well Hermes had decided to retain him and make Cleo available for employment elsewhere. Irritated by this unflattering fiction, she kept not only the Starbuck's mug she'd intended for Hermes, but also the Fran's Gold Bars she'd purchased for Roderick after he shot her a smug look when she stopped by to clean out her desk. He of course hadn't been told about her real assignment. Cleo, herself, was sworn to secrecy. She couldn't tell her parents, couldn't even tell David *if* he ever bothered to call or text.

Besides, she hadn't been told precisely what her assignment was. This week Cleo would work in Athena's department as a temporary executive assistant. Security was borrowing some people from War to provide crowd control during the December festival, Light up the Dark, which started on the winter solstice. From there it was one long roll to, through and beyond Saturnalia. Heavy drinking was integral to the festivities, especially during the Parade of Lights. The route passed through the hotel-studded downtown neighborhood where the magnificent fountain at The Plaza, for that night only, spouted wine.

Tuesday, December 16, 2025

New York City, New York, USA

One thing David Bernstein and his biological father, Saul Crispin, had in common, besides their appearance, was bottomless hunger. By his second full day in New York City it was already routine for the two of them to veer toward the pushcart down the street from Saul's building, the one sporting a bright yellow and blue striped umbrella, each umbrella panel emblazoned twice with a corporate name: *Sabrett.*

"Best damn hot dogs in the city," Saul said, and he'd only had to say it once. David tried the All Beef Natural Casing with onion sauce and the Hot and Spicy All Beef Skinless on yesterday's morning walk, not all that hungry after coffee and glazed donuts earlier at Saul's. Today, though, he was ravenous, and ordered the same as yesterday plus an All-Beef Hot Sausage with sauerkraut. If he'd had more than two hands he would have gotten more. Good thing a pretzel cart was on their route, too.

They strode along, munching companionably as David soaked in the atmosphere. So many people on the streets! Everyone walked fast, most with their heads down, which might have had something to do with the bracing cold. It was a great city for architecture. Yesterday they'd checked out the Empire State Building and the U. N. Today they'd tackle Central Park, Rockefeller Center and finish up at Radio City Music Hall for the Rockettes 8pm show.

"Their Christmas show is a New York City classic." Saul said when he'd mentioned they had tickets. "And here's a little-known fact. Most people think the Rockettes are all the same height. In actuality, they're anywhere between five-foot-six and five-ten and a half."

"Like the difference between me and Cleo." It was the first time he'd said her name since he'd called Saul from Sea-Tac to tell him Cleo wasn't coming. David could see the question in Saul's raised eyebrows. Saul finished his second of two dogs, licked his mustardy fingers.

"What's the matter, kid?"

"Nothing's the matter," David said between bites of the foot-long hot sausage and kraut. "They needed her for some kind of work emergency and cancelled the extension of her leave."

Saul's face relaxed. "That's good to know. She seems like a wonderful girl and I could see right away how dedicated she is to you."

"Yeah." And that was just the start. They'd fallen into a wild, blissful state that was going strong right up to when the text arrived on Sunday morning. Damn that Hermes. David had an ugly hunch Cleo's boss was interested in a lot more than her brain. Who wouldn't be?

"I'd hate to think you two had a falling out."

The last bite of sausage hit David's stomach like lead.

Saul patted David's shoulder. "I've been around a long time, kid."

So, yeah, he told Saul, yeah, he was jealous, and kind of hurt, too, that it had only taken her a nanosecond to change her plans. The past few weeks had been so…

Saul chuckled. "No need to elaborate, I can see the story in your eyes. Why don't you send her one of those text things?" Saul was not big on texting, mostly an email and phone call kind of guy. "You don't have to spill your guts, just tell her you're thinking of her. If she's like everybody else on earth she'll appreciate it."

Would she? Maybe it was his fault for going cold on her. It felt bad when she decided to follow orders without even discussing it with him, after what they'd become—real lovers at last, no more of the "we're just friends" game they'd played for a decade. She'd given up a ton to join his six-month quest to find his biological dad, and it was her determination when he'd all but given up that was the last step to meeting Saul. He owed her a lot, everything, practically, but…

Heaven and Earth, he felt dumped!

He didn't say anything about Saul's suggestion, pretended he hadn't heard it. Saul changed the subject to Central Park, how he'd met the landscape architect—

David stumbled to a stop. "Frederick Law Olmstead? You're kidding me!"

This guy—his *dad*—was like a walking, talking history book. Not many immortals he'd met were like that. Few of them spent much time in the mortal world and paid more attention to the triumphs and downfalls of other gods. But Saul. It seemed like he'd been everywhere David had ever heard of and met every historical figure he'd ever admired.

"We met decades after he designed Central Park, when he was working on the Midway Plaisance redesign after the World's Columbian Exposition. I met him through Sol Bloom, a theatrical entrepreneur I worked for who was a big force in setting up the midway for the expo.

All kinds of theaters, the original Ferris Wheel, loads of international cultural exhibits—big stuff in the entertainment world. That's gone now, of course. Olmstead's job was to convert the midway into a park when the exhibition closed. Ever been to Chicago? The Midway's part of the University of Chicago campus."

"Wow."

Spending time with Saul made something that really bugged David—not the recent stuff with Cleo, but something he'd thought about since he'd first learned he was immortal—rise to the surface. If you went by human years, he and Saul had been alive for about the same amount of time, the difference of a mere twenty-some years. The Bernsteins had protected him for two millennia, renewing a forgetfulness charm on him at regular intervals to maintain the illusion he was mortal and they were a regular mortal family. When the charm was broken, back when he was a barista in Seattle, little bits and pieces of memory had seeped back—not enough to enlighten, just enough to frustrate. If he hadn't been under the stupid charm he'd probably remember a lot of cool history, like Saul. When they stopped at the pretzel cart he floated the idea.

"Interesting thought," Saul said, He took a meditative bite from his pretzel. "Ever ask Thelma about that?"

"Once." He'd brought it up ten years ago, before he'd moved from Seattle to the City of Mount Olympus. "She got all protective, said I might not want to remember some of it."

Saul laughed. "That's the Thelma I remember, a born mom. And she has a point. Getting close to mortals is a setup for loss. I'm an expert in that, and I'll bet the Bernsteins are, too."

David stopped eating, dropped the half-finished pretzel back into the white paper bag and tossed it into the next trash receptacle. He'd been entirely selfish. *Of course* Thelma and Milton would have made and lost hundreds, maybe thousands of mortal friends and associates over the centuries. "I should call them."

"That's a good boy. A little early for them now with the time difference, so maybe when we stop for lunch?"

For a fleeting second David thought about the time difference between New York and the City of Mount Olympus. Seven or eight hours, maybe? Almost the end of the workday at Olympus, Inc., right now, unless Cleo was slaving over some time-sensitive critical project. That ass, Hermes, was sure to be looking over her shoulder, standing way too close.

Blood boiling, David swooped on the next food cart, hardly knowing or caring what was on offer. He trusted Cleo. He *did*. But she was there and he was here and Hermes was a big-shot, two-plus millennia older than David with plenty of bad boy charm. Women practically threw themselves at him, he'd seen it with his own eyes! Heaven and Earth, he wanted to go to her and protect her from that jerk, but she'd walked right into his trap! Cleo was not stupid, far from it. She wasn't naïve enough to—no, he wouldn't let himself even imagine it. He trusted her. He *did*.

When the haze of rage cleared, his hands were empty and greasy.

"Amazing," said Saul.

"What?"

Saul laughed, probably at the stupidly defensive edge in his voice. "You belong in the Guinness Book of World Records, David. I have never seen someone eat two pieces of pizza so fast."

Heaven and Earth, he had to get a grip on himself! He was in New York City to get to know his birth dad, not to make an idiot of himself over the only girl he'd ever loved. At least, the only one as far as he knew.

WEDNESDAY, DECEMBER 17, 2025

Midland, Texas, USA

It was damn cold, a bracing six degrees Fahrenheit at 9am. Edwin B. East (the B stood for Bronchitis, an old family name) peered through the east-facing glass wall of the thirty-seventh floor penthouse office he shared with his twin brother. Too cold to snow now, but downtown Midland had been blanketed with the stuff overnight.

"Damn cold morning," Edwin said to his mirror-image, Cyril B. (which stood for Blitzkrieg, a name he'd selected on his own). The one physical characteristic that made them distinguishable was visible only when they removed their matching generously cut dress shirts.

"Damn cold indeed, if you're a mammal," Cyril quipped, his voice reminiscent of a shrill whistle.

The twins shared a high, wheezing chortle.

"The perfect start to Saturnalia." Edwin continued. He paced the length of the window, feet barely lifting in his long, slow stride. "The exempt staff have received their bonuses?"

Edwin was operations; Cyril was finance.

"They have, indeed."

"Excellent." Edwin rubbed his palms together. He had the usual number of fingers, each exactly the same length as the others, with slightly bulbous tips. It was a point of pride with Edwin to keep his nails perfectly buffed and trimmed. Also, the extra circulation a regular manicure provided faded the slight green tinge in his nail beds. The illusion of normalcy was completed with a single layer of flesh-tinted varnish. Hands mattered. In his line of work he shook a lot of hands.

Cyril rose to join his brother in front of the window. "The Saturnalia party launches at noon. We must keep them happy."

"That we must."

East Fossil Fuels Corporation was the largest employer in Midland, one that paid employees above market and offered a generous benefits package, including two weeks of paid winter holiday leave for corporate staff on a rotating basis. This year's beneficiaries were free December 19 through January 1. If one or two of them did not return?

Tears of joy pooled in Edwin's eyes, irises shining purple with the aid of blue contact lenses. "Attrition is the natural order of things. Such a beautiful time of year."

Cyril huffed in exasperation. "Edwin, you are nothing if not a sentimental fool. We must be serious for a moment and review our Saturnalia plans. Tonight—"

"Role reversal?" Edwin said, head tilted at the angle he employed to look his most winning.

"Yes, let's do," Cyril said, taking in the details of his brother's business attire that exactly matched his own. "We can practice at the party. I will be you and you will be me."

"Splendid! And we will both act as servants to the staff. Who should we choose as King?"

"I was thinking of Perkins, from R and D."

Edwin licked his lips. "He *is* on the plump side."

"With no living family or dependents," Cyril added.

"I'll make sure he gets plenty to drink and offer him a ride home in the limo. Still…"

The downward note of the last word turned them somber. Their identical eyes turned toward the spot on the wall where two gold-embossed certificates hung side by side. The twins inhaled and exhaled in chorus.

"Try as we do to bring culture to our humble lives," Cyril said, "it will never rival our undergraduate days."

Though the hour was early, Edwin shuffled to the bar cart underneath the framed diplomas and poured two generous snifters of rare vintage Remy Martin. He passed a snifter to Cyril. They raised their glasses in unison.

"To Miskatonic University. Long may she reign."

New York City, New York, USA

David awoke on Saul's fold-out sofa, sun glowing around the edges of the lowered shades on the three common room windows. His throat was raw, rawer than his enthusiastic cheering when the Rockettes took their curtain call last night could explain. He rolled off the couch and onto his feet, sinuses throbbing.

"Good morning." Saul, a semi-resolved blur, sat at the far side of the tiny dining table in the kitchen alcove.

David recovered his glasses from the end table.

"Yeah." His voice sounded like a honking goose with gravel in its throat.

"Uh-oh." Saul padded across the Persian rug to the three-quarter bath, the only private space in his apartment if you didn't count the large walk-in closet he used for a bedroom. Sounds of the medicine cabinet opening and closing and water being run preceded his return, one hand cupped, the other holding a small paper cup. "Here, take this. Fingers crossed it will knock down whatever's ailing you."

He set the cup and an oval-shaped flesh-toned pill on the end table, and washed his hands thoroughly at the kitchen sink.

"I've got a job coming up next week, can't afford to get sick," He dried his hands on a blue and white dishtowel. "You better take it easy today. I'll make a run for orange juice and find us something to eat." His keys dropped into his jeans pocket and he was off.

Great, just great. Time in one of the world's most vibrant cities and he was sidelined with a head cold. No fever, though, and his hollow stomach was roaring. Hopefully Saul would remember the old adage *feed a cold*. Thelma was a firm believer in that wisdom, used to make him kugel when he got sick as a kid.

At least as far as he remembered. Heaven and Earth, it bugged him more and more that so much of his memory had been suppressed. Thelma and Milton had apologized about this many times since he'd learned he was immortal. Everyone had thought it was for the best when they'd taken him out of Hera's household as a baby. Without memories, he would never find out that he'd been adopted. He'd never feel the compulsion to search for his birth parents and risk the wrath of Zeus, the cuckolded husband.

At least, now that he knew who he was, he could keep his memories from here forward, and Zeus was no longer an existential threat. They'd formed an okay relationship at Athens U, where Zeus was provost, mostly over a chess board. It was something Zeus did with all graduate students one-on-one. Rumor had it that the chess set had magical powers and there was a lot of speculation about what, exactly, these were. David's gut told him it was probably a life and death thing, though it was incredibly hard to kill an immortal. Still…

Saul had left the bathroom light on. Better to clean up than let the chess board conjecture spin in his stuffy head. The shower enclosure was tiny, tough on the elbows but useful for containing steam. David's sinuses eased. Hopefully whatever it was Saul had given him would clear things up.

He was dressed and sitting on the made-up sofa when Saul's keys rattled in the door. A half-gallon bottle of juice was tucked under one arm. Each hand gripped a grease-spotted white paper bag.

"Oh good, you're up." He set his load on the dining table. "I wasn't sure what you wanted so I covered all the bases. Bagels with the works, chicken noodle soup, rice pudding. Want some coffee?"

"Sure." He started to rise.

"Sit!" Saul commanded. "You are hereby quarantined to the sofa and the bathroom, period. The kitchen and my bedroom are off limits. I'll set up my laptop in here and prep for that job next week."

"Another musical?" Saul had just finished a national tour as Lazar Wolf in *Fiddler on the Roof.*

"Nah." He loaded a plate with bagels and little paper tubs of butter and cream cheese. "Unfortunately, that project was cancelled. Backers nervous about opening for one reason or another, my agent said. Fortunately she got me something else."

"Stage work?"

Saul chuckled. "Not exactly." He set a mug of coffee, black, on the end table and the plate of bagels beside it. "It's live performance, a group I've worked with before. Private event, can't really talk about it. I leave next Monday. Juice?"

They hadn't talked much about Saul's career, not since the night they first met and he'd said a little bit about meeting mortals like Shakespeare along the way.

"Ever do any movies?" David picked up his mug to make room for the juice glass.

"Here and there. I did a couple of silents with Keaton and Lloyd, strictly a bit player. One with Chaplin. When it dawned on me that film was a way mortals could trace me, I gave it up, except working as an extra now and then." He framed his face with his hands. "The name I can change but not this mug. You like films?"

"Oh yeah," David said between bites. Man, the butter was fresh. "Milton's a real movie buff. He's got a million of them on VHS."

"A man after my own heart. I never got used to DVDs, let alone streaming. Everything moves so fast these days. But mortals..."

Saul's voice dropped off, like his thoughts had strayed somewhere sad. "Maybe you've seen this one," he said, brightening. He disappeared into his closet bedroom and, after some rummaging, returned to the living area with a rolling cart. On top of the cart was an old, obsolete television not much wider than the VHS deck that formed its base.

"Streisand." Saul grinned. "One of the greats and always will be. Nice Jewish girl, too."

"You *know* her?"

"Not really. I was just some guy in the background. Great songs, though." He held up the oblong box that rested on top of the television. The young, unmarked face of Barbara Streisand dominated the cover. "Released fifty-five years ago, if you can believe it. Almost fifty-six. Not a great film, but nice. Had to die my hair to get the job, cover the gray. You won't see me until nearly the end. Minnelli used me for background in a few scenes but most of it ended up on the cutting room floor."

David knew the songs. Milton Bernstein was definitely a Streisand fan and the movie soundtrack was one he often put on the stereo turntable. But the movie itself? Saul stood by, VHS in hand, looking wistful.

"Let 'er roll," David said.

Saul warmed a bowl of chicken soup in the microwave while the opening credits ran. A continuous stream of animated rectangular boxes entered the frame and grew small as they reached the vanishing point, very suspense-filled and reminiscent of a Hitchcock movie. Streisand never worked with Hitchcock, did she? The animation and opening credits were accompanied by a choral arrangement backed by full orchestra. David knew the song so well he couldn't resist singing along. The extended vowels in the first line sent him into a coughing fit.

"Easy there, big fella." Saul set a heavy-looking soup bowl on the end table. "More bagels?"

Saul's nurturing was like Thelma Bernstein on steroids. "Aren't you going to have some?"

"Don't worry, I got plenty."

Crappy as it was to be sick, David gave into being gracious and leaned back on the couch. He wasn't a big Yves Montand fan and the guy looked about a hundred years older than Barbara. The Daisy character, the one Streisand played, was undergoing hypnotherapy with Montand as the therapist. She wanted to quit smoking. But then— Heaven and Earth, she was someone else, too! Someone named Melinda, Lady Tentrees…

David set the empty soup bowl aside. Through simple hypnosis, Barbara Streisand had uncovered a past life! Sure, it was reincarnation instead of repressed memory, but…could he…would it…

He reached behind the couch for his backpack and fished out his phone. His gut said Saul wouldn't like it, but he charged ahead anyway, tapping in a query for New York City hypnotherapists. It was crazy, a true longshot, but what if some mortal practitioner could help him unlock his past? He had now through Sunday to set up an appointment and figure out a cover story so he could get away for a couple of hours and find out something, anything, about where he'd been before Salt Lake City, Utah.

Thursday, December 18, 2025

Midland, Texas, USA

Cyril B. and Edwin B. East reclined on matching sofas opposite each other, their feet pointed toward a pile of glowing logs in an open-hearth fireplace large enough to roast an ox. The electric-powered spit had stopped turning at midnight, the moment the skin of Perkins from R & D had achieved a perfect crackling brown. The chime of the grandfather clock in the back of the vast room announced the quarter-hour.

Edwin worked a toothpick in the crown of a molar, freeing the last delicious shred of Perkins. The pile of bones—ribs, arms, legs—topped by the once succulent but now empty skull formed a shape similar to their twelve-foot Christmas tree in the grand entry hall.

"Cyril," he said, pointing to the heap once he'd attracted his twin's attention. "Should we decorate it, in keeping with the season?"

Cyril belched. "Suits me." The room, though cavernous, was toasty warm and his feet were blissfully bare. He wiggled his toes, five of them spaced equidistantly around the curve of his hoof-shaped foot, against the low red firelight. The worst part about working among humans was the footwear. "Of all the holidays, I love Saturnalia best."

After they'd enjoyed Perkins they'd opened their gifts from each other and shared a yip of delight—matching holiday jammies, again! This year plaid was all the rage. A fine MacGregor tartan with lots of red added the perfect note of blood and festivity. How handy it was, not only to be identical in appearance, but to read each other's minds!

"Yes, we'll have to do that first thing on Monday," Edwin said in answer to Cyril's thought. "Can't leave R and D without a shepherd. Will you speak to HR, or shall I?"

"Would you, please, Eddy? You have the better head for what's required. R and D is simply not my forte."

"Easily done." Edwin enjoyed talking to Ms. Allen, the HR head. She was due for extra holiday time next winter and, since she'd started leading the department and now spent most of her time in meetings, had plumped up nicely. "We'll post widely, of course, and have several layers of review for qualified candidates." It was difficult to tell from resumes and references alone whether a job hopeful would successfully align with the corporation's core hiring value: to help those who were properly skilled but, poor souls, had not the joy of living family. Hence their motto: At East Fossil, we *are* your family. "Anything in particular you'd like to see in Perkins's replacement?"

Cyril fell quietly thoughtful. "No, nothing in particular." He belched again and splayed his star-aligned fingers atop his full tum-tum. "I can honestly say there will never be another quite like Perkins."

FRIDAY, DECEMBER 19, 2025

New York City, New York, USA

David Bernstein lay on a single futon—no frame, just six inches of cotton between him and the linoleum floor—in a room not much bigger than a broom closet. It was nowhere close to the plush office Yves Montand had in the movie—no art, no books, not even a window. But Griselda Munch was the first practitioner he'd found with an opening. Saul had grudgingly let him leave the apartment that morning after making him swear on something he held dear (Thelma Bernstein's kugle was the first thing that came to mind) not to over-exert himself.

"Cleo will not be happy with me if you return to Mount Olympus as a mucous-filled sack of contagion," Saul had said.

He'd shrugged in reply. Would Cleo have time for him with her big, important, supposedly crucial work assignment? If he knew more about the past, maybe the present wouldn't seem so important.

David caught the individual-sized bottle of hand sanitizer Saul tossed to him on his way out the door. His head was nearly clear, though residual grogginess from last night's dose of cold medicine lingered. No spring in his step, but one foot fell in front of the other to keep him moving forward. He found the cross-street where he could pick up the needed bus, pulled the wool scarf Saul had loaned him tighter around his neck. The bus was late, and, to Griselda Munch's annoyance, he was late, too.

"Your hour started eight minutes ago," she said without a hello or confirming his name. Ms. Munch pointed to the futon and plopped into a beat-up looking leather recliner, the only other piece of furniture in the place. She tapped a button on her smart phone, summoning music played on instruments tuned to quarter-tones. "Close your eyes and your mouth and breathe!" she commanded. "Relax! Deep inhale, deep exhale."

David focused on his breathing and on the music while trying to erase the sound of Griselda Munch's toe tapping the linoleum. In a steady rhythm…

The scent of oranges. Blue sky overhanging an endless body of water. Sun-warmed shoulders in a suit coat. The cry of gulls.

"Where are you, David?" Munch's voice, soft and steady.

He breathed deeply. "Valencia."

"A beautiful place, Valencia. What's the year?"

"Nineteen-seventeen," wafted on a sigh.

"And you are how old?"

Silly she couldn't see it herself. "A little younger."

"Who are you?"

Standing on the beach, a smile quirked his lips. "Me."

Someone's hand was in his, a soft hand. Her scent mingled with the oranges.

Lucia.

WEDNESDAY, DECEMBER 19, 1917

Valencia, Spain

Waves lapped the sandy shore. Lucia squeezed his hand.

"You'll be going home for the holidays soon," she said.

Chanukah had ended two days ago but Lucia didn't know about that. The Bernstein family had renamed itself Burns when Milton's banking career began, as the majority Christian population of Scotland was inclined toward suspicion of Jews involved with moneylending. Publicly, they were members of the Church of Scotland.

"Yes. My folks expect me in Barcelona for Christmas."

They'd come to Spain for Milton's work. Trade between Spain and other European countries had grown tremendously since the start of the war, and Milton had a brilliant understanding of commodities and currencies. Also, as Thelma pointed out, David would be less at risk. Pressure to join the army had built when Scotland entered the Great War. Some of David's friends had already volunteered—and died—by the time the family relocated. He was now nineteen.

"I wish I could go with you."

"I do, too."

Lucia was a native of Catalonia. Her family was prosperous enough to send her to England for schooling and, later, to pursue nurse's training. Though they'd met only a few days ago, David felt he'd known her forever. Her eyes took on an extraordinary light when they looked into his, a light his heart told him burned in his eyes, too. She'd returned to Catalonia to pursue a dream: to provide nursing services and train others in public health practices. Spain lagged behind most of Europe in matters of health, she'd explained to him. The population was not as dense, with many living in mountain ranges or remote agricultural regions, so new ideas didn't travel quickly. It didn't help that literacy rates were low, especially among women.

David was in Valencia on behalf of his master, the Spanish architect Antoni Gaudi. A mad genius as some called him. Gaudi had, for years, sequestered himself at La Sagrada Familia. The basilica—gargantuan and wildly creative in design—had been in progress for decades. It was whispered the project would never be completed in Gaudi's lifetime.

David had filled a sketch pad with architectural details from religious and secular buildings, plus sketches of local flora as specified by Gaudí for reasons he did not reveal. Such was the nature of working for a genius. When the war ended David hoped to return to the British Isles and pursue his own path to becoming an internationally renowned architect. In the short time they'd known each other, he and Lucia had discussed how easy it would be, with her background and experience, to work anywhere in the world. That she'd live with him was unspoken but understood.

But there was the matter of her parents. The Barbera Cabell family was proud, her father prominent in regional politics and her mother from one of the oldest families in Catalonia. They would never sanction the marriage of their daughter to a foreigner, especially if they discovered he was a Jew.

David slipped his arms around Lucia. *"Mi amor,"* he whispered in her ear. How, in the twentieth century, could two educated, well-traveled people seem as hopeless as Romeo and Juliet?

He was back in Barcelona on Christmas Eve. A pine wreath trimmed with red ribbon decorated the front door. David entered without knocking and followed his nose to the kitchen. His mother was walking the cook through the niceties of steaming a plum pudding.

"David!" Wisps of wavy red hair laced with silver fluttered around Thelma Burns's face. He loved the freckles on his mother's nose, more prominent than ever because of the Mediterranean sun. Her arms flew around him and squeezed. "Your father and I missed you so much. How was Valencia?"

"Absolutely breathtaking, Mother. I—"

"But you must be exhausted." She released him and pushed him away. "Go! Get settled while I finish up with Maria. We have the hard sauce to make yet and your father will be home any minute."

"All right." He longed to tell her about Lucia but also feared what she might say. There'd been a girl in Scotland he'd stepped out with a time or two, a sweet and practical young woman named Katie. It wasn't that Thelma hadn't liked her, but she'd warned David away from getting too close with a cryptic message: *She's not like us.* About being Jewish, he supposed. Thelma wouldn't like that about Lucia, either, an ardent Catholic.

Thelma was right about today's travel, though. David was weary from swaying and bumping over three hundred fifty kilometers from Valencia to Barcelona. The bedrooms were down a hallway, past the dining and drawing rooms. The feather bed in his room beckoned to him to nap.

David set his suitcase alongside the carved chair next to the armoire, dropped into the seat and unlaced his shoes after stripping off his jacket and removing his pocket watch and vest. He stretched luxuriously on the bed and soon fell asleep.

"...count of three. Open your eyes, feeling refreshed and wide-awake. One, two, three."

David Bernstein's eyelids fluttered opened. He reached his hands above his head and stretched, his knuckles bumping the office wall. His throat felt raw like it did when he fell asleep with his mouth open.

Lucia. Dark, intelligent eyes, rosy cheeks, hair worn in a long braid down her back. Her scent a mixture of oranges, carbolic acid, daylight and something undefinably her own. He'd met her, wooed her, held her in his arms. He had, at least once in his earlier life, fallen in love.

"Interesting," Griselda Munch said. "Your name was David then, too."

She pressed him to book another appointment. He said no, he was leaving town in a couple of days. Ms. Munch's skeptical expression made him nervous. David wasn't great at seeing auras, but he took a good look to make sure hers was the pink corona of a mortal. If she'd seen his purple aura tinged with gold, who knew what she'd try to do?

Friday, December 19, 2025

City of Mount Olympus

Hunched at a desk in the War Department, Cleo jockeyed employee names, personnel codes and pay grades, using an ancient spreadsheet program with functions so basic they belonged in the Stone Age. At quitting time on Friday Athena peered over the top of Cleo's cubicle.

"Ms. Petra, please stop by my office before you leave for the weekend."

"Yes, Ma'am." Cleo powered down the old desktop computer. She stretched her arms toward the ceiling. Her spine and shoulders popped like a string of firecrackers.

The door of Athena's office was open. The Goddess of War and Wisdom was ruffling Tim's head feathers and feeding him something crunchy.

"That's a good boy."

He snapped down the last morsel. Athena brushed her palms together and dropped into her chair.

"Tartarus of a week," she said. "Please close the door and sit."

Cleo felt as if the vacant eye sockets of the masks on the wall behind her were boring holes into her back, the same way Athena's silver eyes drilled into her from the front.

"Thank you for picking up the admin slack this week," Athena said. "Dull, I realize, but it only comes around once a year."

"Glad to be of assistance, Ma'am."

"I like a team player, Ms. Petra. Hopefully you'll enjoy the change of pace next week. And for five weeks after that." She handed Cleo an envelope. Inside was a Bank of Olympus deposit slip detailing a generous transfer to her personal account, also an air ticket, departure from Athens International early Sunday morning, destination Washington, D.C.

"A mortal operative has arranged for your training in their world. America, to be exact, at a facility called The Village."

A weekend of laundry and packing. And—

"Can you tell me about my mission, Ma'am?"

The corners of Athena's mouth tilted upward. "Not until you've finished your training. I don't want your magnificent brain inventing real-world scenarios until you've soaked up everything they can teach you. Officially, you're in the mortal world, gathering data on international diplomatic relations. Questions?"

Yes, but knowing she wouldn't get answers— "No."

"Thank you, Ms. Petra, and good luck."

SUNDAY, DECEMBER 21, 2025

City of Mount Olympus

P. B., short for Power Baby until someone came up with a better name for him, sat snuggly warm on his grandma's lap. She, who some called Aphrodite, had wrapped him in a blue, green and yellow blanket of the softest fleece, the colors falling into a celestial pattern of sun, moon and stars. His wee tiny nosey, as Grandma called it, wrinkled under the nip of Mount Olympus after sundown. The longest night of the year, the winter solstice, dark and peppered with an abundance of colorful lights.

It was a perfect evening, out on the town with Grandma, the air filled with excitement and the smart-ass commentary of the God of Shepherds and Flocks, Pan, who announced the passing entries from a P. A. system high up in the reviewing stand.

"These bleachers are fricking freezing," Grandma said to her friend Hera.

They were seated several rows in front of Pan, along with Big-G Gods and other dignitaries who weren't participating in the parade.

"Here." Hera unscrewed the top of a slim stainless-steel thermos and passed it to Grandma. "Toddy."

Now would be an opportune time to fuss and cry. P. B. took a deep breath and let it rip.

"Heaven and Earth!" Grandma swore. She took a healthy swig and set the thermos by her feet. "I can't believe you're hungry again already." She rummaged in the insulated bottle bag, found a white nipple-topped silo and nudged it at his gaping mouth.

Hera said, "He certainly is growing. One month and how many days?"

"Six weeks. Apollo says he's big for his age."

P. B. didn't like the way Hera's eyes narrowed. "Something to do with his *other* father, no doubt."

"That's my guess," Grandma said. "He didn't get it from Hermes, and Monique certainly didn't grow like this. She was always small for her age."

Monique was Mama. P. B. could say her name. He could say most words but innate knowledge cautioned him not to speak them. Not yet. As long as he made the baby noises the adults expected they would let slip everything he wanted to know. Like the fact he had two fathers. One of them was Hermes, who seemed like a smart enough guy but was easy to manipulate. His other father, whom he'd never met, was someone commonly referred to as You-Know-Who.

"And Monique is leaving when?"

That was Hera again.

"After the holidays. She's at home now, writing policies for the microlending bank WomanFront hired her to organize. Which leaves me with Mommy's Little Manniken."

P. B. spit out the nipple he'd been sucking and squealed, his Burp Me cue. Grandma fished a blankie out of the diaper bag and smoothed it over her shoulder. A marching band stomped rhythmically by as she raised him and settled him into place. The band fired up, assaulting the popular tune "Olympus by Night." The reed section squawked like a flock of deranged geese and the cold had tightened the harps to a half-step sharp. The voice of Pan, P. B.'s adored big brother, boomed over the loudspeakers.

"Gods and goddesses, ladies and gentlemen, give it up for the Apollo Middle School marching band!"

A hearty cheer rose from all directions, especially from the people gathered by the wine-spewing fountain across the street.

"The little bandsters get better every year, don't they, folks?"

Bandsters! P. B. nearly choked on his own air bubble it cracked him up so much. That was exactly the kind of thing he'd say when he started talking out loud. But not anytime soon, not while there was so much information to gather. Nothing would make him vary from this plan. It would take dynamite—

"And now, solstice revelers, the arrival of our perennial grand marshal, the reason for the season, Poseidon, God of the Sea!"

Grandma turned him around in time to see a vast silver, blue and green horse-drawn float pull into view, glittery bits of paper glued to a wooden base, row by row and layer by layer, by the Fraternal Order of Immortal Mariners at their weekly ritual night and ale bust. Shapes of waves and dolphins shimmered under strings of twinkling white lights. On a dais at the back of the float stood Poseidon, a tall, muscular man in a blue iridescent wet suit, his trident raised to the heavens in one of his massive hands. The ferocity of the god's expression inspired P. B. with awe. Poseidon was who he wanted to be when he grew up!

"Yes, Poseidon, God of the Sea, the Savior of Seattle, the inventive immortal who saved the lives of thousands with his butt!"

Poseidon's head snapped toward the reviewing stand. "I'll spear *you* in the butt for that, goat brains!" he roared. He leapt off the float and charged into the reviewing stand. Gods and dignitaries scurried from his path.

This topped the Tartarus out of any bedtime story! P. B. slapped his baby palms together with rabid enthusiasm. "Butt! Butt!" His perfectly articulated shout escaped before he realized it.

"Heaven and Earth!" Hera said. "His first word at six weeks?"

Grandma slipped her hands under his armpits and suspended him with his face in front of hers, her violet eyes probing deep within. He attempted to cover the awkward moment with a *goo* and a *ga* but it was too late. Grandma was nobody's fool.

"Butt. Butt," he sniffled and cried, determined this would be the only word he'd speak for the next three to five years. "Buuuuutt!!"

P. B. let loose the water works, crocodile tears sheeting his chubby cheeks.

"Those fools have traumatized him!" Grandma growled.

"Buuuuutt! Buuuuutt!" he yowled.

Hera shot up from her seat and bolted up the risers. An argument with three voices ensued near the top of the bleachers, laced with an abundance of Heaven and Earths and other less common swear words. Also the words Very Real Danger. Grandma slung the diaper bag over her shoulder and tucked him into the crook of her arm. "We're getting out of here!"

Grandma clanked down the steps to the pavement. Poseidon's float clogged the street, a flag unit, a group of tumblers and more bands jammed up behind it. The Apollo Middle School drum section had abandoned their instruments and stood open-mouthed beneath the wine-spouting fountain.

Someone said, "Hey, Aphrodite! Hey, bro!"

Grandma's arm tensed under him. She turned toward Pan, Hera and Poseidon.

"What do you want?" she said through her teeth. "You've scared him half to death."

"Hey, P. B., you're cool, right?" Pan chucked him under the chin. P. B. blinked his eyes and sniffled in response. "You know we were just playing, right? Poseidon isn't really going to hurt me, are you Poseidon?"

Poseidon's scowl was pitch black until Hera elbowed him, hard, in the ribs.

"Uh, that's right." The God of the Sea forced a smile. "Pan and I were fooling around, just part of the show. We didn't mean to scare you."

P. B. had a brainstorm. He reached his chubby hands toward Poseidon and, eyes wide and lower lip trembling burbled, "Butt-Butt?"

Something in the god's blazing eyes thawed. "Cute little tyke, isn't he?"

Security guards shooed the middle-schoolers away from the fountain and began circling it with ropes and stanchions

"Guess that's it for this year's parade," Pan said.

Hera glared at Poseidon and Pan. "Ronnie is going to be livid," she pronounced. That was Veronica Zeta, who was the boss of just about everybody except Grandma and Mama, who had their own business called Love, Inc.

"Oh, I don't know," Pan said, looking around with a shrug. "Looks like it turned out pretty much like always."

Grandma shifted P. B. into her other arm. "We're going. Good night."

P. B. swung his arms violently and wailed "Butt-Butt! Butt-Butt!" just to see what they would do. He threw in a barrage of unrelenting screams and kicked at his swaddling for emphasis. Poseidon took a step toward him.

"I'm not much for babies," he said sheepishly, "but maybe he'd calm down if I held him for a bit?"

Pan whistled low. "Why Poseidon, you old softie."

P. B. kicked and screamed some more to expedite matters. Grandma's sigh came all the way from her toes.

"Oh, all right. You need to support his head." She passed him to Poseidon's outstretched arms.

The god smelled of sweat and salt, the texture of his wet suit slick against P. B.'s cheek. His senses formed a picture of movement and water and playing with dolphins. "Butt-Butt!" he drooled and cooed with delight. He definitely wanted to be a sea god when he grew up.

"Will you be taking him as usual on Wednesday?" Grandma's voice.

"Uhm, no. I need to text Monique about that."

What, no Pan on Wednesday? That was the best part of his week, bonding with his hilarious big bro. If P. B. wasn't so concerned about blowing his cover he'd have let loose a ferocious squall in protest. He lay quietly in Poseidon's arms and shifted his focus to Pan.

"Holidays?" Grandma again.

Pan lowered his eyelids, something he did when he wasn't being entirely truthful, like when he'd assured Mom he'd never take P. B. flying at his tender age. That was the very, very best part of Wednesdays.

"Business. Ag stuff. Athena wants me to consult on some mortal dairy operations. Distribution chains. War on Hunger kind of stuff." Hah! Every word was a lie. "I fly out tonight. Not sure for how long."

That part was true, anyway. But where was Pan *really* going? He was one of a handful of immortals endowed with the power of warp speed flight. P. B. had experienced the thrill of this first-hand when they'd zipped off to Australia last Wednesday, looked at some koala bears while Mom was tied up in a video conference with Elle and Jocelyn Chadwick of WomanFront.

Maybe their mutual dad, Hermes, knew why Pan was going. Hermes and Pan had worked together on an important project recently. Maybe Dad was in on this mysterious scheme, too? Heaven and Earth, if he only had another infant to discuss this with in standard Olympian Baby talk maybe he could figure it out!

In flight, to Dulles International, USA

Cleo Petra, travelling coach, stretched her arms and legs. The flight wasn't crowded, thank Zeus, she had all three seats on her side of the row. A soft chime sounded. Above, the light on the seatbelt icon faded.

"You may now unfasten your seatbelts and power up your digital devices in airplane mode. Our flight attendants will begin serving complimentary beverages and snacks."

She'd never really gotten the knack of flying under her own power. David was really good at it. He'd even saved her from a violent gang that attacked them in Petra last summer, when she'd also learned he could make himself invisible.

Which he had been for all practical purposes since they'd parted at Seattle-Tacoma International Airport. More than a week without a word. No way in Tartarus was she going to cave and text him first.

Cleo retrieved her cell phone from the bespoke exterior pocket of her backpack and dug to the bottom of the bag for one of the Fran's

Gold Bars she'd opted not to give to Waller. The kind with almonds in caramel, coated with dark chocolate, would pair nicely with red wine. Her cell phone blipped. The message icon at the bottom of the screen was superimposed with the number 3.

Veronica first. Athena second. David.

She deliberately read them in order—Veronica's cheery bon voyage, Athena's cryptic sentence about an immortal she'd be partnered with at The Village. Funny no one had mentioned that before. Then:

Happy last day of Chanukah. Saul left for a job. On my way to Mount Olympus, see you there?

Cleo's chest heaved. It all came flooding back, their joyful and intense time in Seattle, the promises they'd made for all eternity. Almost too beautiful to bear and so terrifyingly fragile.

Flying out, can't say where. Gone six weeks at least.

She confirmed receipt of Athena's text and sent an emoji-laced holiday greeting to Veronica. The smartly uniformed Air France flight attendant anchored the refreshment cart in the aisle nearby, asking the person in the row ahead if they'd like a beverage. Cleo ordered a Bordeaux blend of no particular pedigree. Her cell chimed.

Weird. U alone? accompanied by a bright yellow worried-looking emoji.

Yes.

Okay to write?

Would he be able to track her to The Village if she contacted him while there? Would they even let her keep her cell phone during training?

Need to check with Olympus, Inc.

She set the phone aside, sipped her wine, and nibbled the Gold Bar, too preoccupied to enjoy the tastes and textures. Another chime.

IMU with a beating heart emoji.

Cleo chastised herself for the tear streaming down her cheek. She and David had always had rotten timing. Who knew it would hound them forever?

IMU2

She blinked back a new tear and hit send. Something caught the corner of her eye, a blur out the tiny rectangular window. It passed by so quickly she couldn't make out a specific shape. A bird? But what kind of bird could fly so high and so fast?

MONDAY, DECEMBER 22, 2025

Langley, Virginia, USA

Pan landed outside George Bush Center for Intelligence in Langley, VA, CIA headquarters. His mortal get-up of chinos, long-sleeved dress shirt and sports coat had created serious drag on his velocity. He looked forward to leaning back in a shuttle for the ride to training camp.

The CIA campus had many buildings. His rendezvous point was in the original building, a long multi-storied structure in mid twentieth-century style, fronted by a free-standing portico that vaguely suggested mortal notions of the Space Age. His instructions were to join the class bound for the super clandestine, top secret training facility called The Village, at the Memorial Wall in the lobby. Further, he would recognize and approach the yet undisclosed partner Athena had selected to work with him on their coming mission.

He made his way through the main doors and continued toward a few dozen hopefuls, men and women determined to become the new crop of clandestine officers. Flanked with modest amounts of luggage they were gathered in front of a marble wall engraved with multiple rows of stars. Above the stars was an inscription:

In honor of those members of the Central Intelligence Agency who gave their lives in the service of their country.

Pan tamped down his natural extroverted impulses. This was no place to joke around. These mortals he'd train with, eat with and befriend, were willing to die if duty required. He could practically smell their seriousness.

One of them, a woman, had a purple aura topped with a barely detectable sheen of gold. A capped super corona. Pan, a naturally gifted seer of auras had seen this a few times. A deliberate attempt to conceal the Biggest of Big-G Gods signature in one's pedigree for whatever personal or political reasons. She certainly resembled a classic Big-G woman: tall, regal, gorgeous. Cleo something, the one who worked for Hermes.

Cleo wore a dark gray pantsuit, popular with female mortal politicians, and stood perfectly still between two flags that bracketed the stars.

A suitcase and backpack rested against her leg. He bypassed the conversing cliques of mortals, all of whom seemed to know each other already, and approached her.

"Fancy meeting you here." A cliché opener but he was too tired for originality.

Her spine stiffened. She turned around, her large eyes that tilted up at the corners taking him in with disbelief.

"Howdy, partner," he joked, to break the tension.

"You?" It came out loud enough to turn nearby heads. "They sent *you*?" she said a few decibels lower.

"Happy to see you, too, Cleo." Her last name arrived in a mental thunderclap. "Or would you rather I called you Agent Petra?"

She raised her nose to an imperious tilt. "We're officers, not agents. Didn't you read Athena's briefing documents?"

"No time. My orders came while I was announcing Poseidon's damn parade. Anything else I should know?"

Though Cleo Petra was gorgeous, her schoolmarm attitude turned him off. This caper would be a drag if she didn't lighten up.

She looked at the space around him. "Where's your luggage?"

"Didn't bring any."

Petra crossed her arms and scowled. "Gosh, do you think maybe that makes you stand out? Like you're not from around here? These people," she indicated the nearest group with a tilt of her head, "are training to be spies, Pan. They notice things like that."

"Spies?" he said. "I thought we were called officers."

Her face flushed scarlet.

"You," she snarled, "are impossible!" Cleo turned her back to him and resumed her study of the engraved stars.

"Some people," he muttered. Sure, he'd racked up a bad reputation and, until recently, had been nothing but an embarrassing pain in the butt to his father, Hermes, but... Maybe that was it. Maybe she'd heard the old man's complaints one time too many when she'd been his executive assistant. Maybe the arduous role he'd played in the War Against Hunger, work that had elevated him from drunken goat herder to hero, wasn't enough for her.

Off to a miserable start, and not for the first time.

Tuesday, December 23, 2025

City of Mount Olympus

Hermes slumped in his office chair. Waller hovered in the doorway, sheaf of documents in hand. More paper. Where did Waller file all his project proposals after Hermes gave them a cursory review and signed off? And why did he present them on paper instead of transmitting them digitally?

The Messenger of the Gods and bad boy inventor knew the answer: digital files were easy to ignore and he'd done so with abandon. Paper was Waller's workaround. It didn't take the kid long—the irritatingly polite, good-looking, brilliant kid—to adapt to Hermes' curveballs. He'd considered writing Waller up for overuse of resources that contributed to climate change, but once Veronica investigated the origin of Waller's paper pushing she'd bust Hermes good and proper. He'd become a walking, talking rubber stamp, without recourse.

Hermes pointed to his desktop and Waller deposited the proposals—only three today, thank Heaven and Earth. Reviewing proposals was inescapable, but at least he'd sloughed the tedious duty of escorting the newly dead to the River Styx onto one of Heracles' people in Security. This left more time to monitor and subliminally channel tweaks to the projects of inventors in the mortal world, visitations made at warp speed so he'd be home in time to beg Monique for an audience with P. B. every day. The weariness of travel was compounding in his mind and body. He'd get some rest later this week when many mortals paused work to observe their winter holidays.

A solution to the primary problem was nowhere in sight. Where were today's Edison, Fulton, and Henry Ford, who'd had a genius for scalability? The brightest mortal minds these days seemed as preoccupied by platforms and social media as Waller. Waller, the Olympus, Inc., success story of the century. He'd been publicly recognized by Veronica, who'd held a corporate-wide assembly and presented him with the coveted Innovator Award. Hermes, being a mere immortal, felt jealous and rejected, but there were serious issues that concerned him beyond his admittedly petty feelings. He'd seen so much over four-plus millennia, could spot a fad from ten thousand kilometers. How had social media morphed from a simple communications tool to a powerful means of behavior modification? Inspiring mortals to consume less and conserve more was a critical piece in the climate change solution, but it was far from the only piece.

Hermes flipped through the proposals—two tweaks to the overall Green World Works campaign and one about a juice bar in some North American city that made him shake his head in disbelief. For reasons Hermes didn't comprehend (because he refused to read the subsections in fine print), Athena's initials appeared at the bottom of each page. Fine, let the new Golden Boy and Ms. Perfect plunge into some screwball scheme that landed them in the corporate meat grinder.

No longer caring if he landed there with them, Hermes signed, and signed, and signed.

It never got old, driving Mom batshit crazy.

P. B. had heard Monique say it dozens of times, how doing a stint as a volunteer executive for a microloan NGO in a mortal desert was perfectly doable while also caring for a new baby. He was poised to prove her wrong.

Timing was crucial. In the front pack he pretended to doze, lulling Mom into a sense of calm as she studied manuals and toggled between computer screens. Then, when she was deep in thought:

"Butt-Butt!"

He followed this with a barrage of giggles and clapping his plump baby hands. After his fourth assault she reached for her digital device.

"All right, Butt-Butt, if that's the way you want it, I'm calling Grandma." She said it with forced sweetness, like he was a dog and wouldn't understand she was hugely pissed. "Damn Pan," she muttered while she waited for Aphrodite to pick up.

At first P. B. was annoyed when Pan said he had to leave town. For one thing, he loved their Wednesdays—days filled with new and exciting experiences. Also, he'd planned to con Pan into being his ally in the mortal world when Mom started her volunteer work. When the door on Pan shut, P. B. soon realized the window this opened was by far the better route.

~ * ~

Aphrodite answered Monique's request, but she was far from happy about it. In the mirrored walls of the elevator to Monique's luxury condo she noticed the deep wrinkles in her forehead. Her hot pink polished fingertips pressed on the furrowed surface, patting the tension away. Just because she was mad didn't mean she had to look like crap warmed over.

Christmas Eve, of all days, and for once this century she had plans, which were also Monique's fault. Hephaestus, Aphrodite's husband, had noticed the Holly Jolly Love Fest gift bag from Monique under their tree this morning. He'd ordered a romantic dinner from Club Dionysus, due to arrive at 6pm. It was now past two. She'd be home by six, probably, but she'd had her own plans for working up to their at-home date night.

Goodbye to the massage, the soak, the facial she'd set up and had to cancel. Chances were she'd only have time to freshen her lipstick and dive in once she got back.

Monique met her at the door, handed her P. B. in his front pack like he was a parcel.

"I owe you, Mom," she said brusquely and shut the door in their faces.

Aphrodite strapped on her grandson "Your mother is too intense for her own good."

They descended to the lobby and hit the New Mycenae neighborhood street. Her plan was to take P. B. window shopping in the downtown district at Teddy Bears and All the Rest, the best toy shop on Mount Olympus. The three-storied shop had acres of display windows on the ground floor. During the winter holidays they were filled with fanciful scenes from the mortal world—snow-covered villages, top-of-the-line train sets, a band of one hundred automated stuffed animals playing "Jingle Bells." Okay, so that could cause headaches after a couple of minutes, but P. B. seemed to enjoy repetition these days.

"Butt-Butt!" He squealed.

Aphrodite looked up and down the street to make sure Poseidon hadn't pulled into view.

"Butt-Butt, indeed, P. B., but it's getting a little old, don't you think?"

They walked along quietly, the baby's head resting between her breasts. Just like a guy. He craned forward, eyes following a slick new single-horse chariot, the harness decorated with mistletoe and holly, then raised his face to her.

"I think you're right, Grandma."

Aphrodite stopped. She took a hard, unflinching look into his eyes. The look of adult intelligence was undeniable, she'd noticed it a couple of times before, but—

"It's time you and I had a talk." His baby mouth formed the words with precision. "But this will be our little secret. No need to drag Mom into it."

~ * ~

Fun as it had been to drive the grown-ups crazy with his one-word spoken vocabulary, P. B., too had grown to find it tedious. Besides, he needed an ally, someone who could go above and beyond the bottle, the burping, and the diapers. His fascination with Poseidon had more to it than a babyish attraction to glitter and bluster. Something he'd been born with had awakened an irresistible impulse: he had to get to the sea.

Grandma's violet eyes, riveted on his own, blinked.

"What in Tartarus…"

He waited until she started to breathe regularly again.

"You're not hearing things, Grandma, or, at least you're not imagining you're hearing things."

She shook her head. "You little shit." Laughter colored with a note of hysteria burst from her hot pink lips. "You amazing little shit."

He bristled in her arms. "I wish you wouldn't call me that."

"And I wish you wouldn't call me grandma. That word makes me feel older than dirt."

"Fine. Fine already. At least you have a real name, not just a couple of stupid initials that stand for Power Baby. Sounds like a ragdoll on steroids."

Grandma exhaled mightily. "Do me a favor and don't go all passive-aggressive, okay? Why in Tartarus did you decide to come out to me?"

"Easy. You're the most powerful grown-up I have regular access to. And I've got plans—lady." By Zeus this was awkward. "Call me Pablo, okay? And I'll call you…?"

"Aph. It's short and already sounds like baby talk."

He tried the syllable out a few different ways, cracked himself up when he belched it.

"No belching, Pablo," Aph said menacingly. "Remember, I'm a lot bigger than you, even if you can talk the hind leg off an ox."

She started walking again, slowly this time. He'd been working on his pitch all day and rolled out his complicated, brilliant plan. Pablo understood he was asking for a lot, among other things for Aph to take a leave of absence from Love, Inc., at the same time Monique would be away. It was key that the three of them, together, leave the City of Mount Olympus for the mortal world. She'd be powerless to bust him: all he had to do was communicate in front of everyone else the way a normally developing immortal baby would. In the early months mortal and immortal babies were almost identical in behavior and skills, he'd heard it directly from Monique's nurse practitioner, the one called Elle.

"And besides," he said, "we don't really know just how strong my powers are at this point, do we? I might stray to the dark side if there's no one to guide me."

Aph didn't say anything, but the way her body stiffened told him what he needed to know. Willingly or unwillingly, she would be his accomplice.

The Underworld

Persephone studied the faux Elysium sky. As long as she'd been Queen of the Underworld (two-plus millennia!) the high dome had been painted a uniform pale blue. Now, scaffolding climbed hundreds of feet to a large white patch at the apex. Hades, eternally tight-fisted, had been forced to make the repair (the leak originated in the mortal world) but he'd put off painting. Even though he had caves full of treasure and mineral wealth, he moaned about current revenues being down, some problem with gate crashers, and the related lost ferry fares for crossing the River Styx.

She looked away from the eyesore and focused instead on the inmates of Elysium, a sweet group of souls who, of all those in the Underworld, were the ones who qualified for reincarnation. The old nun, the one in the blue-trimmed white habit, hadn't had her turn yet, but she seemed to enjoy her work as an orientation volunteer. She— Teresa was her name—was leading a party of newcomers through the ever-bearing orchard. Teresa's syllables were clipped, her words energetic:

"Do not feel sad because you died during the holidays," she said to the group. "While it is true melancholy will descend on your loved ones each time they celebrate the season, it also brings them closer to the lesson of renewal and rebirth. Sometimes, a death timed as was yours has the power to save someone's eternal soul through self-examination. You must all exist in the hope you will one day be reunited with your nearest and dearest here, in Elysium."

A round-cheeked shade raised his hand.

"Yes, Harold?"

"Is it true, Mother Teresa—"

The nun cocked her head. "First names only here, Harold. Your question?"

"Is it true, *Teresa*, that we're having a celebration today?"

Teresa smiled, her teeth remarkably uniform and pearly. "Yes, that is correct. Our manager, Freya, will commence with her annual Yule observance when our tour is complete."

That's why Persephone was in Elysium today. Freya's Yule bash was the only bright spot on the winter calendar.

"Persephone!" The sweetly golden voice of Freya trilled through the trees.

The goddess herself, a member of the Norse pantheon who'd given up an eternal life of adventure and wealth in favor of the quiet pursuits of Elysium, appeared with hands outstretched.

"I'm so pleased you're here," she said, taking Persephone's hands. Freya's touch was as warm and reassuring as a comfortable pair of slippers. Aside from Cerberus, the three-headed dog who guarded the gate to the Underworld, Freya was the only being down here Persephone considered a friend.

"I wouldn't miss it," Persephone said. "Can I help with anything?"

Freya waved a hand dismissively toward the heart of the orchard. "Nothing to do, it's all set up." She tucked Persephone's hand in the crook of her elbow and escorted her to a long table, covered with snow-white linen and laden with platters of food. Each dish featured ingredients from the orchard, pies and pastries and conserves, and cheeses studded with fruit.

Freya brought her lips close to Persephone's ear. "Any luck with the baby?"

Persephone sighed. They'd had a heart-to-heart when she'd returned from this year's harvest. All her married life she'd longed for a baby but Hades was adamant: children were too expensive. The dream denied had become an obsession after she'd held P. B., a darling infant from the City of Mount Olympus who'd been brought underground as part of a scheme to vanquish a dark force known as The Power. That's what they'd said, anyway, Pan and Heracles and Artemis and Zeus who were all in on it. Persephone longed to keep the baby but Pan, who claimed he was the baby's brother, had taken him away.

"No," she whispered back. "Hades won't hear of it. You know how he is once he makes up his mind."

Freya's laughter filled the air. "Perhaps I can help you."

Persephone realized she and Freya were both tall, slender and blonde, but they were also radically different in appearance. Freya was lithe where Persephone was halting and clumsy. Persephone's hair was pale, the color of corn silk; Freya's was rich with strands of coppery gold. Their eyes were large and well-shaped, but Freya's held a perpetual twinkle where Persephone's eyes reflected sorrow. Freya was the Norse counterpart of Aphrodite, every bit as adept at romantic love and sex, but with an intellectual bent. In contrast to Aphrodite's tabloid and sex toy empire, Freya knew the subtle art of poetry. Erotic poetry.

Freya's voice dropped again to a whisper. "I've poured the Mead of Poetry into Hades' special cup. Once he drinks it, all the romance in his soul will rise to the top for twenty-four hours. With luck, he'll give you anything you want."

Persephone squeezed Freya's arm. "Thank you." Hades loved her, in a way, but the passion between them had been short-lived, a scant few decades after he'd grown magical flowers to seduce her and abducted her underground in his opulent chariot. She hadn't seen the chariot in centuries, but with help from Freya's elixir, maybe…maybe tonight he would cherish her for something more than keeping him company in their loveless castle.

~ * ~

She and Hades left Elysium under the full sun, since the sun never set there. They passed under the portal and started up the path to the castle. The gems in the cavern ceiling glimmered like stars. Anatole, Hades' valet, walked ahead with a lantern. Persephone thrilled when Hades wrapped his strong arm around her waist. He pulled her close, lips to her ear, and murmured, "There once was a girl from Tartarus."

Persephone received his raunchy limerick with outer appreciation though the crude punch line repulsed her. Anything could be endured if it resulted in creating a baby. She clung to that thought as he slipped one of his hands down the front of her toga and fumbled with her breasts.

"Nice titties."

Heaven and Earth, he was coarse! She should throw him off this instant, run back to the castle, and lock herself in her suite—but this would not make a baby. Maybe they could adopt? But no, the Mead of Poetry would wear off before that could happen. She must persevere!

They followed Anatole up the grand staircase and down the cold onyx hall to Hades' wing. The valet shot Persephone a knowing and sympathetic look. She'd seen him talking privately to Freya. Was he in on the subterfuge? When he flashed her a quick thumbs up she was certain of it.

The two of them alone in Hades' chambers, her husband unbelted her toga and eased it off her shoulders. He stood back. A string of saliva fell from his lips and sparkled in the firelight. Hades initiated the removal of his own clothing, piece by piece, each move punctuated with the sly raise of an eyebrow as if he were letting her in on a big, juicy secret.

He approached her with an odd, slinking gait and drew her onto the vast bed, made up as always with black silk sheets not for sensual reasons but because he had sensitive skin. Still, the cool, smooth texture on her bare skin was a delight. Persephone closed her eyes and thought of the baby. Hades lowered his big, hairy body onto her and…

His head fell alongside hers, snoring.

In a way, it was a relief. She'd almost forgotten what a burlesque he made of sex and if it weren't for the baby… She slid out from underneath his sleeping hulk and settled on the other side of the bed. Wounding his vanity would get her absolutely nowhere, and the Mead of Poetry had hours to go before it gave out. Maybe she'd get another chance.

Do I want another chance?

The question made her shiver. But the baby. The baby…

In her dreams her belly swelled and her breasts grew heavy, the miracle of pregnancy and the unbounded joy of creating someone to love who also would love her. Forever and ever.

~ * ~

Freya gazed into the pond behind her cottage.

"Show me what I wish to see."

The surface rippled. The pale blue reflection of Elysium's ceiling deepened to a glossy black. The image of firelight resolved, illuminating the outline of a massive, canopied bed. Two figures, one slender, the other broad.

She wasn't a voyeur. Persephone's desperation and Freya's empathy for the sweet, sad queen had made her curious to see if the Mead of Poetry had performed as needed.

Things looked promising—until they didn't. The Norse goddess of Love, Sex, and many other interesting things waved her hand over the liquid mirror to erase the depressing scene.

Poor Persephone. The woman didn't merely want a baby, she needed one to grow into her own potential. She was a natural beauty with a loving heart and much to give but most of that was squelched beneath the surface. Persephone was a timid iceberg of a goddess, and who could blame her.

"Time for a new approach," Freya said to herself. Hades kept

Persephone under close supervision during her winter months in the Underworld so a near-term intervention was out of the question. Come spring she'd go topside again, far easier to assist. Not that Freya could leave Elysium, ever, but she did have connections. She would watch the pond for her opportunity. With luck, Persephone would become a mother before she was summoned back to the subterranean kingdom.

THURSDAY, DECEMBER 25, 2025

The Village, Virginia, USA

Cleo Petra waited in front of the dormitory for the shuttle, fingering the collar of her dark blue polo shirt. Everyone wore these, standard issue for all officer trainees. Something about the lay of the collar wasn't quite right, sewn on without precision. Normally she'd ignore a detail like this but now was not a normal time. Ever since they'd arrived at The Village the pace had been relentless. So far this week they'd been inundated with technical information, trained on firearms and drilled daily on hand-to-hand combat. Her physical and mental exhaustion was extreme, and now it was time to put whatever she'd absorbed to an early test: role playing.

She'd spent most of her allotted hours for sleep memorizing her cover as Elizabeth Witheridge, diplomatic attaché from the fictional nation of Potark. The exercise would take place in a fully simulated village at the compound, with every detail mirroring reality up to and including personnel engaged to portray the residents. Normally she'd find this kind of challenge stimulating; now, she was just too tired.

But that was the point. Officers in the field had to be alert every minute of the day and exhaustion was an occupational hazard. It was imperative she perform as if she were training for a life and death mission just like the mortal candidates.

Pan was waiting for the shuttle, too. He was talking to one of the other candidates, a guy who knew a lot about American cinema. Knowing she'd be paired with Pan on an assignment in the real-world Cleo had worried they'd be paired together for training, too. That wasn't how it worked, thank Heaven and Earth. Something about him continued to annoy her, though he'd been perfectly decent since they'd connected on Monday. Was it his centuries of lewd and drunken behavior that had sometimes been inflicted on her, or the worry he'd caused Hermes, his dad and her boss? She couldn't erase that past, even after his recent heroic mission in the War Against Hunger. Whenever she thawed toward him her skeptical nature kicked in. Did this isolated incident herald a true change of character, or was it a blip?

Cleo let out a breath so hard the bangs on her forehead danced.

Maybe she was just being a bitch. She boarded the shuttle with the other trainees. They were soon set down in the simulated village, to do reconnaissance of all locations and meet the citizens who worked there.

Reconnaissance was a timed exercise, but she held back a few minutes to watch where the others spread. Many headed for the bar, a likely spot for picking up stray bits of intel but she'd never gone with crowds. Cleo chose the most distant storefront and strode toward it. Though the weather was mild, the village streetlights were decorated with winter decorations—evergreen boughs and red ribbons. Only then did she recall it was Christmas Day.

The shop had multi-paned display windows, decorated on the inside corners with something suggesting snow that likely came out of an aerosol can. Colorful covers of newly released hardbacks faced the street. When she opened the door a bell tinkled overhead.

"Welcome to Evermore Books," the man behind the counter said. Not too tall, forty-something, hair shot with gray, wiry build. His most memorable physical characteristic: aside from his coloring, he looked like an older version of David Bernstein. Though she'd only met him once, shared two rounds of Corpse Reviver martinis with him and David one unforgettable night in Seattle, Cleo was certain of her ID.

"Merry Christmas," she said, one eyebrow raised. "Have we met before?"

He regarded her over the top of his wire framed glasses with benevolent patience.

"And Merry Christmas to you, young lady, though I fear you've mistaken me for someone else. My name is Evermore. Amory Evermore."

"My apologies, Mr. Evermore," she said, her cheeks burning. The trainees had been cautioned that surveillance cameras were everywhere in the village. "You have a strong resemblance to a friend of mine." If a trainer asked about this interaction she'd say she'd been fishing for intel.

"I hear that a lot," he said. "Is there a title I can help you find today? A gift, perhaps, for a friend?"

"No, not today. I'm from Potark, Elizabeth Witheridge with our embassy. I won't see my friends back home for a while." Not a flicker of acknowledgment from Amory "Saul" Evermore. As part of the exercise she'd been given an objective to hone her inquiries toward gathering information for an upcoming embassy party. A bookstore might be the perfect place to learn more about the environment she'd be working in and the people she'd need to influence. She led with a soft opening.

"Burkosia fascinates me, Mr. Evermore. I'd like to know more about it. Can you recommend books on local history or culture, possibly some biographies of leading citizens? Anything you have about local heroes or institutions would be of great interest."

Saul (she chastised herself to think of him as Evermore) tapped his index finger on his chin. "There's the political treatise written by our president when he was a young man. That might be of interest, and a new book on the history of the palace. They've made substantial renovations lately as I'm sure you're aware."

There had been a line or two about that in a briefing: technological upgrades, from smart refrigerators to state-of-the-art security systems. Similar renovations had also been made in the Potark Embassy, where the reception would take place.

"I'll take one of each." She proffered her camp-issued credit card, what she'd assumed was a piece of stage dressing until the officer in charge of approving expense reports clarified real funds were channeled through a real bank on campus. There was a limit on how much trainees could spend in a given day, a collateral skill in fiscal constraint that would be necessary on a live mission.

Evermore perused the floor-to-ceiling shelf labeled Nonfiction and pulled out two volumes. "Can I interest you in some lighter reading as well? Perhaps a suspense novel or historical romance? The president's wife is a romance fanatic. If you ever have the fortune to meet her it would make a natural topic of conversation."

She probably would be introduced to the first lady at the reception. If there was an opportunity to talk...

"Thank you, that's an excellent suggestion."

The book seller set a third hardback on top of the others. The cover art was a portrait of a young woman in nineteenth century dress. The top of the cover ended at her neck, leaving her disconcertingly without a head.

"This is one of her favorites," Evermore said. He penned a hasty note and slipped it into the romance, bundled up the books in brown paper and tied them with a string. "Happy reading, Ms. Witheridge, and Merry Christmas."

"Merry Christmas to you, Mr. Evermore. I'm sure I'll be back."

The shop bell tinkled and she was back on the street. Cleo worked quickly to case the other shops and buildings, entering and exiting other venues, questioning proprietors and employees, studying each building for alternate exits and possible hidden rooms or passages. She'd forgotten to do that at the bookshop, damn it. What if Evermore's place was part of a critical escape route?

And what was in his note?

The village clock tower chimed a melodic code that signaled recall time. Trainees returned to the shuttle. Pan (she'd heard him give his alias as Hermesson) was at the head of the line, in buoyant conversation with a sandy-haired man and a wide-hipped redhead.

"Wonderful pub," he said, clapping a hand on the man's shoulder and winking at the redhead. "Wouldn't be surprised if I stop there again."

Critique of their simulation would arrive by 10pm that evening. Cleo started to second-guess herself. Should she be more outgoing, more engaged with the other trainees? It was imperative she succeed in this training as a prequel to her actual mission. Failure was not an option.

After a bland meal in the sterile, crowded cafeteria and a few hours exploring her new books, a ping sounded from her computer. An internal email addressed to Petra.Cleo read *12/25/25 simulation performance adequate; excessive time in bookshop inappropriate for first reconnaissance but good intel gathered; be mindful of time limits*

There was also an attachment, a document with a dossier on her target at the embassy reception: First Lady Masha Krintz. Plenty of time in the next three days to finish the historical romance she'd already burned halfway through. In addition to the dossier there was an organizational chart of Potark's embassy personnel. Her cover surname appeared on the third level down with two other names, all of them titled diplomatic attaché. The level above was Secretary to the Ambassador: Hermesson. Cleo swore under her breath. She reported to Pan.

City of Mount Olympus

Hermes sat stiffly on the edge of the loveseat, P. B. balanced on his knees. Monique, who'd deigned to give him an audience with his own son, sat across from them in her favorite armchair, the well-padded one upholstered in paisley tapestry that matched the love seat. P. B. squirmed in what Monique called the "darling" reindeer outfit Aphrodite had given him. P. B. shoved back the hood with his perfect pink hands and shook his oversized head as if to erase the feel of stiff felt antlers.

"Don't let him do that, Hermes, I need to take a picture for

Mother," Monique snapped.

The perfect effing family Christmas. Instead of sliding the miserable hood back on his son's head Hermes cooed "Who's Daddy's best boy?" Monique stuck a finger in her mouth and pantomimed vomiting.

Door chimes, tuned to a song by the mortal known as Cole Porter that Monique favored, sounded. Who would drop by unexpectedly on Christmas night? The list was short. Pan was in the mortal world doing something for Athena. Monique had already bitched about how Aphrodite, who'd covered for Pan's weekly babysitting slot at the last minute, had made it clear she was spending Christmas Day at home, with Hephaestus, period.

The door chimes started a second volley. Monique rose with the aid of a cane. In spite of his irritation with her, Hermes felt a pang of guilt. The damage to her reproductive and digestive organs during P. B.'s horrific delivery was mending but, as she frequently reminded him, was still extremely painful. At least she didn't need the walker anymore.

Monique groaned as she stood tall to look out the peephole.

"Someone in effing green glitter," she said. "Must be some drunk." She slid the chain in place and peered through the crack of opened door.

"Sorry to disturb you, Monique." The voice was deep. Holy Zeus, injured as she was did she already have a new boyfriend? "I know it's late but I couldn't let the holiday pass without bringing a little something for the tyke."

"Poseidon?" The bafflement in her voice was plain. "Just a minute." She pushed the door forward and removed the chain. "Please come in. P. B.," she called into the living room in her sweetest mommy voice, "you have a visitor."

The blustering giant of a man shuffled in; his expression surprisingly meek. When was the last time Hermes had seen him, at Veronica and Clifford's engagement party last summer? Then, Poseidon had brawled with Jim Smith, one of his own sons. The fight ended when Pan, wildly drunk and airborne, bombarded Poseidon with a shower of barf.

Monique motioned for Poseidon to go ahead of her. Hermes noted the odd-shaped parcel wrapped in holiday paper tucked under his arm. He should stand and offer his hand, but with P. B. on his knees he simply smiled and said, "Merry Christmas, Poseidon."

"And Merry Christmas to you, sir," Poseidon said with old-fashioned cordiality. He looked down at P. B. "I met this wonderful boy of yours at the Parade of Lights, there with his granny. What do you say, young one?"

P. B. slapped his plump palms together. "Butt-Butt!"

Monique, looking both annoyed and drained, shot Hermes a look that said *you take care of this* and settled back in her chair.

Hermes scooted to one end of the love seat to make room for the sea god. Once they got past the formalities, he offered to let him hold P. B. Poseidon carefully took the baby in his huge hands, the expression on his face pure awe. Hermes held up the Christmas gift.

"Would you like to see what Uncle Poseidon brought you?"

As if he'd been born knowing how to wrap the most powerful Olympians around his pinky, P. B. gazed up at Poseidon and chirped "Butt-Butt!"

"Mother said something about P. B. picking that up from Pan when he emceed the parade?" Monique said.

Poseidon's body tensed so much the loveseat shuddered. Hermes' brain whirled out a rapid analysis. Must be a reference to Poseidon's rescue of the mortal seawall by expanding his body to fill the sink hole underneath? Olympus, Inc., water cooler gossip said his vast, well-muscled buttocks had appeared in the hole on the Underworld side.

The God of the Sea laughed hollowly. "One of Pan's many jests. Since it amuses the tot, I truly don't mind."

Heaven and Earth, maybe Poseidon *was* drunk.

"Look at this, buddy," Hermes said to change the subject. He unwrapped the gift, a plush stuffed animal in light and dark blue with silver points running from the back of its head to its inward curled tail. "Your own seahorse!"

Poseidon grinned. "Squeeze it."

The toy's fat belly resounded with *squee-hee*. P. B. punched his baby fists in the air and cheered.

Hermes could see it now. The moment P. B. developed enough tensile strength he'd be squeezing that thing from morning until night. As Monique raised her phone to record P. B.'s bliss, Hermes resolved to ensure the seahorse would accompany P. B. to the mortal desert, even if he had to send it there himself.

The Village, Virginia, USA

It was close to midnight when Cleo crept into the dormitory bathroom with the headless hardback, *Lady Whatnot's Encounter*. She'd been riveted to a screen for the past hour-plus, studying her assigned role as diplomatic attaché from a fantasy republic. So many details she was required to live for the next five weeks, details she'd be evaluated on. If she screwed up she'd be tagged as killed and bounced out of the program.

Cleo's eyes ached. The overhead light was dim. She selected a stall, closed the door, took a seat and slipped Evermore's note out from under the front dustcover flap.

It was in code. Of course. Cleo scoured her memory for details of the patterns they'd studied so far, a substitution code that had to do with the most commonly used letters of the alphabet, another that used a common word or phrase as the key.

She tucked the note back into her book, flushed the toilet to avert suspicion and washed her hands before returning to her room, a small rectangle with a narrow bunk and tiny desk. Exhausted, Cleo sprawled on the bunk, switched off the bedside lamp and closed her eyes but her mind continued to churn. Saul had written the note after he'd recognized her. That being the case, he might have helped her with the key word, something simple that she'd recognize quickly. She turned the light back on, grabbed the romance novel and a pencil and returned to the bathroom. Cleo scrawled the obvious words at the bottom of Saul's note and tried a few iterations. ACTOR. No. FIDDLER. No. DAVID. It started to make sense...

Make contact at Embassy party. He changed abruptly.

The first part was clearly simulation intel, but the second? That, combined with Evermore's choice of keyword meant only one thing: Something had happened to David, and she wouldn't have a chance to find out what that was for at least five more weeks.

FRIDAY, DECEMBER 26, 2025

Cleo Petra cooled her heels in the chief training officer's waiting room. She had the odd feeling she was facing admonishment but had no idea why. She'd completed all her written assignments on time, and earned a passing score on the interactive digital exams. A seemingly acceptable four and a half days so far, yet she'd been yanked out of a class on brush passes, the art of passing a document to another operative without breaking stride. She'd bumbled the document on her first couple of attempts but lots of others had, too.

The chief's door swung open and her private secretary stepped out.

"You may go in, Officer Petra," the young mortal man who seemed her equivalent age snapped. Heaven and Earth, they were serious here! Necessary, of course, since the mortals were training for circumstances that, for them, meant life or death.

"Have a seat, Petra."

"Thank you, Chief."

The office fixtures were expensive, streamlined, and spare. What there was—two chairs, several neatly filled bookcases, and an ultra-modern desk—was made of glass, stainless steel and black leather. The chief, Ms. Chant, fit her surroundings well. Female, mortal (pink aura visible if Cleo squinted), early forties. Her long dark hair was pulled into a tight ponytail at the base of her neck. She wore the standard issue polo shirt and had the sort of eyes that instantly telegraphed she could see everything. Cleo felt like a document being scanned.

"Important intel to share with you. Classified," she peered over the top of her bulky tortoise shell-framed glasses. "Good," she said the instant Cleo nodded to signal she understood their conversation was confidential. "You've been assigned to deep cover. Research and development department of a fossil fuel company. Texas."

Texas. Cleo riffled through a mental file index, sorting for details from this week's class on regional characteristics of North American countries and states. Tower-topped oil wells. Cattle. The sport the Americans called football.

Chant handed her a single sheet of paper. "Your resume. Your application to East Fossil Fuels will be digital. We have someone working on the inside to ensure you're the selected candidate. Memorize the qualifications now. I'll shred the resume before you go."

Master of Business Administration, Villanova. Undergraduate degree, geology, Arizona State University. Teaching assistant and PhD candidate, ASU.

Her new name was Patricia C. Leo. Easy enough to remember. She handed the sheet back to Chant. The chief slipped it under her desk. The shrill of blades emanated from the knee hole.

"We don't know when you'll be called for an in-person interview with East Fossil Fuels. Until then, you'll be required to perform double duty. In addition to your field ops training, you'll be assimilating your cover for the Texas assignment. You will report back here for additional personal details tomorrow, at which time you will be tested on your resume recall. I urge you to review the information you received today at least once hourly." Chief Chant rose, signaling an end to their interview. "Good luck, Ms. Leo."

They gripped hands and shook once. Cleo wasn't sure if her already-taxed brain would hold up under the new requirement, but what choice did she have? With luck, her real assignment would start soon so she could drop the ops training and focus on just one thing. Once she was released, they'd surely give back her digital device? Then she could contact David, possibly meet up with him wherever she was going in Texas if he wasn't immersed in school by then.

She'd return to the bookshop and ask for books on Texas and her alleged home state, Arizona. Since Saul/Evermore had just toured the southwest in a production of *Fiddler on the Roof*, maybe he would share some first-hand observations?

The next village simulation was tomorrow morning. Of course she would follow up on whatever additional intel Evermore could share about the first lady. Hopefully she could find out more about David, too, though of her three lives the real one was not a priority. She pushed Cleo Petra and Patricia C. Leo into the wings and gave Elizabeth Witheridge center stage.

SATURDAY, DECEMBER 27, 2025

The instant she stepped off the shuttle Cleo strode the length of Main Street to the bookshop. Amory Evermore was waiting on a customer when she passed under the tinkling bell.

"I know you'll be happy with your selection, Mrs. Parsons," he said to the middle-aged woman who waited while he tied up a flat rectangular parcel with string. "The author, in my opinion, is at the top of her craft in this volume. No one can write a spy thriller like she can."

"Thank you, Mr. Evermore. You know I haven't missed one of hers yet," the woman said with pink-cheeked enthusiasm.

Town folk. Mrs. Parsons was, doubtless, another paid actor. There was a scattering of residential neighborhoods between the dormitory and the simulated town. Cleo now realized all the houses were occupied. So many players in this game.

Once Mrs. Parsons was out the door Evermore turned to Cleo. "Good morning, Ms. —Witheridge, is it?" Could the surveillance cameras pick up the I-know-you twinkle in his eye? "How can I help you today?"

She asked for books on Arizona and Texas.

"I have a combined history of Arizona and New Mexico, but the Lone Star State?" He strolled to the section marked "United States History and Politics".

"Sorry, nothing in stock but I'd be happy to look up some titles and order something for you. Let me see…" He returned to the sales counter and tapped on the keyboard. "Texas. Architecture. Geography. History. Culture. Industry. Oil Industry. Politics—"

"Oil Industry, please."

She chose the most current title, also a history volume noted as a classic.

Evermore peered over the top of his glasses. "There's a ten percent discount for prepayment on special orders."

Cleo proffered her credit card. "Thanks." She longed to ask about David but couldn't think of a way to phrase her question—*What do you mean "changed abruptly?"* —without flagging surveillance.

While she waited for the credit card to process, the shop bell sounded. She glanced toward the newcomer.

Pan.

Her insides turned to ice. What if he figured out she and Saul— Evermore—knew each other? David had asked her explicitly not to tell anyone about finding his dad. Word getting out might cause trouble for Saul. Her best option was to get out of there, fast. Cleo thanked Evermore when he returned her credit card and nodded to Pan on the way out.

Suddenly she was starving. The aroma of bacon and eggs wafted from a Mom and Pop restaurant wedged between a bank (closed on Saturday) and a Laundromat where townspeople tended long rows of washers and dryers. Every table in the eatery was taken, except for a small two-top near a swinging door in the back. She followed the hostess, a young woman dressed in jeans and a lightweight sweater, to the vacant table.

"Today's special is French toast, sausage and fresh-squeezed orange juice," the woman said. "Would you like some coffee to start?"

Yes to that, and to the special. A different young woman with a half-apron tied around her hips brought a steaming earthenware mug. Cleo peeled the top off a pod of half-and-half to lighten the very dark cup of java (a word from the mortal slang dictionary Athena had provided).

"Hey!"

Pan. Again.

"Mind if I join you, Ms. Witheridge?" he said, scanning the packed restaurant.

"Not at all, Secretary Hermesson," she said in a pleasant tone while begrudging his rank.

"Great!" He signaled a waitress to bring him a cup of coffee by pointing at Cleo's cup, then pulled out the chair opposite. Pan put his elbows on the table (Cleo's mother, Titania Petra, would have a fit), steepled his fingers and leaned forward. "The guy in the bookshop," he said in a loud whisper over the clatter of cutlery and conversations bouncing around them. "Did you notice his aura?"

"No," she said honestly. Since she knew Saul was immortal she hadn't bothered.

"Pink, like you'd expect for a mortal, but with a purple corona. Odd, don't you think?" The waitress set a mug in front of him. "Thanks, sweetheart," he said as she topped off Cleo's coffee and bustled away.

Cleo willed her face to stay neutral. "What do you think it means?"

"It means, Ms. Witheridge, that Mr. Bookstore Evermore might be one of us. Maybe Athena planted him to check up on us, make sure we're not screwing off. Not that *you* would do such a thing."

Fine, let him think that, it might keep him in line.

"Maybe so."

Seattle, Washington, USA

Jim Smith tucked a third pair of chinos into his suitcase, next to his travel version of *Stratego*. To pack a toga, or not to pack a toga? None of his clients expected it, but if Veronica Zeta called him into corporate for some reason? The CEO of Olympus, Inc., was a stickler for corporate policies, including the dress code. He wrestled a conservatively cut wrinkle-resistant gray toga off its hanger, rolled it up tight to minimize wrinkling, and stuck in a pair of business sandals, too. True, he could buy whatever he needed in the City of Mount Olympus, but he was a hopeless shopper and Candy was staying home this trip.

He should leave for the airport soon. Jim didn't look forward to the Seattle to Athens flight but he just didn't have the stamina to fly on his own after the crazy week of holiday activity. Titus was at the age where he was into everything—sucking on tree ornaments, tearing open presents when no one was paying attention. Somewhere he'd learned about the mortal invention called Santa Claus, harmless in itself, but the boy's incessant cries of "Santa! Want Santa!" whenever Jim or Candy tried to put him down for a nap had them both jittery with nerves.

"Aren't you ready yet?"

Candy leaned against the bedroom doorframe, arms crossed, foot tapping. She wasn't pleased with his summons, but a call from Zeus couldn't be ignored. Most immortals struggled with the holidays, racing around between whatever remained of their own traditions and the newer ones the younger generations expected. Solstice, Chanukah, Saturnalia, Christmas, Kwanzaa, probably some more he was missing. It was enough to give anyone a personality disorder. Or depression. Or a short temper.

"Almost," Jim said, certain he'd forgotten to pack something vital. They hadn't had much couples time lately, first hosting David and Cleo for an extended visit, and then the holidays. He was having a hard time kicking the cold he'd gotten during the tunnel crisis, something he picked up while he'd transformed into a seal to ferry messages between the structurelings holding up the sea wall and Poseidon's team at the sink hole below them in Elliott Bay. He was simply getting too old for that sort of thing. Ralph, who had immediately agreed to come out of retirement and disburse his molecules into the failing seawall, was older still. Word had it that Ralph, too, had come down sick after that adventure. Jim added Ralph's name to his list of people he'd check in on this trip.

The list was getting long.

There was Stella, of course, the eldest of Zeus' siblings who'd recently been through a crisis of her own with The Power, a possession Jim had identified. Her general practitioner, Apollo, had already referred her for a counseling session. The wild card was David Bernstein, who'd sent Jim an email vaguely alluding to hypnotherapy. Something he must have picked up during his months of traveling in the mortal world, Jim guessed. David had been through a lot (who hadn't lately?), finding the father he'd believed to be mortal and long dead. Jim had already talked to David about this confidentially. Given the gravity of Hera bestowing immortality on a mortal, not even Candy knew about Saul. That must be what David needed to talk about. As far as Jim knew, only he, David, Cleo, David's foster parents Milton and Thelma Bernstein, and Hera knew the truth. And Saul, of course.

The condo's intercom buzzed.

"I'll get it," Candy said. "Probably your taxi." Her sandals slapped slowly toward the front door. He loved Candy, and Titus, and their apartment, and the City of Seattle, and, frankly, he was burned out. But...

He zipped his suitcase and rolled it to the front door. Candy had snagged Titus along the way. She passed him to Jim for one last cuddle and kiss. Big toddler eyes studied him solemnly.

"Pa."

Jim held his son close. "See you soon, buddy. Take good care of Mom." He kissed his cheek and handed him back to Candy. "Not gone too long, I hope," he said in an apologetic tone. He took her chin in his hand and raised her lips to his. Something softened in her eyes.

"Miss you already," she said.

The intercom buzzed again. Jim depressed the button.

"Coming."

The penthouse door opened, then shut, behind him. While he waited for the elevator doors to part a scream of "Want Santa!" rose within the condo.

Jim sighed. "Me too, buddy."

SUNDAY, DECEMBER 28, 2025

The Village, Virginia, USA

Cleo Petra sat on the backward-facing seat of a stretch limo. She shared the bench with Mr. Hanks, her fellow attaché. Across from them were Ms. Morton, the other member of their trio, and Pan, who'd been issued a tux for the event. His wild curls were tamed with gel, his face freshly shaved. His posture was different, no longer his usual casual slouch but square-shouldered with chest raised. Amazing how dignified he could look when he tried.

She, too, had been issued clothing to match her identity. Cleo smoothed the front of her conservatively cut pinstripe jacket, the mate to her straight cut skirt that fell just above the knee. Morton had a similar outfit to Cleo's but in navy blue, Hanks a dark gray suit with white shirt and a striped, red tie. Appropriate attire for lower-level diplomats at an embassy reception.

Their European-make limousine that had picked them up in front of the dormitory joined others in a slow advance up the Potark Embassy's circular drive.

Cleo reviewed her mission once more in her head. She would be introduced to the first lady and, during the evening, pass a document to her without being detected. Cleo didn't know the contents of the document, only that the information in it was vital to their overall mission and of a highly compromising nature. If she was caught, she'd be seized by the first lady's bodyguards and interrogated by the president himself.

Satisfied with her recall, she looked at her companions. Morton nodded her head in rhythm, probably reviewing her own orders. Hanks stared out the window, fingertips drumming his knees.

Pan leaned back into the tufted leather upholstery, arms crossed over his solar plexus, his expression smug. Only he knew what each of his subordinates had to achieve. Cleo wondered what piece Pan would play in tonight's espionage puzzle. Again she wondered why in Tartarus *he'd* been selected as secretary to the ambassador and put in charge of the rest of them. Not that even the ambassador was important—Potark was the smallest country in the region. Its only political leverage was being at the crossroads for overland trade, plus a very small annual yield of gold from played out mines. Hardly worthwhile as a target of invasion, let alone an ally. The big fish swam in the pond called Burkosia.

As their limo crawled up the driveway Cleo looked out the window at the façade of the embassy building. The architecture was imposing yet unimaginative: fluted columns, multi-paned windows on the ground floor reinforced with ornate iron bars against the occasional insurrection. The Burkosia government was less than stable, the current leader's tenure so far a scant three years after a questionable election the ruling party insisted was free and fair. President Edward Krintz, one of a multi-generation succession of Krintz presidents, had won ninety-eight percent of the vote on the coattails of his grandfather who, at age ninety, had chosen not to run for his seventh six-year term. The president and first lady were young and glamorous. If their picture didn't appear on the front page of all the local newspapers at least once a week, talk of a coup circulated like a hurricane. Critics of the regime championed an underground newspaper that had dubbed Burkosia a banana republic without the bananas. You only had to spend a couple of hours at a dingy corner table in a local pub to hear it all.

At last they arrived at the grand entry staircase. Pan nodded for them to alight. He walked ahead of their group, Cleo and Ms. Morton side by side behind him, Hanks bringing up the rear. A footman in traditional costume which included two-tone pumpkin pants checked their credentials. They passed through wide double doors, into the grand reception hall, a monstrosity of marble, draperies and gold leaf calculated to telegraph power. They queued up in the receiving line, their destination two couples dressed in impeccable evening wear. At the head of the line was a man of late middle age, tan and gaunt with a leonine head of salt and pepper hair. He extended his hand to Pan.

"Secretary Hermesson," Ambassador Lord Ranko of Potark said. "Thank you for joining us this evening. Ms. Morton, Ms. Witheridge, Mr. Hanks, delighted to see you." Not bad for a man who'd never laid eyes on them before. Cleo smiled primly as she reviewed tonight's cover —Elizabeth Witheridge, second eldest daughter of the Earl of Witheridge—from the crowded storeroom of identities she'd acquired in the past week. Elizabeth Witheridge, not Patricia C. Leo, only child and first to attend college on either side of her family. Not yet.

Lord Ranko touched the elbow of the tall, elegant woman beside him. "You remember my wife, Lady Ranko."

Pan—Secretary Hermesson—bowed over Lady Ranko's gloved

hand. "A pleasure as always, my Lady."

"Mr. Secretary, Ms. Morton, Ms. Witheridge, Mr. Hanks. Welcome," she said in a voice like resonant honey. Cleo wondered what roles Lady Ranko had played on the stage.

"And may I introduce our guests of honor, President and First Lady Edward Krintz."

The president had artificially whitened teeth, his thick black hair cut short and bristled on the top. He wore a dark blue dress uniform with just enough medals on the breast to suggest merit instead of fiction. The first lady was long-limbed and slender, proportioned like a dancer with the posture to match. Her floor-length empire waist dress in sea green silk shimmered with sequins and pearls and her thick braid of dark hair was pinned up in a chignon, studded with more pearls.

"Delighted," the president said, tilting his head toward Pan and ignoring the rest of them.

"So happy to meet you," the first lady said. She nodded to the men and briefly took Morton, then Cleo, by the hand. Her eyes revealed only common courtesy, no hint that she expected an important document to be passed to her this evening.

"Ma'am." Cleo chastised herself for falling into the trap of believing they all had the same script. Maybe the first lady didn't know that Cleo—Elizabeth Witheridge—was her contact, or that she had any contact at all. She'd have to observe Mrs. Krintz this evening, use everything she'd learned about approaching and recruiting a target in the course of three short hours, including a time-killing sit-down dinner.

~ * ~

There were three times as many men as women at the party, reflective of a developing nation's patriarchal power structure. The ladies, as they were recognized in a concluding dinner toast, were dismissed to the formal living room for coffee while the men lingered at the extraordinarily long dining table to discuss matters of state.

Fortunately, coffee was a euphemism. Tea, sherry and brandy were also on offer, with a pleasing tray of petit fours circulated around the room by a handsome young serving man.

Cleo and Morton were not the only trainees in the group. A plump redhead and a short blonde played the role of diplomatic attachés from Cardovia (exporter of crude oil) and two more, both thin brunettes, from Spotan, a coastal principality known as a vacation mecca. Was anyone else charged with making a drop to the first lady? Would the women from the other embassies approach the wife of Potark's ambassador to cultivate her as an intelligence asset?

Aside from the trainees, the other women present were wives of politicians and industrialists. Any one of them could be a potential target and all of them had eyes and ears. Perhaps some of them were cast as informants. Had someone been assigned to watch Cleo, looking for signs of espionage?

She finished a delicious almond petit fours and blotted the thin sheen of stickiness from her fingers with a tiny cloth napkin. Mother, Titania Petra, had given parties like this well into the twentieth century and would feel at home in this setting. The formal living room was vast, furnished with clusters of Louis XV reproduction chairs and settees. The Cardovian redhead was engaged in a lively exchange with the wife of an armaments importer. Her blonde counterpart was seated between the two oldest ladies present, listening intently.

Cleo's target was part of a trio on the far side of the room: Masha Krintz with her hostess, Lady Ranko, and one of the Spotan brunettes. She, herself, had ended up on a settee with the president's mother and the wife of a key parliamentary figure, their group falling together outside the dining room.

"Edward is quite pleased with the reception," the elder Mrs. Krintz said in a languid tone. "Fine in its way, I'm sure, but nothing like the events honoring his grandfather when he held the office. His own dear wife died years ago, of course. It was my honor to serve as first lady at state events. And now it falls to Masha." Mrs. Krintz pursed her lips and shook her head. "I'm sure she'll be fine once she settles in, but I fear she has yet to take her responsibilities seriously. Why just the other day..."

Cleo glanced at the gilt clock on the mantelpiece. A few precious minutes to go until the reception ended. The sealed envelope she was charged to pass to the first lady felt as if it were burning a hole in her breast pocket. All she could think of to extricate herself from the elder Mrs. Krintz and the parliamentarian's wife was to excuse herself to the powder room. On return she would stop where the first lady was seated and—what? Lady Ranko and the brunette attaché wouldn't disappear into thin air just because she wanted them to.

By some miracle Masha Krintz looked Cleo's way when she stood, a fleeting glance without making eye contact but Cleo sensed a moment of acknowledgement. With incredible luck, the first lady would follow her. Cleo looked both ways as she entered the hallway connecting the living room to the powder room, according to the floor plan she'd studied. No one in the hallway. She touched her breast pocket to assure herself she still had the envelope.

An alarm shrilled. The living room doors banged shut, electronic locks clicked instantly. A section of dark paneling slid away. Two armed security guards emerged.

"Stop where you are!" one of them barked.

Cleo froze, her hand suspended over her breast pocket. The muzzle of a gun poked her in the back. Game over.

Instead of being held for questioning by the president himself, Cleo was delivered unceremoniously to Chant's office, handcuffs removed at the door. She'd been bounced! Athena would be furious. She'd blown her mission before it even started. And Hermes. She'd never hear the end of it from him.

The door to Chant's office was open, light spilling in a rectangle into the dark reception area. The chief sat behind her desk, dressed in a plush bathrobe the unexpected color of apricot.

"Sit down, Petra."

Humiliation and bafflement ricocheted inside Cleo, sparking each other to white hot anger. Still, she had sense enough to realize speaking out of turn would make matters worse.

"Busted at the embassy," Chant said. "You know the rules, Petra. One strike, you're out."

She held her tongue.

"Good," Chant said after a long pause. "At least you've learned that much. Here's something else for that magnificent brain of yours to file." The corners of Chant's mouth quirked. "You were set up."

Cleo half-formed the word Why.

"Happens all the time in the field. It could cost you your life. You need to remember that when you get to Midland. You're on the redeye flight."

"I don't understand, Chief," Cleo said. "Why are you sending me on assignment when I washed out?"

"The bust was my method of pulling you from training without arousing suspicion. You interview at East Fossil Fuels tomorrow at 3pm, the first interview in a three-round process, from which you will be selected to fill the vacancy in R and D. Understood?"

Stunned, Cleo nodded.

"Your belongings are packed, ready for check-in before your flight. East Fossil Fuels will send a limousine to the Midland airport. Their driver will be at the baggage claim, holding a card with your name on it. Ticket, passport," Chant slid a manila folder across the desk. "Your cell phone is in your carry-on bag but don't power it up until you deplane at Midland International, we'll have a block on it until then. Questions?"

"Do you want this suit back?"

"It's part of your cover," Chant snapped, as if she were out of patience talking to an inquisitive five-year-old. "Your agency paid for it and four others, including shoes and accessories. Those will be in your second suitcase. Speaking of agencies, this is where you and The Village part ways. Your own people will send the details of your assignment on their own secured link."

Chant rose. "Goodbye and good luck, Ms. Leo."

Cleo had emotional whiplash by the time she folded into the van with a magnetic Dulles International sign on the driver's side door. Three hours in the van to the airport, plus a seven-hour flight with two stopovers. At least there was only one difference in time zone.

At least when tomorrow's interview was over she'd have a chance to call David.

Cleo smoothed the rumpled sleeves of her pinstripe jacket. Funny how Patricia C. Leo and Elizabeth Witheridge had the same taste in suits. The thought struck her in a way that made her laugh.

MONDAY, DECEMBER 29, 2025

City of Mount Olympus

Zeus studied the *Stratego* board, pondering his next move. It was the bombs that preoccupied him. No matter what strategy he employed he couldn't see them coming. They'd barely started the game and already three of his soldiers had been killed.

His opponent, Jim Smith, looked like Tartarus warmed over. Though Zeus always did his own flying and hadn't experienced jet lag himself, he'd heard many a tale about its adverse effects from his colleagues this past century.

After long deliberation he tapped one of his majors against a tile of Jim's.

"Bomb."

Four killed! Zeus shook his head. "I didn't see it coming."

"Hmmm." Jim looked at him quizzically. The counselor had an uncanny sense of when Zeus needed to say something. The Biggest of Big-G Gods slumped in his armchair.

"It's Hera. She's done something terrible." Heaven and Earth it was hard to say. He raked his fingers through his hair and tried again. "I've tried to forgive her, but I...I try to act like everything's fine, that all's forgiven, but..."

Jim was good at silence. Sometimes too good. After a prolonged pause he moved one of his own tiles to a neutral square.

"I can forgive her as a husband," Zeus muttered, "but as a god? She broke one of the sacred laws, Jim. One of *my* laws."

"I can hear how upsetting this is for you."

"Well, naturally! I've been losing sleep over it since I found out. Those laws are for our own safety, Jim, to keep us from harming each other. And it's not the first time she's done it. The first time was with Heracles."

A raised eyebrow punctured Jim's cool neutrality.

"It's not what you think—"

"I'm not really sure what I think," Jim countered. "Can you tell me what happened with Heracles?"

"Everybody knows that old story, don't they?" Zeus blurted. "He did something that offended her when he was a mortal, so Hera tasked him with completing twelve labors. When he succeeded, she rewarded him. With immortality."

It had been a set-up that she hadn't let Zeus in on, a scheme to marry off their impossible daughter Hebe, the bitchy Goddess of Youth and Beauty. Even small-g gods refused to marry her, so Hera had created her own immortal son-in-law.

"Breaking the law is serious, of course," Jim said. "But in that instance, I think you'll agree some good came from Hera's insubordination. Without Heracles, Hebe wouldn't have a husband and you wouldn't have those grandchildren."

Zeus smiled. Spoiled though she was, he adored his granddaughter, Aster. They'd spent a lot of time together when Hebe needed a sitter, before he came out of retirement to become Provost of Athens U and Athens Tech. Just last week Aster had gleefully shredded the wrapping off her Christmas gifts at his and Hera's family party. The twins, Alexiares and Anicetus, were there, too. Handsome boys, and they'd done well for themselves once everyone understood their biggest gifts were physical, not intellectual. They now owned and operated A & A Services, the most popular private security company on Mount Olympus. The boys handled everything from digital home security systems to infrastructure and staffing for major public events.

Jim sat back from the game board. "Your move."

Zeus hopelessly studied the tiles, so distracted he'd forgotten the positions of the revealed bombs. He picked up a colonel. *Boom.*

"Given we all know how Heracles became immortal," Jim said, tapping a tile against Zeus' spy, "I'm surprised I've never heard about Hera's second offense. For a crime so serious you'd think there'd be a myth or two in circulation."

"She *wanted* people to know about Heracles, damn it!"

Jim rested his elbows on his knees and formed a steeple with his fingers. "Ah."

Zeus took a deep breath, then another. "I apologize for my outburst, Jim. Hera...I had no idea she was so adept at keeping secrets. She did it to protect herself, I suppose. You know how I could be in those days. If I'd known about Young Bernstein back then I don't know what I would have done. But this!"

Could he say the words, even to Jim? *Stratego* wasn't the only thing defying Zeus' logical abilities these days: he simply could not cope with the fact Hera had endowed David Bernstein's father—her lover—with immortality. And while she'd been consistent every time they'd rehashed her motive—to keep the man quiet—deep down Zeus didn't believe her.

"Ah," Jim said again. "I'm beginning to understand."

Ah, indeed.

Midland, Texas, USA

Cleo Petra, aka Patricia C. Leo, passed through the street level main entrance of the East Fossil Fuels tower. The building was lavish compared to modern mortal standards of commercial architecture, which tended toward economy and predictably straight lines. It rose thirty-seven floors, tall on the Midland skyline, with successively smaller tiers on each ascending floor. The overall impression was that of a gigantic glass and steel wedding cake.

The foyer was wide and sparsely furnished, the low winter sun bathing the walls in pale golden light. A long reception counter, sleekly executed in mahogany, was directly in front of her, the motto *At East Fossil Fuels We Are Your Family* etched in gold in a matching mahogany awning above.

A rosy-cheeked woman, early twenties in mortal years, stood behind the counter. She smiled warmly as Cleo advanced and gave her name.

"Good afternoon, Ms. Leo, and welcome to East Fossil Fuels! My name is Kendra," she said. "I'll check you in and notify HR that you're here." She gestured to a basket of jumbo-sized chocolate chip cookies to her left. "Please help yourself in the meantime."

Kendra turned toward her computer and briskly tapped the keyboard. Cleo reached for a cookie, leaning forward just enough to glimpse the screen, which displayed an unflattering headshot she recognized from Patricia C. Leo's passport, plus a dozen data fields. The receptionist filled the last blank and hit Enter.

"There, all set! Someone from HR will be down in just a few minutes."

"Thank you." Cleo stepped back from the counter, looked through the foyer windows to the active city street, and nibbled her cookie. Semi-sweet chocolate, butter and brown sugar exploded in her mouth, the calories racing into her depleted body. It was the by-Zeus most delicious thing she'd ever eaten. The meagre airline snacks had left her ravenous and she hadn't had time to eat after checking into the hotel. Every minute had been spent showering off the staleness of travel, redoing her hair and makeup and shaking the wrinkles out of the most attractive suit she'd been provided with—a red linen-textured fabric—all the while running her cover information in her head.

Cleo glanced back toward the desk. Kendra was speaking into her headset and typing rapidly on her keyboard. Cleo finished her cookie and licked the crumbs from her fingers. The elevator pinged and disgorged a young man in a crisp suit. The button on his jacket strained at the midsection.

"Ms. Leo!" He smiled, hand extended. Given his doughy appearance, the firmness of his grip surprised her. "So happy to see you. I'm Jess Travis from Human Resources. I'll be your contact during the interview process. Ready for phase one?"

"Absolutely."

"Good! You received the email I sent with the overview document attached?"

She said yes, though the last time she'd checked, her email access hadn't been restored by The Village.

"Now promise me you won't worry about the test? For candidates at your level it's a mere formality. Just a few questions to help us understand your workplace dynamics so we can anticipate the support you may need. *If* you're the successful candidate!"

His laugh was jovial. Everything about him was jovial.

They stepped into the elevator. Jess pushed a button on the second row from the top, one of two under a single, centered button marked PH. "We're taking the express to HR," he said. "This one goes to the Penthouse," he explained, pointing to the single button on top, "the private office of the East brothers themselves. If you make the final cut, and I dearly hope you do, Ms. Leo, you'll meet them in person. Such generous employers. Won-der-ful benefits! And of course their philanthropic work. I'm proof positive of that."

Cleo's briefing materials had mentioned the East School for Orphans, a top-rated boarding school for gifted children who'd lost both parents, sometimes their entire families.

The elevator chimed and the doors parted, revealing a reception desk and, beyond that, an open floor office with lots of natural light.

"Hi, Richard," Jess said to the young man behind the reception desk. This desk also had a basket of oversized chocolate chip cookies. "This is Patricia Leo. We'll be in Conference Room B for her work style evaluation."

"Welcome, Ms. Leo." Richard pushed the cookies forward. "Please help yourself to our trademark treat!"

The urge to have another was strong but anticipating the test made her stomach flutter. What if they spotted something in her answers that made it obvious she wasn't who she said she was? "Thank you, but I just had one downstairs. The best cookie I've ever eaten," she said in response to Richard's crestfallen expression.

"Maybe on the way out?" he suggested while Jess snagged two for himself.

The HR floor was divided between the sea of desks in the open space—benefits, continuing education and insurance administration, Jess explained—and two corridors with closed spaces. "Half conference rooms, half private offices for the manager and supervisors, for reasons of confidentiality."

Cleo's stomach began to settle. Not much different from the functions of the Immortal Resources Department at Olympus, Inc., where she'd held her very first position in data entry. Time to calm down and feel like Patricia C. Leo on the inside as well as the outside. Conference Room B was comfortingly like most conference rooms she'd seen. A long table lined with matching chairs, with a laptop computer midway down the table. A corner kitchenette unit with sink, coffee maker and a small refrigerator. A whiteboard at the far end.

Jess booted up the computer and pulled out the chair in front of it. "Please take a seat. As you can see the first few questions are on the screen and your name and today's date are at the top. If you become part of the East Fossil Fuels family we'll re-administer the test every six months to track shifts in your working style, if any. Supporting staff is number one at East!"

The friendly people, the delicious cookies, the corporate culture of taking care of staff. It sounded lovely, but taken in balance with what she'd read in the brief it struck a discordant note. Window dressing. It was her job to find something sleazy underneath it all to use as a lever against the climate-mangling Easts.

"Questions? No? Good. I'll leave you to it. When you've finished hit the End prompt. That will notify me to come get you."

The questions in the first section were multiple choice, the five options ranging from Strongly Agree to Strongly Disagree for responses to statements like "I enjoy working with others." Part two was similar, but the statements were no longer work-related and n/a, for not applicable, was added to the options. "I enjoy sharing leisure time with my family" she marked n/a. Patricia C. Leo, single with no children, was an only child whose parents had died in a tragic car accident three years ago. The End prompt was the only element in section three.

"Thank you, Ms. Leo," Jess said from the conference room doorway. "Please come with me and I'll see you out."

I'll see you out. Had she failed already? Probably against policy to say anything that could be construed as encouragement during the interview process, in case an applicant who wasn't hired came back at East Fossil asserting a job offer had been implied.

She tried not to think about it on the elevator ride down, put on her best Patricia C. Leo face for a cheerful goodbye to Jess and to Kendra on her way through the foyer. Her visit had taken less than an hour, yet Cleo was exhausted. She longed to get out of her suit, pumps and that wretched mortal invention called pantyhose, snuggle into a complimentary terry cloth bathrobe, and find out if her email was operational; if she could at last check in with David and find out what had happened to him in New York.

Cleo booted up her digital device in the cab. Thank Zeus her personal internet connection had been restored. Her finger was poised to hit David's speed dial when a snippet of Ravel announced an incoming call from someone with a local area code.

"Hello?"

"Is this Patricia C. Leo?"

"Speaking."

"Ms. Leo, this is Ms. Allen from East Fossil HR. I'm calling to let you know we expect you for phase two of the R and D position interview tomorrow morning at ten, if that's convenient?"

The last knot in her stomach eased. "It is, Ms. Allen, thank you. I'll be there at ten."

Suddenly Cleo was starving. She stopped in the hotel lobby to order room service—a bacon burger, a decadent indulgence David had introduced her to during their travels in the mortal world, and a vanilla milkshake. In her room she kicked off her pumps, peeled off her business wear and spent several luxurious minutes under the hard pulsing shower. Room service arrived shortly after she'd toweled off and wrapped herself in the terry cloth robe.

"Over there, please," she said to the bellhop, indicating an armchair by the window. The cart held a domed plate, a tall stainless-steel cup beaded with moisture and a glass. She handed the bellhop a couple of mortal dollars, and, on her digital device, tapped *Hi, how are you?* to David's account before sitting down to her meal. The bottom corner of the screen showed both the local time, just past 5pm Monday, and that of Mount Olympus. An eight-hour time difference; unlikely she'd hear from him tonight, especially as she intended to turn in as soon as she'd eaten. Fifteen days since they'd parted in strained silence at Seattle-Tacoma International Airport. It seemed like a lifetime, yet she was so numb from the events of the last twenty-four hours their separation didn't feel all that painful or urgent.

Cleo settled in the armchair and lifted the dome, inhaling the steam of beef and bacon. Time to set the day aside and focus on renewal.

TUESDAY, DECEMBER 30, 2025

City of Mount Olympus

Jim congratulated himself on bringing a toga. Through Zeus, Veronica had learned he was on Mount Olympus and had lined him up with the Immortal Resources department to present a best practices session for new supervisors.

He was grateful for the distraction. Yesterday's session with Zeus had strained his nerves to the extreme. It had taken every ounce of self-restraint to not reveal he already knew about Saul's immortality from his earlier session with David, in Seattle. It was good from a counseling standpoint that Zeus knew, good Hera had been forthcoming with him now that the proverbial cat was out of the bag, but Jim felt like he'd fallen into the middle of the scheme.

Thank Heaven and Earth for a bland morning at Immortal Resources to take his mind off the drama. There'd been a hiring spike for entry level staff and lots of promotions lately, due to the corporate-wide climate change initiative. Roderick Waller, the rising star who'd taken Cleo's spot in Hermes' department, was among the trainees. Cleo, he learned, was now reassigned to Athena and diplomacy.

"A lateral reassignment, part of the climate change initiative," Veronica said when she'd met with Jim before the seminar. "Lots of travel. She'll be gone for a few months, at least." Her impenetrable expression signaled she would say no more on the matter. He wondered if Veronica knew about the Saul situation, seeing as it involved her parents.

The seminar was a refreshing change of subject. Waller was indeed a bright light at Olympus, Inc. He'd enthusiastically shared with the class how his Green World Works initiative had already had the desired impact on mortal behavior. Jim was warm to him on the outside but felt a twinge of protectiveness toward Cleo. She clearly loved the work she did with Hermes and had hoped to return to it at the end of her leave. Roderick Waller, however, was congenial and whip-smart, impossible not to like and even admire by the end of the ninety-minute session.

Next on Jim's agenda, lunch with David Bernstein at a favorite Athens U hangout, the College Pub. Jim had a soft spot for the place, modeled on every cozy, run-down watering hole near any mortal institution of higher learning you could name. The décor had changed over the millennia, naturally, but booths were a mainstay. Jim hoped they'd sit at his favorite booth, the one where he'd carved Candy's initials back when he was a student, and she was the prettiest waitress.

David was there ahead of him, good thing because the place was packed. He was seated at the booth next to the one Jim had hoped for. The kid looked exhausted, shoulders drooping and dark circles under his eyes. In stark contrast to his session with Zeus, David couldn't wait to tell Jim exactly what was on his mind. After a quick hello and ordering Jim a beer to go with the nacho platter David had already started on, he dove right in.

"So you know about the forgetfulness charm, right, the one Milton and Thelma kept putting on me, so I'd think we were just a normal, mortal family? It's really bugged me, ever since I found out."

Jim nodded, thinking back fifteen years to when David had discovered he was Hera's son. A mere flicker for an immortal, but David Bernstein had yet to assimilate time in centuries instead of years.

"Okay. So then, when I was staying with Saul I watched this Barbara Streisand movie where she gets hypnotized so she can quit smoking and she finds out she has a bunch of past lives." David shoved a handful of nachos in his mouth, chewed vigorously and washed it down with a soft drink. "So it came to me right away that it would be worth a try, to see if I could recover my past through hypnosis. And I found this therapist—I didn't want to freak Saul out, I mean he's my dad and everything, but I barely know him, and Cleo's gone somewhere on some secret mission," the last two words delivered with a derisive snort. "She's probably not the right one to tell about this, anyway. I haven't told anybody until now. Until you, I mean."

Jim exercised considerable self-control to keep his jaw from dropping when David unrolled his history in Spain and his passionate love for the beautiful Lucia.

"So it ended on Christmas Eve with Thelma and plum pudding and it's driving me crazy to find out more. I really *loved* Lucia, Jim, like I…"

David grabbed another handful of chips. How incredible it must be for him to realize Cleo wasn't the first woman he'd deeply loved, that he'd had that experience more than a century before and only found out now. Jim had dated a few women before settling down with Candy, but of course he remembered those relationships, their strengths and weaknesses, how and why they'd ended.

"I can see it's a lot for you to process," Jim said. How many times had David fallen in love as he moved through his young adult centuries? How many times had it ended, and the memory been repressed by the well-intentioned Bernsteins? The situation had more potential as a minefield than *Stratego*.

"It's all I can think about, Jim, and the new decade of my master's program starts next month. How can I focus on that if I don't figure this out?"

Jim sipped his IPA. If David wanted what Jim guessed he wanted, doing it would almost certainly open a huge can of worms.

"You've gotta help me, Jim," David pleaded. "I have to find out what happened back then or I'll lose my mind."

Hypnotherapy was not Jim's favorite technique. He hardly considered himself an expert, but if he didn't help now, David might go to someone with questionable ethics. There were a few hypnotists in the City of Mount Olympus, their practices tending toward the self-improvement part of the continuum. Given David was Hera's son, the temptation to take advantage of the situation might...

"Let's look at a time for tomorrow," he temporized. "I'm staying at the Mountain High Plaza Hotel. We can meet there if that works for you."

David accepted immediately. They agreed to meet at 2pm, enough time, Jim figured, to reset after his 10am with Stella.

Though he longed for a nap after the IPA, Jim said goodbye to David and called Ralph, hoping to see him sooner rather than later. Brianna answered, said Ralph was still recovering from the cold he'd caught while reinforcing the failing Seattle seawall. She said absolutely no visitors but when Jim said he, too, was recovering from a cold contracted on that same job she relented, and invited him over for an early dessert.

"Feed a cold," she muttered and gave Jim directions to their vacation condo.

He'd barely knocked before Brianna threw open the door, grabbed his elbow and escorted him to a love seat facing an identical one bearing Ralph, wrapped in a quilt and cupping a steaming mug of something nastily aromatic in his big hands. His nose was red, his eyes a little glassy.

Brianna sped away and came back with two heaping plates of fruit, whipped cream and cake. "Trifle. Good for what ails you," she said. "You have twenty minutes, Jim."

When she turned her back Ralph made a face. "Overly protective," he wheezed after Brianna bustled away. "Still peeved I came out of retirement for the emergency."

Ralph had been a structureling, a type of immortal trained to disburse his molecules into mortal-built structures to reinforce them when the engineering was sub-par. Brianna had worked as one, too, brutally hard physical work that had recently been converted to digital. Good as the new technology was, sometimes the immortal-operated computers simply couldn't cut it.

They chatted about family and the holidays. In spite of a violent coughing fit, Ralph insisted he was nearly mended. Brianna showed Jim the door as soon as he'd finished his trifle. Lulled by a full stomach, he took a chariot back to the Mountain High Plaza Hotel. The Extra King bed called to him. Time for a nap, then to start his refresher on hypnotherapy. He was out the instant his head hit the pillow.

WEDNESDAY, DECEMBER 31, 2025

Hera paced the length of her corner office from window to window. The city below was overcast, reflective of the foul mood that had settled on her in mid-November and remained. The holidays—praise Heaven and Earth they were nearly over—had been a master class in presenting a calm exterior that bore no resemblance to her inner state. Zeus, too, was unsettled, though the face he wore in public said otherwise. They'd maintained the artifice of affection, especially in front of the children, but had lost the hard-won ease they'd cultivated in the past fifteen years, the only years in thousands where she'd felt equal to him, and genuinely loved.

Damn Saul Crispin. And damn David for finding him.

She paused and looked at her hands. A few age spots, impeccable ruby red nails. Strong hands that had made heroes out of nobodies, had raised legends and built up the most profitable department of Olympus, Inc. Why give her the power to make things if stodgy rules were used against her?

And why was Zeus the one who made the rules? Damn him, too!

It was all about power. That's what galled her most. His jealousy she could have worked with, could have acted contrite to counteract his wounded ego like she had when he'd first learned about the origins of David Bernstein. Ridiculous, of course, when one considered all the times Zeus had cheated on her. But that was beside the point, now. She'd escaped punishment when she'd given Heracles immortality, once she'd walked Zeus through the necessity of finding Hebe a husband. Heaven and Earth, miserable Hebe would still be living with them if Heracles burning on his funeral pyre had been the end of the story!

But giving Saul immortality…

Exasperated, she turned from the view, intent on the credenza aka liquor cabinet, Hera's work-around after Ronnie had forced the removal of its predecessor the mini-bar. The small hand on the clock overhead was at XI, a good thing as this meant the sun was over the yardarm somewhere. She liberated a bottle of Chardonnay, sipped, and thought. With Heracles, she had shown Zeus the overriding benefit of granting him eternal life. What she had to do now was illustrate why making Saul Crispin immortal was also of benefit. It would require a considerable amount of spin, but...

Hera set her empty goblet on an end table and strode to the office door.

"Gilda!" she shouted to her executive assistant. The middle-aged guardian of the Department of Marriage bustled to meet her, digital pad in hand. She peered through her thick-lensed glasses as intent as a hunting dog on point.

"Yes, Ma'am?"

"Is that Jewish holiday over yet? The one that changes dates every year?"

"Chanukah?" Her face brightened as it always did when she didn't have to research an answer. "It ended the day after the solstice, Ma'am."

"Excellent!" Her so-called love child should be home. "Put a call through to David Bernstein, Gilda, and tell him it's high time he had lunch with his mother."

"Yes, Ma'am. Right away, Ma'am."

Surely after spending days with Saul *he* would have gleaned something that made the man worthy of immortality? Some globally determined humanitarian award, perhaps, or a souvenir from one of the appalling mortal wars in which he'd saved thousands of lives, single-handed? The invention of a plague-defeating medicine? She wasn't asking for much. Even that idiot, Pan, had recently become a hero for saving the blasted mortals.

Gilda returned.

"Mr. Bernstein confirmed for lunch at noon on Saturday, Ma'am."

"What?!"

Gilda reared back, iron-colored braids swinging. "I'm sorry, Ma'am! He was just now on his way to an appointment and has orientation the next two days for the new decade of his master's program."

Hera took a deep breath and let it out slowly. "No need to be alarmed, Gilda," she said, cranking a stiff smile into place. "I'm just a devoted mother, eager to see my dear son. I'm going for some air now." She pushed past Gilda.

Gilda padded behind her. "Ma'am, you have an eleven forty-five with Ms. Zeta."

"Cancel it!" Hera said over her shoulder. Ronnie would give her Tartarus for cancelling but if she had to deal with one more family member right now she'd explode. Goddess of Marriage and Family might sound like a soft-power job, but Hera had been at it long enough to know it was quite the opposite. The covering up and posturing she'd suffered ever since she'd confessed to Zeus about Saul's immortality had pushed her to the brink, and David's refusal to meet her for lunch today was the straw that sent the proverbial camel to the chiropractor. She had two possible outlets for her frustration: a lunch-hour Five Thousand and Over Zumba class or a quick glass, or two, or more, at the Grape and Grain open 24/7.

At the elevator she pushed the down button and waited, toe tapping. The highly polished doors reflected a red-draped tower of rage. Checking first to confirm no one was around, Hera shook out her shoulders, tossed back her waist-length silver hair and straightened the belt of her signature ruby-colored toga. No point in looking like donkey droppings, no matter which venue she chose.

"Come on, come on!" she muttered as the pulleys hummed. The doors parted on Aphrodite, perfectly turned out in a hot pink mini-toga and a forest of platinum blonde hair extensions.

"I was just coming to see you," the Goddess of Love said.

"Excellent!" Hera strode into the car and pushed the inverted triangle icon with such violence she broke a fingernail. "We're going down."

~ * ~

Aphrodite swayed in a hanging basket chair, a fixture in the Free Love room she'd had installed in her corridor of therapy venues. Half of the original fifty counseling rooms remained intact; the rest had been sacrificed to the manufacturing division of Love, Inc. On the other side of the superbly insulated partition wall was a hive of activity—cutting, sewing and pressing fantasy costume pieces for the end consumer, one of the lucky millions to purchase a Love, Inc., patented Gift Bag for Lovers. The division's manager was excellent, of course, and the floor supervisor was an organizational genius as well as an inspiring leader. It would be hard to let go overseeing this process, though. The time she'd be required to chaperone Pablo while Monique worked in the mortal world stretched before her, undefined.

"Very kitschy," Hera remarked, seating herself in the matching basket chair opposite. She kicked off her sandals, tucked one leg underneath herself and adjusted the cushions behind her back. "The tie-died pillows are a deft touch."

"One of my most popular counseling habitats," Aphrodite said. Immortals followed and often adopted fads in the mortal world. She, herself, always had plenty to keep her engaged in life, but for some immortals eternity weighed heavy on their hands. Half the people who came to her for advice merely suffered from boredom. Dionysus, the God of Wine, put it best: trying out new and novel things helped to pass the time.

Hera's eyes tracked the shifting colored lights that blobbed up and down the white walls in imitation of a lava lamp. "All that's missing is sitar music."

"Coming right up."

Aphrodite tapped a button hidden in the frame of her basket chair. A recording of Ravi Shankar (such a lovely man for a mortal and how she missed him) welled from concealed surround sound speakers. She pushed the environmental aromatics switch for good measure. A slow release of jasmine scented the air.

"Breathe in, breathe out," Aphrodite coached. On the exhale, Hera's shoulders eased from square to a mild slope. After three more rounds of breath Aphrodite said, "Do you want to talk about it?'

Thank Heaven and Earth she'd intercepted Hera in the elevator. Her mother-in-law, and, after a lifetime of bitter rivalry now her dear friend, was on a downward slide. The thermos she'd passed Aphrodite at the Parade of Lights wasn't the spiced wine she'd expected but a ferocious hot gin punch laced with brandy. Why hadn't Zeus been with Hera at the parade? The two of them had independent lives and interests, didn't live in each other's pockets by any means, but at traditional public events they'd always made a showing. This year, Zeus had avoided the parade all together.

"Such a dull story," Hera said. Her snapping eyes inferred the opposite. Anger? Fear?

"Good holidays?' Aphrodite said, looking for a back entrance.

"Hah! The usual wretched routine, with Stella thrown in. Fortunately she didn't want to see us anymore than we wanted to see her, but Zeus insisted we make the effort after all she's been through. I still don't think of her as family—my sister, Heaven and Earth!"

Aphrodite wasn't crazy about Stella, either, after the role she'd played, hosting Pablo's malevolent half-father during Monique's pregnancy. Clearly Stella had been a pawn as much as Monique had been, drawn into the game of creating an heir for the ancient force of evil. Aphrodite didn't pride herself on maternal warmth, but a fierceness sprang alive in her when her children were threatened. Even after Apollo told her of Stella's near death during the crisis she felt no empathy.

"Time should make it easier," Aphrodite said, as much to herself as to Hera.

Hera raised an eyebrow. "We shall see." She peered around the room, decorated with an eye to freedom and transcendence. "Have you got any wine in this joint?"

She hated to enable Hera's self-destructive crutch, one she, herself, knew from the inside. Drinking worries away was a temporary fix at best. But something to lower Hera's inhibitions might facilitate Aphrodite's fact-finding mission. She tapped the button that buzzed direct to Eros, the best personal assistant on Mount Olympus. The room number would light up on a digital display in his office, prompting him to bring a tray of herbal tea and drug-infused sweets, what the mortals had dubbed edibles.

"Did you see your kids?" Aphrodite continued. "David must be back by now."

A noise like a growl vibrated in Hera's throat. "Is it too much for a boy to prioritize lunch with his mother? He's been back for days and not so much as a digital message. I reach out and he puts me on hold for three days. Three days!"

Ah. "Breathe in, breathe out," she prompted again. "I've ordered some refreshments. Let's just relax and breathe for now. We'll only talk if you want to."

Eros soon arrived, costumed in embroidered bell-bottom jeans and nothing else. Hera snorted when he handed her an earth-toned pottery mug, wisps of herbal steam rising over the top and floating down like a cloud of dried ice. She selected a piece from the edibles tray, muttered something about being too old for Turkish Delight but licked her fingers when she'd finished.

"Good." It wouldn't take long for the relaxant to kick in. Aphrodite set her own tea on a tall rosewood end table alongside her basket chair and leaned back into a sea of pillows. "I'm sure David's busy, getting ready for the new term," she said in a tone calibrated to soothe. "You mustn't take it personally, even if you are his mother." Excellent advice that Aphrodite, herself, had never been able to follow. "Let's look deeper. Your feeling might not have anything to do with David at all."

Hera's eyes closed. "It was so long ago," she murmured. "Desperate time. Didn't want to lose Zeus, didn't want to..."

"Didn't want to what, Hera? I promise you, as a counselor and as your friend, I will keep whatever is said in this room entirely confidential."

"Hmmm. Tiberias. Hot springs. Had to get away, couldn't take the …Zeus. Cheating all the time. Felt worthless, so old so ugly. Had to go… All those banquets, and afterwards with… Didn't think I could conceive at forty-six hundred but…David…wouldn't go away. Had to make him." Her mouth pinched as if trying to hold something in. "Go. Had to make him…"

Aphrodite worked slowly and methodically to overcome Hera's resistance, prompting her with simple questions until—Heaven and Earth!

She couldn't speak through her own shock. It wasn't the affair, something she'd known about for years. Even at her worst she wasn't hypocritical enough to judge Hera for that. But… All the Big-Gs had the power to gift mortals with eternal life, but who would be fool enough to tamper with that particular—that *sacred* aspect—of human existence? Hera had committed a serious crime in violation of Zeus' Laws. The punishment, if found guilty, was severe. She'd been acquitted when she'd made Heracles immortal, her act determined to be consistent with family and dynastic considerations. The jury (of which Aphrodite had been a member) had found unanimously in her favor.

There was another issue to consider, a matter of simple humaneness that did not concern the Court of the Twelve Great Olympians. Heracles could and did live with other gods. Not so for Saul Crispin. How could an immortal, born or made, bear to exist only in the mortal world, to survive again and again as everyone he knew and loved died? The prospect struck her dumb.

"Hera," she at last managed to say, "I need you to say that again, to make sure I understand."

"Saul. David's father. He's alive."

~ * ~

When David arrived for his hypnotherapy session, Jim was in a buoyant mood. He recounted his morning with Stella, the non-confidential parts, as he was quick to point out.

"Beat me three games straight at *Stratego.*" he'd crowed, "even when I tried a new strategy that I knew would win. Same wicked sense of humor as ever. She seems happy at Olympus Rest assisted living."

"Neat." David had a hard time picturing Stella as anything but cruel and hateful but, hey, getting major things resolved like no longer being possessed by a force of pure evil could probably change a person for the better. His own problem, though...

"I need to know what happened to us—to her, I guess..." David felt disloyal to Cleo to even think it, but if he wanted to get things straight with himself... "It was real, Jim, back in Spain, it wasn't like watching a movie. I was there—body, mind, all my senses. I can still smell her hair."

"That must be difficult, falling in love with a mortal," Jim said. "Why don't you lie back, take a few deep breaths to a count of ten for each inhale and exhale."

David reclined on the sitting room sofa; Jim seated nearby in a wingback chair.

"Take yourself back to the Bernstein house in Barcelona. You're on the bed in your room, waking from your nap. It's Christmas Eve. The sun is down. You..."

The shirt he'd traveled in was rank with perspiration. David stripped down to his undershirt and dropped the soiled shirt in a hamper for the maid. One bathroom, a luxury for families of middle class means, was between his room and that of his parents. The water from the hot tap soon warmed and he filled the sink. Incredible how fast his beard grew these days. He ran a soapy washcloth over his face and under his arms before working up a mug of lather to lubricate the work of the straight razor.

Refreshed, he selected his Sunday shirt from the armoire, attached a clean collar, and donned a dinner jacket. He first looked into the kitchen, the room astir with the cook and her assistant. Thelma had progressed to the dining room. She straightened a centerpiece of candles and made small adjustments to formal place settings for three.

"In here, David." Milton's voice, from the adjoining drawing room. Father rose from his favorite chair, one upholstered in leather that had come with the furnished house. Both parents had stressed to David the virtue of being adaptable to a change in household, something they did a lot, it seemed, compared to other families.

Milton extended his hand. "Merry Christmas, son, or nearly." Father was not given to fanciful conjectures, holding to available facts as one would expect from a banker. Except when it came to music. He adored Gilbert and Sullivan operettas. *The Pirates of Penzance* quavered through the Victrola horn.

"Merry Christmas to you sir," David said, matching Milton's

friendly grip, "or nearly."

"Hah!" Milton clapped a hand on David's shoulder. "What's your pleasure, my boy, a touch of sherry or something with a little more bite for the holiday? Some very fine brandy arrived from France while you were away."

"Thank you, sir." David leaned against the mantle, enjoying the radiant heat of the fire. He sighed, contented, his heart filled with the magic Lucia inspired. He'd tell them tonight. It wouldn't be like last time, when Mother had warned him away from the sweet girl in Edinburgh. Too young, she'd said, and perhaps she'd been right because that love had faded. But now, with Lucia…

"Here you go." Milton handed him a crystal snifter with a healthy topaz-colored pour. "What shall we drink to, David?"

"To love," said David, touching his glass to Milton's.

"Ah." Father's expression was indecipherable. "Ah," he said again, and took a drink.

Milton's silence was maddening! "Her name's Lucia," David said, unable to contain his urgent news. "I met her this trip, up the coast at Valencia. She's a remarkable girl, Father, a nurse, trained in England."

Milton appeared to study the contents of his snifter. "I can see she's made quite an impression on you, and quickly, too. You've only been gone a week."

"Yes. Yes, I realize that, Father." Zounds, it was hard to remain patient with him! "But surely you know how it is with love? When you met Mother and you all at once realized she was the one? I want to spend my life with Lucia. I know it as well as I know I'm your son."

Father opened his mouth to reply then abruptly shifted his gaze to a spot behind David. "Thelma, my dear, join us won't you?" Milton poured another snifter of brandy, handed it to Thelma and raised his glass. "To our family." Their three glasses clinked. "May we always be together, on this Christmas and many more to come."

"Hear, hear," David said reflexively, but the sentiment felt hollow. Why didn't Milton want to know about Lucia?

Milton turned to Thelma. "David has informed me that he is in love."

For an instant Mother's lips tightened, so quickly David barely saw it. "Well," she said, her mouth blooming to a rosy smile that did not reach her eyes. "Well. Isn't that something?"

Two, three. The snap of fingers.

David's eyes blinked open to the bland décor of a twenty-first century hotel room. He felt remarkably relaxed but...

"David. How do you feel?"

He rubbed his hands over his face. "Uhm, fine. I guess. But it's weird, Jim."

"I'm sure it must be."

"It's *real*." David sat up. "Heaven and Earth, Jim, how could I have forgotten her, what did they—?"

"Forgetfulness charms are powerful," Jim said. "I want to help you, David, and I will help you, but please consider the danger this could bring. Knowing and reliving the past could create difficult personal consequences."

Heaven and Earth, he felt down. The Bernsteins had behaved so strangely, like they were in an episode of *The Twilight Zone*.

"Yeah. I guess." David ran a hand through his hair, his mind scrambled. He had to talk to somebody. Sure, Jim was a friend, but it felt weird now that he knew—whatever it was he knew. Cleo was gone, Saul was working somewhere where there was no cell phone service. No way was he going to ask the Bernsteins about this, not after seeing how creepy they'd been in the past. Who could he just hang out with who would get it? All kinds of people must know about the forgetfulness charm by now. Veronica, for sure, but she was always busy and besides, she and Cleo were friends and if Veronica told Cleo about Lucia—

Jim rose and headed for the minibar refrigerator. "Buy you a beer?"

"No. No thanks."

He turned back toward David, arms crossed, head tilted to one side. "Are you okay?"

He could hear Jim's concern but sheesh, he really needed to get out of here.

"Yeah." He slipped on his sandals, put a hand out to Jim. "Thanks for helping me today."

"I'm here for another week. I've got some openings if you want to meet again. Hypnotherapy if you decide that's how you'd like to proceed, or we could just talk."

"Thanks."

He felt like a jerk, leaving, but there was too much to think about. He also felt deeply lonely. Weird that he didn't jump at having Jim's company, but that wasn't what he needed. He needed to talk to someone who knew what it felt like, to live and love and lose in the mortal world without knowing you were a god. He was half-way back to the Athens U when he realized who that person was.

Friday, January 2, 2026

Heracles had a code of behavior with many subsections. Part of the code was to arrive at appointments ten minutes early. As such, he was cooling his considerable heels at an underground drinking establishment favored by students.

The College Pub. Not where he would have chosen to meet a chum for a beer, but the Bernstein kid, who was family in a roundabout way, was his host, and his own mortal mother, Alcmene, had raised Heracles to be a gentleman so he'd accepted without comment. Not a bad place, the pub, but the booths were cramped for someone his size. He squeezed into a booth, and facing the door, watched and waited.

It wasn't easy, being tall and broad and as muscular as an ox. Heracles had started off mortal (though Zeus was his father) and had lived to adulthood. It had been a life loaded with incident, nothing like the carefree crowd that packed the tables around him. He was probably the only one present who hadn't come from a life of ease, with family affiliations at Athens U or Athens Tech. His own education had been excellent in all areas of learning that befitted a young nobleman, including a wide knowledge of arms and armaments, courtesy of his foster father, Amphitryon, the famous general.

None of that counted here. Most people here only knew about his heroic exploits and his work as head of Olympus, Inc., Department of Security. He did his job well but socially he was a fish out of water. The one immortal he could relate to was his half-sister, Persephone. Like him, she was compelled to live in a world where she didn't belong. The Underworld was precisely the wrong place for her willowy beauty and sensitive nature, even though she only resided there three months a year. When she lived above ground, performing her agricultural duties spring through fall, her mother, Demeter, worked her to a crisp. Sad, sweet girl. She deserved better than she'd been given. He shut out the dream of how their lives would be, together.

The green entry door swung open. David Bernstein walked with his torso angled forward, like a pup straining on a leash. Wild black hair, not unlike Pan's. Thick glasses. Dressed in mortal wear—jeans, turtleneck sweater, leather shoes instead of sandals. Just returned from an extended stay in the mortal world. And, for some reason, Tartarus-bent on talking with Heracles.

"Excuse me, sir? Heracles?"

Heracles half-rose, the table tilting up on his thighs, and lightly took the hand David extended. Restraint was his watchword, ever since he'd recovered from a deadly fit of madness in his mortal days. The tragedy had gnawed on him ever since.

"Thank you for your invitation, David. It's very nice to see you."

"Thanks for making time for me." The kid slid onto the opposite bench, smiled awkwardly. Worried. Why? "Have you ordered yet? My treat."

They ordered a pitcher of IPA and a platter of potato skins to share.

"So how's Hebe?" David said.

Heracles winced on the inside. Expected, as Heracles' wife was David's half-sister but he did not relish thinking or talking about her. He offered his standard reply.

"She's as always."

The bills she'd run up for the holidays were the worst yet. He wasn't sure they could cover the minimum payment this month on her Bank of Olympus platinum card. They'd had a row about it before he'd left for work this morning. Doubtless she was laid out on a chaise, having one of her migraines. That was her favorite weapon, next to taunting him about what had happened with Megara and his mortal children.

"Good, I guess, right? So."

The pitcher and skins arrived. David filled two chilled pint glasses to the top.

"Cheers," they said in unison as their glasses clinked.

Heracles carefully forked a potato topped with the works onto his plate, loathe to spill crumbled bacon on the tabletop. David had no such compunction, picked up a skin with his hand and gulped it down before Heracles had taken his first bite.

"So." Thank Heaven and Earth David had swallowed before talking. The last thing Heracles wanted to do was perform the Heimlich maneuver on his host. David took a swig of beer, wrapped his hands around the pint and stared at Heracles, his dark eyes huge behind the lenses. "I have a kind of problem that maybe you can help me with. You were mortal once, right? That's not just a myth?"

He took a long sip of IPA, rounded his grief into a manageable ball. "Right. It's not just a myth."

If David knew about Heracles' past, all of it… But perhaps he didn't. David had been raised a mortal, after all. Maybe he'd only had the usual exposure to the story of Heracles' life the average young mortal would have, read a sanitized telling in a book written for children or seen one of those embarrassing sword and sandal films the Italians made in the middle of the last century. His own sons had ridiculed him mightily about that.

"Good. Because that's kind of what my problem is." David picked up the pitcher and topped off their pints. The muscles in his face, especially around his mouth, were tense. Didn't want to talk but had to talk. "I, uh, I'm two thousand years old, but I don't remember most of it. My foster parents used a forgetfulness charm on me to keep me from realizing I was immortal. Hera's orders."

Hera's orders. The very thing that had turned Heracles, himself, into a murderer.

"I know it's kind of the opposite of your experience, you being mortal first and all, but you're the only one I can talk to about…" A tear welled behind David's lenses. "Heracles, I'm starting to remember some of it, about a hundred years ago. I met this girl and…"

Heaven and Earth. Heracles had performed many arduous tasks in his mortal and immortal lives, but he'd never shouldered the duties of an agony aunt. Even his own boys hadn't confided in him about their romantic lives, they'd simply announced who and when they'd decided to marry and that was that. David Bernstein, Hera's son, looked for all the world as if he needed a shoulder to cry on. Another one who didn't quite fit in, he realized, just like Persephone, just like himself.

"Take your time, son," he said. "I'm here to listen."

~ * ~

David was careful not to mention Saul. If Heracles knew that particular story, so similar to his own, it could be pretty upsetting. Plus, Heracles might consider him a security risk and he sure didn't want to get Saul into trouble.

He did share the details about his hypnosis experience in New York, though, and his session today with Jim.

"I feel kind of excited about it, kind of creepy, too, but mostly I want to know what happened to her, Heracles. I loved Lucia. I still love her."

Heracles' fingers were woven together, his hands resting on his heart. He looked incredibly sad.

"What would you do if you were me?" David said, both afraid of and desperate for an answer.

Heracles drew a deep breath. His shoulders sagged as if he carried the world on them. "I can understand your curiosity to know more about your own life, but David, brother, some things are better left unknown."

David raked his fingers through his hair in frustration. It was not supposed to turn out this way. They were natural allies, weren't they, a couple of guys who'd been messed with by the immortals? Sure, Saul had mentioned his own experiences with love and loss, how crushing it could be to realize everyone around you would die in a mere number of decades. For your own safety, your own sanity, you had to learn not to care. He tried again.

"The mortals you knew. I barely know you, Heracles, but you seem like a really nice guy. The family you grew up with, the people you loved, don't you miss them?"

"Yes. Of course. Every day."

The words came out like nails being pulled.

"I've never had the chance to feel that way," David said. "I can see how sad it makes you, but you're the lucky one, don't you see? Now that I've had a taste of what happened, not an imagined thing but something real, I *need* to know how it turned out!"

"David." Heracles made his name sound like a warning. "I'm going to tell you something most of the Big-Gs know, something Hera, herself, cursed me to do, though that doesn't excuse my actions. I did, as you say, love. My first wife, Megara, was the daughter of Creon, King of Thebes. She was given to me in marriage as a reward for defending Thebes from the Minyans. We were happy together and had children." The corners of his mouth tilted briefly upward but settled into a hard line. "I'm one of Zeus' bastards and Hera's hated me my whole life, then even more than now. She couldn't abide my happiness, sent me into a fit of madness. I killed my wife and children, David."

"Heaven and Earth! Heracles, I'm sorry, I didn't mean to—"

Heracles held up his hands, palms out. "No need to apologize. It has nothing to do with you, except to show you that terrible things, once seen, can't be unseen. Think of all the sorrow you've been spared, buffered from two thousand years of loss."

"Oh, man." David sagged into the booth. "Oh, man."

"You'll make your own decision, of course," Heracles said. "And

I'm glad you confided in me. Honored, really. The City of Mount Olympus can be a lonely place for people who don't fit the template."

The big man swallowed him in a hug when they said goodbye. "Take care of yourself, little brother," he said. "If you want to talk again sometime, I'm here for you."

David waited at the cashier station, his mind swimming. Lucia. Cleo. Saul. Heracles was great to talk to, but he couldn't make up his mind for him. Make another appointment with Jim? More hypnosis? Did he have the courage to face all of the hurt he was certain would come?

~ * ~

Zeus came home after his lunch meeting with the deans of Athens U and Athens Tech. There was much to do in his role of Provost with classes resuming next week but he simply couldn't focus. Not since Monday, when he'd told Jim about Hera and how she'd broken one of his laws. Again.

He paced the marble hallway at their penthouse condo, struggling to organize his thoughts. Hera had complained about his restlessness last night, how he'd kept her awake with his tossing and turning. By daybreak he'd figured out the problem—much as her making a mortal into an immortal gnawed at him, telling Jim about it had felt like a betrayal. He laid in bed, relieved to at last understand his feelings but stumped as to what to say to her.

Hera, my dear, I told Jim Smith you willfully broke one of my laws, but keeping it in was bothering me so much I...

Wimpy, at best.

Hera, as the Biggest of Big-G Gods and your husband, I must inform you that...

Too pompous and too much like a form letter.

Hera, my love, I'm so sorry I...

Groveling.

He looked up from his pacing at the sunburst clock in the entryway. IV XXI. She'd leave the office soon and, since she didn't have Zumba today, would come directly home. Was there a good way to break bad news? If there was, he'd yet to find it. Important, though, to point out Jim was bound to client confidentiality and could claim immunity from divulging whatever Zeus had told him in a court of law. On the other hand, that would suggest her crime might be brought to trial. He retired from the hall and stepped into the butler's pantry. Hughes, their butler since time immemorial, rose from his personal armchair and switched off one of his few guilty pleasures, his afternoon soap opera.

"Sir?"

"Hughes, when convenient, would you bring me a glass of ale? I'll be in the den."

"Very good, sir."

Zeus studied the décor in the den with fresh appreciation. Hera had excellent taste, insisting the Barcaloungers and big screen television be replaced with twin chaises, low tables, indirect lighting, and a jungle of potted plants. He paced some more, too agitated to settle on his designated chaise with built in massage and heating features, though his back and shoulders ached with tension. Part of it, he had to acknowledge, was his wounded ego. Something about this man, Young Bernstein's mortal father, had inspired her to gift him with immortal life. Heaven and Earth, if Zeus had done that for his own mortal consorts the world would be brimming with them! Zeus, the Thunderer and Lord of the Heavens, would not stoop to such improprieties. Affairs of the heart were one thing, but—

The sound of Hughes clearing his throat broke Zeus' musings.

"Your ale, sir." The butler lifted the cold sweating glass from the silver tray he carried and set it on the long, low table between the chaises.

"Thank you, Hughes."

"Anything else, sir?"

"No, Hughes." And the fewer ears, the better. "In fact, why don't you take the evening off? Hera and I can fend for ourselves."

"Very good, sir."

Zeus sat, sipped, and reeled back his jealous anger. It wouldn't be productive to dredge up Hera's criminal act again. The crucial thing was to simply tell her Jim knew about it, too.

Saturday, January 3, 2026

Hera arrived at the Grape and Grain twenty minutes early to get a booth instead of a table. The carafe of house white she'd ordered, down by half, was simply a coincidence.

The front door opened, flooding the dingy and none-too-clean interior with winter-bright light. A male figure, short and wearing the unattractive mortal invention called jeans, broke the light with a dark silhouette.

David shaded his eyes with his hand. The windowless interior had that effect on newcomers. Hera had learned to don dark glasses for a few minutes before entering this dubious den, not one of her regular hangouts but a venue she considered a friend in need.

He peered around, his nose wrinkling as if he smelled something bad, which was likely. When he spotted her in the booth farthest back he lowered his hand and shook his head. Disgust? Revulsion? Hera was beyond caring what he thought. This was not a feel-good mother and son tête-à-tête. She was here to get the facts and to convince him by whatever means necessary to keep his mouth shut about Saul Crispin.

David slumped into the other side of the booth. "Hello, Hera."

"So nice of you to lunch with Mommy," she said with acid.

He crossed his arms and glared at her. "What do you want?"

Heaven and Earth he was the spitting image of Saul, what she could remember of him after all these centuries. It would serve David right if she transformed him from immortal to mortal, and maybe she would, *if* she had that power.

"Menu." She pushed the acrylic holder that displayed a brightly printed postcard toward him, a short list of greasy entrees. "I recommend the Double Double Burger with Bacon."

Lull him with food. If he got up to use the restroom she'd dump the truth powder from the hidden compartment in her snake-headed ring into his drink to expedite things.

A waitress with mussed hair and dark circles under her eyes slouched over to their booth.

"What'll you have?" she muttered, pencil poised wearily over pad.

"Double Double with extra Cheese," Hera said. Hearty enough to soak up the wine.

David slid the menu back toward her. "Greek salad."

Hera bit the insides of her cheeks to mute the tirade she longed to spew at him for this petty act of aggression.

The waitress finished scribbling and looked pointedly at Hera's carafe. "Anything to drink?"

"I'm fine, thank you, and please bring a glass for my son."

"I'll have an Arnold Palmer," David said. That wretched mortal concoction of cold tea and lemonade he'd taunted her with the last time they'd lunched. That time she'd graced him with a mother's care, teaching him Biggest of Big-G cloaking as a bon voyage gift, a powerful spell that made the practitioner invisible even to Zeus.

The waitress sauntered off. With effort Hera arranged her facial expression to one of benign interest.

"Tell me about your trip, David."

"Why? You already know the punch line."

Hera burned to know how he had found out about Saul, to know who had betrayed her. She had told no one about the gift she'd bequeathed to Saul, not even her trusted servant Thelma Bernstein, who'd become David's foster mother. But much as she hungered for this information, something more important dangled over her head. She reached across the table and grabbed David's wrist.

"Listen to me, David. You must not tell anyone about Saul. Must. Not. Tell." He pulled back but she tightened her grip. "Even someone as naive as you must see he'd be in danger if word got out. If you care about him *at all*, keep your mouth shut. I mean it!"

Spent with emotion she released his wrist, heart pounding. It was dangerous enough Zeus knew. As he'd reminded her in their horrible conversation last night, charges could still be brought against her, as breaking Zeus' Laws didn't have a statute of limitations. Thank Heaven and Earth he still had enough love for her to hold back. For now.

Jim Smith knew. Surely the Petra girl must know? Had Cleo or David said anything about Saul to Jim's wife, Candy, who'd hosted them during their stay in Seattle? And now, Aphrodite, though she was bound by confidentiality. Five people, at least six if you counted Saul, himself, who hopefully had the sense to keep well hidden. Too many people were in the know. If even one of them didn't know Zeus' Laws—didn't understand the gravity of breaking them—and passed this information on as if it were merely titillating gossip? Tears brimmed in her eyes.

The food and David's loathsome beverage clattered onto the

tabletop.

"David, I—"

He slid out of the booth and shot to his feet. "Save your breath. I've had it with you and your self-pity."

She reached toward him. "You don't understand. Please come back, there's—"

"Goodbye, Hera." He spun on his heel and strode through the gloom toward the sunlight.

A presence hovered nearby.

"You want a box for that?"

Hera looked down at the soggy assortment of cucumber and tomato, and the grease bomb she, herself, had ordered.

"No. No thank you. Here." She fished out her Bank of Olympus Platinum Card. The caustic sweetness of the poor-quality Chardonnay had worn off midway through her second glass, which seemed a long time ago. Hera topped off her goblet. She should have let Saul die, should have killed him while it was still possible instead of suffering like this two millennia later for her stupidity. He'd better keep his mouth shut. Everybody had better keep their mouths shut.

~ * ~

David Bernstein walked for miles, didn't register where he was going after his derailed lunch with Hera. How dare she! He would never do anything to hurt Saul, even though he barely knew him. Saul hadn't had a choice about being absent from David's life, that had all been Hera's decision. She'd passed him off to the Bernsteins like a bag of dirty laundry. Now he didn't trust them, either. Sure, he didn't know his entire past in Barcelona but he had a very strong feeling Milton and Thelma had put an end to his relationship with his beloved Lucia. How many more times had this happened since he'd been old enough to fall in love?

By the time he noticed his surroundings he was in the posh New Mycenae neighborhood. Though exhausted, fury still simmered within him. His whole life had been a farce and all because of Hera. David longed to kick one of the fancy Art Deco-style lampposts that lined the street but, thank Zeus, had the sense to realize what a bad idea it was to kick anything when wearing sandals.

Instead, he sagged against the nearest lamppost. Tears pooled in his eyes. A farce, a lie, a huge deception, but the deception was over. It had ended with the hypnotherapy session in New York. Or was that just the beginning of a new and horrifying reveal? Heaven and Earth.

"Bernstein, I say, is that you?"

A voice rained down from above. He looked up into the worried face of his imminent brother-in-law, Clifford Essex. Made perfect sense, now that he realized he was in front of Clifford's condo building.

"You'll excuse me, old chap, if I say you look a wreck. Heaven and Earth, what's happened to you?"

"She…I…" Tears tumbled down his cheeks.

Clifford tsked. "Problems with the fair sex." He glanced at the digital device strapped to his wrist. "I was just on my way to meet Veronica but give me a mo' and I'll dial her up."

David wiped a hand across his face. "Don't change your plans, Clifford, I'm fine, I—"

"And I can see that you're not. Honestly, Bernstein, I've never seen a man more in need of a stiff drink. Won't be a minute."

David stood quietly by as Clifford engaged in a volley of texts. "She's not at all keen on this, but there are times," Clifford muttered. "I've got us an hour, my friend." He nodded toward the entrance door, indicating David to follow. In the foyer they waited for the elevator. Clifford tapped his device again. "Better send flowers, to be on the safe side."

He edited his story in his head as the elevator ascended to Clifford's condo. Telling him about the hypnotism, Barcelona and Lucia would be plenty to explain the tears without going into anything about Saul. Clifford was an aficionado of high-end Scotch and took joy in generously sharing his treasures with friends. David would really have to watch what he said. Especially on an empty stomach.

Clifford seemed to listen, topped off David's Scotch and soda before he could object. He seemed distracted, though, checking his digital device when it pinged and sighing like a man condemned. When the allotted time had elapsed Clifford raised his glass.

"Here's to the ladies."

Not the most tactful toast, but it covered their mutual troubles. David set down his half-empty glass and thanked his host.

New Mycenae was a long way from graduate student housing at Athens U. David ambled, slowed by the effects of Scotch. The air had cooled. Consulting his digital device he saw it was ten past four. He shivered, ducked into the first coffee shop he came to and ordered a double mocha with whipped cream. And a bagel, make that two, and a walnut brownie. What was this day about? What was his *life* about? Nothing and no one seemed solid anymore.

The calories started to kick in and quiet the questions in his head. He could find out more about Lucia through hypnosis, but did it really matter? It wasn't like he could time travel, like he could go back to her, pick up that life where he'd left it and live it through until... Obviously she'd be dead by now, probably had been for decades. How would it have been for her to grow old, but not him?

Yet there was something more, he knew it with gnawing certainty. It wouldn't have ended simply because Milton and Thelma had told him no on Christmas Eve, 1917. The passion he'd felt was real, that life was real. Lucia was real! How could his life move forward if he didn't know what had happened to her?

Two ways to do this. He tapped a quick message to Jim—had he said he'd be in the City of Mount Olympus for a week, or was it for the rest of this week? So he just typed *Hi, can we get together before you leave?* and hoped for the best. If he couldn't schedule another hypnotherapy session there was another alternative: research. Maybe he could even get permission to visit Barcelona if he made it central to a project. A paper on Gaudi's architecture would be a natural.

Ping. David looked down at his digital device. Not Jim, as he'd hoped. Cleo.

He hesitated before tapping the subject line: *Job.* Their email exchanges had resumed this week but his replies had been terse and she'd mirrored it back, which was weird because she was usually a chatty correspondent. Before they'd had their fight, anyway.

Got a job. Talk this weekend?

It was an eight-hour time difference, she'd mentioned earlier. Nearly five here was 9am that morning in Wherever-She-Was, Texas. Heaven and Earth, it was hard to navigate his feelings. Part of him wanted to tell her everything but another part held back to protect— what, exactly? His anger that she'd immediately agreed to get swept up in some crazy work scheme Hermes had orchestrated? His frustration over being out of touch? Was he trying to protect Lucia, the girl he'd loved a century ago, or Cleo, the girl he'd been madly in love with and if the noise in his head would ever clear, realize he probably still was?

Way to go he wrote back, letting her question hang.

MONDAY, JANUARY 5, 2026

Midland, Texas, USA

Monday morning Cleo gazed appreciatively around her suite. She'd been given another week at the hotel to allow time for apartment hunting, which was extra wonderful as valet service was included. Her five suits had been dry cleaned and pressed. The four she wasn't wearing were in the closet, shrouded in plastic garment bags.

She'd selected the pinstripe from the disastrous embassy party for her first day at East Fossil. Hard to believe only a week had passed since then. She'd been swamped, interviewing, and reviewing her cover. Over the weekend she'd read the policy, history and employee manuals Ms. Allen had sent, filled out a bundle of employment forms for payroll and benefits, and signed a letter stating employment verification and terms. Was seventy-five thousand dollars annually a lot in mortal money? Cleo queried the local cost of living. The local index was less than the national average but more than the average for Texas. Midland per capita income was just under thirty-two thousand. She figured she'd do pretty well.

There was more information from Olympus, Inc., background information on the East brothers, Edwin and Cyril. They were twins, and had established their business sometime in the mid-1970s following something called the OPEC Oil Embargo. There were clippings from *Fortune, Forbes* and *The Wall Street Journal*, some with photos of the Easts. Cleo charitably described their appearance as "blocky" in build, with "interesting" faces.

Another briefing document detailed the Easts' involvement in industry organizations and lobbying. In their early years they'd made substantial contributions to several non-profit environmental agencies but that had ended sometime in the 1980s. Also at that time a separate division of their research and development department that addressed the impact of fossil fuels on the environment was absorbed into general R and D.

Her mission had come separately in a brief email. *Be all eyes and ears for anything suggestive of secret dealings, bribes of public officials and/or illegal activities. Transmit your observations to Olympus, Inc., Department of War at this link:*

A specially encrypted communications portal. There was no mention of Pan, no estimate of his time of arrival or what role he would play in their investigation.

Cleo reported to HR at East Fossil Fuels shortly before 8am. A woman named Carol Allen, the HR manager who'd called with the job offer on Friday afternoon, said the first day was strictly orientation. Carol Allen was waiting for her in the lobby. She smiled broadly and extended her hand.

"Welcome, Patricia, to the East Fossil family!" Ms. Allen's enthusiastic two-handed shake was brief. She spoke with a drawl Cleo had noticed in many of the East employees. "I know everyone will be delighted to meet you and I guarantee you'll feel right at home. Cookie?" she said, snagging the basket from the reception counter and holding it toward Cleo.

"No thank you," she said. "I had an excellent breakfast not long ago."

Coffee and a banana snagged at the hotel coffee shop, but Carol Allen didn't need to know the details.

Ms. Allen, herself, took a cookie before replacing the basket. "I know I shouldn't," she said with an apologetic grin, "but these things are my weakness."

Cleo noted Ms. Allen's bulging waistline, compliant with previously observed corporate standards.

"We'll tour the building and introduce you to every department this morning," Ms. Allen said in a chirpy voice. "The afternoon is split between R and D orientation and coffee with the East brothers. They pride themselves on personally welcoming new members of the East Fossil family, along with some other employees to make a friendly gathering."

It seemed an impossible task, to buzz through all thirty-six floors in one morning. Some departments occupied more than one floor, twelve departments in all. She and Carol Allen stopped on the floors with the main reception desks. Janitorial, housekeeping and maintenance on the ground floor, R & D on two through four, and so on. Engineering had more floors than anyone, five in total, and also enfolded exploration activities. Marketing and its smaller sibling, Public Relations, was the second largest department (*Public image is everything* had been stressed during Cleo's interview). HR, of course—it had one modest floor. Legal was near the top, floors thirty-five and thirty-six. "The personal province of Cyril East," Carol Allen noted as the elevator doors parted, revealing an ebony reception desk. A brisk-looking young man sporting dark brush-cut hair with a bleached stripe down the middle was the guardian.

"Patricia, I'm delighted to introduce you to Michael Guy. Michael, this is our new R and D manager, Patricia Leo."

"Pleased to meet you, Michael," Cleo said.

Michael rose from his ergonomic chair, pressed his palms together and drew his hands toward his heart. He bowed his head. "*Namaste.*"

Ms. Allen chuckled. "Michael is our corporate yogi. He leads a class Tuesdays and Thursdays at the gym, twelfth floor. He's been a wonderful addition to the family, joined us just before the holidays."

Cleo noted his grey pinstriped suit fell smoothly over his still-trim torso.

"No previous experience is necessary and newcomers are welcome," Michael said, a twinkle in his dark eyes. Mischievous, almost. "If you join us, East Fossil will reimburse you for the purchase of yoga clothes and a mat."

"Our excellent benefits strike again," Carol Allen said.

Michael guided them down a corridor lined with gilt-framed abstract collages. "A favorite local artist of Mr. Cyril B. East," he explained. After showing them into yet another conference room with yet another gathering of employees he withdrew. Ms. Allen introduced Cleo and dipped her hand into the ubiquitous basket of chocolate chip cookies, number five since Cleo had arrived. The others present had one, too, as they had at every reception that morning. Corporate culture or cult? She'd mention it in her report to Athena and let her evaluate the importance, if any.

Lunch was in the corporate cafeteria, floors fourteen and fifteen. An atrium filled with lush plants, thriving under artificial full-spectrum light, joined the floors in the middle.

"So important during the winter months," Carol Allen commented as they stood in line. The space was similar to the Olympus, Inc., cafeteria, though at least double the size. Approximately eighteen hundred employees, overall. "The exact number is a moving target," Ms. Allen said, "especially at this time of year. We lose more right after the holidays than any other time."

"Interesting. I wonder why?" Cleo said.

"I've run an analysis on that for years but it's hard to tease out," Carol Allen said. "Some of them who get the bonus holiday time off don't return. Sometimes I wonder if they're planning to look for work elsewhere when their turn comes up, and take advantage of the extra days to apply for other jobs. That's the way it was with the person you're replacing, Mr. Perkins."

This, too, would go in her report.

They reached the table with the trays and started the slide down stainless-steel runners. Four Cheese Lasagna. Meatloaf. Macaroni and Cheese with Bacon. Vegetables were represented by overcooked broccoli, baked beans and candied sweet potatoes, the salad bar heavy on creamy gelatin-based items and cold pasta. A lonely pan of shredded iceberg lettuce was the only fresh selection in the fatty food panoply. Cleo chose that (thank Heaven and Earth there was Italian dressing) and the least lethal looking of the pasta salads.

"Both of my favorites today." Carol Allen beamed at her plate that was half lasagna and half candied sweet potatoes. She glanced at Cleo's tray. "That's all you're having, Patricia? Hardly enough to keep you going all day. Eat up!" she added brightly. "It's the East Fossil way!"

Cleo mustered an appreciative smile when Ms. Allen dropped a trademark East Fossil chocolate chip cookie on her tray. It wouldn't serve her mission to stand out on the very first day.

After lunch Carol Allen released her into the care of Madalena Lopez Rojas, temporary R & D manager. Madalena showed Cleo the mid-sized office of the departed Perkins, walked her through the necessary programs on a large screen desktop computer, and explained how to navigate the East Fossil phone system.

"It's important to make contact with the subcontractors, definitely by the end of the week. Many of them are local. I strongly recommend in-person meetings when possible, to introduce yourself and assure them the projects they're working on will continue. Perkins really left us in a lurch," she said. A crease deepened in her brow. "Left without notice. No one from wherever he's working now called HR for a reference, can you believe it? All he did was send an email during the holiday break. So irresponsible."

One more item for today's report to Athena.

"I'll get up and running on this first thing tomorrow," Cleo said.

"I'll leave you to close that down," Madalena said, pointing at the computer. "The bosses expect you in fifteen minutes."

After a quick stop by the restroom to freshen her lipstick and verify she didn't have lettuce between her teeth Cleo boarded the elevator for the thirty-seventh floor. Two other employees were in the car, one she'd never seen before in a maintenance department uniform, the other a thick-spectacled woman who said she was from marketing. Another rider joined them from one of the finance floors, a middle-aged man named Grant. When they reached the top, the party of four approached the reception desk, its curving legs carved with cherubs under gold leaf. Behind the desk sat a blonde cherub-cheeked woman with a beatific smile. Soft instrumental music wafted from a surround of hidden speakers.

"Welcome to afternoon coffee at the executive penthouse," she said, her voice like a sweet silver bell. "Mr. and Mr. East happily anticipate your arrival."

The oak wall to her right rolled away, revealing an inner office staffed by a woman with a short grey pageboy. She rose from behind a clear desk, made from Lucite or some other durable material but faceted in a way that refracted light like crystal.

"Greetings to you all," she said with a short bow. "I am Mrs. Weatherby, executive secretary to Mr. Cyril and Mr. Edwin. They are ready to receive you."

The wall behind Mrs. Weatherby parted in the middle, retracting to the width of a double door. The employees from maintenance and marketing entered first, Cleo and the man from finance behind. The high-ceilinged space was illuminated by a half-dozen chandeliers, patterned after the Solar System. The exterior wall to their right was glass. A matched collection of overstuffed armchairs and loveseats arranged in a crescent faced the view. To one side, a man in a short white jacket and tapered black slacks stood beside a large rolling cart. The cart supported a silver coffee and tea service and several tiered plates of finger sandwiches and miniature pastries. And, of course, a generous basket of chocolate chip cookies.

"Welcome, all, to a simple afternoon with the East Fossil family!"

The voice squeaked from the far side of the room. It belonged to one of two identically dressed men, large men with bodies that subtly but distinctly widened from the top down, like sacks of potatoes standing on end.

"I am Edwin B. East, CEO and co-founder of our little enterprise," the one on the left said. He gestured toward the other man who resembled him in every feature. "This is Cyril B. East, CFO and co-founder of East Fossil, and, I rejoice to say, my identical twin." Their mouths widened to display glistening white teeth. "Please be seated, wherever you choose, and we'll proceed to get acquainted."

The Easts lumbered forward. Each settled on a loveseat, the four employees in wing-backed chairs. Each seat had its own end table, the perfect size and height for the waiter to deposit selections of coffee, tea and finger food

"Surely you want more than *three* sandwiches, Miss Leo?" Edwin —or was it Cyril—said to Cleo.

The others, all with bulging waistlines, had stacked their plates two layers deep. Cleo signaled the waiter and asked for a cookie, too.

"That's the spirit, Miss Leo!"

"Now Eddy," Cyril said (for it must be he by process of elimination). "You know you must call her *Ms.* Leo. We don't want her reporting you to our Ms. Allen in HR."

The two of them chortled, bits of food spewing from their lips.

Cleo conjured her sweetest smile. "No harm done, Mr. East." There was something odd about the pair of them, in addition to their unusual physiques, old-fashioned way of speaking and identical dress. Some sort of energy or force? When the conversation flowed to a dialogue between the Easts and the woman from marketing, Cleo squinted at them. Murky green-gray halos emanated from their heads. She made a quick check of the others before refocusing her eyes, confirming that each had a pink mortal corona.

Both Easts insisted on shaking everyone's hands when they parted.

"So pleased to meet you at last, Ms. Leo," Edwin said, his hand engulfing hers like a manicured grizzly bear's paw. His fingertips were bulbous, his palm clammy. It was the same shaking hands with Cyril.

"I hope you'll treat yourself to a healthy dinner," Edwin said. "Now that you're part of the family we'll work you very hard indeed."

~ * ~

Cleo was exhausted when she got back to the hotel but there was still much to do. She asked for copies of the daily newspapers at the front desk, changed from her work clothes into leggings and a sweatshirt, and studied the "for rent" sections. There were several listings priced at one thousand dollars a month, the limit she'd set for herself based on salary. She made an appointment to see a furnished studio the following evening. She'd miss Michael Guy's yoga class, would have to buy yoga clothes and a mat first—one more errand to run.

She put a wrap skirt on over the leggings, ventured to the deli in the lobby, and purchased a chicken Caesar salad and a split of white wine to take back to her room. Between nibbles and sips she drafted her report for Athena—the prevalence of chocolate chip cookies, the near universality of overweight employees, the mysterious circumstances of Perkins quitting his job, the unusual auras of the Brothers East. Edit twice, review one time more, hit send.

As she poured the last of the wine into her glass her digital device pinged. David, probably, with a two-word reply to the four-word email she'd sent yesterday

Not David; Athena. Her heart sank a little, then a lot when she read the message.

Auras highly concerning. When in contact with East brothers exercise extreme caution. Will further research with Apollo for medical opinion/determination of species.

Species? Cleo bolted the rest of her wine. The people she'd been sent to investigate weren't human? Were they some sort of animal that thrived in a carbon-rich environment? The carbon reduction trials she'd run for Hermes had indicated plant life was agreeable to that kind of atmosphere. Could the Easts be sentient plants, capable of presenting like humans? But how was that possible, since they'd eaten twice as much as everyone else at afternoon coffee? Plants did not metabolize human food. As far as she knew...

Cleo filled her tub with steaming water and dumped in two loads of bath salts. She was investigating beings that were probably not human, who seemed bent on destroying the Earth in a way that would end human survival, mortal and immortal alike. Heaven and Earth, how was she supposed to solve this mystery? Who was her contact at East Fossil, when would they make themselves known, and when the Tartarus would Pan be here to help?

CUESDAY, JANUARY 6, 2026

Cleo's morning passed in a haze of phone calls and emails, reaching out to the subcontractors she'd inherited from Perkins. Her considerable experience in business administration served her well in staying organized and on task. She had just enough science in her background to articulate project basics—one more thing to study at night. Cleo couldn't help but wonder what Roderick Waller was doing at her old desk with his Green World Works campaign. Probably receiving all kinds of accolades from Veronica on down.

"Hey, Patricia, how's it going?"

It took Cleo a moment to realize someone was talking to her. Madalena, today sporting an aqua skirt with yellow linen jacket, hovered in the doorway.

She shrugged. "Pretty good, I guess. It's taking me a while to work down the list." She turned the monitor toward Madalena.

"You're all the way to Southwest Techtonic?" Madalena said.

"More or less. I had to leave messages for some of them."

Madalena whistled. "Boss, you've earned yourself a coffee break!"

Cleo sat back and rotated her shoulders. She'd been so preoccupied with her task she hadn't noticed how stiff they'd become. The clock in the lower right-hand corner of the screen had advanced three-plus hours since she'd started.

"Guess I lost track of the time," she said.

"We can't have you burning out your first week," Madalena said and shooed her to the elevator.

Cleo rode alone on the up bound elevator, the time late for coffee but early for lunch. She took a deep breath and blinked. Working through the contact list, the one task she required herself to finish today, was a welcome reprieve from the constant observing and absorbing of East Fossil culture and personnel. Living her cover was important, but she also needed to maintain vigilant eyes and ears on her coworkers. No better place than the employee cafeteria.

She stepped up to the espresso bar and ordered a double latte, asked for a skinny but the barista explained they only used whole milk, and selected a puff pastry filled with spinach from one of the Lucite shelves along the line to the cashier. Two dollars even, in true East Fossil feed-your-face style.

The dining area was sparsely populated. She spotted Michael Guy by himself at a table for two, a copy of *The Wall Street Journal* propped against a large sugar dispenser in front of him.

"Hi Michael. I'm Patricia Leo, we met yesterday?"

He set his paper aside and looked up. "Yes, of course."

"Mind if I join you? I'm interested in your yoga class, and I have a few questions."

"Be my guest."

He told her about a shop at a Midland mall that sold yoga clothes. East Fossil provided mats but if she wanted her own she could purchase it and be reimbursed. Classes were one hour, Tuesdays and Thursdays.

"Room for twenty yogis and we have a few spots open," he added. "Generous as East Fossil is with health benefits, employee fitness is not exactly their focus."

She mirrored his smirk. "I can't start tonight, I'm looking at an apartment, but please sign me up for Thursday."

"Consider it done." Michael Guy ran a hand over the peroxide stripe that divided his dark hair. "Back to the grind for me. See you on Thursday."

He picked up his empty cup and newspaper. Where the *Wall Street Journal* had been was a folded piece of paper. Cleo picked it up, "Wait, Michael, you—"

She turned in the direction he'd gone but he was nowhere in sight.

Cleo made a quick visual scan for security camera lenses, unfolded the note in her lap an inch or two under the tabletop just in case. The message was two words:

Contact. Destroy.

WeДNesДay, January 7, 2026

City of Mount Olympus

From his fourth-floor kingdom at Olympus, Inc., headquarters, Hermes ascended in the highly polished elevator. His shoulders stiffened as each succeeding number lit up on the panel above the doors, marking his journey to the eleventh floor CEO suite.

He'd been summoned—summoned! —by Veronica Zeta, his former admirer and ally who treated him like an underling now that she'd determined he was the god responsible for climate change. Her whipping boy, that's what he'd become. His mind reeled at how quickly she'd transformed from someone who respected him, collaborated with him, and had shown a touch of giddiness when meeting with him, into his indisputable boss.

The elevator doors opened on a more-or-less greenhouse. Afternoon light glowed benevolently through the glass ceiling. The abundance of thriving plants exhaled so much oxygen you could smell it. Hermes didn't bother to flirt with Alexandra, the executive assistant posted at a desk in front of the elevator. He passed her with a curt nod and strode directly to Veronica's desk in the middle of her executive jungle.

"Good afternoon," he said, tight lips holding back *What is it this time?*

The CEO of Olympus, Inc., looked away from the super-sized screen on her desk. "Hermes, please have a seat." Veronica rested her elbows on the desktop and steepled her fingers. "Did you have a chance to review the conference schedule I sent?"

The effing climate change and agriculture conference. He'd quickly scanned the file, scoffed at the generalist tone of the workshop and lecture summaries, and dismissed the three-day event as a boring waste of time. He nodded.

"I want you to attend the day sessions, especially the panel discussions, to expand your world view of what's at stake. Your trips to monitor mortal inventors," she said, tapping her keyboard and glancing at her screen, "are concentrated in North America, Africa and Europe. You need to broaden your focus. Network with the presenters, especially ones from South America, Asia and Australia. You need to evaluate inventions addressing crop failure, famine, and the expansion of deserts, and add them to the climate change reduction plan."

The damn plan. Heaven and Earth, Veronica had become a thorough bureaucrat now that she had the bit between her perfect teeth, confident she could solve every problem with a spreadsheet and an outline swarming with subsections. His mind didn't work that way. Hermes was certain this forced regimentation of thought had stalled his problem-solving genius. When Veronica forwarded a project tracking template to him, what doubtless appeared on her screen now, he'd sent it straight to Waller without a second glance.

"Fine." He'd go to the damn conference, what choice did he have? But it would aggravate the other factor distracting him from his work. P. B. was leaving the City of Mount Olympus next week. The conference felt like a load of bricks compacting the time he'd planned to spend with his boy before a six-month absence. Six months! How would he survive being separated from P. B. for what used to be a blink but now seemed like eternity?

~ * ~

Heracles walked the custom-carpeted grand entryway of the Odyssey Hotel, flanked by his adult sons, Anicetus and Alexiares. The boys had invited him to their pre-conference security walk-through and urged him to point out anything they might have missed.

"The inaugural climate and agriculture summit." Anicetus (who had a fading scar on his right temple, the remnant of a fraternal childhood fracas) spread his arms wide as if the vast corridor was a side-show and he was the barker. "Part of the new climate change initiative you folks are doing at Olympus, Inc. Ms. Zeta's got the whole world in on this thing. We're expecting bigwigs from every pantheon you've ever heard of."

"And then some," Alexiares chimed. Except for Anicetus' scar and the small mole behind Alexiares' left ear it was impossible to tell them apart. That, plus Alexiares' lifelong habit of topping everything his twin brother said.

"Given the high visibility of the attendees and the international scope of this gathering, we're taking extra precautions. You know how it is, Dad. Reducing carbon emissions isn't popular with everyone, and some people don't want things to change. They could do any number of things to throw a crowbar into it. We'll have luggage pre-check at the entrance to keep anything dangerous from coming through." Anicetus pointed an index finger in the air and drew a circle above his head. "Security cameras will monitor all movement in the entry hall. Same in the Grand Ballroom."

"But twice as many cameras."

They veered into a ballroom so vast it dwarfed the grand entryway. Heracles and Hebe had been married here more than two millennia ago; a solemn ceremony decorated with enough flowery frippery to give the entire Roman legion hay fever. Zeus and Hera had spent a bundle on all that—couldn't swing an ox without hitting a pink champagne fountain. Hebe had had a dozen bridesmaids, all of them even rounder and shorter than she was. Theirs was a strained union from the start, an arranged marriage that had yet to find the path to contentment. When Hebe went into labor with the boys she'd said outright she wished he, Heracles, was dead. She hadn't let him touch her for centuries afterward.

His loathing for the room, its custom carpet woven with a pattern of waves realistic enough to make him seasick, had been immediate and lasting. He'd been summoned back here thousands of times since. Family parties, always family parties, with hundreds in attendance. So many parties and so many guests Hera had a full-time staff member who organized these monstrosities. Like Veronica and Clifford's engagement party last June. Heracles wasn't the interfering kind, but with this family —Hebe's family—he'd considered more than once taking Clifford aside for a god to god chat. They weren't bad people, just completely inflexible about getting their way. The women, especially.

"Event staff at all entrances and exits," Anicetus said. "Plus the elevators, and on every floor with guest rooms. Each of them fitted with a body cam."

"The newest generation of body cams. With double the employees at peak times."

"Secure valet chariot parking in both the main and overflow lots."

"Twenty-four seven."

Ah, for the old days when security meant swinging a club until the enemy, however many individual soldiers or robbers that entailed, was out cold. The boys were part of a new era of security, hand in gauntlet with Hermes and all the latest digital gewgaws.

"Well done," he said, patting their shoulders. "No recommendations for improvement."

"Thanks, Dad."

"Thank you very much, Father."

The two of them pushed through swinging doors in the back that led to the kitchen.

"One last word about table cutlery."

"*And* background checks on the servers."

The doors swung shut on whatever else they said.

Alone in the ballroom, Heracles took a long, standing stretch and ambled back to the grand hallway. A mound of paperwork waited on his desk at Olympus, Inc., headquarters. In the hallway three tables had been set up and put together in one long unit. Two young people in house-keeping uniforms smoothed white linen cloths over the tops. A pale, thin woman with hair the color of corn silk watched them, a cardboard file box cradled in her arms and another on the floor beside her.

"Seph!" Heracles raised a hand and waved. "Hey, Seph!"

"Hey, Clee!" She set down the box and hugged him. "Are you here for the conference?"

"No, just a security walk-through with my boys. Glad to see you topside. How'd you manage it?"

Persephone wrinkled her nose. "Mother's doing. She insisted I be the registrar. I hate doing things like this, you know, dealing with so many people."

Seph was definitely on the shy side and having a possessive brute of a husband didn't help. "Nice to get out and away, though?"

"*Very* nice."

Poor Seph. They'd met long ago when Heracles, still mortal, came to the Underworld to rescue a misbehaving hero named Theseus from the Chair of Forgetfulness. On that adventure Heracles and Persephone had bonded over her dog, the three-headed hell hound who guarded the gates of Hades' kingdom.

"How's Cerberus?"

"Oh!" She beamed. "He is *such* a good boy, and he's learned to shake. I didn't know what he was doing at first, holding up a paw when I brought him bones."

Her delight warmed him. He'd been the one to teach Cerberus that trick when he'd covered for Hermes last fall, leading the souls of the newly dead to the Underworld.

"Holidays okay, then?"

Her smile faded. "Are they ever?"

He shrugged.

"How've you been, Clee?"

"Oh, fine. Fine." But it was far from true. Ever since talking to David at the pub he'd been thinking about Megara and their children. Why couldn't Hera have left them alone to live and die their mortal lives in peace?

"Excuse me, Ma'am?" One of the hotel housekeepers was at Persephone's elbow. "I'd like your opinion on the setup." She tilted her head toward the linen-draped stretch of tables. "Is that how you want it, Ma'am?"

Persephone circled around to the front of the registration area, Heracles beside her. Two easels had been set up, one at either end, supporting colorful cardboard placards. One announced the conference name above the word *Registration*. The other advertised some sort of dance workshop tomorrow evening.

"Yes, that's exactly right," Persephone said. "What's that, a door prize?" She pointed to a large cellophane-wrapped basket in the center of the table.

"No, Ma'am. There's a card with your name on it. Delivery person brought it a couple minutes ago."

Persephone gave a squeak of surprise and reached toward the offering.

"Not so fast, Seph!"

Heracles stepped in front of her. What the boys had said about possible terrorist attacks had made him jumpy and here was something suspicious already through the door. It *appeared* to be an innocent fruit basket but could, in actuality, be something capable of inflicting bodily harm. No way was it from Persephone's wretch of a husband who, in addition to being irrationally jealous, was also notoriously cheap. "I'll have the boys check it out before you get any closer."

He summoned Anicetus and Alexiares on his wrist device, the only one of Hermes' inventions he found much use for. The twins appeared, rosy cheek by youthful jowl, their detector wands poised. Anicetus waved his wand slowly over the top of the basket. Alexiares scanned both top and sides. Not a blip, not a beep.

"Negative."

"Confirmed."

"Thanks, boys," Persephone said.

Anicetus raised the digital device strapped to his wrist and said,

"Arco, put two inspection personnel on the front doors, ASAP." A confirming noise answered back. "Periphery inspection next," he said and strode toward the automatic doors to the outside.

"Hotel, annex and parking lots," Alexiares added on his way out.

"They certainly are thorough," Persephone said. She reached for the card, supported by a plastic trident anchored in the basket. "Ohhhh! From Freya. How sweet of her. Fruit from Elysium." She turned her pale, smiling eyes on Heracles. "You know how awful conference food can be."

It took so little to make her happy. Heracles felt the impulse to pull her into his arms and make the world right for her. In the real world, the best he could do was hope she'd meet someone who could, and would, give her what she needed and deserved.

"Gotta run," he said. "Paperwork."

"Good to see you, Clee. Thanks for saying hi."

One of the things he appreciated most about Persephone: she had never once asked him to give her love to Hebe.

Thursday, January 8, 2026

Persephone cowered behind the registration table. Her nails were bitten to the quick. Why had Mother volunteered her as registrar for the first ever All Pantheon Agricultural and Climate Summit?

Her raw fingertips drummed the linen-draped table, channeling her anxiety. Demeter had insisted she was doing Persephone a kindness. "My poor dear, trapped for three bleak months in the Underworld! I have to get you topside, darling, before you fade away like the dead heroes in Asphodel. A mother knows these things."

Persephone stopped drumming. She checked her wrist chronometer. The conference doors opened in five minutes. She smoothed her hands over her thighs in a futile effort to iron the wrinkles out of last decade's toga. It was her very best, pale blue reminiscent of an early spring sky with a border of white irises at the hem. Not quite right for the season but Hades wouldn't spring for a new winter frock. Though he was hours away and miles underground, his gruff words ricocheted in her brain.

"A new winter toga is a waste of money when all you do is hang around the castle."

He was the cheapest god in the pantheon, and she was shackled to him for eternity. He'd even cut off her Bank of Olympus card, not a platinum card like all the other goddesses had, but a regular one, which ruled out shopping even now that she'd escaped to the city. And not allowing her to have a baby, based on economic considerations! He'd tricked her when she was young, abducted her to the Underworld and—

"Greetings, my dear."

Ganymede's smooth voice interrupted her irate musings. Youthful, blond and clean-limbed, the Cup Bearer to the gods swooped in front of the registration table and deposited a stack of colorful postcards before her. "Discount coupons for the open bar," he said as if describing a tantalizing special on today's menu. "Dionysus wants to keep things flowing after the participants use up their complimentary drink tickets."

"Thanks, I'll make sure to point them out. Hang on a minute." Her inflamed fingertips danced through the registration box to the letter G. "Here's your packet. Please wear your nametag and check the meal vouchers to make sure you got what you ordered."

Menu planning had been a nightmare. Immortals from around the world were attending the conference—so many different cultures and dietary codes. Half the sea gods demanded fish at every meal but for the other half that was taboo. Lots of vegetarians, naturally, as so many worked with crops. And since when did immortals have food allergies? Serving a dessert with nuts in it could cause an international incident.

Ganymede waved his registration envelope above his head. "Absolutely perfect. See you at the bar." He sped through the wide portal behind her, into the ballroom.

A mellow chime resonated through the hallway. A trio of radiant females, varied in shape and size but each dressed in a dazzling shade of gold, collected their suitcases from the luggage check in the foyer. The entryway sliders, etched with sea serpents, rolled open. Sun goddesses. They were always the first to arrive at any gathering.

Persephone forced a terrified smile. "Welcome, ladies."

"Good afternoon! Registration for Sol," the tallest said, her cheekbones sharp enough to slice tomatoes.

The petit one with straight black hair spread her arms wide, giving the impression she was receiving an ecstatic round of applause. "My name is Amaterasu."

The curvaceous one with a broad smile chimed in. "I'm an A, too. Arrina." She fanned her face with her hand. "Is it just me, or is it hot in here?"

The three of them fell into a fit of giggles. If all the visiting immortals were as cliquish as this trio it was going to be a long three days. Amaterasu didn't like the color of her nametag (Sorry, it's the only color we have) and one of Sol's meal tickets wasn't right (*Really* sorry! I can trade you a roast pheasant ticket for your pasta).

"I'm parched. Where's the bar?" Arrina said.

Continual thirst was an occupational hazard for sun deities. Persephone nodded toward the portal behind her. "Main ballroom, back corner. You'll want one of these," she added nudging the stack of discount postcards across the table. Arrina snapped up five.

The three of them linked arms and floated away. Persephone inhaled deeply and breathed out her mantra. *Not my problem. It is not my problem.*

The next two hours swung between feast and famine, with dozens seeming to arrive at the same time, their voices rising in animated conversations about everything from emerging wind patterns to the migration of tree species. Dying coral. Failing crops. Water shortages. Some were gracious about the slow-moving line, others not so much. The discount postcards were extremely popular. The building roar from the back of the ballroom stopped people from asking where to find the bar.

Twenty more minutes to go in the official registration slot. Three lonely packets remained in the box. Ares, the conference chair, stopped by to tell her one of these wouldn't arrive until tomorrow. That left two Norse gods, Thor and Frey. Thor was a VIP, part of an all-star discussion panel with Zeus and the colorful Mariamman, Hindu goddess of rain.

Persephone had immediately felt a bond with Mariamman—the way kindness radiated from her joyful face, the vivid red and gold of her close-fitting tunic and harem pants. Such a freeing way to dress! Mother would faint if Persephone wore harem pants to work; definitely not up to Demeter's standards for feminine dress. But no one would dare to criticize Mariamman, the main mother goddess of South India, and rain wasn't her only skill. Tonight, before dinner, she would lead a half-hour folk dance session. Persephone hoped to close registration in time to attend. She fingered the two soon-to-be claimed packets.

"Thor can be on the brusque side," Ares warned Persephone. "He can turn from jovial to vengeful on a drachma if he detects the merest hint of disrespect. The usual big god with small hands problem," Ares said with a smirk. "He's always late, sorry to say. I know you've had a long day already, Seph, but for your own safety please be as cordial as you possibly can, and if he reaches for his hammer, duck!" He patted her shoulder. "Can I get you something from the bar?"

"Mai Tai." She laced her fingers and stretched her arms up over her head. Crack went her shoulder blades. "Make it a double."

Heaven and Earth, she'd been so busy today she'd missed lunch and there was every possibility she'd miss dinner, too. The basket from Freya sat unopened under the registration table. Persephone received few gifts. This one was so pretty she'd resisted opening it to save it as long as possible. But now…she really shouldn't suck down a double Mai Tai on an empty stomach. The green and gold cellophane crinkled under her shaky fingers. A perfectly ripe, perfectly round, perfectly red and gold streaked apple was on top. She polished it on the front of her toga and nibbled a break in the skin.

The flavor—a burst of honey and sunshine with the perfect hint of tartness—exploded on her tongue. The full weight of her hunger descended, suffusing her body with a burning desire for more. Persephone bit deep into the flesh, heedless of juice trickling down her forearm. She consumed the apple, seeds, core and all, and licked her sticky fingers with joy. Heaven and Earth her body tingled!

Ares shouldered his way through the crowd at the ballroom entry, gingerly holding a brimming full glass. "Sorry it took so long, it's a jungle in there."

Damn, Ares looked good. Why had she never noticed it before, the classically handsome tilt of his chin? He handed her the drink. The strangest look came over his face when she brushed her fingers over his.

"Thanks." Her voice was low, husky.

"Uhm. No problem." Ares backed away, eyes wide. "Gotta go. Time to introduce Mariamman and start the folk dancing." He turned on his heel and dove into the ballroom throng.

Persephone smiled at the sweating glass, the dainty pink paper parasol jutting from the top, and the generous curve of pineapple hanging on the rim that reminded her of something she couldn't quite identify. They made everything so pretty topside.

"Whoa!" She set her glass down after the first potent sip. Dionysus had been heavy-handed with the rum. Half-way down, twirling the liberated paper parasol between her thumb and index finger, she toyed with the idea of ordering another. She sucked on the rum-soaked slice of pineapple before gobbling it up and took the last sip. Through the bottom of her glass came a man the size of a mountain and another guy.

"Hi there!" she shouted, shooting out her hand to the big guy. "You must be the famous Thor!"

The giant pumped her hand with his disappointingly small paw. "You may call me the God of Thunder," he boomed, then pulled back into a pose, chest raised. What was she supposed to do, chisel a statue?

She would have giggled but one of his little hands was resting on the hammer lodged in his belt. Recalling Ares' warning, she segued to a radiant smile.

"Here's your conference packet, Oh Honored Guest. Don't forget to wear your nametag." Like anyone wouldn't know who he was at a glance. "I've checked your dinner tickets for you. Ox at every meal. Bar's in there," she said, swinging an arm toward the ballroom entrance. "Drink tickets are in your packet."

Thor nodded as if to dismiss her and strode, chest first, into the raucous crowd. Her head swiveled after him.

"Excuse me."

Oh. Right. The other one. She swung back to her duties and—

Oh my.

Looked into the most beautiful eyes she'd ever seen.

"I'm Frey." And such a sensual smile.

"Persephone," she said.

He rested his hands on the registration table and leaned forward. "I believe you have a packet for me, too?"

"Yes," she sighed. "Yes," she said again. "Sorry, it's been a long day. Here." Maybe it was the Mai Tai, but when she handed him the manila envelope, even though their hands didn't touch she felt a jolt. His beautiful eyes looked all the way into her, knew all her secret desires in an instant.

Divine music—harmonics, what they called half-tones, maybe—ebbed in the ballroom, slowly and sinuously overpowering the alcohol-fueled chatter. Mariamman's dance class. The music circled around them. How did Frey's aura shine like that, white, dark green and magenta, the colors pulsing like the Northern Lights?

She released his envelope and slipped around the front of the table. In a gesture of unspoken consent, they touched palms and started the dance.

Elysium, the Underworld

The goddess Freya sat back on her heels at the edge of the pond, delighted by the scene in her magic mirror. The arrival of her twin brother, Frey, at the conference was an unanticipated plus. Naturally Persephone would select his radiant sexuality over any other male present. Primed as she was by the apple loaded with a compound that, when consumed, created a super-sensitivity to male pheromones, Persephone was well on her way to a night of procreation play.

Midland, Texas, USA

Yoga class, at last!

Cleo welcomed the moment to relax and let all the chaos of the week go for one luxurious hour. The women's locker room was furnished with spacious lockers, plenty of benches and a Jacuzzi in the shower area. An entire wall was devoted to a sauna. The fragrance of redwood and steam mingled with scents of chlorine, sweat and hair products.

She'd visited the yoga outfitter yesterday after work, selecting lavender leggings and a cute lipstick red crop top. The garments, adult size large, looked like they were sized for an anorexic preteen. But the fabric had a lot of stretch and fit pleasingly like a second skin. Her mat, in turquoise, was six inches longer than standard, a recommendation from the salesclerk given Cleo's height. It came with a bag and a long strap that fit neatly over her shoulder, reminiscent of the quiver of arrows she'd carried at summer camp when she was a kid.

Out of the suit, into the yoga kit, onto the gym floor with a handful of people—eight students, total. Michael Guy stood under a netted hoop at one end, a piece of equipment used in some beloved mortal game with a name she couldn't recall. She rolled out her mat at the end of the second of two rows.

"Welcome, Yogis," Michael said. His raised his arm and pointed toward her. "And please welcome our new member, Patricia Leo, who joined R and D this week." Polite applause echoed around the gym. "Let's get started."

Michael pushed a button on his digital device, summoning instrumental music, slow and soothing.

"We'll begin in Child's Pose. Big toes together, knees wide, forehead nestled on the floor between your biceps. Breathe. Reach into the four corners of your mat."

Cleo had a little bit of experience with yoga but was no expert. She appreciated Michael's clear and detailed instructions, the way he walked between their mats and made gentle adjustments to their postures as he continued his narrative.

"Remember your breathing. Lips sealed, in through your nose out through your nose, equal lengths of inhale and exhale. Inhale, High Halfway Lift. Exhale, Forward Fold."

Every so often he'd have them pause in a comfortable pose to focus on breathing and feel the change in their bodies.

"Lift your heart toward your thumbs, shoulders down. Breathe."

Her lunges were clumsy, and she wasn't the only one. The man on the mat next to hers missed his footing going into Warrior Two and fell over.

"Find the balance between effort and ease. Distribute the weight evenly between the ball of your front foot and the knife edge of your back foot."

The pose called Figure Four, done on the back with the ankle of one leg crossed over the thigh of the other, unlocked her hips. Too much time at the desk these past few days. She let that thought drift away and flowed with the feeling of release. At last, Shavasana, morbidly known as Corpse Pose. Complete and total relaxation. Stretching. Fetal Pose. Pushing up into a seated position.

"Heads bowed, hands to heart center. Inhale. Raise your hands to the third eye between your brows. Bow forward, honoring the light in each other. I honor you and say *Namaste*."

"*Namaste*," they repeated. Silence.

"Wonderful work, everyone," Michael said, breaking the spell. "See you back on your mats on Tuesday."

Her fellow Yogis, some of them so relaxed they looked dazed, wandered toward the locker rooms. Michael remained, his perfectly rolled mat under his arm. He looked at his digital device. Cleo began rolling up her mat but it started going at a diagonal. She muttered under her breath, started again.

Michael paced toward her. "How was that for you, Patricia?"

She laughed. "I'm a little rusty but I think I'll get there."

"Side Plank is difficult for many people," he said. She blushed, reliving the moment of awkwardness, struggling to get one leg on top of the other. "Once you feel the shape of it you'll be fine."

It was the first opportunity she'd had to talk with him since their encounter in the cafeteria. "I have a couple of questions about the class if you have a minute."

Michael's eyes shifted up and to the right. Security cameras? Why not, since they seemed to be everywhere at East Fossil.

"Glad to help but at the moment I'm badly in need of restoration. There's a juice bar nearby, if you don't mind?"

"That sounds good."

"See you out front in ten."

Two of the yoga women were still in the locker room.

"Great class," Cleo said.

"Lucky to have it," the taller one said. She was lean in build with a slight bulge around the middle. "Helps balance the free corporate cookies. Those things are addictive."

"I'll say," the other one said, a pudgy, perky redhead. "I gained five pounds my first month here!"

Cleo toweled off the traces of sweat, didn't bother to shower, certain she needed to wash today's blouse before wearing it again. Now, at least, she had an apartment, a semi-furnished studio with a washer and dryer on the same floor. Two more nights at the hotel. Saturday morning she'd call a cab and move her luggage, then venture out on public transportation to buy supplies for the kitchenette and bathroom. Like most immortals, Cleo had never learned to drive. The only internal combustion vehicles in the City of Mount Olympus were Aphrodite's gold stretch limo and Hephaestus' motorcycle.

Michael stood in front of the East Fossil building, huddled in a wool topcoat. Olympus, Inc., Field Ops, had provided Cleo with a trench coat which, thankfully, had a zip-in winter lining. In the few days she'd lived in Midland she'd observed the air cooled quickly in the evening, despite highs in the 60s. Michael asked about her apartment. His brow furrowed when she named the building.

"What is it?"

"I'll tell you at the juice bar."

Two blocks later they rounded a corner and faced an attractive storefront of east-facing windows filled with a jungle of potted plants. The front of the striped awning read *Green World Juice Works*.

A flash of recognition—Roderick Waller's digital PR campaign, Green World Works. Coincidence?

Michael's posture relaxed the instant they passed beyond the potted plants. They were in a juice bar, all right, with tall sleek tables and no chairs. State of the art juicing equipment hummed behind the counter and a colorful chalkboard menu was suspended above. There were a few patrons, mostly in business wear. She squinted to confirm their pink auras. The young woman working the juice bar had a healthy shield of purple.

"One of us," she whispered to Michael.

He nodded. "Backup," he murmured. "And no surveillance cameras. If something goes wrong at East report here as fast as possible." He gestured toward the menu. "My favorite is pomegranate-banana with wheatgrass and a pinch of brewer's yeast. What appeals to you?"

She chose the Green World Special, described as "loaded with antioxidants."

The person working behind the bar (Michael referred to her as a juicer) set two color-filled pint glasses on the pickup end of the counter, smiled at them and said, "What can I make for you?" The name Kari was stitched on the upper left side of her greengrocer's apron.

Michael gave their order and introduced Cleo.

Kari beamed. "Nice to meet you! Any time you need something just ask, I'm here Monday through Friday, eight to eight."

"Long shifts," Cleo commented.

"The overtime's nice, and lots of people work late in this part of town. Gotta admit though, I love the weekends." Kari's eyes flitted over the seating area. Her buoyant expression turned serious. "Open twenty-four seven," she added quietly. "Safe house door is around the back."

They waited at the table farthest from the other patrons, side by side, facing the roar of the juice bar.

"So what's wrong with my apartment?"

"What?"

"Your brow furrowed deep enough to plant corn when I said the name of the building."

"Oh," he said. "Nothing you can't handle, just that it's one of *their* holdings. I've been doing some digging into other corporations they hold—lots of rental properties and a horror-themed chain of amusement parks in the southern states. There's evidence pointing to some offshore LLCs and a bank in Central America, but I've yet to find solid leads on those."

"And that's why you're here?"

"Initially, yes. Athena was hoping I'd find enough evidence of illegal activities to bring them down. A while back I uncovered another possible line of inquiry. That's why they sent you."

She waited for him to say more. He didn't.

"The East brothers," Cleo said to restart the conversation. "They're …different."

"Hah! To say the least."

"I got a look at their auras."

Michael nodded. "The color of mud. Did you see the alert from headquarters last night? Apollo himself thinks they're from an ancient race." He said it so quietly she barely heard him over the roar of the industrial-strength blender. "An older race than we are by many millennia. They came from the stars."

"What? You're joking, right?"

He sighed. "I wish I were. They express themselves in old-fashioned ways and appear to be slow, but they're really incredibly intelligent and powerful."

"They seem to like humans," she said, looking for the positive.

"Certainly." He looked directly into her eyes. "For dinner."

"Holy Tartarus." She took a moment to clear the grizzly imagery from her imagination. "But they're bent on destroying the earth, right? Why would they do that and endanger their—" she took a deep breath to tamp down nausea "—food supply?"

"Order up for Michael!" Kari set two glasses, filled to the brim with contents in unappealing shades of green and beige, on the pickup counter. Michael retrieved the drinks and handed the green one to Cleo.

"I don't think I can," she said, grimly regarding her Special.

"My dear Ms. Leo," he said, "I assure you it tastes better than it looks."

"It's not the color," she clarified. "It's the eating of human flesh."

"Tiny sips with long breaks in between," he said in his yoga teacher voice. "There's something going on in R and D. Olympus, Inc., needs you to find out everything you can about all the ongoing projects, including the ones hired out to subcontractors."

A sick thought occurred. She set down her nearly full glass.

"What really happened to the person I replaced?"

"You mean Perkins?" The casual way Michael said the name chilled her from head to toe. "It helped that he'd reached prime obesity and was also on the list for extra paid time off during the holidays. I slipped some information to the Penthouse to put him on their radar. The Easts got him tipsy at the corporate holiday party and took care of the rest."

"You aided and abetted them?" she said.

"Don't sound so disgusted, Ms. Leo. It was our first opportunity to get you on the inside. If you're successful in this mission, think of all the mortal lives you'll save, all the innocent species you'll save that are nearly extinct. Think of the polar bears."

"Excuse me." She made it to the restroom stall just in time to hurl her smoothie. Espionage. The disgusting, nauseating, horrifying world of espionage.

FRIDAY, JANUARY 9, 2026

City of Mt. Olympus

Persephone awoke in a king-sized bed. Frey's voice, lively with song, emanated from the shower. The small hand of her wrist chronometer was past VII. She hastily pulled on her toga and, sandals in hand, tip-toed to the door of room 2307, opening it just enough to look both ways. No sign of security personnel in the hallway. Was there a camera somewhere, recording her this very moment?

Too late to worry about that now. Registration for day session participants opened at eight. She trotted to the elevator bay and pushed the down arrow. If fortune favored her she'd make it to her single queen on the sixth floor in time to shower, change and snag a donut and coffee at the hospitality table in the lobby.

She thought of Frey as the droplets pulsed on her head and shoulders. How could he be so gentle yet so—commanding? That wasn't quite the right word. All the clichés from her avid reading of romance novels eluded her. The night with him had been glorious, dangerous, and oddly soothing. His room had an en suite Jacuzzi and…No! No one, absolutely no one, must suspect she'd breached marital fidelity. She had to keep her tryst a secret because she longed to do it again.

Frey's song, words forming in her mouth in a language she didn't understand, burst from her bruised lips. It was sheer madness, sheer wonderful madness, but she didn't have time to linger, had to keep moving. Everything depended on her being where she was supposed to be, when she was supposed to be there. She untangled her hair—a shade of gold richer this morning or did she imagine it—and plaited it into a single braid. Her reflection showed pink cheeks in full bloom. She was alive!

Persephone gathered up yesterday's toga, the cloth heavy with Frey's delicious sun and rain-drenched scent, and indulged in a prolonged inhale before tossing it on the closet floor. Two choices of togas, neither of them touching the glorious freshness of her mood but the peach-colored one was newer than the sadly faded green. Lace up her sandals, set the wreath on her head, and she was done.

The wreath! Heaven and Earth, she'd left it in Frey's room. What if housekeeping found it, what if—? There was no time to think. She dashed out, pulled the door closed behind her, spied the crowd at the elevator bay. Persephone sprinted to the opposite end of the hallway and barreled down the stairs. She arrived at the hospitality table at five minutes to eight. Mother was lecturing a bus person about keeping the donut trays full. Persephone pretended she hadn't seen Demeter, tried to sneak by but—

"Goodness, Sepphie, I've never seen your cheeks so pink. Do you have a fever? And what on earth have you done with your wreath?"

"Running late, Mom, have to go." With Frey on her mind would her cheeks ever cool? She snatched the last donut, a round chocolate-glazed one, from the tray and thanked the dryad overseeing the urns for drawing her a cup of regular, not decaf. Not that she needed the octane, no, not at all. A splash of hot liquid escaped the paper cup when she lurched into her chair behind the registration table. One more packet, for one of the Greek Pantheon's own, Eirene, Goddess of Peace. She'd been detained by some round of mortal détente or other but was scheduled to lead a panel on geopolitical issues this afternoon. Frey, not only a god of rain and sun but of peace, had mentioned he was on that panel when they'd stopped their lovemaking for a few minutes over a glass of wine. Deliciously bright wine that made her feel full of hope and promise and…

She floated away on a dream-built cloud, hands resting on her love-warmed belly. Frey, as it happened, was also a god of fertility.

~ * ~

Hermes listened to the agricultural panel discussion from the sound booth, behind smoked glass. He'd quickly become persona non grata with this crowd, once everyone had made the connection between climate change and his involvement in the exploitation of fossil fuels. The Asian, South American and Australian gods Veronica had ordered him to schmooze were reluctant to share their solutions-in-progress with him, except for Huayra-tata, an obscure wind god. After Hermes had plied him with a few drinks he'd grudgingly talked about an invention that showed promise in sucking carbon from the air. Hermes could barely contain his irritation when he realized Cleo had run a simulation using this invention in the Olympus, Inc., lab last June. Complete and total failure.

He'd wasted two days on this drivel. What was Veronica trying to do by forcing him to be here, punish him some more for screwing things up?

On stage Kokopelli, a big deal god from North America, took the mic.

"We've been asked to describe conditions in our individual regions. I must tell you, the outlook in the American Southwest is grim. Not only are we experiencing increasingly dire weather conditions, with far greater frequencies of hurricanes, floods, scorching summers and brutally cold winters, we are home to some of the most ruthless mortal players in the fossil fuel industry. They threaten and bribe their elected officials into providing subsidies and spreading misinformation about renewable energy sources, they…"

Hermes yawned. He was far from indifferent to the issues Kokopelli raised but he'd heard it all before, hundreds of times from hundreds of sources because Veronica sent him every damn link she could find on the subject. Hermes waved at the sound guy, Chet, his ears covered with headphones, eyes glued to the level indicators on the multi-channel soundboard. He knew a way out through the kitchen, would take a walk, message Monique to see if she'd let him take P. B. for a few hours this evening. Heaven and Earth, they were leaving—leaving! — for a Zeus-forsaken mortal desert next week and there was nothing he could do about it. Everyone, from Apollo to Veronica, was on Monique's side. Did anyone appreciate that he'd miss out on his son's babyhood? Did anyone care?

His hands landed unintentionally hard on the swinging doors to the kitchen. A young guy on the other side, wearing a white chef's toga, jumped.

"Tartarus, you scared the crap out of me!" The guy waved the formidable knife in his hand. "I'm dicing vegetables, man. I don't need to lose a finger doing prep!"

"Jerk," Hermes said under his breath, though he knew he was at fault. No matter where he went, no matter what he did, life sucked. These days no one around him offered the easy camaraderie he'd enjoyed all his life. Waller was a nice kid but had no personality outside of his work. Pan was gone, Cleo, too, working for Athena. They were undercover, and the Goddess of War had banned all contact with them. He couldn't even send them a selfie!

Hermes wove through the vast, crammed kitchen, through a mass of prep cooks and a half-dozen sous chefs, identifiable from the silver stripes down the sides of their togas. Some lifestyle article he'd read a while back claimed the hotel had a separate sous chef for each entrée.

Hermes did a double take on an unusually large, blocky guy in a sous chef uniform, as big in the shoulders as Heracles but built on the bottom-heavy side. The hem of his toga brushed the floor. The image didn't linger, his thoughts reaching for P. B. as he passed through the service entrance and into the open air.

That night, following the banquet, everyone who ordered the fish came down with a wicked case of food poisoning.

SUNDAY, JANUARY 11, 2026

Persephone woke nestled spoon style with Frey. She took a deep, satisfied breath and hummed a little moan of pleasure, her body alive and thrumming from crown to toe. He rose on one arm and pressed his lips to her temple.

"Good morning, Goddess."

She rolled into his embrace. Their mouths met and merged in deep, luxurious kisses. Never had she felt such sensations, such desire. This was the opposite of marriage; this was being forged together in fire. Yet she didn't fret about their imminent parting, him back to his northern kingdom and her back to…

His hands, masterful and expressive, launched an exploration down her body. Shoulders, breasts, belly, thighs. A new thought was born in her brain. Though she wasn't due topside again until the spring she wouldn't return to the Underworld. The gift she carried within was hers alone. She wouldn't squander it in the realm of Hades.

They made love again. And again. At half past X the wake-up call Frey had ordered alerted them to the XI checkout time. A last deep kiss, no promises made, they parted.

Persephone peered into the deserted hallway. No security personnel. Everyone else had probably checked out already. Her hips swayed with confident pleasure as she sauntered to the elevator bay. When she arrived at her own room the phone was ringing. Unhurried, she lifted the receiver and said hello to the dial tone. She shrugged, dropped the receiver back in the cradle. Her suitcase waited on the bed, packed the night before in anticipation of making every moment count. She tidied her hair and her person as quickly as living in a dream allowed and wended her way to the lobby.

"Sepphie!"

Mother's screech burst through the parting elevator doors. Demeter abandoned her place at the marble and gold hotel registration counter and strode fiercely toward Persephone. "Honey, where have you been? I've been ringing your room all morning. Hades is having a fit, says he hasn't heard from you since Thursday afternoon. Is your digital device malfunctioning?"

Persephone answered with a Mona Lisa smile.

"Heaven and Earth, you look delirious!" Demeter pressed the back of her hand to Persephone's forehead. "Hmm. No fever but your skin has the strangest glow. I'll call Apollo right now to have a look at you. You were in contact with absolutely everybody who came through registration. If a virus circulated around the conference we'll never hear the end of it."

Someone stirred in Persephone's belly.

"I wouldn't worry about it, Mother. Whatever I have, I'm positive it isn't catching. But just in case, I'll quarantine at the Mountain High for a week. I'd hate to go home too early and infect the Dead."

Demeter's attention had already wandered to Guanyin, the Chinese Goddess of Mercy, and her entourage. Mother had been cultivating a relationship with this eminence since the crop failures began. Guanyin helped the distressed and hungry. Her patronage was critical until climate change was arrested. "Message me when you get home," Mother murmured, and was gone.

Thank you, Mother, but I shall decline.

Persephone would not message Hades either, not until she'd registered at the Mountain High Plaza Hotel, one of the finest in the City of Mount Olympus. Frey had gifted her a generously funded Norse Bank debit card and encouraged her to buy some new togas befitting her status as the mother of his *in utero* child. That left plenty for a week of spa time and room service. The baby, she was sure, would appreciate that.

She left the Odyssey Hotel and Conference Center, towing her second-hand suitcase behind her. Head high, heedless of the way the badly worn wheels tugged the case to the right, she didn't notice the oddity of nature occurring in her wake. As she passed the winter-fatigued sidewalk planters, frost-slimed stems stood tall and suffused with chlorophyll, pushing blossoms from their tips.

The Mountain High was just a few blocks from the Odyssey. She strode up to the automatic doors, confident and defiant, the opulence of the lobby barely making an impression as she approached the registration desk. The person behind the desk, a woman with straight blunt-cut hair and subtle but discernable makeup, flicked her eyes over Persephone from head to toe, as well as her shabby bag.

"How may I help you, madam?" The flat line of her lips fell short of welcome.

Bitch. Persephone, bathed in the afterglow of a weekend of love-making with a hot fertility god, firmly but sweetly said, "I need a room for one week."

That should be plenty of time to find an affordable flat, some-where close to Athens Tech and Athens U where inexpensive housing was abundant. Anywhere would be better than living in the icy black opulence of Hades' palace.

"Let me see." The woman tapped her keyboard. Her lips formed a pout. She looked back at Persephone with a cool stare. "I'm afraid we're booked solid for the next two days."

Persephone reached into the side-seam pocket of her toga. She held up a large gold coin and dropped it on the desk with a resounding clink.

"See if this won't clear things up." It was one-fifth of the hard money Frey had given her but well spent to see the snooty ninny's face turn red, then pale. The woman's fingers flew over the keyboard.

"My mistake. They upgraded our software at the start of the year and it still has a few glitches. I see now that we have a single queen and a suite available. Which do you prefer?"

It would be highly satisfying to take the suite, to see how low the desk clerk would grovel, but why should she give someone who treated her rudely more commerce than necessary?

"The single queen, please." What a lovely string of words. Yes, she would take one and, Zeus willing, one day she'd *be* one.

"Your name, ma'am?"

"Persephone."

"And your surname?"

"Just Persephone."

The clerk did a double-take. "Oh. Yes." A smile cringed on her lips. "Of course."

A bell hop was summoned to drag the pitiful suitcase to her room. She tipped him with some copper coins of her own, closed the door behind him and checked out her temporary home. Comfortable looking bed, sleek desk and straight-backed chair, a sofa situated toward the view. The room overlooked the Plaza Fountain. Though the temperature outside was cool she slid open the glass door, stepped onto the tiny balcony and stretched her arms to the sky. Half a lifetime since she'd been free.

Persephone messaged Mother first, the single word *Arrived.* To Hades she wrote *See you in the fall.* Maybe.

Elysium, the Underworld

Gazing into the pond, Freya watched the story of her protégé unfold. Carrying a baby had transformed Persephone from a cowering, discontented wife to the child of Zeus she truly was. The gold coin she'd presented at the reception desk was pure Frey, but how many had he given his consort? Through magic and means of her own, Freya conjured a debit card in Persephone's name and transferred a princely sum from her own Norse Bank investment account for the balance. The card would arrive at the Mountain High Plaza tomorrow, complete with a deposit slip showing an amount that should carry Persephone through the birth of the baby. She also hacked the website of the best women's toga shop on Mount Olympus into Persephone's browser, a simple operation given lax IT security in the Underworld thanks to Hades doing everything on the cheap. If she, herself, could leave the Underworld, what fun it would be to join her friend for a day of shopping, girls' lunch out and finding a place of her own.

City of Mount Olympus

Hermes made the thirty-seventh adjustment to the minute tracking device with pliers a fraction of the size of tweezers. He slid the magnifier goggles up on his forehead, sat back from the lab bench microscope and pressed a key on his personal digital device, praying to Heaven and Earth this tweak was the final piece of the solution.

Geographic coordinates for his Olympus, Inc., lab flashed on the screen.

"Perfect."

He rubbed his bleary eyes and ran his hands through his shaggy, graying hair. The tracking device was ready, just in time for his last parental visit before Monique whisked P. B. away for six months. At least he'd know where his son was during their separation, could get to him in case of emergency. Small comfort, but it was the best he could do in the circumstances. Hermes' recent track record with Monique was crap. He was confident he could irritate her enough to make her leave the room for a few minutes, time enough to numb P. B.'s thumb with a drop of topical anesthetic and slip in the device. A dirty trick, but these were dirty times.

MONDAY, JANUARY 12, 2026

Midland, Texas, USA

Edwin East was dragging when he arrived at the penthouse office. It had been a long, cold swim home once he'd completed his mission at the conference in the City of Mount Olympus, effectively cancelling the Alternatives to Fossil Fuel Extraction roundtable on Saturday. A pinch of salmonella in the filet of sole did the trick.

Cyril greeted him with a heartening, clammy smile.

"My dear Edwin, how I missed you!"

"Cyril, my dear, how have you been keeping yourself?" The brothers exchanged a fraternal hug. "So thoughtful of you to lay today's suit out for me so I wouldn't have to think of what to wear."

It was a pity flowing robes were frowned upon for menswear among American mortals. He'd relished the freedom of movement in his sous chef toga, not to mention the salubrious benefits for his skin. So much lovely air circulation.

"Mission accomplished?" Cyril prompted.

"Naturally, my dear."

"Well done! One more victory for the East boys. And I must say I'm highly pleased with Perkins's replacement—"

"Lovely, lovely Perkins." He could taste the juicy crackled skin even now.

"Indeed he was. But as I was saying, your person in HR—"

"Ms. Allen, yes, delightfully plump woman. She was an absolute genius, culling the top ten candidates from a virtual mountain of resumes. And now the charming Ms. Patricia Leo is part of the East Fossil family."

"I hear Perkins's former subcontractors are delighted with her. The clever thing has met with half of them in person in one short week!" The poor souls had been neglected for over two weeks, such a long time for mortals, especially during the holidays. The dears got so anxious about money at that time of year.

"That may well be, Cyril, but I do have one complaint against her." Edwin slumped onto one of the loveseats facing the east window. "She's a mighty light eater."

"Yes, she is that." Cyril hesitated to share his second piece of news regarding Ms. Leo, reluctant to upset poor Eddy after his long swim, but being forthcoming was always best. "I regret to inform you she has also joined the twice-weekly yoga class."

Edwin clapped his palm to his chest. "Oh, my dear, why did we ever allow such a thing?"

"Recall, dear brother, it was part of our hiring arrangement with young Michael Guy in Legal. He came highly recommended, and of course the absence of any living family put him at the top of the list. Ms. Allen said he had an excellent offer from one of the big regional firms in his pocket, and was certain we'd lose him if we didn't bend."

"Ah." Edwin nodded in sympathy. "And what terrible pain it caused you, I am certain. But take heart, Cyril, dear. We've fattened skinnier fish than Ms. Leo and Michael Guy."

The brothers erupted in a duet of guffaws.

"We have indeed, Eddy my sweet. We have indeed."

Cyril's laughter came to an abrupt halt. He goggled at his brother.

"What is it, my dear?" said Eddy.

"You look peaked, dear chap. Your color is definitely off. Such a long and grueling excursion you've had. Perhaps some inhalants are due? Please oh please consider taking the morning off and returning to our abode for a dose of carbon dioxide. The spa was cleaned just yesterday. The reverse ducting from the oil furnace was working perfectly the last time I required treatment."

Edwin drew a hand across his weary brow. "Precious Cyril, you unfailingly have my best interests at heart! I will do as you recommend, dear brother, but first I must fuel myself with alternate comestibles for the journey."

Cyril fetched a burgeoning basket of chocolate chip cookies and a half-bottle of brandy from their penthouse stores. He poured each of them a snifter.

"To your health, dear Edwin," he said, snifter raised. "To your health."

In a Mortal Desert

Pablo, in Aph's arms, watched his mom from the opening of the MicroLend International tent. Monique Reynard studied her client's face as a flurry of syllables flew from the woman's mouth. The device tucked in Mom's ear translated the local language into English. To Pablo's delight, he understood every word without digital aid. A genetic gift from his "bad" dad? Whatever the source, he'd take it.

Monique was impressive—serious, jotting notes on a yellow pad when the client (mortal, thirty years old but she looked more like fifty) used phrases like *big global market*. Mom's follow-up questions were concise and relevant. The woman, a weaver, wanted to borrow the equivalent of two hundred US dollars to purchase a loom so she could make large-scale blankets and wall-hangings. She handed Monique a letter of confirmation from an interested buyer in the United Kingdom, stating the quantities they hoped to purchase and at what price. If sales came through as expected, the loan would be repaid in two months.

"When the money comes I will pay the loan, buy better food for my children, and fit our tent with solar energy. Then I can work at night as well as day, and my children can study."

The solar energy program was a subdivision of MicroLend, with the goal of moving households away from fossil fuels. Oil lamps and cook stoves that created unhealthy airborne particulates would, hopefully, become a thing of the past.

Through a tiny digital microphone pinned to Monique's khaki shirt collar she told the client her loan was approved. The woman's face bloomed with joy.

"Butt-Butt!" Pablo squealed, clapping his chubby hands. Mom looked up, smiling but her brow furrowed.

"That's enough for now, manikin." Aph delivered her line perfectly. "Nap time."

Pablo was happy living in a tent, and who wouldn't be since indoor plumbing wasn't his personal issue? Bottles, burping, diapers—it was universal stuff, as long as supplies held out. Not a problem at Beta Village, where babies came first. Social life was stimulating, too. In the two days since their arrival Aph had taken him to what the mortals called a Play Group. Everything from babes in arms, like himself, to toddlers. Mortals, naturally, but the lingua franca among his physical peers was the pared-down language of Global Baby. One of the guys was a genius at twisting the syllable *goo*. Those three letters could mean dozens of things, depending on intonation, volume and inflection.

These babies had seen a lot. Pablo was impressed and a little frightened when they told their stories of fleeing war-torn villages while *in utero*. Hardly anyone had a dad anymore. He didn't mention he had two of his own, though one of them had been absorbed into the Chair of Forgetfulness in the Underworld. Kind of like having your dad shot by a firing squad.

So yeah, he was learning a lot, and more grateful than ever for his own familial and immortal circumstances.

Aph played up the grandma routine when they were in public (or, for that matter, with Mom). She wasn't happy about leaving her business and her mansion and her husband back in the City of Mount Olympus, but he'd caught her good and tight in his net, making her worry about his potential for evil if left unsupervised. Now that they were poised to enact the afternoon nap, he'd explain his plan to her in detail.

She stood near the tent opening with him cradled in her arms, singing a lullaby, calling him her little manikin and saying how she was ready for a nap, too. After a few minutes of this window dressing she set him in his camp crib, a nifty construction of wood and canvas, and stretched out on her cot. Aph raised one of her hands in front of her face for inspection.

"Would you look at my fricking fingernails?" she moaned. She didn't leave Mount Olympus much these days and had forgotten to pack both nail polish and remover. "And it's so dry here. I can literally feel my skin turning into leather. The sooner we get out of this dump and back to civilization, the better. By Zeus, I wish you'd picked someone else to enable you."

He thought it impolitic to tell her his first choice was Pan, who'd been summoned who-knew-where for who-knew-what for who-knew-how-long. Probably something to do with climate change, like what most gods were working on these days. The bastard could at least have sent him a postcard.

"We won't be here forever," he said.

"Hah!"

"I'm on the level, Aph. This place is great for me but it sucks for you. What I propose is a complete change of scenery."

"Good!"

"I need to get in touch with my father's side of the family, and I'm not talking about Hermes."

Aph sat bolt upright and swung her legs over the side of the cot. "You've got to be by-Zeus kidding! Don't tell me we're going to see that —that *thing's* kinfolk."

Though it hurt to hear one of his dads called a "thing" Pablo let it ride. "The part you don't understand, Aph, is that The Power—" evil of him to take joy when the words made her flinch but a baby had to have some fun "—that is, my other dad, is the proverbial black sheep."

He'd need some serious thumb-sucking time to remove the beacon Hermes had tucked under his skin the night before he and Mom and Aph had left for the desert. Aph could sew it into the underside of his Beta Camp cot cradle to create the perfect diversion.

"We're going to a place with wealth beyond belief, Aph. We're going—" he paused for dramatic effect "—to the Mariana Trench."

ThURSDAY, JANUARY 15, 2026

City of Mount Olympus

Hera sat heavily at her desk. Out the picture windows the clear sky and bright sun mocked her dark mood. If the windows were a type that opened she'd fly away now, soar into the sky and head to some no-count fishing village, hide at the edge of the sea, any sea, until the danger passed.

If it ever passed. That was the problem with granting someone immortality.

She'd had some follow-up sessions with Aphrodite, talking about her fears, trying to figure out what to do. But Aphrodite was gone, off looking after her Spawn of Evil grandson while Monique did something involving money and impoverished mortals.

And now Veronica was coming down from the CEO suite to talk with her for reasons undisclosed. Hera could count on one thumb the number of times Ronnie had come to her office instead of summoning her upstairs, and that visit hadn't been good. It involved a bunch of gobbledygook about performance metrics that Veronica, her own ungrateful child, had decided to use to evaluate Hera's performance. Ronnie had had a nasty controlling streak since childhood, something parenting hadn't been able to drill out of her completely.

The device on Hera's desk pinged.

"Yes, Gilda?"

"Ms. Zeta is here."

Hera drew a deep breath and counted to ten as she let it out. "Send her in, please."

Ronnie expected people to rise when she walked into a room these days so Hera didn't.

"Hello, Mother." She sat stiffly in the seat opposite Hera's. "Thank you for seeing me today."

Her salutation sounded petulant instead of thankful.

"How can I help you?" Saying the cold words warmed her, anger in advance of accusation. Accusation? Heaven and Earth, is that what she was expecting? Sharing her secret with Aphrodite suddenly felt dangerous, in spite of client confidentiality. If Ronnie found out about Saul—

"I'm doing this in privacy to spare you embarrassment," Ronnie said, her lips pinching the words. "Mother, you've been spotted at the Grape and Grain during the workday four times this month. Can you tell me about that?"

So she didn't know yet and, by Zeus, Hera hoped she never would. She formed a bitter smile. "Like what? That it's open twenty-four seven?"

Ronnie's expression darkened. "Don't take that tack with me, Mother. I'm trying to help you."

"Really? It sounds more like you're planning to give me a reprimand."

Veronica rose. "I've made an appointment for you with an in-house drug and alcohol counselor." She produced an appointment card from her toga side-pocket and slapped it on the desk. "I'll hear about it if you're a no-show, so no tricks."

Hera watched her daughter sail through the office door like a ship rigged tight enough to snap the mast. For a moment she felt a tinge of maternal pity. The new bottle of Chardonnay in the credenza beckoned as a more appropriate response.

FRIDAY, JANUARY 16, 2026

The Village, Virginia, USA

Pan leaned against the wall of an architecturally real but substantively false storefront. Another reconnaissance on the make-believe main street. He yawned, didn't bother to cover his gaping mouth. The business inside sold menswear, as if the trainees would ever require something besides their polo shirt and khaki uniforms and the undercover disguises provided as needed. At least the sun was out today. He basked in the rays and felt a sentimental tug for the temperate winters in the City of Mount Olympus.

The mortal trainees needed refresher after refresher. They were by-Zeus slow on the uptake. What would their big surprise be today—a pretend suitcase nuclear bomb? A make-believe riot? A cartoon coup? Bumps and bruises could be earned in these training exercises, not to mention emotional strain, but what good was it if it didn't incorporate actual danger?

He was no one to criticize, of course, being immortal. But still… How, out of his dunderheaded classmates, had intelligent, well-prepared Cleo been the one nabbed at the embassy party? He'd been briefed in advance one of "his" attachés was a double agent so it wasn't a complete surprise. It had to have something to do with their overall mission; that was the only reasonable explanation. With luck, he'd be busted soon, too, and sent somewhere more interesting.

The menswear shop was near the end of the street, kitty-corner from the bookstore. Pan had been there again since he noticed the proprietor's pink and purple aura. His initial reluctance to confront Amory Evermore was now replaced with curiosity. It was the only interesting mystery in this made-up place. Did Evermore work for Athena too? If so, he might know where Cleo had gone.

Pan shoved his hands in his pockets and strolled across the street, whistling like a mortal movie detective to appear nonchalant. He greeted Evermore as he passed into the bookshop, slouched around the shelves, and pretended to peruse the inventory.

"Do you have anything on Greek mythology, Mr. Evermore?"

"Hmmm. Let me see." Evermore scanned the section labeled

World Religions, three scantly stocked shelves below World Geography. "I usually have the Robert Graves books, the two-volume set, but I seem to be out. I can order those for you and get them here in two business days. Is next Tuesday soon enough?"

Pan hadn't read the Graves himself but he'd heard someone hooting over it in a pub when it first came out. "You should see what he says about the Big Twelve," a sloshing patron two stools down from him had said. "Sex and violence, all of it! Maybe in the old days, but the way they are now? Tied up with corporate business and saving the bloody mortals from themselves every minute of the day. Almost makes me feel sorry for them."

"Works for me," Pan said to Evermore. It might make for fun recreational reading. Maybe he'd pick up a few tidbits about himself that had been invented through the ages. Besides, it gave him a reason to return to the bookstore next week.

Evermore returned to the sales counter computer, tapped at keys and flipped through a series of screens. Pan once again studied the pink aura topped with purple corona. A case of mixed mortal and immortal parentage? The immortal trait passed to a very small percentage of such children. He surveyed the man's features. Coloring similar to Hermes, but too close in age to be his offspring. Nose somewhat familiar, but like no one of the older generation. Short—maybe he was one of Zeus'?

"You'll be paying with your card?"

Stupid question since trainees weren't allowed any other means of payment, but all the false businesses asked.

"Yes." He proffered his small plastic rectangle.

"Pan D. Arvis," Evermore read before swiping the card in the reader. Pan and his two surviving diplomatic attachés had been issued new identities since the embassy party simulation, the Ambassador of Potark and his wife returning home after their embassy was seized by the Burkosian Army. "Sounds like a Greek name. No wonder you want the Graves."

Was that an opening?

"Yes," he confirmed. "I got the bug to know more when I was visiting family last year. They live near Mount Olympus. Perhaps you've been there?"

Evermore's eyes met his. "I haven't had that pleasure."

The credit card machine spit out a slip. Pan signed. Evermore handed the duplicate to Pan when he'd finished.

"Put this in a safe place," Evermore instructed. "You'll need it next Tuesday."

"Thanks." Pan tucked the slip and the card into the back pocket of his khakis. "See you then."

He had half an hour to kill before the shuttle was due, time for a pint at a pub and a listen to the local gossip, loaded with clues so simple a toddler could discern them. Pan slid the sales receipt out of his back pocket at the same time he retrieved the card to pay for his drink. There was handwriting on it, coded, like several other receipts he'd collected in the false town. Silly business; as often as not the code key was the day of the week.

But in the dormitory bathroom stall that night, *Friday* did not break the code. He tried *Mount Olympus* with limited success, then *Greek* (better still). *Graves* applied to the alphabet yielded *who sent you and what do you want?*

Bingo.

MONDAY, JANUARY 19, 2026

Casablanca, Morocco

Aphrodite stared up at the ceiling fan, the wide blades creaking in slow rotation, too slow to cool the humid Moroccan air. She'd remembered Casablanca as a romantic destination, filled with long evening feasts, and all-night lovemaking on a sumptuous silk-dressed bed.

It wasn't supposed to be like this, laid flat by the stifling air in a once grand but now down-at-the-heels tourist hotel, sharing a lumpy mattress with an infant. Usually it was a plus that Pablo was a gifted conversationalist. This afternoon, after flying with him in her arms, hundreds of miles from the WomanFront village to this dump, she longed to switch off his motor mouth and sleep.

"You'll need to get us outfitted and reserve our cabin on the boat. That'll get us to Panama. We can fly across the isthmus and…"

How in Tartarus had he talked her into this, and how had she persuaded Monique that taking Pablo on a cruise of the Nile (a cover he'd fabricated in his fertile two-month-old imagination) was a good idea? Okay, so the infusion she'd slipped into Monique's morning Chai explained that part. But, really, why was she going along with this madness?

"Then, when we get to the Mariana Trench and make contact with the Old Ones, they can…"

Aphrodite rolled off her back, propped herself up on one arm and immediately wished she hadn't. It had been centuries since she'd flown as far as she had today. Pablo's baby body hadn't felt like much at first, but time and the additional drag had stressed her biceps to the limit.

"What makes you so sure they'll want to help us fight climate change?" she snapped. "From what I remember chthonic monsters are remorseless thugs. The ones that tried to invade Mount Olympus, back when—"

"Media spin," Pablo said, dismissively waving a chubby hand. "Maybe they'd seen the future and were coming after Hermes when they found out he'd inspired the mortals to invent the wheel. It's not a black and white world, Aph. We need to think in shades of gray."

Heaven and Earth that was exactly the color her hair was turning.

Never in the past two thousand years had she permitted her roots to grow out without a touch-up. Maybe there was someplace in Casablanca that—

"You do swim, right?"

"Well enough to rise out of the sea foam the moment I was born," she retorted. But not so much since then. Bathing in asses' milk was more her style.

"You don't sound one hundred percent confident on that, Aph. You can train while we're at sea. Be sure to book a ship that has full athletic amenities."

Grandson or no, if Pablo wasn't immortal she'd strangle him. It was one thing to serve as ground transportation and companion in a refugee camp, but to go dashing off on a wild caper to the deepest place on Earth? Sure, her body would survive a thirty-six-thousand-foot dive, but it would play havoc with her skin elasticity, possibly turn her into a platinum blonde pancake with all the external pressure.

"Tell me again how you'll make contact, once we get there." She would, of course, derail their expedition. But Pablo was smart, and who knew how powerful. She needed to play her hand with care.

"There's a signal," he explained in a patient tone. "It's inside of me, Aph, maybe the only thing my other dad gave me. That's how I know he was an outcast, and also," Pablo's baby eyes grew moist, "that he was sorry about a lot of things. If I can talk to the Old Ones about that, maybe they'll help us with the rising seas." He sniffled. "That would help my other dad, too."

Pablo's mouth opened wide, releasing his anguish in baby-speak. It was stupid of her, but when he cried for real and showed his vulnerable side she melted. She gathered him into her arms and pulled him close.

"Shhh, shhh, shhh. Don't worry, baby, we'll find them." He heaved an ear-splitting yowl and fell into muted sobs. "We'll find them."

TUESDAY, JANUARY 20, 2026

The Village, Virginia, USA

Pan pushed through the bookshop door Tuesday afternoon. He'd borrowed one of the campus scooters to make the unscheduled trip and was surprised to find businesses up and down the street open and ready for custom. Made sense, if the actors who lived here had to shop and bank and get their hair cut.

Evermore was working at the computer. He looked up when the bell chimed, bruise-colored circles under his eyes.

"Mr. Arvis, back for your books." He reached under the counter and pulled out two paperback volumes. The one on top sported a cover photo of ancient pottery decorated with a primitive depiction of Heracles. He looked like a damn fool in a lion skin, the head worn as a helmet.

"Interesting," Pan said, inspecting the picture. "Heracles is a major player, of course." They'd worked together just two months ago, vanquishing the dark force known as The Power. "Personally, I'd rather work for someone like Athena."

"Ah," Evermore said in a bland tone. If he knew anything, he was damn good at hiding it.

"She's more or less the patron of special agents," Pan continued. "Goddess of War and Wisdom. A woman with the smarts to gather intelligence before she makes a strategic decision."

"Very interesting," Evermore said. "I've never thought of her in a contemporary setting."

"She'd definitely be a take-charge type, and detail-oriented, too. Would want her agents well-trained to make sure they could sustain a cover, for example."

"I see. Well, then." A trace of anxiety in his eyes? It came and went so quickly Pan couldn't be sure. "Is there anything else I can help you with, Mr. Arvus?"

"Thanks, but I think our business is finished."

Amory Evermore dipped his head in acknowledgement.

"Enjoy your evening, Mr. Arvus."

"You, too, Mr. Evermore, and thanks for the books."

Pan slipped his books into one of the scooter's saddlebags, perplexed. What was Evermore doing here? No way to ask headquarters about it now, with his digital device impounded. But later…

~ * ~

Saul Crispin, in the privacy of his townsfolk cottage, poured his third glass of wine. Working at The Village had always been a welcome change of pace, with good pay and an opportunity to get out of the city. The CIA provided identities and histories. Actors had room to make the characters their own, provided the basic storylines stayed intact. Not everybody was briefed on the same aspects of town life, which kept things interesting. Some characters were direct players in crisis scenarios created for the trainees while others were sources of relevant information.

Connections formed between players. Merchants collaborated on street-wide sales events. Restaurants learned customers' preferences and modified the menu. Relationships developed, mostly friendships but every so often romantic attraction created new couples, eroded sham marriages and shook up the fabricated social scene. Saul wouldn't let that happen to him. Centuries of passing for mortal had made it clear: falling in love with a mortal was a probable route to being outed.

And now his safety was compromised by that curly-haired trainee, Pan Arvus. Somehow that guy knew Saul was immortal. How could he have figured it out after such a short, impersonal acquaintance?

Saul declared it drink an entire a bottle night. He refilled his glass, rummaged a half-loaf of Italian bread, some cheese and olives from the small but serviceable kitchen. Why did Arvus mention Athena? David had told Saul every immortal in Greek mythology lived and worked in the City of Mount Olympus. Had his own immortal status surfaced on the Mount Olympus radar, and Arvus sent to hunt him down?

Wine dulled the shiver in his spine but another stronger one came. Where was Cleo? He hadn't seen her for weeks. Had she tipped off Arvus, pointed Saul out like Judas pointed out that other guy two millennia ago? Had she betrayed him? Why would she betray him?

Saul sipped deeply and pondered how to defend himself. His iron-clad contract for this stint ran through the end of January. Surveillance was excellent at The Village. At least if security was breached and he was extracted by immortal agents they'd see it happen. But what could they do? Big-Gs were powerful. Hera, herself, had granted him immortal life. The destruction any Big-G could cause could be devastating.

The wall-hung pendulum clock chimed a late hour. Eleven more days and nights, if this one still counted. Did David know what was going on with Cleo and the Arvus guy? Saul glanced at the telephone, a late twentieth century model that plugged into the wall. It worked, but only on site. Cast members relinquished their personal phones at check-in; he couldn't call anyone until he left.

Saul tipped the last of the bottle into his glass. Life as a wandering Jew had never been easy but he'd never feared the future in this way before, as if punishment were waiting to be rendered. Even if he'd been disinclined to become Hera's lover, which he hadn't been, he wouldn't have had much choice. He'd been a member of Herod Antipas' household where it was either do the lady's bidding or die. He'd learned she was immortal only after David was born and was spirited away by the Bernsteins. He'd begged her to let him raise their child if she didn't want David for herself.

You are not capable of raising him because he will live forever.

Hera's words, cold and precise.

You will leave me now.

Saul refused.

She raised her hand, and eternity began.

THURSDAY, JANUARY 22, 2026

The Moroccan Shore

Pablo gazed upon the Atlantic Ocean, yearning his thoughts beyond the vanishing point, across South America and into the Eastern Pacific. The Old Ones were quiet this morning. Morning in Morocco, anyway. His baby mind, though brilliant, was challenged by concepts of time and distance. Understandable, he realized, as his options and schedule were severely limited by the needs of his infant body. He shifted in Aph's arms, puffing fussy noises through his lips.

"What's the matter *now*?" she asked in a distinctly un-grandmotherly tone.

So many things. The inability to act on his own. The stupidity of the grownup immortals who couldn't see the obvious starting place to curbing climate change was recruiting the help of the Old Ones. The load about to explode in his diaper. But the worst problem was Aph. Ever since they'd arrived in Casablanca she'd been raising barriers to his cunning plan.

They want passports was her first excuse. Well, not an excuse exactly, he'd heard the cruise ship ticket agent say so with his own baby ears since Aph couldn't leave him behind when she'd gone to make arrangements.

No, she said, she didn't have the skill to forge a passport herself. Hah! What good was being one of the Twelve Great Olympians if you were incapable of committing a tiny little felony? But no, she'd explained, the issuance of false documents was under Athena's purview and there was plenty of red tape to navigate. In a pinch, Hermes, the eternal trickster, might be persuaded to whip one up, but they couldn't go to him. Hermes hadn't wanted Pablo to leave the City of Mount Olympus in the first place.

Okay, so maybe she wasn't sandbagging but that did nothing to stem his frustration. He had to get to the Old Ones, had to save the world and save his Dads' reputations! Pablo reached deep down inside and seized the last available tool to launch his plan.

"Whaaaaa!" he shrieked. "Butt-Buuutt! Butt-Buuutt!!!"

"Tartarus, you're bursting my eardrums!" Aph snapped. She set him down on the shore. He screamed some more, kicked his chubby baby legs loose of the swaddling, let a huge load rip into his diapers, and screamed again.

"Butt-Buuutt! Butt-Buuutt!!!"

The waters before them erupted in wave and foam. The sturdy, sparkling figure of a man rose from the sea and strode toward Pablo, shooting Aph a sharp look on the way.

"What is the meaning of this?" Poseidon bellowed. "Aphrodite, what have you done to this child?"

"For Zeus' sake," Aph spat. "You know nothing about babies, Poseidon. Indulge him like this and he'll be spoiled for life! Mind your own business and go back to the briny deep."

"Hah, like you could make me!"

Pablo stopped wailing and listened in fascination.

"Any day of the week, fish boy!"

"Tart!"

"Takes one to know one. Since when did you care about babies? You've certainly left all your children on their own."

Nice one, Aph.

"Like you have room to talk, you she-wolf!"

"You never lifted a trident to help the children you fathered on me, you deranged, scaly masher!"

Wow! In his two months Pablo had picked up some bits and pieces of gossip about Olympian promiscuity but never anything this good.

Aph dropped to her knees in the sand and scooped Pablo into her arms. "We're leaving," she said as she scrambled to stand. "Don't try to follow us."

The look she gave Poseidon must have been killer from the expression on his face. Aphrodite kicked through the sand, bearing Pablo toward higher ground. Dramatic, and a dandy metaphor, but this would never do.

"Waaah! Butt-Buuutt! Butt-Buuutt!!!"

Travels with Poseidon would be rough and ready, but his masterful plans would come to nothing if he couldn't get to the Mariana Trench.

Wet smacks of Poseidon's web-toed feet slapped behind them. Pablo felt it all the way to his baby bones. His plan was going to work. It *had* to work.

A Boutique Hotel, Paris, France

"Frig, frig, frig fucking frig!"

Aphrodite paced in front of the faux marble faux fireplace in her posh Paris suite, arms crossed tight over her solar plexus, chipped fingernails digging into her biceps. How in Tartarus was she going to explain to Monique that Pablo had been kidnapped by Poseidon, and was off on some insane undersea adventure that would require weeks if not months? Hadn't it been enough she'd schemed on behalf of the little turkey to get him away from the desert camp, with the intention of curbing his craving to visit a colony of slimy ancients in the Mariana Trench? Heracles had fought off these clammy jerks when they'd attacked Mount Olympus. They were the Bad Guys! But how to explain that to Pablo, who, though articulate, was not, in her opinion, wise beyond his years?

"Frig!"

The extra curse was for herself. She'd been too slow, damn it, had never dreamed Pablo could best her.

P. B., she corrected herself. She'd have to use his official name when she talked to Monique. But not today. No, not today, she was done with the conniving little bastard and his bullying fishy friend for today! By Zeus, what she hadn't done to aid Pablo in his time of need—interrupted her own life, gone to the driest spot on Earth with close to zero amenities, including a nail salon. When she'd arrived in Paris this afternoon, travel tattered, hair blown in a dozen directions as if it existed to show off its gray roots, the desk clerk had raised an eyebrow.

"Madame might enjoy our spa services," he'd blandly suggested. Any other time she might have blasted him a new orifice in a creative location but today she grasped his point. "We have an opening early this evening—"

"I'll take it!" She slipped the woven travel tote off her shoulder, a product of one of Monique's clients, whipped out her Bank of Olympus Platinum Card and slapped it on the registration desk.

"Do you need assistance with your luggage, Madame?" the clerk said while they waited for the chime of credit approval.

She tapped a ragged fingernail on her bag. "This is it. I'm here for shopping, luggage included."

Retail therapy was a stupidly mortal way to let off steam but her choices were limited. An evening at the spa would be pure ambrosia.

A cheerful *ping* issued from the credit card reader.

"Very good, Madame. Henri!" He snapped his fingers at a uniformed young man standing near an antique elevator with gold-toned retractable grille. The thin, pimply bellhop strode forward to take a large brass key from the desk clerk. "See Madame to her suite, number seven."

Number seven overlooked the Champs Elysees, as the bellhop pointed out. He paused, expectantly, waiting for a tip.

"Sorry, it's all I have with me," she said, handing him a wad of Moroccan dirham, virtually valueless in relation to the Euro. She conjured her most seductive smile to offset his financial disappointment, realizing she must look about as enticing as Medusa after today's flight.

She paced and cursed in front of the fireplace, hungering for the restoration of her appearance and dignity an evening at the spa would bring. Time to put thoughts of everyone who vexed her aside. In the mortal world, Paris was her favorite restoration destination. Her time. To Tartarus with them all!

Except for Hephaestus. They didn't keep tabs on each other by any means, but he'd appreciate hearing from her and knowing she was all right. She pawed through the scant toiletries and dirty clothes—a call to the valet would be next—for that silly but admittedly convenient digital device everyone carried these days. *Bonsoir, Hef!* she tapped with her index finger. *Guess where I am?*

Atlantic Ocean, off Morocco

When Poseidon dove into the Atlantic, breaking the waves with one arm and carrying Pablo in the other, three things became apparent. First, and most critically, Pablo could breathe under water. Second, he had to tell Poseidon where they were going. Third, there was a load in his pants and no one had a diaper bag.

Sound moved slowly under water. It took Pablo a few tries to form words that could be understood as anything but *blub*. At last he managed to shout his rescuer's name.

The big sea god stopped. He held Pablo in front of him, staring. *What did you say?*

Pablo heard the words not with his ears but in his head.

"Surface," Pablo said with tremendous effort, the water pressure heavy on his lungs. "Talk."

Poseidon shot up to the surface. "You can talk! Aren't you a little young for that?"

"It's kind of hard to explain," Pablo said. "I need to tell you where we're going."

Poseidon squinted, shook his head as if to loosen something that was stuck.

"Must have encountered a red tide without noticing, inhaled some toxin or other."

"No, Poseidon, you're not imagining this. I can speak, and I have complex thoughts. But the important part is, I'm on a mission."

"Oh certainly. Of course. This is some sort of trick Aphrodite's playing on me, isn't it?"

Pablo wriggled to rearrange the uncomfortable mass in his diaper, his patience at the breaking point. "It's no trick, dude, don't be an idiot."

Poseidon turned a violent shade of crimson, pulled Pablo close to his face. "Why you cheeky little—"

"Don't threaten me, man."

"Hah!"

"I mean it, Poseidon. You know who my dad is."

"What?" he roared. "Hermes? I could take him down in—"

"The other one. Ever heard of The Power?"

"Impossible," Poseidon said, though the color drained from his face.

But he was conversing now instead of doubting. In a few minutes Pablo laid out his plan and the reason for it.

"Let me get this straight," Poseidon said. "You call yourself Pablo. You want me to take you to the Mariana Trench, where you will hobnob with a hoard of ancient and aggressive monsters in order to convince them to help Olympus, Inc., save the Earth from climate change."

"I didn't say anything about them being aggressive, man, they're family."

"If you'd seen what I've seen," Poseidon said, "you wouldn't want to mess with that bunch. The time they invaded Mount Olympus—"

"Ancient history. Are you going to help me or not?"

Poseidon's expression shifted from puzzlement to hurt. "You set me up for this, didn't you, you little bastard? Right from the start. Knew you needed the most powerful swimmer of all to get you to their deep-sea lair so you could spin your line of bull."

"Wouldn't have occurred to me until I saw you in person," Pablo said. "I mean it, Poseidon. When I saw you riding on that float in the

Parade of Lights, decked out with your crown and your trident and exuding your incredible force of power to the cheering crowd I was captivated. You're a true hero, saving the Seattle waterfront and Elysium in one bold move."

Poseidon bowed his head. "Any of us would have done what we could."

"But you were the one who did it, the only one who could. That's why I need you for this mission. Skill, brains, strength—you've got it all."

Plus the sparkling wetsuit, but Pablo kept that to himself. Baby eyes were dazzled by that kind of shit, speaking of which—

"I don't suppose you can help me with a diaper issue?"

Poseidon roared with laughter. His big hands were ill-suited for the job of undoing safety pins, but after a brief struggle and a couple of pokes he freed Pablo of the blasted thing and tossed it away.

"Cloth," Poseidon said, as they watched the diaper bob a few times and sink. "Biodegradable. I appreciate that."

The route was contrary to Pablo's original Isthmus of Panama course but Poseidon said this was shorter by far. They swam south along the African coast, Pablo blissfully unencumbered, the water caressing his bare bottom.

Paris, France

Aphrodite—showered, swathed in a thick terrycloth bathrobe, and restored by a split of complimentary champagne—padded down the hall to a modern elevator that went directly to the spa. The doors opened to the soothing fragrance of essential oils and soft pink lighting, flattering to all ages and complexions. A peaceful individual, trim and androgynous in appearance, sat on a tall stool behind a high desk. No computer on the desk, just a simple ledger and a potted orchid in bloom.

Perfect. Absolutely by Zeus perfect. No hydration-sapping desert, no Casablanca dive, no naughty little bastard of a grandbaby to use her and cast her aside for Poseidon—Poseidon! After all she'd done for Pablo he could at least have replaced her with someone who wasn't a complete and total macho jackass.

Breathe. Time to take the advice she most frequently offered her counseling clients and let it all go. A restorative evening of pampering, a ton of sleep in a posh hotel, retail therapy in the heart of mortal fashion tomorrow, and a few days beyond that. She'd turned off her digital device. After the abuse she'd suffered, if the immortal world wanted to find her for the next few days they'd have to look very, very hard.

FRIDAY, JANUARY 23, 2026

Midland, Texas, USA

Cleo Petra, aka Patricia C. Leo, rolled back from her desk in her state-of-the-art ergonomic chair and let out a hard breath. The analysis of R and D projects she'd labored over was conclusive: much as Marketing asserted otherwise, East Fossil funded no climate change research. Some of the project names were blatantly misleading. The file on Clean Air Options from subcontractor Pure Earth, LP (she'd read it to the last detail before meeting with their general partner) was really about new technologies for locating undiscovered Arctic fossil fuel reserves. When she'd questioned the general partner about this he'd started to sweat, said the entity name was one Perkins, her predecessor, had recommended they adopt in order to, as he put it, square things with marketing.

Pure Earth was one of many such examples from subcontracted research groups. In-house, proposals aimed at reducing atmospheric carbon dioxide and other pollutants were stored in a file titled Proposals Rejected. None of the authors of those proposals, she'd noted, now appeared on the weekly list HR sent her for payroll approval.

In-house corruption, subcontractor corruption, and Perkins, a critical witness to these shenanigans not only dead but eaten. If Cleo had uncovered a scheme like this at Olympus, Inc., she would have taken it straight to Veronica. Not so with the Easts; their signatures appeared at the bottom of every accepted proposal. Clearly the window dressing was unethical, but was it enough to press charges under mortal law?

Cleo made circles with her head to pop the tension out of her neck, shrugged her tight shoulders up and down. Heaven and Earth she needed a break.

Minutes later she stood at the cafeteria's espresso counter, brain fogged, bleary eyes moving uncomprehendingly over the chalk board menu above. She'd summarize her analysis for tonight's report to Athena; some legal expert in Diplomacy could figure out what action to take, if any. Afternoon coffee breakers trickled in by ones and twos as she numbly pondered whether she wanted an Americano more than a double mocha. A pair of men—one a rumpled individual she recognized from Legal, the other a stranger in an impeccably tailored suit and overly shiny shoes—stepped up to the counter and placed their orders.

"After all the money we've poured into him he's become recalcitrant," the snappy dresser said. "Needless to say, the Easts aren't pleased. Who do you have to blow to buy a congressman these days, anyway?"

The man laughed heartily at his own joke. Cleo, whose hearing was excellent, barely heard the guy from Legal say "*Sotto Voce.*"

Corruption on the outside as well as the inside? That might give the mortal legal system something to sink its teeth into. Her efforts distilled to a satisfying clarity. Tonight's report could be the driver for the hoped-for sting.

SATURDAY, JANUARY 24, 2026

City of Mount Olympus

Ping!

Athena, goblet of Syrah in hand and comfortably reclined on a chaise in the New Mycenae condo she shared with the owl Tim, reached toward the coffee table for her digital device.

"A goddess of war and wisdom's work is never done," she said to her companion, who roosted on an elegantly carved perch nearby. The owl hooted at their well-worn joke.

The screen displayed the time—II:IV AM—and a text message. Athena scanned Cleo's findings on East Fossil's misleading R and D projects, not remotely surprised at her conclusions. But the paragraph at the end…ah, yes, the underhanded work of a corrupt mortal lobbyist.

The corners of her mouth lifted. The owl hopped from his perch to the back of the chaise and hooted quizzically. Athena set down her goblet and reached up to ruffle his head feathers.

"It's what we've been waiting for, my friend," she said. "It's time to deploy Pan."

MONDAY, JANUARY 26, 2026

Pacific Ocean, Mariana Trench

Zipping through the Atlantic Ocean was great fun. At first. They shot past many varieties of aquatic mammals and fish, even the sailfish which Poseidon pointed out as the fastest fish in the world. The God of the Sea, himself, could travel four times the speed of the fastest submarine, clocking in at 300 kilometers per hour. If Pablo wasn't as bald as a cue ball he would have worried his hair would be pulled out at the roots.

But it was a long way from Morocco's shore at Casablanca to the Mariana Trench. Even though Poseidon stayed awake for the entire trip and maintained his top velocity, it took more than three days.

"Almost there," Poseidon said.

At last it was time to dive deep, deep down, nearly eleven kilometers to the bottom. Pablo felt the pressure of the water everywhere, but especially on his lungs. It took his eyes several minutes to adjust to the pitch-black darkness. Pale embryonic fish with fat bodies and long wispy tailfins scoured the ocean floor.

"Mariana snail fish," Poseidon, who was talking with Pablo head-to-head, said. "The top predator at this depth. Better hope they don't have a taste for babies."

Pablo tried not to let what sounded like a joke bother him. He set to work looking for a hatch or a doorway that led to the Underground Kingdom of the Old Ones. They'd sensed him coming and had sent out a message on a frequency that could only be heard by those of chthonic blood. The signal was faint, but "glowing entry" was repeated enough times to convince him he'd heard correctly. He'd passed this information to Poseidon.

"See anything?" Poseidon said. "At this pressure we can't stay down here more than a few minutes."

"Swim the length, slowly," Pablo said. He turned his head from surface to surface, searching for—

"There!"

A thread of gold defined a large rectangle to their left. The shape of a star glowed in the center. Poseidon edged closer so Pablo's out-stretched palm could touch the surface.

The door shot away in a nanosecond and they were sucked in faster still. Poseidon landed on his bottom with Pablo clutched to his chest. The opening behind them clapped together and solidified into a seamless wall. The seawater that came in with them puddled underneath Poseidon's bum. They were in a rock-walled chamber. Torches in wall brackets provided illumination.

"Hello!" Pablo called. The word echoed down a long rock tunnel in front of them, carved with pictograms and dissolving into darkness. "Hello!" he called again. When the second series of echoes died away it was replaced by the sound of flesh dragging over rock, far down the tunnel. As the sound grew louder, torchlight cast shadows on previously darkened walls. Large, lump-shaped shadows, like boulders or giant beehives, advanced. When the first members of the party resolved into solid form they began singing. It was a simple language with a few syllables repeated over and over. Pablo somehow knew one of the words meant *kinsman*.

He felt Poseidon draw in his breath. Pablo, too, gasped at the splendor of the oncoming assembly, giant lumpish bodies, yes, but dressed in long flowing robes woven from silver, gold and copper, and sparkling with precious gems. The two in the lead wore tall conical hats and carried staffs.

"Whoa, dude," Pablo whispered to Poseidon.

The procession stopped a meter or two in front of them. Poseidon rose slowly and rested Pablo in the crook of one arm.

"Welcome, oh kinsman of the Old Ones, Son of Your Wayward Father who left us for the temptations of the Above. We rejoice in your return and shall escort you and your slave to a celebratory feast."

"I, Pablo Raison, accept your welcome with thanks, oh Ancient Cousin," Pablo said, the foreign words filling his mouth as if by enchantment. He tried to add *as does Poseidon, God of the Sea* but the enchantment did not play along.

The two priests stepped apart, making room for a litter borne by four of their kind, also dressed opulently but clearly of a lower rank.

"What in Tartarus have you gotten us into?" Poseidon muttered.

Determined to look cool and in control, though he wondered the same thing, Pablo pretended he hadn't heard.

City of Mount Olympus

Hermes shifted in his chair, feeling both tedium and the sensation the vacant mouths of the masks hanging on the wall behind him whispered curses at his back. Blah, blah, blah, Athena might as well have been saying. Cleo was successfully embedded at East Fossil Fuels in R and D, a dead end as he'd tried to explain weeks ago but the Goddess of War and Wisdom was numb to his opinions. She and Ares were hung up on the East brothers being some variety of chthonic monsters, a big So What as far as Hermes was concerned. There were beings like that scattered all around the mortal world, remnants of a once thriving population that had peaked a millennia ago. Okay, so they didn't usually run mega corporations based in Texas, but…

Damn, he could use Cleo's help right now. The tour of Asia Veronica had ordered him to make had actually rendered something of interest and he needed someone with Cleo's analytic abilities to run an independent evaluation of what he'd found. Chinese inventors had come up with several seemingly viable designs for small, economical nuclear power plants. Cleo had the kind of mind that could figure out how to make the prototypes scalable. Then Waller could let 'er rip on social media, persuade the rest of the mortal world to set aside politics for once and adopt the Chinese designs in their own countries. He felt reasonably certain this could knock coal-powered energy out of the mix for good, if he had enough time and goddess-power.

He perked up when Athena shared the lurid detail about the Easts eating some of their employees. Was she born yesterday? Happened all the time in the mortal world. He bit his cheeks not to laugh.

The digital device strapped to his wrist vibrated. Hermes glanced at the small screen.

Beacon no longer transmitting.

The message kicked his heart into his throat. P. B.'s implant. If he couldn't monitor his infant son's location—

Hermes bolted from his chair and strode out of Athena's office. The owl on her shoulder screeched.

"Where are you going?" Athena said in a matching tone. "I'm not finished with the briefing."

"Emergency," he said over his shoulder.

On his way to the elevator Hermes messaged Monique, something he'd vowed he wouldn't do to maintain his sense of pride, but if P. B.

was in danger he had to know.

Where in Tartarus have you taken P. B.?

Athena's receptionist came out from behind her desk and tried to block him but he pushed past her and dashed for the stairs. Hermes ran down and down and down, eyes glued to his screen. He'd just passed the fifth-floor landing when a message appeared:

WTT? He's with Mother.

Where?????

The Nile.

The Nile? He shouted in fury, his cry echoing up and down the Olympus, Inc., stairwell. Why in Tartarus had Monique insisted on taking P. B. with her if she'd already sent him off on a holiday with Aphrodite? Zeus on a crutch, what was wrong with her?

He pulled up Aphrodite's contact code.

Where in Tartarus are you, Aph?

Five seconds, ten, twenty, a minute and thirty-seven seconds—

Ping!

Hermes stared at the screen, unbelieving.

Service for this account is not available. Please try again.

He shook his head to clear the panic, took the last few stairs to the fourth floor and raced to his desk. Bad connection? Possible in the mortal world, but the Olympus, Inc., digital system was robust. He pulled up the analytics app and queried Aphrodite's account. She'd shut off her device, the bitch! But the tracer function would at least give him a location. One click took him to Paris, France.

Paris, France

Aphrodite woke to a horrible electronic siren. Heaven and Earth, was the hotel on fire? No, it was that blasted device on the nightstand. She swore she'd turned it off days ago but it screeched ever louder, spiraling to ear-splitting volume. She pushed the hair out of her eyes and rolled toward the monster. Incoming call from Hermes. Hermes?

Aph what in Tartarus is going on?

Merde. Try to get some rest and relaxation after an incredibly trying time and what happens? Tracked down by the Digital Devices bloodhound.

Everything's fine. Take a pill.

It wasn't like she'd been irresponsible. She'd checked in with Poseidon daily and talked to Pablo, too. And yes, it had been a hair-raising time, worrying about them dodging sharks and Zeus knew what else to get to the chthonic settlement and the ancient race who lived there. After Poseidon transmitted *Working on strategy they are eager to assist* late yesterday, she'd put out the *ne pas déranger* sign and turned in for a long day's sleep.

Aphrodite rolled away from the offending screen and put a pillow over her head to mute the siren but it only grew louder. She removed the pillow and typed: *If you get an incoming message from Poseidon, pick it up.*

Poseidon?! WTT Aph?

She terminated the connection with Hermes and put a hand over her ear while she pulled up Poseidon's account.

Tell Pablo to call his dad.

The siren continued to wail. Fine, if that's the way he wanted it! Aphrodite rolled out of bed, opened her window, and pitched her digital device so hard it crashed against the Arc de Triumph with a satisfying *crunch*.

THURSDAY, JANUARY 29, 2026

En route to the Mariana Trench

For three days Hermes waited in agony. When a text at last arrived from Poseidon he shot up from his desk, threw open the office window and flew southeast at warp speed. Why was P. B. with Poseidon and why in Tartarus did that swaggering macho fish think the Mariana Trench was an appropriate place for a baby? Did Monique know about this? Not that it would make the whole thing any less crazy. Had they all gone crazy?

Adrenaline pushed his thoughts aside. Hermes set his wrist device to navigate mode and concentrated only on speed, willing the eleven thousand-plus kilometers to melt away. He barely noticed when the device vibrated, alerting him he was within minutes of his target. An X on the screen marked Poseidon's location.

Hermes broke the surface of the Pacific with a perfect jackknife. With luck, he'd have P. B. in his arms in minutes and take him home where he'd be safe. Down, down, down he went, five kilometers, six kilometers, more. The weight of an ocean pressed down on him, made his eyes feel like they were being pushed up the sides of his head, but he couldn't stop, he wouldn't stop.

Thunk!

His forehead hit something so hard it felt like his skull had cracked. Invisible barrier, transmitting a message.

By order of Chief of the Old Ones, no admittance.

The words echoed in Hermes' throbbing brain. He raised his wrist to his blurred eyes, saw Poseidon's X pulsing big on the screen. They were definitely on the other side, *if* he still had P. B.

No! The bubble surrounding Hermes' cry floated up, toward the surface. No time to look for a way in—the compression was crushing him. Heartbroken, he started for the surface. Hopefully he had the strength to make Japan, stop to rest before winging back to the City of Mount Olympus and from there to the mortal desert if needed. Some-one, maybe several someones, had some explaining to do.

SATURDAY, JANUARY 31, 2026

Dulles International Airport, Virginia, USA

Saul Crispin passed through the TSA checkpoint shortly before midnight. His cell phone, sequestered since late December, slept in the pocket of his leather jacket. He'd powered it up in the van to the airport but hadn't checked messages yet. His sense of foreboding—what if the Mount Olympus people had found him and had summoned him to face the consequences of his actions two millennia ago? —was at last overcome by curiosity.

He settled in the end seat of a linked row of stainless steel and leatherette chairs and began the digital excavation. The one on top was from Andrea, his agent. *Welcome back. Audition tomorrow 1pm, cat food commercial. Text ASAP when you get home.*

A cat food commercial. Hopefully the audition wouldn't involve actual cats, to which he was violently allergic. Next was an announcement from a New York jazz club he frequented when he was in town, a list of Thursday night concerts in February. Several from David, from as far back as December 22 to say he'd arrived safely at Athens U. Another one from Andrea about an audition two weeks ago that ended with *Oh, you're gone. Never mind.*

Once he'd scrolled through all the subject lines he went back to David's first entry and read them all, in sequence. There were several each day from December 31 through January 4, cryptic snippets about Barcelona and queries about Saul's experiences when he'd *you know, fallen in love and stuff* over the centuries.

Saul didn't realize how tight his shoulders had been until they started to relax. Normal young man stuff, nothing about a goon squad of Olympians being dispatched to capture Saul and—what? They couldn't kill him. Life in prison with an ample heaping of torture? What kind of a guy was Zeus? Had his feelings about a 2000-year-old affair mellowed with time?

He resolved to let it go, told himself his tryst with Hera was ancient news. Not even a vain, cuckolded husband could care by now. Life moved on, even eternal life.

On the way home from a job Saul typed to David. *Busy day tomorrow.*

Will try to get back to you tomorrow night. Sounds like life is interesting for you? He meant to inquire about Cleo until he realized David hadn't mentioned her once.

SUNDAY, FEBRUARY 1, 2026

New York City, New York, USA

Saul stumbled into his studio, wheezing. The audition had turned into a disaster the moment he met his co-star, Mister Bon-Bon—asthma at first sight. Fortunately tomorrow was clear so he could baby his languishing lungs. Saul put the kettle on to boil water for a cup of Colds and Allergies tea. He snagged his inhaler from the medicine cabinet and administered two puffs. In minutes the tea was steeped. Soothing steam rose from his *My Favorite Martian* mug (he'd been a guest star on the series in its second season and had loved working with Ray Walston—what a hoot!). He settled at the table with his cell phone, tapped *Never again* in reply to Andrea's post-audition inquiry and brought up David's address.

Barcelona—que tal?

David was awake and highly communicative in spite of the six-hour time difference. When Saul read a lengthy, impassioned description of a beautiful nurse named Lucia David had fallen in love with in Valencia, 1917, his heart fell. He'd been there—not in Spain but in New York City —in 1918. When the pandemic hit he'd given up his place in the Ziegfeld Follies and volunteered for eighteen-hour days as a hospital orderly, knowing he couldn't die.

City of Mount Olympus

David Bernstein hungrily tapped in the return message to Saul. His frustration level was totally ginned up. No one he'd talked to could tell him what he needed to know. He was no longer sure what he hoped to find—some kind of answer or solution or resolution to the heart-breaking pull he felt from the past. It had been a huge struggle to con-centrate on his studies. He'd totally bombed on the first paper of the new term, an assignment on mortal psychology and how it affected architectural design that should have been a no-brainer.

All he could think about was Lucia. A follow-up hypnotherapy session with Jim had gotten him to January, 1918, a quick trip up the coast to see her in Valencia under the duress of Milton and Thelma's disapproval. Nothing wrong with the young lady, they'd said, instead decreeing that at nineteen he was too young to take on a wife and, very likely, children. On the Mediterranean shore he'd held her close, gazed into her soulful, liquid eyes, vowed his eternal love and that he'd find a way for them to be together. They took a cottage for two nights, made love, held each other, wept.

What happened next? His gut told him it hadn't ended well. How could it? Even if they'd married and lived happily together she'd be dead by now. Thinking about Heracles and his tragic life as a mortal plunged David deeper into despair.

Cleo. Another knife in his gut told him not to share his new sorrow with her, though she'd been his confidant in the past. It was different now that they'd been lovers, especially since she'd chosen her work over him. Yes, he had been childish about this, he'd known it as soon as he'd gotten on the plane to New York, alone. Now she was half a world away, in Midland, Texas, for reasons she couldn't—or wouldn't—share. Sure, she'd reached out first, but their correspondence had been terse and then stopped all together. Probably his fault, again.

Heaven and Earth it felt awful to be at odds with Cleo. He never would have found Saul without her determination and persistence when his own will to stay on his quest had flagged. Now his list of support was down to one person, and Saul's message back was short.

Hard to win against the past. You can break your heart trying.

The sick-to-his stomach feeling that had lifted when the message came in returned. No easy answer or positive insight. The pictures in his head, the feel of her body against his, the scent of her hair spun in his brain, haunting him, yet he couldn't bear to let it go. He'd be all alone again if he let it go.

I need more information, he typed back. *I need to know what happened to her.*

Milton and Thelma would know, but his trust in them was low. He hadn't communicated with them since he'd learned about Lucia.

How do I find her, Saul?

After a protracted pause the answer arrived.

First, look at the place and its history. Then, death records.

David swallowed, the taste in his mouth bitter. He knew she was dead; he didn't want her to be dead.

It seemed wrong he could find the answer in a book, though that's where he'd always started before to solve life's big questions. Love was different, wasn't it? There had to be some kind of magic involved, something that defied convention and could carry him back to her. Something beyond hypnosis.

"I'll find you, Lucia," he said through his tears. "Somehow I'll find you again."

THURSDAY, FEBRUARY 5, 2026

It took Hermes two days to get home after his fruitless mission to the Mariana Trench. He'd checked in with Poseidon dozens of times, seeking assurance P. B. was all right. The sea god had once used the word "mastermind" for reasons Hermes couldn't fathom. What he'd texted about the Old Ones accepting P. B. as one of their own at least had some root in reality: The Power. That damn guy would always be a presence in P. B.'s life, regardless of being absorbed into the Chair of Forgetfulness.

Action. That's what was needed. He remotely installed an app on Poseidon's digital device that would sound an alarm once they left the Undersea World of Big Slimy Guys.

Once that was in place, Hermes barricaded himself in the lab to think and think and think. He had to save the world from climate change, save the world for P. B. Hundreds of mortal inventions he'd studied streamed through his brain. After days of isolation he emerged, bleary-eyed, determined and grim. Yes, there was a solution, an elegant solution with a dual nature. If successful his invention would restore Earth's atmosphere to wholesome pre-industrial levels. If it failed, it could potentially obliterate every form of life on the planet.

Hermes made a quick trip to his condo, showered for the first time since his wild flight, packed a bag and returned to the lab. There'd be no more meetings taken, no more being summoned to the CEO suite for reprimand; just monitoring Poseidon's movements, with every other waking second devoted to the creation of the splendid new machine dancing in his imagination. A mechanism of salvation or doom.

FRIDAY, FEBRUARY 13, 2026

Midland, Texas, USA

And just like that, Texas had a new US House Representative.

Congressman-Elect Pendarvus Fotakis swept the special election easily. Not a landslide—that would have engendered suspicion and a wave of investigative reporting—but an indisputable five points ahead of his rival. The incumbent had been rumored in December to possibly be the subject of an ethics scandal. Athena's agents had laid the groundwork immediately, dropping hints of a dark horse candidate into the 24/7 media cycle, a candidate who would appear ideal to the Easts. Meeting the criteria to enter the race was ridiculously simple: one must be at least twenty-five years old, a resident of the United States for the past seven years, and inhabit the state they hoped to represent at the time of the election. With some artful hacking the requirements were eased into the necessary databases. On January 31 Pan exploded on the campaign trail.

"Opportunity for all Texans through fossil fuels" was the heart of his message. His staff, headed by Olympus, Inc., operative Maida Steele (not her real name), ran a major get out the vote campaign, targeting a large and frustrated contingent who couldn't imagine an economic path forward for themselves without vast increases in the extraction of oil.

Too bad about disgraced Congressman R. T. Truly, of course. He was indeed indicted in an ethics scandal that even the media was reluctant to pursue. The murmurings about livestock involvement were unfortunate.

Pan ran as an Independent, positioned as a wild card who would not hesitate to ply his agenda to either side of the aisle should he prevail. Donations from Big Oil flooded in. His closest rival, a protégé of Truly's who currently served in the state legislature in the majority party, was crushed in a blitz of television spots and finished second.

The new representative was now engaged in a victory tour, making a quick sweep through the state to thank major donors before flying (this time in a plane) to Washington, D.C., for the swearing-in ceremony. Today's first stop: East Fossil Fuels.

Bunches of balloons decorated the lobby packed with dozens of cheering people who wore everything from utilitarian jumpsuits to pinstripes. Pan was presented with a horseshoe-shaped wreath of red roses, a hamper loaded with enormous chocolate chip cookies and a sturdy-looking aide to carry it. A small, enthusiastic brass band accompanied him to the lift, the one with *Private* etched above. The welcome reminded him of his return to Olympus, Inc., headquarters last fall, after single-handedly defeating the gangs of desert warlords who'd been hijacking truckloads of humanitarian aid bound for displaced women and children. The one difference: that time he'd actually achieved something.

The swag-burdened aide pushed the top button and up they swept. They emerged on the top floor and passed between two lines of cheering folks that formed a runway. One familiar face flashed in his periphery. Cleo Petra, one of the suits.

The lines broke behind him, pushing him like a tailwind into a vast office suite with one wall entirely of glass. Standing in front of an imposing marble-faced gas fireplace were two of the ugliest beings he'd ever seen, dressed in identical, expensive business wear, their livery lips spread in twin smiles.

He'd never met the Easts in person. Their money had been passed through whatever legal and illegal channels flowed to his campaign coffers. The pictures of them Maida Steele had pulled up on her digital device in the airport limo hadn't captured the muddy auras. For a sickening moment Pan wondered if they could see his aura, too.

"Welcome, Congressman-Elect Fotakis!" one said. His mouth, when speaking, took on a distinct resemblance to an anus.

"Yes, welcome, dear sir!" The other one extended his slab of a hand, the fingers bulbous at the tips. "My name is Edwin and this is my dear brother, Cyril. We're absolutely delighted about your victory, Fotakis, and look forward to the bright future your tenure will bring to our fair state."

The employees who'd greeted him when he got off the elevator had formed an arc around the Easts. Most of them were thick around the midsection.

"Allow me to introduce our human resources chief, Ms. Allen," Cyril said, gesturing toward the woman who'd moved in beside him. "We'd be up a stream without a paddle without Ms. Allen to keep our people happy. That's really what East Fossil Fuels is about, my dear Fotakis, keeping people happy."

A quick wink followed Cyril East's statement.

"And these are our marvelous department heads," Edwin said. "This is Mr. Jacobs, from Legal. Mrs. Sprink from IT. Mr..." He indicated each person who'd joined the line alongside him with a roll of his hand. "And last but not least, Ms. Leo from Research and Development."

Patricia C. Leo, according to Athena's briefing. Pan lingered in a handshake with Cleo, let his eyes spark when he said, "*Very* pleased to meet you."

They adjourned to a long buffet table, groaning with meaty hot dishes and an abundance of desserts. Pan piled his plate high, his excuse for eating instead of talking so he could also observe.

Cleo hovered at the edge of the crowd, nibbling crudités. Pan double-checked to make sure hers was the only purple aura in the crowd. Everyone else, except the Easts, exhibited the normal mortal pink.

"Delighted to have your ear for a few minutes," Edwin said—or was it Cyril? Whichever it was had been talking nonstop while also eating. "I'm sure a bright and promising young man like you will not hesitate to carry our *concerns* to the federal government." Another wink. "We can hardly afford to let extraction rates decrease, my dear man, and put all these wonderful people out of a job. So difficult to get hold of new drilling sites these days, so much fuss about the ice cap and the polar bears. Stuff and nonsense, I say. What are polar bears compared to people?"

The other laid a heavy paw on Pan's shoulder. "Please consider yourself a member of the East Fossil family. We'd be honored if you can spare a few minutes of your valuable time to chat with the young lady who manages Research and Development. She can tell you about our projects that will be of interest in Washington, D.C." He raised his other paw and waved. "Yoo-hoo, Ms. Leo!"

Cleo set her mostly full plate on an end table and walked toward them. At the Embassy party simulation she'd been done up in gray pinstripes, somber in her role of diplomatic attaché. The mortal get-up she wore today was more flattering, a turquoise linen suit with a tuck at the jacket's waist. Her smile was warm but he saw the calculation going on beneath.

"Ms. Leo, Congressman-Elect Fotakis is eager to hear about our drilling simulations. Would you be so kind as to indulge his curiosity?"

"Of course, Mr. East, it will be my pleasure."

Pan extended his hand for another prolonged shake. "*My* pleasure, Ms. Leo, and please call me Pen."

"We'll be wrapping up here shortly, Ms. Leo," Edwin, who'd been described in the dossier as the dealmaker of the two, said. "If you'd have the kindness to brief our friend Fotakis and arrange to have his little gifts sent to his limousine, I'd be most grateful."

"Of course, Mr. Edwin," she said, with extreme business cool. "Mr. Fotakis, I'll wait for you at the elevator." On her way out she spoke briefly with the swag aide. The lad scooped up the cookies and roses and made a quick escape.

After a hearty round of handshakes and backslaps Pan also made his exit. Cleo waited at the elevator, the mild boredom of nine-to-five employment settled on her face.

"Fancy meeting you here," Pan quipped after looking around to assure they were alone.

"Careful, Mr. Fotakis," Cleo said, tilting her head in the direction of a security camera—careless of him to miss it. "You don't want anything questionable on your record now that you're in the limelight."

It was incredibly hard to ride to the ground floor in silence. Pan's limo waited at the curb. Maida Steele, half-eaten chocolate chip cookie in hand, instructed the aide on the placement of the goods in the trunk.

"I'm aware of the secrecy required when discussing R and D, Ms. Leo. In the interest of confidentiality, would you join me in the limo? We can take a loop around town and return you here when we're finished."

Cleo arched an eyebrow. "If you don't mind, Mr. Fotakis, I'd be more comfortable if you'd accompany me to our neighborhood juice bar. It's not far, and your driver can follow us."

The moment they got past the jungle of potted plants at Green World Juice Works Cleo gave him a thumbs up.

"Petra, what is it with all the fat people?"

"Oh. That." An expression of distaste crossed her visage. "They eat them."

~ * ~

Cleo introduced Pan to the barista and ordered their drinks.

"Now, Congressman-Elect Fotakis," she said, "Let me fill you in on the cutting edge of fossil fuel technology."

She gave a brief summary of the yawning gap between the dearth of climate change experiments in R & D and Marketing's misrepresentation of East Fossil's commitment to saving the planet.

"More like saving the planet as a carbon farm for their personal consumption," she said, before launching into her discovery about lobbyists and bribes. "So that's where you come in."

Cleo wasn't a bit surprised to hear a lobbyist had already sent Pan a congratulatory email and an invitation to lunch.

When their drinks, a pair of Green World Specials, were ready, Cleo picked them up at the counter and handed one to Pan. He studied the pint glass at arm's length.

"What do they put in these things, frog intestines?"

"It's an acquired taste." She told him about Michael Guy, mostly a positive report but she mentioned he could sometimes be arrogant. "He tends to swagger—"

"That's not a crime," Pan said.

Cleo laughed. "It might be, the way *you* do it. He's completely the opposite when he's teaching yoga, very supportive and considerate."

"Yoga?"

"Tuesdays and Thursdays, after work. The Easts have a huge employee gym with every amenity you can think of."

"Sounds like you've had it rough."

"Hah! Life in have-another-cookie land isn't as sweet as it appears."

A new customer walked in, someone from Legal. Pink aura. Cleo resumed her cover.

"Congressman-Elect Fotakis, what kind of legislation will you propose to help the fossil fuel industry?"

Pan babbled in circles, saying absolutely nothing.

"It must be exciting for you, the move to Washington, D.C.?"

Under the roar of the turbo-charged blender Pan mouthed a response. She stepped close and said in his ear, "From what Michael Guy's seen in contracts, the Easts have their slimy fingers in every fossil fuel pie. Fracking, coal extraction, the works. Lots of companies rolled up in the parent. Zero research on limiting carbon emissions, unusual for a company this size according to industry publications. What species do you think they are? I've never heard about anyone like them."

"Humanoid enough to pass," Pan murmured. "Did you run it by Athena's department?"

"Yes, the day I met them," she said. "Apollo's guess is that they're a race more ancient than humans and came from the stars. But his analysis was inconclusive. Now he needs a DNA sample to narrow it down."

"Holy Tartarus, how will you manage that?"

"Not sure. Michael Guy is working on getting me access to the in-house security systems but—" Contemplating a break-in set her nerves on edge. "Maybe I'll steal something one of them has handled the next time I'm in the penthouse?"

For a fleeting second Pan looked worried. "Promise me you'll be exceedingly careful, okay? Anyone who routinely eats their employees won't hesitate to play hardball."

"I'll be as careful as I can," she said, mulling other possible strategies. Drugging the Easts, their executive secretary, the receptionist and then—no, too messy and too complicated.

Pan tapped a fingertip on their table. "Safe house."

"Yes," she confirmed. "But don't you find their choices odd? The Easts, I mean. What's their motive in exacerbating climate change? If they use humans as livestock, why are they bent on destroying the metaphorical grazing land? That's the part I don't understand."

Pan shrugged. "Maybe when we know their species it will be apparent. I'll see what I can dig up on them in Washington and about the rest of it. Shouldn't be too difficult, with dozens of lobbyists poised to become my new best friends." He cleared his throat and squared his shoulders into a camera-ready pose. "Thank you, Ms. Leo," he said, taking her hand in a firm but relaxed grip, "for your valuable time and the highly interesting beverage. I'll tell everyone in D.C. to make Green World Juice Works a part of their day."

She followed the direction of Pan's gaze. Maida Steele stood near the entrance looking pointedly at the digital device on her wrist.

"And thank you, Mr. Fotakis, for giving me a place in your busy schedule. I hope you'll visit East Fossil the next time you're in town."

"I wouldn't miss it, Ms. Leo," Pan said. "Watch your back, Cleo," he added through gritted teeth.

Maida marched Pan out the door. Cleo sipped her Special to the dregs, thinking. She had to get the DNA sample ASAP. And if she got caught? The Easts probably couldn't kill her, but were they ruthless enough to eat her alive?

Tuesday, February 17, 2026

Washington, D.C., USA

Pendarvus Fotakis was sworn in at 10am in the Capitol Building, repeating a solemn oath in opulent surroundings. Pan stifled a yawn as his colleagues advanced through the agenda—something to do with taxes and another concerning security—and noted many of the other representatives doing the same.

When the session broke for lunch he was escorted out of doors, past a building called the Library of Congress—a collection of sweeping stairways, columns and archways—to his personal office in the Longworth Building. It was a graceless hulk compared to the Capitol, a fancied-up rectangle with columns and pediments tacked on to carry the theme of the older structures.

Maida Steele greeted him in a tight, sparsely furnished office off a nondescript basement hallway. "Good thing they don't spoil you freshmen representatives," she quipped, arms crossed over her midsection, her expression one of disdain. His escort, some page or other, left. "Lucky to find you a desk," Maida said, bumping her hip against the scratched and battered monolith with an oak veneer. "They promised to bring a chair to go with it by the end of the day."

Pan dropped his briefcase on the desktop, bored already as he thought about the reports and whatever else was inside that he'd have to read sooner or later. He had to live his cover to keep the East brothers convinced they'd really, truly purchased themselves a member of Congress.

Knuckles tapped the door frame.

"Representative Fotakis?" A big-shouldered guy in a dark suit stood in the opening with another gods-awful horseshoe of roses.

Pan nodded.

"Delivery for you, sir. I ran a metal detector over it. It's clean."

The plain clothes man (if an impeccably tailored suit, custom shoes and an earpiece with a spiral cord that disappeared down the back of the jacket qualified as plain) balanced the floral monstrosity on the three-legged stand that came with it and strode off.

Maida plucked a card out of the arrangement. "From your friend

Anonymous. How very clever. I wish the slobs had sent a file cabinet instead."

Word of the floral horseshoe had arrived in the Capitol chamber by the time he reported back for the afternoon session. The ethics chair took him aside, said he'd cut Pan some slack because he was new but he should have refused the thing and needed to dispose of it ASAP.

"My pleasure," Pan said.

"Get some seasoned office staff and they'll take care of this kind of thing before it has a chance to get you into trouble," the ethics chair advised. "I hear it's damn ugly, but it's the giver and the dollar value that count."

"Got it."

Representative Fotakis braced himself for a dull afternoon but grew surprisingly engrossed in the debate over immigration policy. During a break the other representatives from Texas introduced themselves. He was delighted to discover being an Independent truly did make him an object of political desire.

"Nice to have fresh blood," a middle-aged Republican with rosacea said as he vigorously pumped Pan's hand. "R. T. Truly was a fine man, of course, but he didn't know when to keep his pants zipped."

For a brief moment Pan indulged in the fantasy of flying above his House colleagues wearing nothing but a loin cloth.

"I'll take that under advisement," Pan said.

Some of the males surrounding him chuckled. A stern-looking woman in a purple suit shouldered her way through them.

"Representative Fotakis, I see you're interested in the immigration debate." The chuckling shut off as if she'd thrown a toggle switch. "I'd be happy to arrange for you to audit the open meetings of the Immigration and Citizenship Committee."

"Give him a break, Sheila, it's his first day," the rosacea guy said.

"And he's only got a few months to make an impression on the voters before the midterm," Sheila Who-Ever-She-Was fired back. "Why don't *you* try that for a change, Hayward, and do something for your constituents besides suck up to big oil?"

The rosacea marks disappeared in Hayward's blood-suffused face. He clamped a hand on Pan's shoulder. "She talks big, son, but I can tell you where the *real* power is."

Pan bit the insides of his cheeks to keep from laughing. Mortals.

Apparently, they were still as feckless as he'd once observed to a play-wright drinking buddy a few centuries back.

"What did you just say?" Will had asked then, passing him the wineskin and picking up a quill to scratch one of Pan's *bon mots* on a scrap of parchment.

"I said, What fools these mortals be."

FRIDAY, FEBRUARY 20, 2026

City of Mount Olympus

David Bernstein stood in front of the bathroom mirror in his studio apartment, reviewing his appearance in the small, cramped frame. He'd chosen the simple trousers, waistcoat and jacket of a workman, someone who would easily blend into the crowd in Valencia, October 30, 1918. A Catalonian newspaper he'd traced down through reference books, courtesy of the extensive Athens U library, had noted the arrival of a nurse, Lucia Barbera Cabell, in a group with five others at Saint Vincent of Saragossa Hospital the prior week.

He fitted a dark gray homburg over his unruly curls. The crowning touch as he'd be noticeably out of place moving through the outdoors hatless. His clothing was newly made from period appropriate materials, courtesy of a Mount Olympus tailor. The spell book, open to the relevant page and resting on the vanity, had come from a cellar bookstore frequented by occult enthusiasts on Mount Olympus. The spell on the right-hand page required the traveler to possess one authentic article from the time period being traveled to and one from the present to travel back. A watch certified as made in 1915 was at the end of the chain that crossed his waistcoat, snuggled firmly in its own small pocket. On his right index finger was a plain silver band. He'd watched the jeweler forge it at a crafts fair celebrating Saint Valentine's Day, a holiday heavily promoted by Aphrodite's company, Love, Inc., for obvious reasons.

Excited, nervous, heart aching with pain and love, David studied the words one more time, tore the page from the book and read them out loud. He invoked the final words, "Take me to the side of Lucia Barbera Cabell."

White hot pain surged through his body as he was pulled violently back at the waist, bent double as he swept backward into a cyclone of spinning bands of colored light—blue, green, white. His brain throbbed hard against his skull, felt like it would burst. Gravity crushed down on him. Velocity doubled. Air shrieked past his ears.

Crack!

He stopped moving as abruptly as he'd started. Frozen in a ball position and shivering, he slowly opened his eyes onto an interior court-yard. The sun was low, didn't clear the walls—rising or setting? The air temperature was mild.

From his vantage point in a corner he noted the urn-shaped stone fountain that anchored the center of the space. Alongside it stood a statue of a somber looking man in flowing robes. No doubt the saint who was the place's namesake. A pigeon rested on the saint's head. Stone benches surrounded the fountain but otherwise the courtyard was bare.

David drew a deep breath, willed the shiver out of his body, and assessed his condition, moving his arms and legs, feeling his ribs. The spell had warned the user would pay a price. He ached with cold but nothing seemed to be broken. His right hand clutched the page torn from the spell book.

"Thank Zeus," he said and folded it into his coat pocket.

Using the wall behind him as a support he eased himself to his feet, shook out his limbs, brushed off his clothes with his hands. Three sides of the courtyard resolved into archways that framed a continuous walk. He perceived the outline of doors in the dim area beyond.

To cloak or not to cloak? Before his travels last year Hera had taught him how to conceal himself with Biggest of Big-G Cloaking. He looked his question to the pigeon, the only other living being in the courtyard. He read the coo and a slow blink as *Yes*.

The clatter of heels on cobblestones drew his eyes left. Two young women with white aprons over their dresses and white rectangles over mouth and nose tied by ribbons in the back strode by. One of them wore a straw boater, which she exchanged for a simple white cap as she walked. They were either arriving for work or coming back from a break.

Bliss coursed through David's veins. He'd done it! This had to be the right place, the right time. Invisible, he followed them with quiet feet, bound for a rendezvous with his dearest Lucia.

WEDNESDAY, OCTOBER 30, 1918

Valencia, Spain

Sister Lucia Barbera Cabell was assigned to one of many wards for soldiers at *San Vicente*. She'd volunteered to work an isolation ward, separate from those wounded in battle, for victims of the flu.

Her duties were simple but endless. Administering medicine, giving sponge baths, emptying bedpans. The need for basic nursing was so great that the specialized training she'd received in England was not, at this time, relevant.

"Good morning, private," she said to a gaunt young man, pale and dazed on a bed in the ward's double row. The beds were closer than they should be, less than a meter between them but space was at a premium. "How do you feel today?"

His face screwed up with pain. "Weak, sister," he whispered.

The effort to speak kicked off a deep, wet cough. When the spell passed she helped him raise his head for a sip of water. Once he was prone again she took his wrist between her thumb and forefinger, thankful for the double thickness of cotton cloth covering her nose and mouth. The flu, fairly mild when it first arrived in the spring, had accelerated to a pandemic in September. The best analysis tied the spike to the return of soldiers from the battlefields of the Great War. Contagion was escalating and everything used to treat flu patients was in short supply. She'd insisted on carbolic acid for herself and the other nurses to disinfect their hands but rationing was so tight the small quantity they were allotted was likely not effective. At least her baby was safe, the little girl born in a convent three weeks ago and in the care of a cousin, a nun who was assistant to Mother Superior.

Lucia entered the pulse rate on the patient's chart and hooked it over the iron railing at the foot of the bed. A draft of odd warmth grazed the back of her neck. She touched the spot between her collar and cap in reflex.

Another six patients to complete her first pass through the ward today. All of them too young, too sick, too plainly mortal. She used her dwindling supply of carbolic acid sparingly when she finished the round, not much more than a spoonful poured into a basin and rubbed diligently on and between fingers, palms and backs of hands. She drew her cape over her shoulders and exited the ward for a breath of air in the colonnade.

Saint Vincent of Saragossa's back was to her, a pigeon on his head and another on his shoulder. Legend said ravens had protected Vincent's body after he'd been tortured to death for refusing to consign the Scripture to the fire. They'd saved him from the ravages of vultures until his followers were able to collect the body. A grim tale, but seeing his statue guarded by pigeons made her laugh. There'd been so little laughter since the flu had come.

"Lucia."

She spun to the voice behind her. A young man in simple attire, Homburg in hand, a riot of dark curls on his head. Lucia gasped. Her hand flattened on her heart. So many times she'd dreamed, and yet...

"David." His name came out in shock and wonder. "What are you doing here?"

He grasped her hand and drew it away from her chest. "Lucia, I've been so worried about you. Ever since—"

"You left me!" She pulled away from him and wove her fingers protectively against her belly. "I wrote to you but you never wrote back. Did you never receive my letters? In the spring, in desperation I wrote to Señor Gaudi. One of his clerks informed me you and your family had returned to Scotland."

~ * ~

David saw the heartbreak on her face, a face rounder than he remembered. Her eyes hurled knifelike accusations at him. Why hadn't he had the guts to work with a new hypnotherapist after Jim had returned to Seattle? Maybe he had a deep-buried memory of exactly what he'd done to her but had been afraid to excavate it.

"I didn't want to hurt you." *Lame!*

She pushed past him and headed for her ward. He grabbed her arm.

"Please, Lucia, I can't explain what happened but I'm here now. I've come back for you."

Lucia shook off his hand and rounded on him. "Why should I believe a man who promised he'd never leave me? Now go away."

He didn't follow her. Not until he'd resumed Biggest of Big-G Cloaking, an underhanded maneuver but he had to know. Somehow he'd wronged her. He had to make it right.

Lucia veered to an alcove in the colonnade, a half-rounded indentation with a short, curved bench. She sat heavily and bent over double, hands covering her face. Every tear tore his heart anew.

At last she straightened up, consulted the watch pinned to the bib of her apron. Her expression of grief was reset to one of resolve. She dabbed her eyes with the hem of her apron, tucked escaped tendrils of hair back under her cap. A wet spot had spread on her bodice. Had she cried that many tears? Lucia squared her shoulders, rose, and, chin high, strode back to her duties.

He had two choices: either speak the incantation and return to the present or wait for her to get off work and try again. Though ravenous, he ignored his rumbling stomach and rested his back against the arch nearest Lucia's ward.

~ * ~

"Goodnight, sister, may God keep you safe."

The words startled David awake. He looked up from where he sat, arms wrapped around his bent legs at the foot of the arch, his limbs fizzing with sleep. A woman stood three feet from him, her back toward him.

"And to you, sister, as well."

That voice was Lucia's. *Sister.* Had whatever stupid and horrible thing he'd done to her make her decide to become a nun? Heaven and Earth! He rose gingerly, shaking life back into his arms and legs, and followed her from a distance.

The air had cooled. The sun declined to the west. His pocket watch showed it was just past six. The darkened colonnade was illuminated by yellowish electric light, globes shining at the tops of stone torches mounted on the wall. Watching her figure, ahead, he could see she'd grown wider in the hips, her step weighted where before she'd moved like a dancer. Was she the sort of girl who would eat to ease her sorrow? He wouldn't have figured her for that, but loss changed people.

Loss caused by me.

Outside the hospital, a few farm carts lined the cobbled street. Vendors flanked the wagons, bargaining for fruit, vegetables and eggs with women in house dresses. Everyone had rectangles of fabric covering their nose and mouth. Though invisible, David drew a handkerchief from the breast pocket of his coat and tied it on in the manner of a bank robber. The Spanish Flu was running rampant now, as he'd read in a Catalan history book.

Lucia ignored the calls of the vendors, her step quickening as if she were running a gauntlet. Past the carts there were shops, most of them shuttered for the day. A man in a skeleton mask leapt at her from a recessed doorway, shaking his gloved fist that was decorated with bones.

She didn't shy or shriek, simply sped up. A pantomime of the Plague or a rehearsal for Day of the Dead? Lucia appeared unimpressed.

The cobblestone street narrowed and gradually tapered off to a dirt road. He followed Lucia up a gentle slope through fallow fields. A long, low stone building stretched in the distance. As they neared it, a half-dozen lights appeared in the windows.

In the lintel was carved *Convento de Santa Clara*.

~ * ~

Every day Lucia visited the convent, though since returning to work she was no longer allowed inside.

Amàlia.

If she tapped at a certain window and waited patiently, Sister Jospeha would bundle up the baby and bring her in view.

Oh, how she'd grown, even since yesterday! Lucia's fingertips pressed against the glass, longing to touch the pink softness of Amàlia's cheek. Already she could lift her head for a few seconds. She seemed to be looking, really looking, at Lucia tonight. Lucia experimented with her fingers, moving them side to side on the pane, filled with joy greater than she'd ever known as the baby's head rolled gently back and forth to track them.

"My precious girl," Lucia cooed. "My beautiful angel."

~ * ~

Concealed under cloaking, David watched, stunned.

He was a father. The beautiful rosy-cheeked baby was his.

Why this hadn't occurred as a possibility until now seemed an insane oversight. When people made love they could make babies, especially in older times when birth control was uncommon. Especially in a Catholic country like Spain where birth control was considered a sin. Heaven and Earth, he'd been a fool!

He was a father, and had likely been a coward, too.

After several minutes of beaming love and adoration through the glass panes Lucia made a sign of farewell to the nun who held the baby. She turned away, pulled her cloak tight, bowed her head and walked slowly on the path toward town. He lifted the cloaking, heart beating wildly as he came alongside her.

"Lucia, please."

She accelerated her pace. "How dare you follow me here! I told you to go."

"Lucia, please, I didn't know! Please believe I didn't know."

She stopped and rounded on him, eyes cold.

"You didn't know you didn't love me enough to stay? Is that what you didn't know, David Burns?"

"But I do love you, Lucia, and I'm here now. I'll make it right to you and our baby, I swear I will. I'll do whatever you want me to."

"Then go back to Scotland and leave me in peace!"

She ran from him, down the path to town. The weight of love and regret dropped David to his knees. He shouldn't have come, he understood that now. Lucia had survived his betrayal and moved forward in her life. How brave she'd been. How deeply she must have suffered.

And there was nothing he could do about it to help her heal, to help himself heal.

He soared into the sky, released a heart-tearing scream on the ascent. Why had he left her? She wouldn't tell him. But the Bernsteins—they would know exactly what had happened.

David looked down to get his bearings—the Mediterranean Sea was to the east. He set a path northwest, aiming for Scotland. Where had they lived? Glasgow was the largest city but would Edinburgh, the capital, be the banking center? He'd try one, then the other. Milton Burns couldn't be too hard to find.

Eight hours into his journey David was so exhausted he had to land. The sun glowed on the horizon to his right and spilled light across an expanse of open country, dotted with small structures spaced far apart. Central France? He resumed cloaking and burrowed into a haystack near a barn to sleep.

The sound of hooves woke him, striking hollowly on hard-packed earth. He parted the straw just enough to peer out at a rough-looking wagon pulled by a skeletal workhorse and driven by a thick, slouch-shouldered man. The land beyond was a gray tangle of flattened vegetation. War, he was certain, had passed this way, crops trampled whether shots had been fired or not.

David's stomach rumbled so hard it echoed but he had no inclination to ask the farmer for food. The man's posture showed clearly enough how much he'd suffered.

In the late afternoon he glided over a large city on Scotland's east coast. David had no recollection of Edinburgh. He looked for wide, busy streets, ones that looked promising as homes of commerce and banking. Cloaked from mortal view he flew low for a closer look and eventually lit in an alley alongside an impressive façade signed as Dundas House, Royal Bank of Scotland.

Icy cold penetrated his jacket. David shivered, his hollow stomach making him weak. He hadn't planned for this, had pesos, not pounds in his pockets. Would this bank be capable of exchanging currency so he could feed himself before he collapsed? Would any of the bankers know Milton Burns, international banker recently returned from Barcelona?

He uncloaked, stepped into the gray daylight, and approached the Palladian style bank building. Two men in tailcoats and top hats descended the front stairs, one talking animatedly as he pulled on a glove.

"I tell you, sir, the rates are too high for my liking." His voice was just shy of losing its burr. "Given the collateral offered—" his head swiveled in David's direction. "I swear by Almighty God is that you, young Burns? I saw you not five minutes ago, inside. What's happened to you, lad? You look as if you've been in a scuffle."

The man said his name was McVey, and did David remember they'd been introduced when he'd started at the bank after returning from Spain this past spring?

"I've just now finished with your father, David Burns. Should I take you to him?"

"Thank you, no, Mr. McVey. I'll be fine." Heaven and Earth, he hadn't considered his younger self would be here, too. How would he navigate that?

He pulled the brim of his travel-battered Homburg low and ascended the wide sandstone stairs with tentative steps, his brain scrambling for a plan. Two solidly built men in plain clothes stood just inside the doors, eyes anchored on the entryway, hands clasped behind their backs. The one nearest David stepped forward, overshadowing him.

"How may I help you today, sir?" The voice was low, not menacing but tinged with the question as to whether David belonged there or not.

"I'm here to see Mr. Milton Burns," he said.

The guard raised an eyebrow. "Name, please?"

How to get Milton's attention? He answered slowly, improvising. "I'm Mr. David, recently of Barcelona, but—" *Think. Think!* "We met in Tiberias, many years ago. He particularly wants to talk to me about Tiberias," he emphasized. "Mr. David, from Tiberias."

The guard nodded curtly and veered toward a row of glassed-in offices on the left. Straight ahead were teller cages, a half-dozen men working behind a marble counter, separated from their clients by gilt bars. The third one from the right looked startlingly familiar, his dark curls slicked down at the sides of his head, a shorter than average young man, wiry before the addition of another century and the advent of a modern diet. David half-hoped, half-feared his younger self would spot him. That was a bad thing in time travel, he remembered from some short story or other he'd read. He'd been careless, hadn't considered his trip might alter history.

"Mr. David, is it?"

Milton had returned with the guard. His face registered all kinds of crazy things—shock, fear—still, he extended his hand. David met his grasp and simultaneously pushed back the brim of his hat. "Heaven and Earth," Milton muttered. "Please wait outside, Mr. David. I'll get my hat and coat and join you."

David's foster father bustled him into an enclosed horse-drawn cab and gave the driver the name of a nearby pub. "Merciful Zeus, what have you done?" Milton said over the clip-clop of hooves.

"I traveled from the year twenty twenty-six," David said. "I'm looking for answers, Milton. I need some answers."

ThURSDAY, OCTOBER 31, 1918

Edinburgh, Scotland

Milton "Burns" Bernstein quickly put down a pint of ale, then another. Hera would be livid if she heard about this, an unimaginable security breach after two millennia of pristine caution. It was damn difficult, what he and Thelma had been tasked with, keeping David anonymous and safe from the wrath of Zeus.

Thelma. Heaven and Earth, she'd kill him in his sleep if she found out about this, even if he was immortal.

Questions bounced between them. This was a David he didn't know, a David who now understood after centuries of painstakingly renewed forgetfulness charms that he was not a mortal, that he was the bastard son of a goddess. In this David's time it was known all over the City of Mount Olympus that Hera had cuckolded Zeus and left evidence in the form of a son. Hera, Zeus and David lived amicably now, with David attending Athens U where Zeus was Provost!

It was incredible enough Zeus had given up control of Olympus, Inc., to a successor, let alone all the rest of it. Including that David had tracked down and met his biological father, Saul Crispin. Milton tried not to worry about that now. It wouldn't happen for more than a century. Doubtless they'd suffer many trials before then.

This David had somehow learned about the love affair with the Spanish nurse, a lovely girl by all accounts, but mortal. This David was wise to the Bernsteins and their forgetfulness charms. This David had demands. This David, who was polishing off his second meat pie in spite of their intense conversation, was not a boy, he was a man.

"There's a baby, Milton," he said between bites. "I wronged Lucia. We all wronged Lucia, and the baby is not just her responsibility, it's mine too. I need you, now, in this time, to do something about it."

The question kept dying in Milton's throat, but the third pint loosened it.

"Is the child mortal or immortal?"

FRIDAY, NOVEMBER 1, 1918

Valencia, Spain

It had taken every ounce of Milton Bernstein's strength to make the flight from Scotland to Spain, even with David towing him most of the way. He hadn't told Thelma about the journey, except through a note delivered by a bank messenger: *Urgent business. Back soon.* Containing this unfathomable encounter was critical. Milton prayed to Heaven and Earth the actions he was taking now wouldn't tamper with the future, but if they did it couldn't be helped. Future David made it clear he wasn't going back to his own time until Milton made things right for Lucia and the baby.

They landed in Valencia in the early evening. David set down near the rural convent where he said the baby was kept, isolated from the pestilence of the city. The newspaper headlines often featured the second deadly wave of flu pandemic sweeping Spain and other parts of the world. He followed David's example of making a triangular mask with his handkerchief, thankful Thelma always insisted he carry a spare.

Milton's stomach was painfully hollow. They'd stopped twice, in northern and southern France, but not long enough to find, let alone eat, a decent meal.

"What do we do now?" Milton said, hoping David would say something about scraping up dinner somewhere.

"We wait."

His face was so hard it could have been carved from stone.

A candle flickered to life, illuminating one of the front windows. A figure stood in the light, clothed in dark robes, her hair covered with a veil. She left and soon returned with an oblong basket cradled in her arms. She placed the basket on the table bearing the candle and hovered over it, lips moving, her hands reaching gently down.

A lump stuck in Milton's throat. Thelma was the gifted one when it came to seeing auras, a far keener observer of people than he. She'd probably see it radiating up from the basket even before she saw the baby.

It hadn't felt cold when they'd landed but the combination of standing still and the sinking sun deepened the ache in his joints. If only he'd brought his topcoat.

"How long?" he asked.

"She'll be here soon. Her hospital shift ends at six."

Milton's heart ached for the young woman, clearly someone of empathy and courage to take on nursing soldiers felled by the lethal flu. It hadn't been their choice, his and Thelma's, to keep David ignorant of his own immortality. Hera, herself, had trained them to administer the forgetfulness charm. To protect David, she'd said. Heaven and Earth, he'd like to give her a piece of his mind about that.

A rectangle of white moving up the path toward the convent caught his eye. The girl's dark hair was visible on the sides, beneath her cap. Pretty eyes with a hard expression—a blend of determination, exhaustion and heartache. The expected pink aura of a mortal.

Her step lightened as she neared the candlelit window, chest rising, her face warming to a smile. When Lucia was in front of the window, David gestured to Milton to draw nearer.

Milton tamped his spectacles firmly down on the bridge of his nose and moved forward, several feet from Lucia but close enough to admire the baby's fat, pink cheeks. The aura was identical to its mother's.

"Well?" David said.

"Mortal."

David's shoulder's drooped. What had he planned to do, take the baby and raise it himself if she were immortal?

"You'll set up the trust fund." An order, not a question.

"We need to discuss the arrangement with the mother, first."

"She won't talk to me, Milton," David said with heat, loud enough to break Lucia's love trance at the convent window. She spun toward them and planted her hands on her hips.

"You again," she hissed at David. "And this time you've brought a friend. I thought I made it clear I don't want to see you. Get out of my sight. Now!"

She turned back to the baby, her shoulders raised to her ears, the spell of maternal adoration broken. Milton turned to leave but David grabbed his arm.

"We *wait*. I can't leave her like this."

Milton stood alongside David, eyes closed, mourning the loss of trust from someone he truly did love like a son. When at last Lucia blew the baby a kiss and turned back toward the town, David nudged Milton ahead, indicating he should walk alongside Lucia, and trailed behind them.

"Pardon me, Miss Barbera Cabell?"

Her chin tilted sharply upward but she did not reply.

"Permit me to introduce myself. I am Milton Burns, David's father."

She doubled her pace. Exhausted as he was from the flight, he could barely keep up with her.

"I don't blame you for hating me, Lucia. I admit I was the one who forced David away from you. There's something you don't know about him, something I can't tell you but—"

"Save your breath, Mr. Burns," she snapped through the cloth that masked her mouth and nose. "I don't need to know any more about him than what he has already shown me by his cowardice."

"I-I'm here," Milton said, panting to keep up. "Here about the child."

She darted in front of him and pushed her hands violently into his chest, sending him stumbling backward into David.

"You will not take my daughter from me!"

"It's for her future, Lucia!" David said, tears in his voice. "She's my daughter, too, and I want to provide for her. For you, too, if you'll let me."

"My Amàlia and I are not for sale!"

She turned on her heel and ran down the path. David followed her. Milton threw up his hands in frustration. Fine! Let them work it out between them. The sooner they settled it, the sooner he could go back to Edinburgh.

~ * ~

Heaven and Earth, Lucia was stubborn! How had he missed that under hypnosis? David finally persuaded her to sit on a bench on the edge of a square somewhere near her wretched hospital and explained to her the arrangement he'd worked out with Milton. A trust fund would be set up for their daughter, with provision for her upbringing should anything happen to Lucia.

"And now you threaten me!"

"No, no, my love." The word felt foreign on David's tongue. Milton had been right to say he'd been blinded by youthful infatuation. He had no one to blame but himself for tearing off in a hot-headed rage and consummating his passion for Lucia with no thought of the consequences. Who could blame her for turning on him?

He started again. "You must admit your work puts you in great danger. I could never forgive myself if our daughter was left alone in this world—"

"I am not interested in you forgiving yourself," she muttered.

"You won't have anything to do with me, Lucia, and you won't let me take care of her myself. I'm sorry it's this way but it's the best I can do."

There was a long silence.

"Say that again," she said quietly.

"It's the best I can do."

"No. Before that."

"What?" he said, his mind numb from endless flying and lack of sleep.

"That you're sorry. Say you're sorry, David."

"Oh, Lucia." He took her hands, saw the tears brimming in her eyes. "I am sorry, so very, very sorry. You are a beautiful, strong woman and you deserve a man far better than me." She sniffed. "We'll meet tomorrow, with whatever lawyer you choose, and get your security established."

"Only for Amàlia, I will take nothing for myself."

He sighed. "As you wish."

He and Milton had difficulty finding lodging and food, what with fear of strangers during the flu epidemic, but at last settled at a rustic inn for a meal of stew and bread, and a restless night's sleep. Tomorrow morning they'd meet Lucia by the bench where she and David had negotiated their truce, and move forward to protect Amàlia.

His daughter. With luck she'd grow up, marry, and have children of her own. He would never see any of it, would never share the joy and heartbreak of the life he'd helped make. His heart beat slow and hollow.

FRIDAY, FEBRUARY 20, 2026

Midland, Texas, USA

Cleo Petra, undercover as Patricia C. Leo, R and D Manager of East Fossil Fuels, listened with a frozen smile as a coworker unspooled his epic about house breaking his Labrador retriever puppy.

"Uhuh." "I see." "Yes." "So what did you do then?"

Apollo's request for a DNA sample had taken on new urgency. With Pan in D.C. the sting was unfolding. A cursory look at the security system blueprints Michael Guy had hacked was enough to convince her breaking and entering was not a viable option. Today's reception was her best chance.

She tried not to be obvious, sneaking glances around the penthouse suite, watching the East brothers converse with other employees. Today's afternoon coffee honored a stout woman from Sales who'd just been chosen to succeed her accounts manager. Word was the manager had retired, but no party had been held, not even a mention in the online in-house newsletter. Had this person gone the way of Perkins?

"Excuse me," she said to the dog daddy. "I need some coffee. Can I get you some?"

He declined and turned his story full force on another listener.

Cleo eased through the crowd at the buffet table and filled a fresh cup. To her right was Edwin East (identifiable from the telltale crease in the back of his jacket she'd noted earlier), facing the glass wall and talking to the honoree.

"Think of it, Ms. Fields, your new office will face this magnificent view!"

His words were mushy, typical of both Easts who frequently talked with their mouths full.

Cleo drizzled some cream into her coffee and listened intently.

"I'm so honored and excited, Mr. East!" Ms. Fields said.

"You must celebrate to the fullest, my friend," Edwin encouraged. "Here, try a bite of cream puff, they are exceptionally good today."

Ms. Fields giggled. "Right off your plate, Mr. East?"

"Why of course, my dear. Here, I'll take the first bite to assure you it's wholesome. And now—"

A tremendous wheezing hack tore their conversation.

"Mr. East! Oh my goodness!" Ms. Fields squeaked. Cleo turned and saw Ms. Fields thumping Edwin's back. "Oh my goodness, oh—"

An explosive sound, thick with cream and mucous, echoed off the glass.

"Mr. East, are you all right?" Ms. Fields had him by the elbow. "Let me help you to a chair so you can catch your breath. Would you like a glass of water?"

Cleo worked quickly amidst the chaos. She scraped a pale, disgusting blob off the glass wall with a clean napkin and slid it into the plastic bag she'd stowed in a pocket. Olympus, Inc., had sent a sample collection pouch; courier service to Apollo was only a text away.

SUNÒAY, NOVEMBER 3, 1918

Valencia, Spain

The lawyer was a favorite cousin of Lucia's, who had agreed to meet with them on Sunday.

"The sooner we resolve this and you leave Lucia in peace, the better," the lawyer said.

Documents were drawn up, the first one for a trust, to be funded on David's behalf by Milton, to assure Amàlia's maintenance and comfort for life. Milton presented their proposed amount for the corpus and his projection of how this amount would pay out over time. After a brief discussion Gomez Barbera agreed to the sum. He specified the bank and the trustee.

The parameters of the second document proved more difficult to negotiate, Lucia sitting on one side of a conference table with her cousin, David and Milton opposite.

"If I die before Amàlia comes of age I will not entrust her to anyone but the Sisters of Saint Claire. Not even you, Guillem," she said to her cousin. "Families are not to be trusted. This I learned the hard way. They would never allow me to marry outside the Catholic faith even though Mr. Burns, at that time, vowed to them we would wed."

She wouldn't look at him. He wasn't sure he wanted her too, her eyes so cold above her mask.

"We will have to get consent from Reverend Mother," Gomez Barbera pointed out.

"I suggest we do so immediately so as not to further inconvenience these *gentlemen*."

This involved a trip back to the convent and the holding up of a succession of written notes through closed windows. David got close enough to drink in every detail of Amàlia's face, the dark, feathery eyelashes that brushed her round, pink cheeks. His arms ached to hold her, just once, but the convent's quarantine rules would not permit it. Even Lucia was banned from that joy until the contagion got under control.

There was nothing left to do except sign the documents and assist Milton back to Scotland. This time they stuffed their pockets with rations, would travel more slowly so as not to tire the older man completely.

They left Valencia the afternoon of November third. When they stopped that night along the French coast, far south on the Bay of Biscay, David asked Milton if he would tell the younger David about the baby and the legal arrangements.

"Unless we lifted the forgetfulness charm, he wouldn't know what I was talking about," Milton answered after a long silence. "That would be too great a risk. You realize you've already played with fire, coming here in the first place? I hope to Tartarus this won't rewrite history."

They didn't talk much after that.

David and Milton touched down in Edinburgh the evening of November sixth. The necessity of getting back to 2026 had grown in David's mind with each mile. Only then would he know if his plan had worked. Heaven and Earth, he hoped he'd done more good than harm!

Milton gave him enough pounds to put up in a hotel for the night. David promised to return to his own time as soon as he'd rested. They shook hands.

"See you later," Milton said, his eyes twinkling for the first time since their adventure began.

"Take good care of Thelma and me," David said, shaking his head at the oddity of the situation. He watched Milton step into a nearby cab, touched his left index finger and thumb to his right index finger to feel the silver band ring and found it—gone!

David moved zombie-like through a hot bath and dinner, his mind numb with the realization he was stuck in time and had no idea how to get back. The page from the spell book was still in his pocket, thank Heaven and Earth, but there was no guidance on how to perform the reversal if the return token was lost. Though every muscle ached, and the hotel bed was the best place he'd slept in days, he remained hyper-awake.

How many days had it been? Surely someone at Athens U would notice he was missing his classes and report it to Zeus. He should have told someone about his plans, at least Jim who could have kept it confidential. From the start David had sensed what he'd done wasn't entirely … "legal" wasn't quite the right word. The spell book said there wasn't exactly a law against it, but noted time travel was notorious for creating unintended consequences.

David tossed from his right side to his left. He'd go to the bank tomorrow and ask Milton what to do.

No. *Toss.* He'd already put his foster father in a tough enough position.

Saul was somewhere out there in the world but how would David find him with the available technology? Besides, Saul had changed his name a bunch of times. In 1918 he probably wasn't even Ari Cantor yet, like he was when he'd been a crooner of Frank Sinatra songs in the 1940s.

No. *Toss.* Who else did he know, anybody?

All his immortal friends, family and associates were somewhere in the world. Of course none of them knew about him, yet. He remembered a photograph Cleo had in her office when he'd first met her. She was dressed in a kind of safari suit. She'd said the picture was taken at an archaeological dig near her family home in Petra, Jordan. He'd been to that place, a mansion hidden in the cliff behind the tomb known as The Treasury.

No. *Toss.* Cleo's mother hadn't liked him when they'd met last fall and her opinion had barely thawed one degree by the time he'd left. And even if he could find Cleo, why would she be impressed with him? It had taken a decade for her to fall in love with him even in the best of circumstances.

Ralph was doing what right now—working as a structureling, holding up London Bridge? Had Jim been transferred to Seattle yet, or was he still Continental Manager of Australia? Not that it mattered, because neither of those guys would know him in 1918 either.

Toss. Aside from the Bernsteins and Saul, there was only one immortal in 1918 who knew about him. She would recognize him now, because he looked so much like Saul.

The only one who could help him in the Zeus-forsaken world of 1918 was Hera.

SATURDAY, FEBRUARY 21, 2026

City of Mount Olympus

Persephone reheated a slice of yesterday's College Pub pizza in the kitchenette microwave. Her mouth watered in anticipation. Hades had never allowed her to try anything new during her marital imprisonment in the Underworld. Though she had resolved never to return there again, Persephone was well acquainted with the capriciousness of fate. Her short-term plan was to seize whatever caught her fancy and enjoy it, just in case.

Once she'd eaten, her mouth lightly burned from the pleasures of overheated pepperoni and black olives, she rinsed her hands and took a few short steps to the full-length mirror mounted on the bathroom door. Persephone turned sideways. Six weeks plus a few days since her romantic encounter with Frey. If she smoothed her hands over her belly just so, pulling the raw silk fabric of her new sky-blue toga just right, she could almost see it. She could definitely feel it, forming inside her.

Exhaling a contented sigh she took two steps more to the daybed, plenty for her now but soon she'd need a crib. Persephone reclined on the grass-green chenille bedspread decorated with crocheted daisies she'd found at a thrift store in her University District neighborhood. Her eyes trailed up to the ceiling. The vine of a hearty philodendron, a once-scrawny plant abandoned in the apartment building lobby with a placard reading 'FREE' propped against its pot, now draped lush and full-leafed between three hooks.

Life was filled with light, peace and joy. How easy it was, once she'd received the new debit card that had to have come from Frey, to build her own little island, hers and the baby's. A young neighbor had shown her how to block incoming calls and messages on her digital device. No more Hades. No more Mother. Not until she, Persephone, said so.

ThursDay, NovemBer 7, 1918

Edinburgh, Scotland

Fueled by two hours of fitful sleep, David donned his freshly valeted suit, wolfed down a double breakfast of oatmeal, sausage, potatoes and eggs, assumed Biggest of Big-G Cloaking and soared away from Edinburgh before the sun rose, his course to the southeast. Even flying at his top speed it would be an eight-hour flight. His stiff, overworked muscles complained bitterly.

He touched down several times to rest. What he saw of Western Europe was discouraging, all of it war-weary and straining under the flu pandemic. His only meal consisted of hotel scones he'd tucked in his pocket and bruised, wind-fallen apples from a picked-over orchard in Austria.

There was no Athens International Airport yet, no signage marked with words only immortals could see, directing them to warp speed chariot service to the City of Mount Olympus. The portal he'd passed through on his first visit must be in place, though, since the Parthenon had been there for centuries. Something about concentrating on certain columns at the back of the temple, blurring his eyes, and—what? He paid for a tourist ticket at the kiosk and climbed up the broad marble steps of the Propylaea to the Acropolis, the City on the Hill.

The small number of visitors didn't surprise him. He'd masked his nose and mouth with his handkerchief the instant he'd landed. The flu couldn't kill him but who knew how sick he might become if he caught it? Medical treatment in 1918 was something he did not want to experience.

The sky was heavy and gray, mid-autumn instead of the white-hot summer day when he'd first come here, the first time he remembered coming here, anyway. The Parthenon, Athena's temple, rose before him, rendered in yellowed marble, endowed with the weight of human history.

Seeing it triggered the details of his prior visit. The portal was at the west end, third column from the left. He needed to blur his vision and head toward the designated column until he saw a golden light.

David removed his eyeglasses and squinted. The edges of the column softened, and golden light danced up the edges. He closed his eyes and paced forward...

"Tartarus!"

His handkerchief was on fire! David speedily unknotted it and threw it to the ground, stomped out the flames not on yellowed marble but on verdant green grass.

"Whoo-hoo, that was a close one! Never seen it happen to a second-timer."

An ancient man in a toga stood before him, sky blue eyes crinkling with laughter.

"Myclops?"

"Well, aren't you a sharp one! Myclops, Brother of Cyclops if you want the full pedigree. I remember you, too. You're from the outside."

"But..."

"You're not the only one who's done some time traveling. David something-or-other if my memory's working proper? From, let's see now." Myclops tapped his index finger on his chin, deep in thought. "About a century from now, I reckon. Don't get a lot of time travelers these days, it's out of fashion with the Big Twelve and where they lead their immortal flock follows. Speaking of following, come along with me. The route's a little different now than it will be the first time you come. But first—"

Myclops shot out a hand, palm up. An offering, David remembered from before.

"Nothing bloody, that's my only rule," Myclops said. Last time David had found a disposable razor in his backpack but today he had no luggage, only the clothes on his back. He didn't dare part with the watch, the token he'd used for the back in time part of the spell.

"Here." He popped off the dark gray Homburg.

Myclops grasped the brim with both hands and settled it on his own head atop his waist-length snarl of white hair.

"Oh-ho!" He tapped the crown, beaming. "Now *this* is what I call an offering! Follow me, David Something-or-Other—"

"Burns," he said.

"You sure about that? Sounds shorter than I remember. Oh well." Myclops shrugged. "I guess you know your own name better than I do."

The first hill was the same verdant rise he remembered, but when they crested the next one it was terraced from top to bottom and planted with grape vines.

"Different, isn't it?" Myclops said. "They drink more now than they will in the future. Following the mortal trends for something to do, don't you know?" He led David up a path in the middle of the vineyard.

"Now this'll knock your sandals off, when you see what's on the other side. Completely different setup than your first time," Myclops said.

The view from the hilltop staggered him. Nestled in the hillside, in place of the eleven-story Olympus, Inc., corporate building was a longer, lower structure, neoclassical in design with two floors and a dome rising from the center. The city beyond was built in a similar style, bereft of skyscraping hotels in the downtown tourist district and sleek blocks of high-priced condos in the New Mycenae neighborhood. On the edge of the developed area was a familiar sight, the pale green marble of the sanitarium, Olympus Rest, with its column and pediment façade. The only other buildings he recognized were on the other side of town at Athens U and Athens Tech—the scale model of the Parthenon, the admin and classroom buildings, and the track. The dormitory that had been his home for a decade did not yet exist.

"Wow." The old go-to word he'd tried to excise from his vocabulary was the only one that adequately expressed his feelings.

"Good luck to you," Myclops said, giving him a slap on the back forceful enough to start him downhill. "And thanks again for the fine offering!"

~ * ~

A spear-wielding, toga-wearing guard atop the wide marble steps leading up to Olympus, Inc., looked David up and down, scowling. David squared his shoulders under his travel-trashed jacket, ran a hand through his wild curls in an effort to tame them.

"State your business," bayed the doorman.

David, three steps below, puffed up his chest. "I'm here to see Hera, Goddess of Marriage," he said with confidence he didn't feel.

"Whatever makes you think she's *here*?" sneered the guard. "No women at corporate. Marriage is in the annex, same as the Department of Home and Hearth and whatever it is that Demeter does."

"Agriculture?"

The guard descended and came face to face with David. "Think you're a smart one, don't you?" The man's fetid breath made David far less self-conscious about his own state of dishevelment. "Well let me tell you something, Mister Outside World, we don't take kindly to smart ones here at corporate."

Obviously.

"Fine. If you'll point me toward the annex I will trouble you no more."

"Don't you take that fancy tone with me!" The smell of sour ale curdled in David's nostrils. "Down to the corner." The guard pointed his spear to the right. "Turn left and you're there."

The annex was built from a lesser grade of marble than the corporate building, with few attractive veins and a notable number of pockmarks. Single story, no dome, no one guarding the two shallow steps leading to the entrance. Inside was a meek-looking young woman in a shabby pale pink toga.

"Hello," she squeaked. "How can I help you today?"

When he asked to see Hera a look of terror crossed the receptionist's face.

"Are you sure, sir?"

"Positive."

She leaned forward as if to share a great confidence. "Do you have an appointment?"

"Yes," he bluffed.

The receptionist looked down at a ledger on her desk, flipped some pages and frowned. "Are you certain? It's nearly closing time and there aren't any appointments written down for her here."

"Must be an oversight," he temporized. "Just tell her David Bernstein is here."

She looked at him like he'd asked her to cut off her hand. "Are you sure, sir?"

"I'm sure."

She scuttled down the long main corridor and turned right.

In her absence he studied three life-sized statues tucked into a large alcove with benches that must be the waiting area. Hera; Hestia, Goddess of Home and Hearth; Demeter, Goddess of the Harvest. His mother and his two aunts, sisters to Zeus, Poseidon and Hades, segregated here, away from the seat of power. Maybe missing the first two thousand years of his life hadn't been such a bad thing after all.

A section of wall to the left of the alcove hinged open. The receptionist peeked out, eyes large and face bloodless.

"Quick, Mr. Bernstein! Follow me."

~ * ~

Hera paced the Turkish carpet in her private office. How could Thelma Bernstein have let it slip that she, Hera, was David's real mother? He was going to blackmail her; she knew it in her bones. She'd have to charm him, or, failing that, put a charm *on* him. If word of this reached Zeus she didn't care to speculate what might happen to her. Disgrace? Banishment? Divorce? He'd done that before, with Demeter. Though it might be advantageous to unshackle herself from (to put it charitably) a very difficult marriage, the fall in status would ruin her future and that of her children. Especially Veronica, who showed such promise in business and leadership. Ronnie was the one who might, at long last, raise the women of Mount Olympus to equal status with the men. The spawn of her illicit desire must not be allowed to derail this possibility.

She stopped in front of a mirror to check her appearance. The loathsome High Olympian style that Zeus demanded she, as his wife, embrace grated on her sense of fashion. Everything white, from toga to sandals to hair that was coiffed according to regulation. Regulation! An impossible number of braids and curls encircled her scalp, her thick, waist-length hair bound in tonsorial slavery. Maintaining the look required the daily services of an historian turned hairdresser named Janet. It was an idiotic waste of time and money, a stale tradition Zeus refused to drop.

A weak knock tickled the wall. Hera drew a deep breath and summoned her most imperious tone.

"You may enter."

Mousy little Phaedra (no one would mistake her for the long-dead, infamous mortal queen) scurried in and frantically waved in the person behind her, a medium-short young man in a rumpled suit, his hair springing in every direction.

Hera took another deep breath. If she discounted the eyeglasses, he looked just like Saul.

"Mr. Bernstein, please take a seat," she said, voice determinedly steady as she indicated one of two Savonarola chairs some decorator or other had inflicted on her. "You may leave us, Phaedra. When we've finished I will show Mr. Bernstein out."

~ * ~

David had forgotten how starchy Hera used to look in her classic goddess wear, like a flawlessly draped statue sculpted by an artist who specialized in facial scowls, cold as the marble it was carved from.

Behind him, the door to the secret passageway closed. They were alone.

"I won't beat around the proverbial bush, Mr. Bernstein, I know who you are. Your resemblance to your father is strong and your coloring is much as mine used to be."

Not only was her outward style different, but her bearing was different, too. Her shoulders were rounded forward whereas he'd only known her, the future Hera, with shoulders proudly squared. The brutal humor he remembered in her eyes wasn't there. Instead, anxiety etched her forehead. Whatever had changed for her after 1918 must have done her a world of good. For today's Hera, he felt an unanticipated pang of empathy.

"I apologize if I've startled you, Hera. I'm not here to cause you pain—"

"Hah!" she snapped. "If you tried, I'd have you thrown in prison!"

"Please let me explain. We meet in the future," he said, keeping it simple.

"Who told you about me?" she demanded. "I'll track Thelma Bernstein down and flail the skin off her if she broke her promise to keep your true parentage a secret."

"Not Thelma. I never doubted she and Milton were my parents until you told me so yourself."

"Why should I—"

"I don't know why you told me," he cut in. "We met under pretty strange circumstances in an American city called Seattle, and there was this weird, scary crisis and I guess it just kind of came out?"

Hera leaned close and gripped David's forearm. "You're not to say a word of this to anyone, do you understand me? Not a single, solitary word. If Zeus found out—"

"No, of course not. I'm not here to make a claim or anything, I'm here because I need help, Hera, and you're the only one I could think of who knows who I am."

He quickly relayed his decision to time travel, the spell book he'd used, his situation with Lucia and the baby and how he'd recruited Milton to help him address his parental responsibilities.

"Once we got back to Scotland I planned to return to my time the next morning, but then I couldn't find the silver ring that was my return token. It must have slipped off my finger in flight. Now I don't know what to do, and I'm hoping you can help me. I need you to help me get back, uh, forward, I guess, to twenty twenty-six."

"Heaven and Earth," Hera said under her breath. She rose and crossed the room to a tall cabinet, opened the double doors in front and pulled out a decanter and two glasses. "I need something to clear my thoughts. Do you like wine?"

"Sure."

She returned with two goblets, brimming with pale gold.

"Some lovely stuff from France," she said, handing one to him. "Something or other blanc." She took a long pull from her goblet.

He, too, raised his glass. The wine was light and fruity with a tart edge.

She studied him, cold-eyed, over the rim of her goblet. "You need to get away from here as soon as possible for both our sakes. It's a matter of survival so don't mistake this for maternal affection. I make no promises, but I will do what I can to help you."

He reached for the paper in his pocket. "I have the spell with me—"

"A wise precaution but since you've lost the token we'll need to find another way. My youngest daughter is enrolled at the university. I'll ask her to check out all the spell books in the collection."

Veronica. She'd be in a post-graduate business program now, working on her masters or maybe her PhD.

"What can I do to help?"

"Nothing! But it's imperative you stay hidden. Zeus has spies everywhere. You'll have to go somewhere you won't be noticed. Do you have any work skills?"

He told her about his barista experience.

"Like the Arabs," she said. Her reference didn't register with him, but she seemed to understand. "I'll send you to Dionysus, he runs the largest eatery in town. He's always looking for staff and doesn't ask questions." She gave him directions to the venue and had him repeat them back to her. "Nothing in writing," she emphasized, eyebrow arched. "And you'll need a different surname. Milton is well known here as a tax preparer."

"Wow."

~ * ~

David, surname Petrarch, slogged through an unrecognizable section of the city, what would become the hotel district, to Chez Dionysus.

The restaurant was in the same location as Club Dionysus from his own time but the building was different. It was cold and bright, compared to the future intimate eatery favored by lovers. There were tables for two and four draped with white linen cloths where a few couples and groups were seated, the hour early for dinner. The high ceiling was decorated with pressed tin tiles. Tall windows dominated the street side. A man in a tuxedo was pulling the last pair of heavy red drapes closed against the darkness. The man was clearly the maître d' by the authority with which he strode to the podium near the entrance. He eyed David with disapproval.

"How may I help you, sir?" he said, peering down his long nose.

"I'm looking for work," David said. "I have lots of experience as a barista and some tending bar."

"I'm afraid we can't—" the maître d' began but the entrance of a couple in expensively tailored togas seized his attention. "Welcome!" he said in an oily, melodious voice. "Mr. and Mrs. Papadakis, your table is ready. Come right this way."

David took advantage of the distraction to dart past the high carved bar toward a pair of swinging doors in the back.

The kitchen was alive with activity, three long counters for prep and plating, and a bank of ovens that set the temperature swelteringly high. A trim blond youth in dark slacks, starched white shirt and a red cropped jacket brushed past him, corkscrew in hand and wine bottle nestled on his forearm. Ganymede, David's friend from the future, who'd changed careers from Cupbearer to the Gods to head sommelier and never looked back.

Invisible in the chaos, David navigated his way to an open door on the left. Inside, seated at a desk with a candlestick telephone raised to his mouth and ear, his future friend Dionysus barked commands at the unfortunate party on the other end.

"I expect the lamb to be tender, Mr. Ryopolis, not as tough as the sole of a sandal found at an archaeological dig! Send me a suitable replacement immediately or my business with you is done, sir!"

Dionysus grabbed the glass of clear, effervescent liquid resting on his desk, drank it down in one gulp, held his fist to his heart and burped. His eyes lit on David and narrowed.

"Who are you?" he snarled. "What do you want?"

David stepped back. The Dionysus he knew, and knew pretty well, was laid-back and gracious. Whatever the next century would bring must have improved his circumstances as much as it had improved Hera's.

"I'm looking for work," David said.

"Not hiring. Now get out of here, I'm up to my ears in it."

David took a deep breath. "I was sent by a lady," he said. "By *the* lady."

"Heaven and Earth." Dionysus threw his hands up in the air. "I don't care if she *is* the number one female on Mount Olympus, I—"

Someone standing behind David cleared their throat.

"Ganymede, what in Tartarus?"

"It's Argus, sir. Called in sick again."

"Jumping Zeus, can't you handle it by yourself on a Thursday night?"

"Normally, sir, yes, but we're running a champagne promotion tonight and we're booked solid from seven until closing."

Dionysus turned fierce eyes on David. "You any good at serving champagne?"

"Well, I—"

"I'll take that as a yes. Get the kid in a monkey suit, Ganymede, and show him the ropes." He turned back to David, "Make it through tonight without a major screw-up and you're hired."

~ * ~

The mechanics of opening champagne were different than what David had seen in movies. Remove the foil, twist open the wire guard and gently twist—not pop—the cork. Ganymede coached him through opening a bottle of inferior grade, one that would be shared among the kitchen staff, before turning him loose in the dining room. The service aspect wasn't all that different from working as a barista, any remarks on his part confined to congratulating the patrons on their excellent choice but with Madame and Monsieur thrown in.

"Seven until closing" found David serving his last bottle of bubbly at five minutes to 2am, bar time. Adrenaline had carried him through the evening with only two minor mishaps—retrieving an escaped cork that rolled under a table and over-pouring a coupe for a middle-aged woman who, fortunately, had a sense of humor about champagne dousing her bread plate. By the time he changed from his uniform into his street clothes, the long day filled with travel, work and emotion caught up with him. He could barely keep his eyes open.

Ganymede laid a hand on his shoulder. "Well done. Staff dining table is in the back," he said, pointing to the rear of the kitchen.

The hollow cavity where his stomach used to be rumbled. David joined the handful of men at a long wooden table with benches on either side. At one end a cast-iron pot steamed with the delicious aroma of herbs, vegetables and meat. A man in chef's whites ladled the thick stew into earthenware bowls. Raw-tasting red wine splashed into short stem-less glasses, loaves of bread were torn into manageable chunks.

"A madhouse tonight, eh?" someone said, initiating a recap of the evening's highlights that would have been amusing if David were more alert.

~ * ~

David awoke, joints stiff, looking up at the underside of the bar. "Wow."

A thin pad of some sort cushioned him from the hardwood floor. He rolled over, relieved his head, at least, didn't hurt. Not that it should after one glass of wine. The floor behind the bar was sticky. He slowly got to his feet and looked out into the dining area. Bright daylight edged around the heavy red curtains, still drawn from last night.

"There you are, sleeping beauty!" A squat, middle-aged woman wearing a calf-length toga rested on the handle of a mop. "Just in time for me to swab down the floor back there. Between you and me, those bartenders can be such pigs."

David pulled the watch from his waistcoat pocket. The hands had stopped at two-twenty. He looked up at the clock behind the bar, set the hands to five minutes later than what the face told him, and wound the stem until it resisted. Just past noon. Someone must be in the back, may-be a prep cook. If he was going to be stranded in the City of Mount Olympus for a while, he needed a place to stay.

He found a youngish man in the kitchen, hotly engaged in conver-sation with someone delivering an order of goat cheese.

"You can tell Pan from me this price hike is outrageous!" the kitchen man said, pointing his finger at the other man's chest. "Dionysus said he'll go out to the farm and settle it himself if necessary."

The other man, by far the shorter of the two, took a step back and pulled the shearling vest he wore over his toga tight around his torso. "No need to threaten me, I'm only the messenger."

"Then I hope to Tartarus you'll deliver that message!"

The kitchen man slammed the door shut between them. He

deposited the box resting heavily on his hip on the staff dining table and blew out a breath.

"Excuse me—"

The man spun toward David. "And who in Tartarus are *you*?"

David explained himself to the man who identified himself as Valerian, kitchen day manager and, as he crudely put it, the by-blow of one of Poseidon's romantic adventures.

"Not that being his son will get you anywhere, there are so by-Zeus many of us," Valerian groused. He unlocked Dionysus' office and took an envelope out of a desk drawer. "Last night's pay. Your shift starts at six and you'll need to change before that."

"I need a place to stay," David said. The envelope was light, only a few bills inside from the touch. Enough for one night, he hoped.

"I'll give you the names of a couple of dumps nearby." Valerian held out his hand for David's envelope and scribbled on the back. "Don't pay for board if you can help it, the food's better here."

~ * ~

The room was inferior to the one he and Milton had secured in pandemic-ridden Valencia, eight feet by ten, divided by a curtain for privacy from the guy on the other side. This was the City of Mount Olympus, for crying out loud, home to the Greek Pantheon, the immortal beings who ran the mortal world from behind-the-scenes! What wasn't downright Dickensian was reminiscent of the Pottersville scenes in that old movie *It's a Wonderful Life*. Everyone surly, everything dingy and down-at-the-heels. David had the feeling if he asked anyone what was wrong, no one would know what he was talking about.

The room was so dismal he left as soon as he'd paid for it and rambled around the city. Some of the major streets were named as he remembered them. He walked to the green marble splendor of Olympus Rest, admired its pediment carved with the Rod of Asclepius. Cries of the mentally unhinged echoed from within. Sick at heart, he turned away and set a course for Athens U, figuring a few minutes of quiet in the full-scale reproduction of the Parthenon, complete with giant statue of Athena, would bring him solace. When he arrived the steps were roped off. A sign in front read *Closed for Renovation*.

He arrived at Chez Dionysus an hour early. At least serving the Friday night crowd would give him something to think about besides whether he could get back to his own time. It came to him as he changed into his sommelier uniform: what would happen if he got stuck here? Would a duplicate of him show up in 2015 when he'd first visited the City of Mount Olympus? There was that younger self back in Scotland, too.

A chill juddered through him.

"Hey, Petrarch!"

It took David a moment to remember his temporary surname.

Valerian stood in the changing room doorway, stance wide, thick forearms crossed over his chest and eyes narrowed.

"There's some girl here to see you. She's out back. Make it quick, Petrarch, this is a restaurant, not a matchmaking service."

Standing in an alley, her hair and shoulders covered with a shawl, was Veronica. Her questioning eyes darted up and down, scanning him from head to toe. A stack of ancient-looking, leather-bound books was cradled on her hip.

"You're Mother's friend, Mr. Petrarch?" she said, skepticism clear in her tone.

Her ankle-length toga was made of a gray pinstripe fabric like she'd worn when they'd first met, all those years forward and back ago, in Seattle. His intense and supportive half-sister was a stranger to him now.

"Yes, I'm David Petrarch."

She looked from side to side as if she feared being spotted. "I'm not supposed to have these, they're from a restricted area of the library but Mother said it was imperative I bring them to you." Veronica leaned forward to whisper. "She said it was a State security issue."

He couldn't think of an answer to this. Veronica's single nod seemed to take his silence as confirmation.

"She said I could help, and save you time by finding certain… *entries*. I marked them with slips of papyrus." Veronica handed him the books. They were heavier than he'd anticipated, and pulsed, somehow, as if they were alive.

"Be very careful with these, Mr. Petrarch," she cautioned. "If anyone finds out I've removed them from the Athens U library I'll be expelled, and I must not be expelled, Mr. Petrarch. The future of Mount Olympus depends on it."

"What do you—"

She turned away and ran down the alleyway, her tread so light it made no sound. Veronica *knew*. She knew what was wrong with the gods and their city. Reference to this dark time hadn't appeared in the standard text for all incoming Athens U students *A Brief History of Mount Olympus*. Either it was a deeply guarded secret or...

The butterfly effect. Had his trip back in time, an immature and self-indulgent tantrum he now realized, somehow robbed the city and its people of every shred of beauty and grace?

He hid the ill-gotten books under his street clothes. A faint greenish glow emanated from underneath. Hopefully, none of his overworked coworkers would notice.

SATURDAY, NOVEMBER 9, 1918

His shift, the last for two days, was jam-packed with ardent wine-drinking customers from start to finish. Thankfully, the books were where he'd left them and didn't appear to be disturbed or tampered with. David's stomach rumbled but he dared not eat with the other employees, didn't want to tempt fate with the books being discovered. He wrapped them in his jacket and snagged a dark, hearty-looking loaf from the long table. It would have to do for now.

His boarding house roommate snored like a sawmill. David settled on his side of the curtain, lit the candle he'd purchased from the landlady at an outrageous price and read as he munched: *A Spell for Moving out of Time, F'wrd & Beck tro Tyme,* and the intact page of the spell he'd brought from 2026.

Wait, though! That page was from the future. So were the clothes he'd had made in preparation for this trip. Could these things serve as return tokens?

David studied the ripped page, silently read it a half-dozen times before pulling a button off his waistcoat and clenching it in his free hand. He drew a deep breath and murmured the reverse spell out loud.

Nothing.

A Spell for Moving out of Time had a glossary: "Token—An object that tangibly represents the result desired."

Did the watch he'd used to get to 1918 represent time? Did the ring he'd lost stand for love? He searched his brain for the symbolic meaning of his waistcoat, trousers, shoes, his whole limited wardrobe that might fuel his return to 2026, and came up dry.

A Spell for Moving out of Time had a spell substantially the same as the one he'd used. It, too, required tokens, but as for *F'wrd & Beck tro Tyme—*

Viewing the volumes together on his narrow cot he realized the latter book was the one casting the greenish glow. And the weird spelling. The glow was so strong he could have read the book without candlelight but instinct told him not to douse the flame. It was hard to pick out the meaning of some of the words, either misspelled or at least an antiquated spelling. He moved his lips in phonetics. This book addressed the loss of a return token:

Trvlar messt mk blud sacrfic n wsht nu tk'n n blud

David closed the book and shivered. Would he have to kill something—or somebody—to return to 2026?

MONDAY, NOVEMBER 11, 1918

Phaedra looked up in alarm when David entered the Annex Monday morning. She asked no questions, didn't utter one word but simply gestured for him to follow her to the secret access to Hera's suite. They stood outside the hidden door, listening. Silence from within. Phaedra rapped once from the tunnel side.

"Rats!" Hera, loud and clear. "When will we be rid of the eternal rats?"

Phaedra timidly opened the door.

"Tartarus." Hera pointed to the glowing book tucked under David's arm. "What have you got there? Leave us, Phaedra," she added as if it were an afterthought.

Phaedra nudged David into the room and scurried away, closing the door behind her.

Hera glared at him. "Don't tell me *this* is one of the books my daughter brought you?"

"I'm sorry, I didn't—"

"Of course you didn't! This whole adventure proves you're incapable of thought. How any child of mine could—"

"I didn't know, Hera. I would never purposely do anything to hurt Veronica—"

"You know her *name?*" Hera said, her voice rising to a shriek.

"We meet in the future," he said. "I—"

"I swear to you, David, son or no son I will destroy you if you in any way harm her. She's the only one who can reason with Zeus, our only hope."

Frustration at being in the dark overwhelmed him.

"Is that what's wrong with this place?" he blurted. "Something to do with Zeus?"

"Heaven and Earth, what did you think? Of course it has to do with him. The City of Mount Olympus *is* Zeus. He built it on a foundation of his own vitality and now he's..."

Hera bit her lower lip.

"Is he sick?" Maybe he'd somehow caught the Spanish Flu.

"Yes and no."

"I don't understand."

Hera let out a hard breath. "It's a man thing. You'll find out about it when you're older."

So it wasn't him, the time traveler, who'd crushed the city's soul. David's shoulders, up around his ears since he'd first read about the blood sacrifice, relaxed. Heaven and Earth, how they ached.

"You need to get out of here before he hears about you. The whole place will fall down if he finds out that I—"

"Okay, I get it," David said. It all turned out fine in the future, if he could get there. "There's something in here," he said, holding out the book to her. "It's about how to make a replacement token for travelling forward in time but it's kind of, uh, grim?"

Hera took the volume gingerly and held it at arm's length on the trip to her desk. She slid a gilt-painted fingernail between the bookmark-ed pages, sat, and gestured for him to sit in the chair opposite. Her eyes flitted back and forth, working down the page, head nodding, until—

"Ah. Blood sacrifice." She looked up, her eyes meeting his. "We don't do that anymore."

"Sorry?"

"The temple priests and priestesses were always complaining about how hard it was to clean blood off the altars, and the smoke—such headaches! Hestia's migraines were through the stratosphere. Trust me, if the Goddess of Home and Hearth isn't happy, nobody's happy. The whole thing's been codified."

"Codified?"

Hera huffed a huge exhale. "Zeus' Laws, you fool, punishable to the full extent of the law if someone is found guilty of breaking them. I can't be involved."

David shot out of his chair and planted his hands on the desktop. "Fine, you don't have to be involved. But you want me out of here, right? Can you at least tell me exactly how this is supposed to work so I don't screw it up?"

What she said horrified him, but if it was the only way to get out of this crazy and depressing version of Mount Olympus, Heaven and Earth, he'd do it.

~ * ~

That afternoon David stood on the green marble steps of Olympus Rest. The button he'd pulled off his waistcoat was in his coat pocket. He pulled a cleaver he'd nicked from the Chez Dionysus kitchen from the back of his trousers waistband, extended his index finger as far from the rest of his right-hand fingers as possible, raised the cleaver in his left, and…

Voices.

"I don't know where he came from, sir, I just heard him howl on the front steps and ran out to see what happened."

"Heat the cauterizing tool and be quick about it," snapped a different voice, familiar except for the hard edge.

David opened one eye. A man hunched over a burner held the cool end of a rod lapped in white flame; the other man was gone. He fought to remain conscious long enough to fumble the waistcoat button out of his pocket, roll it in the stump of his index finger until it was coated with blood. David tucked the hand holding the button into his trousers pocket, closed his eyes, and girded his will to endure the cauterizing before he spoke the words that would carry him home.

~ * ~

David Bernstein woke up on a hard surface. His right hand was a mass of gauze, stained brown where his right index finger used to be. He got to his knees. His head throbbed like a boiler ready to burst.

So this was what happened when you fell in love.

In time he levered his hands on the bathroom sink and got to his feet. His digital device was on the vanity where he'd left it. He tapped the home key with his left index finger. The device was fully charged. The display at the top of the screen read Friday, February 20, 2026. His thirteen days in the past had taken thirteen minutes.

MONDAY, FEBRUARY 23, 2026

City of Mount Olympus

David's visit to the Athens U infirmary generated a notification to Zeus, as Provost, given the severity of David's injury. This resulted in a one-on-one meeting in Zeus' office on Monday afternoon.

They sat in the well-used armchairs, facing each other across a game table topped with the fabled chess set. A new log caught fire on top of a red-hot stack in the fireplace, its radiant heat soothing the raw ache in David's right hand. He made his opening move, his color the lighter of the two as always when playing Zeus. The pieces weren't black and white but lighter and darker shades of gray. It was awkward, manipulating the pawn (who bore a strong resemblance to Pan) with his left hand. Zeus' opening mirrored David's. He set the dark pawn down on a new square and looked up, the expression in his eyes somber.

"Will you tell me how it happened, David?"

"It was an accident, sir."

"So I would hope." The God known as The Thunderer leaned forward. "Your aura has a faint black corona, the residue of dark magic."

Heaven and Earth, there was no getting out of this, but he stalled anyway. "Sir?"

"I need to know the details of how and why you lost your finger. It's a matter of security. Whatever power forced this on you—" David winced involuntarily "—yes, I can see that much already. A determination must be made as to whether that power is still present, and whether it can cause harm beyond the harm it inflicted on you."

Zeus' stare wielded its own irresistible power, strong enough to force a confession. David started at the beginning.

"You enlisted the assistance of Hera." Zeus said it as a statement, not a question.

"Yes, sir. I didn't know what else to do. She was the only one in the city who knew of my existence then."

"And what was her attitude when you made your appeal for help?"

"She was frightened, sir, that's the best way I can describe it."

"Afraid for you, David?"

"Maybe, but mostly afraid for herself, sir." A pulsing in his orphaned knuckle made it impossible for him to couch what he needed to say. "She was afraid of what you'd do if you found out about me."

"Yes." Zeus leaned back into his chair and shifted his gaze to the fireplace. "My behavior at that time frightened most people. An important mitigating circumstance to weigh against the known violation of law by both Hera and Veronica. But you." His eyes returned to David. "Were you afraid of me, too?"

Honestly, Zeus' wrath was small potatoes compared to being stranded in the past.

"No, sir."

"Yet you willingly broke the law by time travelling and making a blood sacrifice—"

"I didn't know about those laws when I started my journey, sir," he broke in. "But yes, I did find out about the blood sacrifice when Hera told me. It seemed worth the risk."

"Do you know what the remedies are for your actions, if you are found guilty by the Court of Twelve?"

The Court of Twelve? David shook his head.

"For lower tier laws, which cover time travel and dark magic, our goal is restorative justice," Zeus said. "The convicted must make amends in a manner appropriate to the situation. Violation of my Great Laws are another matter," he added, as if to himself.

David's heart fell to his sandals. "Will there…will there be a trial, sir?"

"That's unclear at present," Zeus said. "You need to be under observation for a period of quarantine. Two months is the average. You'll be sequestered at Olympus Rest until Apollo is satisfied contagion is not an issue, and will participate in your classes remotely. If the spread of dark magic is detected during quarantine the gravity of the charges will require trial by jury to determine guilt or innocence. Restitution, if deemed appropriate, will be determined at that time by a judge. If the accused is found innocent, a course of corrective action for the individual charged will be determined by me." Zeus nodded toward the chess board. "Your move, David."

David was so distracted by thoughts of courtrooms and trials he fell to Zeus' checkmate in a half-dozen moves.

"Go home and pack what you'll need, David. I'll arrange for your transport to Olympus Rest."

Normally they'd shake hands at parting. Instead, David folded his wounded hand over his heart and bowed.

~ * ~

Zeus had seen it on the chess board, whose sole power was revealing the future of his opponent. David would not be convicted. His actions would be mitigated by the relatively short time he'd known he was immortal and not growing up in that culture. Sentencing would include a course in Olympian law with emphasis on Zeus' Laws. There would be another component as well, in consideration of the mortal child David had fathered. Aside from that, permanent loss of his right index finger seemed an appropriate if grim punishment.

If only David had chosen differently. But he hadn't, no more than Zeus had in the early twentieth century when he'd let the City of Mount Olympus fall into ruin because of his own conceit and distress. Zeus the Thunderer, legendary seducer of women mortal and immortal, had been ill-prepared for an aspect of aging he now understood affected many men, a part of nature he'd taken as a personal insult. He'd vented his frustration on everyone around him. If someone else had written the Great Laws, he might well be on trial himself.

TUESDAY, FEBRUARY 24, 2026

Midland, Texas, USA

Cleo, sluggish from an hour of mandatory time management training, studied the preliminary report on monthly R & D budget variances. Employee benefits were substantially over budget, payroll far below. Accounting error? It had to be. She flipped to the footnote page, the crease in her forehead deepening.

She was poised to dial the payroll department when her digital device shrieked. It was a ringtone she hadn't heard in weeks, the opening bars to *Fiddler on the Roof.* Concentration shot, she tapped the green icon, the receiver of an old-style telephone.

"David. Hi."

"Uh. Hi."

He'd never been great at openings but this was lame even for him.

"Haven't heard from you for a while." The rush of adrenaline cautioned her to stay neutral, though she wanted to shout *Where in Tartarus have you been?* Being estranged from him for two and a half months, hard on the heels of being brand new lovers and having their first real fight, had made her wary.

"Yeah. I was kind of on a trip."

"Really? Athens U extended your leave?"

"Uh, not exactly. It's hard to explain."

She counted to ten, waiting for him to say more.

"I'm at work right now," she said. "Pretty busy."

"Oh. Yeah. Sorry, I kind of forgot about the time difference thing."

Would he ever stop sounding like a boy? His conversational quirks used to charm her; now, the three-century age difference between them felt like a yawning gulch.

Cleo assumed her phone voice smile. "I really have to go, David. I'll call when I get a break, okay?"

"Uh, yeah, okay."

She tapped the disconnect icon, pulled her suit jacket from the back of her chair, snuggled it over her shoulders and reached for the variance report.

"Ow!" A narrow red stripe bloomed on her index finger. She pressed down on the paper cut with a tissue and headed for the restroom where a first aid dispenser provided, among other things, bandages. Once she'd bound the paper cut and returned to her desk an irresistible urge prompted her to turn off her wrist device.

At lunchtime Cleo set her Caesar salad at a cafeteria two-top and powered her device back up. He'd sent a text:

Sorry I was vague. It's kind of hard to explain.

A good reason not to call him back.

"Mind if I join you?"

Michael Guy, crisp as ever in his pinstripes.

"Not at all." She gestured for him to sit. He'd chosen the vegan lasagna.

"I'm thinking about adding another yoga class," he said as he lifted his fork.

Yoga was their code word to signal he needed an off-campus meeting.

"Sounds great. What night?"

He finished his mouthful. "The lasagna really isn't up to snuff today. What do you say we make a quick trip to Green World and pick up some smoothies? Better go quick, so we're not late coming back."

His voice didn't sound urgent but his eyes said otherwise. They dumped their leftovers in the nearest bus tub and strode off.

They covered the blocks between corporate and the juice bar so quickly she was panting when they arrived.

"What is it, Michael?" she murmured when they'd passed through the greenery.

"Order first."

They moved to their usual table as the juicer growled to life.

"Fotakis comes back to East Fossil on March third. Headquarters wants both of you in place for the sting. The more secure the Easts feel, the better your chances. The two of you are under orders to become lovers."

Lovers, with Pan? The idea made her sicker than the sight of her Special waiting at the pickup counter. She faked a look at her digital device.

"Look at the time!" She stepped back from the table. "Finance will have my head if I don't get them the budget analysis right away. Gotta run."

Cleo's heels beat a hasty staccato back to East Fossil. She wasn't exactly a prude but lovers, with Pan? She wanted to save the world as much as anyone, was as loyal as anyone to Olympus, Inc., but this was too much. They couldn't make her do this. *Could* they make her do this? David's face, pale with incomprehension, materialized in her mind. Maybe it was the shock of being romantically paired with Pan. Or maybe she still loved David after all.

City of Mount Olympus

David squirmed in his chair, hating himself for it but the way Veronica stared at him, as if she were looking at an insect through a magnifying glass, unnerved him.

Dinner, takeout from Club Dionysus she'd brought to his Olympus Rest quarantine suite, congealed on the dining table. A double portion of meatloaf for him, vegan pasta salad for her, fresh fruit and dark chocolate brownies to share. He was starving, like always, but how were they going to eat if Veronica didn't take off her respirator? His new clumsiness with a fork was problem enough. Why were they even pretending things were normal?

"I need you to tell me what happened, David, from beginning to end."

She'd brought food like a normal big sister but really, she was here to interrogate him, some kind of thing she had to do as CEO of Olympus, Inc., a document for the Court of Twelve, all highly confidential.

"Well. Uhm…"

She looked weird, her hair stuffed under a cap like someone working in an operating room, gloves, too. Personal protective gear. Everyone who came into contact with him while he was in quarantine had to wear it. He felt as human as a toxic landfill.

The unopened bottle of Dionysus Red Blend amidst the entrees taunted him. David let out a breath and started, made it all the way from the beginning through his chess game with Zeus. Veronica listened in silence, her digital device recording it all.

"Let me clarify a couple of points," she said when he'd finished. "You say you saw me in the City of Mount Olympus in nineteen-eighteen. I have to tell you, David, I have no recollection of meeting you then. I don't recall bringing you—*stealing* for you—the spell books from the Athens U library."

"There wasn't much to remember," he said. "I recognized you, of course, but you didn't tell me your name or anything. And you didn't really look like you. I mean, your face and everything, yes, but you seemed really nervous, scared, almost. Like someone was following you, or like you were worried you'd get arrested or something."

"How strange." Her eyes momentarily flitted to the bottle of wine. "And it was Mother who asked me to do this for you?"

"Yeah. Like I said, she was the only one I could think of who would know me back then. I figured she was the only one who might believe me enough to help me."

Veronica's brow furrowed. "It's funny. I have a general recollection of Mount Olympus being in a state of constant construction back then, but not much else."

"I hope I don't get you into trouble, too," he said. Heaven and Earth, what a mess he'd made. Veronica reached across the table and lightly rested a gloved hand on his wounded one.

"I'm sorry, David, about Lucia and the baby, and about your finger. That all must have been awful for you."

"Yeah." His lips curled ruefully. "I guess this is what they mean when they say curiosity killed the cat."

Someone rapped the outer door.

"Sorry to interrupt." It was Apollo, also suited against contagion. "I have the DNA analysis on the sample from field ops," he said to Veronica. "Would you like to hear it now or would you rather stop by my office on the way out?"

Veronica shot David a glance. "Not a word about this, okay?"

David, relieved to be off the hot seat, nodded.

"Go ahead."

"Turns out the oilmen aren't quite men after all," Apollo said. "There's a small percentage of human DNA but the majority is classic chthonic, straight from their home star system. The twist is, about twenty percent of their genetic makeup is that of plants."

Veronica's laser stare locked on Apollo. "Have you told Athena yet?"

"Yes. We're relatively certain the genetic makeup would facilitate the ability to absorb nutrients from both a human type of diet and carbon."

"That would explain their passion for fossil fuels," Veronica said.

Apollo concurred.

"And the eating of human flesh?"

Eating of human flesh? David's eyes landed sickeningly on the meatloaf.

"Possibly part of a religious practice, or maybe just a kink. Questions?"

"Not for now, thanks," Veronica said.

Apollo left them.

"Thank you for your deposition, David," Veronica said, like everything was normal. "I hate to rush off, but I need to get Mother's deposition this evening, too." She glanced around his quarters, complete with home movie theatre, a complicated universal exercise contraption and a small wall-mounted screen with the expansive Olympus Rest menu, available 24/7. "Are they treating you okay here?"

"Yeah, it's good. They even have me set up for classes, remote," he said, nodding toward a laptop on the corner desk.

"Good." She touched his shoulder. "Hey, I'll visit when I can, okay?"

"Yeah," he said. "That'd be nice."

And then he was alone. Six months travelling in the mortal world, weeks out of touch with Cleo, a traumatic trip to the past that had telescoped down from days to mere minutes in real time, and now two months of quarantine. Did he even exist anymore?

David flopped on the sofa, brain numb with the weirdness of it all. Yeah, he definitely existed. Anything that sucked this much had to be real.

Thursday, February 26, 2026

Hera pushed the elevator button for her floor, hyper-aware she was late. She was groggy and short on sleep after Veronica's interrogation last night, compounded by Zeus confronting her earlier in the week about that insignificant episode in 1918, barely worth mentioning except as a matter of historic interest. The offending spell book had never made it back to the Athens U library shelves. She'd dosed it with a charm of her own, to self-immolate the instant David catapulted out of that cursed year and back to now. Decades had passed since she'd thought about it.

For a reason known only to itself the elevator car took half an eternity to arrive and part its polished doors. She loathed tardiness, in herself or anyone else. Time seemed to distort itself to a viscous state, moving thick and slow. No appointments until ten so at least she wasn't keeping anyone waiting.

"Good morning, Gilda," she said to her executive assistant as she passed through the double doors of the Department of Marriage executive suite.

Gilda, whose face was perpetually set with anxiety and an aversion to disorder, sprang from her desk and scurried in front of Hera, blocking the door to her suite.

"Gilda, what in Heaven and Earth—"

"I told her to wait out here until you arrived," Gilda said in a horrified whisper, "but she went right in, said it couldn't wait. And she told me to hold all calls!"

The throbbing Hera thought she'd resolved with aspirin thundered back into her head. "*Who* has committed these blasphemies, Gilda?"

"Ms. Zeta." Gilda cowered when she spoke the name.

Ronnie *again*? What could she possibly want now? "Well, for the love of—at ease, Gilda. I'll take it from here."

At least the ungrateful chit wasn't sitting behind Hera's desk. Her youngest child had the decency to rise when Hera strode to the chair of authority and didn't sit again until Hera was seated. Maybe she was here to ask a favor instead of delivering an admonishment.

"Good morning, Veronica," Hera said with forced cheer. "To what do I owe the pleasure?"

Though Ronnie was skillful with makeup there were dark circles under her eyes. Another spat with her fiancé? They'd been coming thick and fast since the engagement was announced last summer.

"May I close the door, Mother?"

Meek tone. Interesting. Maybe not a spat after all as disagreements with Clifford tended to infuse Veronica with fire.

"As you wish," Hera said, magnanimous with curiosity.

Scurry, close, back to the desk. Silence.

"Well, what is it, Ronnie?" Hera finally asked.

"Mother, we need to talk about a strictly private and confidential matter. I need you to tell me more about nineteen-eighteen."

That wretched year again!

"Delightful. A walk down memory lane, is that what you want? You of course remember our mortal friends were falling as dead as dominoes from their flu."

"I'm not interested in general history, Mother," Veronica snapped. "It's something that happened to me."

The ghost of Chardonnay, the full bottle she'd consumed after last night's deposition, rose in her throat. "What in Heaven and Earth are you talking about?"

"Mother, you coerced me into aiding and abetting you and David in the commission of a crime."

Tears welled in Veronica's eyes. She was and always had been a stickler for pristine ethics, part of what made her a good CEO.

"For Dad's sake, Ronnie, put aside the courtroom drama and calm down."

"But I don't remember any of it, don't you see?" Tears raced down Ronnie's cheeks. "What did you do to me, Mother?"

Tartarus. The petty infractions were adding up. Forgetfulness charms weren't precisely illegal, but they were definitely frowned upon in polite society. She explained her actions to Ronnie awkwardly, leaving out the part about how she'd threatened to stop payment of Ronnie's tuition if she didn't smuggle the restricted books out of the library. Cruel, but effective. When Ronnie arrived home after making the delivery Hera had whisked her into her bedroom and zapped her with twenty-four retroactive hours of forgetfulness.

"So that's why I failed the presentation I'd crammed for all day Friday," Veronica said with wonder, "that special project session for doctoral candidates, the half-day on Saturday. How could you do that to me, Mother? It took me months to regain my confidence."

Hera folded her hands on her desktop, trying her best to look wise. "A small price to pay for an alibi, don't you think, Ronnie?"

In truth she'd been scared to death Ronnie would tell Zeus what had happened, provoking him to come after them both. His male vanity was already in shreds that year. A few episodes of erectile dysfunction had shaken his self-confidence so deeply it nearly took the City of Mount Olympus with it. She'd almost welcomed the tantrum he'd thrown not long after, soaring away from his responsibilities into the arms of some mortal concubine who puffed up his ego and a few other things during a two-year tryst. When he eventually sobered up from his spree and humbly asked Apollo for practical medical advice the city regained vitality. Everyone around him had paid a miserable price during the episode, but it had led to something good and needed: the energy of the city was at last disconnected from Zeus' mojo and was now serviced by a super-computer designed by Hermes.

"Veronica, I hope you can forgive me. Try to imagine how it felt when David, whom I hadn't seen since he was a baby, showed up in the middle of when Dad was—*sick*."

Ronnie nodded soberly, understanding the euphemism.

"I feel terrible for you, and for David, of course, but it was the only solution available at the time."

And what if Zeus had found out about Saul back then? He would have done something far worse to her than the statutory penalty for making mortals immortal, terrible though that was. She turned her thoughts away from the issue, lest she slip and mention it to Ronnie.

It would be Tartarus on skates if Ronnie ever learned the truth about Saul.

Friday, February 27, 2026

New York City, New York, USA

Saul Crispin walked head-on into the biting February wind, shoulders hunched inside his down parka against the cold. An audition awaited him a few blocks away and he had to clear his brain before he got there. David's incredible story—time travel! Even though Saul, himself, was proof of life's paranormal detours he'd never imagined the H. G. Wells kind of stuff was real. He tried not to blame himself for providing the seed that had grown the mighty oak of David's desire to see an old love again. Damn Streisand movie, anyway. All so he could show off some job he'd had as an extra that didn't even pay residuals.

Crazy—crazy! The kid had cut off a finger and incurred who knew what kind of emotional damage from his caper. Had not Saul, himself, told David it's better to leave the past in the past? Mortal or immortal, the most impossible task on earth was trying to persuade someone else to benefit from one's own wisdom and experience.

David wanted to know: if Saul were in his place, what would he do now?

It had been on the tip of his tongue during the call: *They're all dead, David.* But he hadn't the heart to say it. How could David resist learning more, now that he knew his daughter's name, knew about Lucia's cousin the lawyer, and the religious order where the baby was temporarily fostered?

They're all dead, David.

Why hadn't he had the guts to say it?

Merciless gods, it had been a lonely existence, life as the veritable Wandering Jew whose only crime was fathering an illegitimate child. How many lovers, spouses, children, and friends had he loved and lost before he'd closed his heart against the burgeoning pain? A life of exile, living with beings who looked like his own kind, yet weren't. An immortal sentenced to life among mortals. Hera couldn't have chosen a crueler punishment if she'd tried.

At least now he knew David. And Cleo. And Pan Arvus from the CIA training camp, he recalled with a shiver.

He pushed away worry and dread and focused on the job before him. The audition was for one of the father roles in a revival of *The Fantasticks*. He'd been the perfect father onstage many times, not so hot in real life. If he made the cast Saul promised himself he'd cull the libretto for helpful parenting hints.

SATURDAY, FEBRUARY 28, 2026

City of Mount Olympus

It was a relief to request the census records remote. David got the creeps even thinking about the Athens U library, where *F'wrd & Beck tro Tyme* had once resided. Scrolling through computer files in search of Amàlia, Lucia, the Sisters of Saint Claire, and Lucia's cousin Guillem Gomez Barbera was mind-numbing to the extreme but he had to know what happened. He may as well have "Total Loser" tattooed on his forehead if he didn't find out.

Lucia's name appeared first in chronological order. She was listed in the Valencia newspaper of record as dead, November 11, 1918. The day he'd come back to the present.

He blamed himself, cried, tried to convince himself the timing of her death was coincidental. Her small estate was settled by the end of the year by cousin Guillem, including the permanent transfer of the custody of the baby to the nuns. The funds he and Milton had put in trust for her were transferred to the convent at that time.

A century of obituaries, fortunately, was available online. Amàlia had lived to eighty-nine as Sister Leo Maria of the Sisters of Saint Claire.

David leaned heavily back in his chair.

"Wow."

A person of his own creating had lived a long life and died, yet he was more or less a 20-year-old guy. A loss out of order. The baby he'd seen in the window, his daughter, had been in her grave for nearly twenty years.

He closed the files and powered down his laptop. Was there something he should do? She'd been a nun, so there'd be no children, no one to take care of now, no chance an octogenarian grandchild would show up on his doorstep searching for their roots. Still, it was too much to wrap his head around. It didn't feel right to call Saul again. Talk to Milton about it, maybe? Call Cleo? Heaven and Earth, how would he explain this to Cleo? If she even cared.

Tuesday, March 3, 2026

Midland, Texas, USA

Cleo Petra, aka Patricia C. Leo, peered out her open office door. Red, white and blue bunting was draped all over R & D. Earlier, she'd observed baskets of chocolate chip cookies topped with patriotic sprinkles alongside the espresso machine in the break room. A banner welcoming US Representative Pendarvus Fotakis had already been deployed above the reception desk at the main entrance when she'd arrived at work this morning. The congressman the East brothers believed they had bought and paid for was due for his hero's welcome in forty-five minutes.

Grateful she'd been excused from the frenzy of preparation, Cleo sank back into her chair and tried to concentrate on a proposal from a lab developing a giant suction machine that would, supposedly, suck carbon dioxide out of the atmosphere. There was also a new brochure from Marketing to review, a promotion of East Fossil's "extensive" investment in solar energy. Lots of images of attractive people frolicking on sunny beaches and vast arrays of solar panels in alkali deserts. She'd done enough digging, with assistance from Michael Guy, to discover the solar panels belonged to an entirely different organization; East Fossil's holdings of such were limited to the panels atop the East brothers' mansion, installed purely for the reason of receiving a tax credit. The marketing claims were complete and total falsehoods, and Pendarvus Fotakis was the one who would make sure the American public never found out.

According to texts Pan had sent over a secured Olympus, Inc., Department of War connection, East Fossil-backed lobbyists had paid him extensive court during his first two weeks in Washington, D.C. The plan, as handed down from Athena, was for Pan to flagrantly flaunt various bribes, paving the way for charges to be pressed against the fossil fuel mega-conglomerate.

Timing was everything, and the timing was at Pan's discretion. Would he do it today? Cleo felt sick to her stomach just thinking about it.

The cloying fragrance of red, white and blue star lilies tainted the air in her office with a floral fog. An ostentatious display, courtesy of Representative Fotakis, who had leaked to the media he'd taken a shine to a certain transplant to Texas. Their photos, appearing side by side on a cable celebrity gossip show last week, had gone viral. All part of their cover. Now Cleo had a plausible reason to spend time alone with Pan without raising the wrong eyebrows. They had a reservation at the Venezia Restaurant tonight (romantic, by Midland standards), and plans for a long, private conversation in the back of his limo after dinner.

Cleo sneezed and swore under her breath. The lilies irritated her, the cover even more so. Why was she perpetually paired with weird, short guys with wildly curly hair and incredibly strange pasts? David had sent her dozens of vague texts, clearly wanting something but not saying what. The beautiful romance they'd lived and breathed for a few weeks last fall now seemed entirely imagined. After using her intellectual and emotional resources to the fullest to convincingly hire on and work at East, there wasn't much left for daydreams.

She almost—almost—wished David would vanish from her life as abruptly as he'd entered it. A shard of love and longing surfaced long enough to push a single salty drop from her eye.

In half an hour she checked her makeup and reported downstairs. Naturally she had to be part of the welcoming scene, prominently placed in the background where photographers could easily capture her in close proximity to Pan. So much of undercover work was in the storytelling. Thank Heaven and Earth she wasn't required to show overt affection for him in public; ladylike, politically calculated restraint with a touch of fawning was the proscribed behavior for the paramours of elected officials. As subtext, she imagined herself as someone who aspired to be first lady of the United States of America. Her own class-conscious mother, Titania Petra, would be thrilled at the prospect; for Cleo, it was a struggle to get past *Yuck*.

Her main consolation—slowly, but surely, they were getting the goods on the East brothers, the ammunition to interrupt the activities of these earth-endangering fossil fuel exploiters, a major domino to topple in the fight against climate change.

In the lobby she smilingly declined a patriotically decorated chocolate chip cookie that a temp hired for today's event tried to force on her. She hadn't allowed herself to eat one since her first week, when she'd started to wonder if a secret ingredient in the cookies made the majority of East Fossil employees not only fat, but docile. Maybe poor Perkins had been stuffed with the things and, happily inebriated, walked into a waiting oven.

She edged her way through the crowd of hundreds of East Fossil employees. They represented every department and had attained the honor to be here by lottery. Red, white and blue "Fotakis in 2026!" buttons, anticipating his campaign to retain his House seat, adorned every chest. She took her own from her jacket pocket, grimaced in anticipation of the hole it would leave in the tight-woven, lightweight wool when she pinned it to her lapel. One cheerful thought occurred: their mission should be over well before Pan had to bluff his way through the November congressional election.

She arrived near the bunting-draped podium just before a deafening cheer bounced off the lobby floor, ceiling, and walls. The crowd had been choreographed via email:

1. Cheer for arriving limo
2. Those to the left of the entrance shout "Fotakis!" when the Representative enters and makes his way to the podium
3. To the right, alternate "Now!" with "Fotakis!"

Cleo turned her head toward the glass double doors. A shiny black limo with miniature flags of the United States of America and the State of Texas fluttering from all corners pulled neatly to the curb and disgorged the man of the hour, flanked by Maida Steele and three broad-shouldered men in dark suits. Glass doors parted and Pan burst through, hand raised high in greeting, his smile electric.

"Fotakis!"

"Now!"

"Fotakis!"

"Now!"

Some young woman emerged from the crowd and held out a baby for Pan to kiss. He took the baby in his arms, gazed at it in adoration and touched his lips to its cheek.

The crowd's chant dissolved into a rowdy cheer. Pan handed the baby back to its mother and, with both hands, blew the crowd a kiss. The decibel level doubled.

He was way too good at this.

Cleo sought his eyes with false enthusiasm, beamed her practiced smile—practiced to go all the way to her eyes though that was the last thing she felt. A burst of empathy for the significant others of successful politicians surged through her.

At last the cheering crested. Pan shook dozens of hands as his security crew cleared his path to the podium. His eyes met hers, twinkled as he mouthed the word "darling." He settled easily behind the podium (a custom-made one to compensate for his short stature) and launched into a speech touting Fossil Fuels Now, Fossil Fuels Forever.

~ * ~

The Venezia Restaurant. Pan rolled his eyes as he and Cleo passed under the awning and through the front doors. Anyone but a Texan would have called it Venezia Ristoranti.

He'd learned a lot about Texans from the ones he'd met the past few weeks, the ones who continually and ardently pushed the big oil agenda to him in D.C. Some of their characteristics he admired—the unabashed confidence, the proclivity for living larger than life, the vintage Cadillacs ornamented with bovine horns. But some of their bravado and swagger, the part that insisted on Texicanizing everything they touched, was just plain tacky.

Maybe these behaviors were affectations, like playing a part? Easy to relate to, today in particular when the Lone Star State paparazzi elbowed each other out of the way to photograph his actions, catch his every word and mood.

Cleo was holding up well. Elegance in bearing served her perfectly —excellent posture, shoulders squared but relaxed. She didn't hunch or round her shoulders in deference to being half a head taller than he was, which, he realized, made him stand a little bit taller.

The restaurant itself belied the Texicanization of its name. They were shown to a corner table draped with white linen, not so different from Club Dionysus, the go-to romantic eatery in the City of Mount Olympus.

The table was set for two. Maida Steele and the three secret service men sat at a four-top nearby. The men were silent, bodies tense, scanning the room for threats. Maida tapped her digital device and scowled like she always did. Not the ideal circumstances to pursue a budding romance, but such was a politician's life. His flight back to D.C. left at midnight.

The evening was filled with *Sirs* and *Mademoiselles* and considerable pride on the part of the sommelier about the award-winning wine list. Pan bluffed his way through, happy to hide in Pendarvus Fotakis instead of facing the challenge of sincerely relating to the woman sharing his table. Heaven and Earth, how long had it been since he'd been on a date?

Historically, back when he'd been an unrepentant drunk and proud practitioner of lewd innuendo, whichever lady in question would ultimately
walk out on him. A slip up like that now would have him up on House
ethics charges before they could bust him for illegal activities with the
Easts. He deferred to Cleo's choice of wine (a gold medal Merlot) and
ordered himself a Perrier.

"Ms. Leo," Pan said when the sommelier brought their order and
Cleo pronounced the sample he poured her as good, "I'm sick to death
of talking about legislation and regulations and budget committees." He
raised his glass of mineral water to her. "Right now, I'd like nothing
better than to talk about you."

This was a pre-determined phrase to initiate a conversation about
the timing of their sting. She touched her glass to his and laughed.

"I don't know if there's much to tell, Congressman Fotakis."

"Pendarvus, please. Or Pen, if you'd rather."

He threw in a little eye sizzle for good measure. Two of his security team were operatives through Olympus, Inc., but the third one,
Harrelson, was American Secret Service, someone Maida Steele had
arranged to add credibility to Pan's cover.

"Thank you, Pen," Cleo said, wrinkling her nose in a way that
conveyed it would be a struggle for her to do so.

"Good. And I'll call you Patsy."

"Patricia," she immediately shot back. "No one's called me Patsy
since my parents died."

"Sorry, Patricia, I didn't realize. You're very young to have lost
them both."

She told her cover story about their accidental death, the signal
for him to tell her when the East Fossil scandal ball would start rolling.

"I still have Mom," he said, though in truth he'd been such an ugly
baby none of the Pleiades would admit which one was his mother. "Dad
died when I was eleven, though."

March eleventh, the day someone would discover the evidence
that would lead to his indictment for bribery.

"That must have been hard on you, and your mother. Did she ever
remarry?"

"Yes. She met my stepfather when I was seventeen."

On March seventeenth Cleo would contact the Department of
Justice and alert them to a startling discovery at East Fossil. Their point
of no return.

"She didn't accept his proposal at first," Pan continued. "Too afraid he'd die on her, too, I think, but he still roams the earth, healthy as an ox. He has a kind of a glow to him."

Cleo nodded. The stepfather stood for Olympus, Inc., Pan's assurance Athena's operatives would be close at hand, ready to protect them as needed when—not if—things got rough. Plus a reminder she could identify friendly agents by their purple auras.

ChuRSDaY, MaRCh 5, 2026

Mariana Trench

Pablo, supported at the negotiation meeting in Poseidon's arms, fought the urge to put himself down for a nap. Man, the Old Dudes were hard to talk to. They were super-intelligent beings but their language was hampered by a limited vocabulary that required a string of modifiers to describe things. If they'd ever seen a zebra they would have called it something like "Black and white striped African equine with bristly mane that grazes and is eaten by lions." What Pablo had anticipated would take a week to ten days to discuss, plan and implement was now in its sixth week.

The Old Ones, themselves, were very big on global health and a clean environment. Their own bodies were quite sensitive to pollution. He'd seen the protective suits they wore when they ventured beyond their sealed-in city at the bottom of the Mariana Trench, dull instead of shiny like the wetsuits Poseidon favored, gigantic onesies that made the wearers resemble something commonly found in sewage systems. In spite of the unattractive appearance that suggested inertia, they could swim as fast as torpedoes.

Their military chief, Throqutp, had the floor this morning. After he'd dispensed with two hours of required rituals and greetings he got to the heart of the matter.

"Star-fingered and outside our laws mutations of fish frog mountains of sinister destruction and food enough to choke a city rip and pull and pump from up above us dirt-making warmth and ways for wheeled motion," Throqutp growled. "From us but not us spoil pure in the sky and in the water and in the ground. I find them on this dot of flat dried pulp." He touched his fingertip to a spot on the vast map of the world that covered the war room table. The spot was in the northwest quadrant of a weirdly shaped patch in the United States of America's southwest, what looked like a boot stuck on top of a chicken breast with the wing still attached.

Throqutp raised his other hand into the air, fist clenched. "There must we go with arms and legs through water and arms and legs through sky. To find star-fingered and outside our laws mutations of fish frog mountains of sinister destruction and food enough to choke a city. To bind those from us but not us and end spoil pure in the sky and in the water and in the ground."

Pablo looked up. Poseidon's bearded chin sagged above him.

"Pssst! Wake up!"

The chin rose abruptly. "Just resting my eyes," Poseidon grunted.

"They have a plan, man."

Throqutp shot Pablo a disgusted glare. "Miniscule and pink alarm-raising quarter relation not to speak. More."

Pablo shrugged. "Sorry."

"Move with arms and legs through water when night orb next full round. Twenty-eight trips around day orb."

"We're waiting to take down the bad guys for an entire *month*?" Pablo said, unable to contain himself. Life under the trench had its charms, but four more weeks in this place?

Throqutp leaned down across the table, so close his carthy breath filled Pablo's nostrils. "Twenty-eight trips around day orb, miniscule and pink alarm-raising quarter relation. So it must be." He straightened up to address the assembly, two dozen commanders in all. "Then to start from here, with arms and legs through water and arms and legs through sky, to Midland, Texas."

WEDNESDAY, MARCH 11, 2026

Washington, D.C., USA

Pan had taken pains to decorate his congressional office. Red-flag window-dressing was essential. The furniture was all new, the latest and sleekest and most expensive available (Maida Steele had a genius for spending money). One original Remington hanging on the wall was questionable in terms of ethical propriety, the second one blatant. He would, of course, tell the ethics panel they were merely on loan from a donor, that he really didn't glean any pecuniary benefit from the paintings, just wanted to show the proper level of Texas pride to folks who visited him in the nation's capital. Which donor would that be? Gosh, he'd have to get back to them on that as it had slipped his mind.

The diamond cufflinks? He'd had those for years, college graduation gift from an indulgent grandmother. Then why had one of his staff noticed them being delivered to Congressman Fotakis's office in a pale blue Tiffany & Co. box? He'd sent them out for cleaning, naturally.

What about the photos and eyewitness accounts from several members of the press who'd seen Congressman Fotakis being wined and dined and accepting a fat envelope in the men's room of D.C.'s most prestigious restaurant since his recent return from Texas?

You know how congressmen all look alike. I have my appointment diary with me. You can see for yourself I wasn't there.

Sleazy cheating lying weasel. Pan grinned. And, oops, a well-placed trail of documentation breadcrumbs would lead the ethics panel straight to the door of East Fossil Fuels.

Tuesday, March 17, 2026

Midland, Texas, USA

High noon. Cleo rolled back from her desk, caught a downward elevator and walked briskly out the main door of East Fossil Fuels in spite of her heels and pencil skirt. She quickened her pace over the blocks to Green World Juice Works. Once she cleared the potted plants she punched the recently programmed button on her digital device. One ring. Two. Three.

You've reached the United States Department of Justice. Our regular business hours are Monday through Friday...

She signaled Kari the juicer to make her current favorite and listened to the menu, heart thudding under her linen blazer. *To report a crime, please press...*

A twelve-ounce glass of Strawberry-Mango Delight was delivered to her table. She waved her credit card at the server. The young woman took a small oblong device out of her half-apron pocket and ran the strip down a recessed track. The device made a contented *blip*.

For white collar crimes, please press...

Antitrust? Likely, but her evidence didn't support that particular transgression. *For intellectual property crime*—who could say? *For public corruption.* Bingo! *Please press three.*

You've reached the United States Department of Justice.

Instead of screaming, Cleo drew a long sip through her straw. Surely they hadn't bounced her back to the main menu?

To report suspicion of the white collar crime (pause) *public corruption* (spoken by a different automated voice) *please call the Federal Bureau of Investigation Local Corruption Hotline or submit an FBI Tip online at...*

She set her smoothie on the marble tabletop and furiously queried for the FBI website, wondering how many crimes went unreported due to bureaucratic red tape. More waiting, more button pushing. Her lunch break was nearly over when she was connected to the El Paso field office.

"Bribery of a member of congress?" A female voice, someone who'd identified herself as Special Agent Jamie Garcia.

"That's right." Seven minutes late already and she needed another ten to get back to her office. If anyone asked she'd say she'd been detained at an off-campus subcontractor meeting. HR had access to her networked scheduling app. Hopefully no one would check. Cleo silently berated herself for not putting in a dummy appointment as a contingency.

"I'd like to keep this communication brief, Ms. Leo. You know Beal Park?"

Cleo split her screen view and quickly typed in the name. "I can find it."

They arranged to meet at 6:30 that evening. "Dress for a brisk walk. I'll be at the skateboard park in a turquoise jogging suit."

~ * ~

The sunny day had cooled substantially. Cleo shivered in her jeans and windbreaker, the one she'd purchased in Seattle last fall at David's insistence. She'd arrived a few minutes early. The kids using the skateboard park, mostly boys with two girls, all of them in their middle teens, she guessed, soared up and down walls executing potentially neckbreaking flips at the peak. Amazing what mortals could do.

At precisely 6:30pm a wiry woman in a turquoise track suit, her dark hair slicked back in a ponytail, ambled into view. Cleo joined her at a nearby bench, both of them faking prior acquaintance with their relaxed body language. They fell into a series of leg stretches.

"Let's do our usual route," Garcia said and headed toward the fishing pond. They passed in front of a keystone sign, painted with the names of Midland Parks and Recreation donors. East Fossil Fuels topped the list. Cleo glanced around, searching for objects that might harbor surveillance cameras. Looking back, she noted tall light poles surrounding the skateboard park. Would someone at East know what El Paso special agents looked like? Had they been spotted already? The sun started to set.

"Fotakis," Garcia said, like the name tasted bad. "We've had an eye on him, like we do with anyone new to Congress. Pretty much came out of nowhere from what we can tell. You sleep with him?"

"What? No." She should have expected that, shouldn't have sounded so shocked. "Not yet," she amended.

Special Agent Garcia snorted. "You in love with him?"

"Not yet." It was funny, though. In the restaurant, when they'd been playing their parts, she'd noticed some of the same bad boy suavity in Pan that had tickled her in her former boss, his dad, Hermes. And, like Hermes, he was lighting smart. Great at thinking on his feet and why wouldn't he be, after a career of getting himself out of trouble?

"Tempted, though, by the fame and the power," Garcia said as if it were a fact. Cleo fuzzed out her vision to get a better look at the special agent's aura. Pristine mortal pink, not a fleck of purple, or, thank Heaven and Earth, that sludgy corona unique to the Brothers East.

"But not the corruption," Cleo said. "I'm sure you've seen pictures of us together? I think every photojournalist in Texas followed us to the restaurant that night."

"Oh yeah. We watch the regular news outlets and social media, too. Lots of talk about running Fotakis for president in 2028 with you for his first lady. If we bring him down, the people who rally around him now will shred him. That worry you?"

"I haven't done anything," Cleo said, planting a trickle of fear in her voice.

"You work at East. Got anything on them, besides your suspicion they're bribing your boyfriend?"

Cleo's face flushed. "A friend of mine in Legal said something about shell corporations but he didn't go into detail."

"Another boyfriend." Garcia said, again like it was a fact.

"No! He's a *yoga* instructor." Heaven and Earth, how did people with real secrets to hide make it through this kind of bullying without a meltdown? "I'm trying to do the right thing, Agent Garcia," she said in a prim tone. "You're not making it easy."

"None of this is easy, Ms. Leo," she admonished. "It sounds like Fotakis is our best lead. Congressional oversight requested a dossier on him last week, as I'm sure you're aware."

Good to know their carefully choreographed non-encoded video call over the weekend had been captured by the FBI, as they'd hoped. Pan had insisted he was being subjected to a witch-hunt; Cleo had portrayed shock, followed by a vow of her undying belief in him and her unwavering support.

"The ethics chair set up a hearing for next week," Garcia continued. "The more we can get on Fotakis, the sooner this circus will end. Are you willing to work with us?"

"Yes, of course. That's why I called you."

"Good. Doesn't it seem to you, Ms. Leo, that this weekend would be an excellent time to jet to D.C. and do what you can to reassure the congressman?"

Cleo stopped walking, as Patricia C. Leo would if she suspected something questionable loomed on the horizon.

"What do you mean by reassure?"

Agent Garcia spun around and walked back to her.

"I mean, Ms. Leo, in the interest of taking him down and, incidentally, saving yourself from prosecution as rendering aid to a target for federal corruption charges, will you sleep with Pendarvus Fotakis?"

SUNDAY, MARCH 22, 2026

City of Mount Olympus

"Ooof."

David Bernstein set aside a weighty mortal-authored civil engineering text, rolled his shoulders until they cracked and lunged toward the mini-fridge at his Olympus Rest quarters in search of a caffeinated drink. A single can of Mount Oly Java Bomb, the brand favored by Athens U graduate students, remained of the six pack he'd requested yesterday. He popped the tab and guzzled, tossed the empty in the recycle with a *tink* against the others.

A Comprehensive History of Geotechnical Engineering had just about finished him off, but Professor Bumby required it for his "The Myth of Mortal Engineering Infallibility" seminar, to be discussed in a group (David to participate via a video call) next Monday. The thing weighed as much as the *Riverside Shakespeare* he'd languished through as an undergrad, when he was still under the illusion that he was just another bored young mortal guy who couldn't figure out his major.

The caffeine pumped new energy through his veins but his neck, his shoulders—too much hunching over the desk.

He fished his digital device out of his jeans pocket—no need to wear a toga in isolation—and slouched over the small screen to surf the net.

The Seattle public radio station was a fun browse. He scrolled through the KUOW website, regional news first, which mostly had to do with the college basketball tournament and yeah, he was a fan but had kind of fallen out of the habit. He tapped the National Public Radio button and linked to their website. The top feature was on the economy, blah, blah, scroll, scroll, scroll—Whoa!

What a picture! A total babe in a red sequined dress with a plunging neckline, and plenty of leg showing through the high side-slit. She was getting out of a limo, some short idiot in a tux taking her hand.

"Damn."

Cleo. She'd never looked so hot. The short idiot looked one Tartarus of a lot like Pan. *Freshman Congressman to Answer for Ethics* shouted the headline under the photo. David clicked on the irresistible bait, eyes devouring the article about new Texas Congressman Pendarvus Fotakis.

Fotakis denies all wrongdoing and proclaims the upcoming ethics hearing a politically motivated witch-hunt. He was spotted with Ms. Patricia C. Leo, employee of East Fossil Fuels of Midland, Texas, Saturday evening at the Sofitel Hotel on D.C.'s Lafayette Square.

Patricia C. Leo—hah! David queried the hotel website, every morsel of information over-the-top romantic, and French. This was Cleo's work? This was why she'd barely replied to his texts for a month, to make the news looking so...

David scrolled to the top of the article, eyes glued to the photo. His heart thundered in his chest, not only on account of heavy-duty caffeine. Whatever she was doing looked absolutely crazy but with Pan there, too, it had to be authorized through Olympus, Inc. Heaven and Earth, he'd been a fool to pick that fight with her back in December, and now...

If he ever got her back he'd never, ever do that again.

He returned to his home screen and pulled up her contact page.

"Hey," he typed. "Wow."

WEDNESDAY, MARCH 25, 2026

Washington, D.C., USA

Pan settled into his slick yet personable Pendarvus Fotakis demeanor during the limo ride to 425 3rd Street S.W., Suite 1110, home to the Office of Congressional Ethics. It was a striking building, nine or ten floors in white with plenty of glass. He hoped his hearing would be conducted in one of the corner units with long, tall windows that met at the angle. As the patron of shepherds, he worked best when close to nature.

His equally slick lawyer, recommended through discreet channels by the East brothers, sat on the backward-facing bench seat, designer briefcase balanced on his knees.

"The most important thing to remember, Congressman Fotakis, is to not give the board any additional information when you answer their questions. Start with a simple Yes or No and make *them* work to get to the point."

"Understood." After the first few questions he'd open up like a sieve. Pan patted his own briefcase, an insanely expensive brand that was even more coveted in D.C. circles than his lawyer's briefcase. Inside was the loan agreement for the Remingtons that failed to specify the paintings would be returned to East Fossil Fuels when Fotakis left office, in direct violation of House Ethics Committee requirements. Bank statements? He had those, too. Even a financial dunce couldn't miss the transfers between the campaign money market account and his personal checking. He blew on his right diamond cufflink and polished it on the lapel of his bespoke Italian suit. Payment for this showed up on his personal credit card statement. A smart investigator would notice that no travel expenses to Italy appeared between the beginning and end statement dates.

Out of the kindness of their hearts they loaned me their corporate jet for the final fitting. Truly no big deal.

He grinned. His nonchalance would tie the Board in knots and ensure a referral of the investigation to the House Committee on Ethics. If Cleo hadn't flown back to Midland on the Sunday night redeye, he'd take her out to dinner tonight at Marcel's and put it on his office credit card.

So hang me for living the American Dream! If he could fit that remark into his testimony he'd make all the national conservative talk shows.

Pan's grin deepened. Cleo had been a champ last weekend, flashing her perfect teeth and stupendous cleavage at the cameras whenever she got out of the limo. When they retired to their suite at the Sofitel, reserved specially for her visit, she'd promptly retired to the dressing room to change out of what she called her clown clothes (that red sequined evening gown would pack the stands of any circus) and into sweats, ready to review the details of their next public appearance. They slept in the same king bed to keep the maids from talking but Cleo's sweats remained firmly in place. Okay by Pan. Cleo wasn't his type—too confident, too urban. His personal kink was peasant girls, especially ones who did macramé.

MONDAY, MARCH 30, 2026

City of Mount Olympus

Persephone read the text from Demeter with trepidation. Somehow, the message had overridden the block she'd put on Mother's account. Heavy frost in a prime cherry growing valley that straddled the US and Canadian border had compromised the 2026 crop and she was commanded to report to work.

The thought of leaving her topside nest and working outdoors was appealing, given daily bouts of nausea, particularly in the mornings. But what about the earlier threats Hades had made? She tried to discount his digital rants as hollow, but what if he really did have "agents abroad," stalking her, poised to drag her kicking and screaming back to the Underworld?

And why was it that, outside of Frey, no one ever asked her *nicely* to do something? All the major changes in her life, prior to her affair at the conference, had been conducted with ham-fisted force. It went all the way back to Hades' courtship. At least then he'd had the sensitivity to lure her with a field of enchanted flowers before he'd abducted her—abducted her! —when she was a mere, innocent girl. Mother had done nothing to save her, had stood by absorbed in her own grief over her stolen child on the one hand but, at the same time, shrugged it off as an inevitable event in the lives of immortals. It was simply what happened to females.

A dark thought occurred. Mother had sent the text to help Hades, to flush her own daughter out of a safe space and into the greater world where she'd be vulnerable to attack!

Nausea sent Persephone charging to the bathroom. When the upheaval was complete she rinsed her mouth, suddenly starving for Kalamata olives. Her fingers plunged into the nearest jar in the mini fridge and scooped out a pitted dozen. They paired nicely with squares of 85% cacao chocolate.

Thus sated, common sense returned. No, Hades had not hired "agents" to stalk her, he was too cheap for that. No, Mother was not in league with Hades. She'd be thrilled to have her beloved daughter topside. Persephone checked the weather report Demeter had reposted. It wasn't a hoax. The mild winter had ended just ten days ago. It wasn't at all uncommon for a warm winter to be followed by an unusually hard frost.

Persephone shrugged into the mantle of duty. It would take more time than usual to fly to the Okanagan Valley. She didn't dare use warp speed for fear of harming the baby.

She left the philodendron with a neighbor, tucked three days of emergency provisions into her toga pockets, slid open the balcony door and balanced on the railing. Her bump had grown but the baby was still so small it required only a little extra effort to get airborne. Persephone soared into the blue cloud-flecked sky, bearing northwest.

Elysium, the Underworld

In the mirror-surfaced pond Persephone glided into the sky, radiating bounty from every molecule of her being. Joy in the baby, Freya sensed, but also joy in returning to work. Perhaps her protégé could use another gift. A simple shifting spell transferred a portion of the agricultural goddess's fertility to her tears.

Okanagan Valley, Washington, USA

Adjusting for the time difference, after many hours of flight Persephone arrived in the Okanagan Valley at 11am, March 30, two hours after she'd left Mount Olympus. Though she longed for a nap, check-in time at the motel Demeter had booked on the corporate account—a cozy Ma and Pa concern made up of a dozen rustic tourist cabins—was three hours in the future. She circled a large acreage orchard under a milky sun and dark, overcast sky. Why hadn't she thought to bring a shawl?

Pale blossoms crowned the cherry trees. Surely the freeze had damaged them? It was too sad to think about, trees bereft of yield. Sorrow leaked from her eyes, sprinkling the orchard below.

Color rippled through the trees like wildfire—the burst of green shooting from branches, followed by round, green fruit that swiftly swelled and rounded and reddened. Surely she was seeing things? Persephone circled down.

The fragrance of ripe cherries filled her nostrils. She laughed out loud. The air was warm now. Had the rapid movement of fruit and tree molecules generated heat?

A voice shouted in the distance, faint but the direction it came from clear. Peering past a sea of trunks she spied the pink aura of a mortal man. He gestured wildly with one arm, the hand of the other jamming a thin black rectangle against his ear. She landed and crept amongst the tree trunks, close enough to hear him yell "Don't argue with me, Mike, I'm telling you the cherries are in and they're *ripe*! Call the unemployment office and the homeless shelter and see who we can get out here. We gotta pick these babies now and get 'em in storage." There was a pause. "What the hell do you mean, am I *on* something? Get out here and look for yourself if you don't believe me, but make the damn calls first or you're fired."

Persephone scurried to the edge of the orchard and took to the air. She had a certain skill for moving among mortals undetected but if the trees were suddenly flooded with pickers—in a crowd, one or more of them might have enough of a sixth sense to spot her.

Bacon. There was a diner down the road from the motel that served breakfast all day. She'd get some bacon on board before reporting to Mother, but how would she explain what had happened? Demeter was expecting a frost damage report, not the heaviest harvest in years, and three months early!

Surely the damage would be limited to this one orchard? After she'd eaten sufficient bacon she'd fly the entire length of the valley and assess every orchard. But bacon, first, and thank Heaven and Earth for Frey's debit card.

~ * ~

After a long afternoon of cruising up and down the cherry growing region that reached from Washington State, USA, well into British Columbia, Canada, Persephone, replete with bacon to the point of bursting, had seen it for herself. Vans from local television and radio stations from every city within two hundred miles choked the roadways. People dressed in dungarees and thick shirts swarmed among the cherry trees, climbed ladders, groaned under the weight of overflowing buckets and aprons and crates. Semi-truck flatbeds pulled in easily and pulled out grinding their gears under the weight. Every warehouse with excess capacity in the Pacific Northwest was on standby to receive delivery.

Equipment rental trucks from Spokane, WA, and Vancouver, B.C., brought lights attached to stanchions so harvest could continue through the night.

Aside from observing, there was nothing she could do.

At the motel, Persephone rolled onto the sagging Queen bed with the television remote and a bag of cheddar flavored pretzels.

"—unmitigated agricultural disaster," a local news anchor said.

"Or an agricultural miracle, depending on how you look at it," the perky cohost said.

Persephone surfed the channels, growing more depressed with each tap of the button. One of the national channels had picked up the story and was running with it.

"—believed to be collateral damage of climate change, according to our expert, Dr. Margi Parsons, agricultural epidemiologist. Dr. Parsons, to what do you attribute—"

The digital device on Persephone's wrist vibrated, as it had every minute or so since she'd been in the C-store buying the pretzels. The newest message showed at the top of the screen. One word. *Report!*

From Mother, of course. But Heaven and Earth, she was so very tired. Persephone typed in five letters as her eyelids drooped.

Sorry.

She rolled on her side, pulled the quilted synthetic bedspread decorated with a hunting motif over her bone-weary body and powered off the wrist device. If only it were this easy to turn off the incredible power of fertility she'd acquired, a power, she now feared, that could disrupt food supply chains around the world.

tuesday, march 31, 2026

Midland, Texas, USA

Cyril B. East paced in front of the east-facing expanse of glass, bulb-tipped fingers laced behind his ponderous back.

"Eddy, Eddy, Eddy," he said, shaking his head in disbelief. "Our Congressman Fotakis is proving a grave disappointment. I shudder to say so, but I believe we've purchased ourselves a pig in a poke instead of an elected official."

Edwin B. East, dressed identically to his twin brother in a mournful suit of dark gray, languished on a loveseat, hands pressed to his heart.

"It cuts me to the quick, Cyril, it truly does. We've been more than generous with him. The campaign contributions. Our precious Remingtons. All to an imbecile who seems intent on throwing himself under a political bus and us along with him."

"It's only a matter of time, Eddy." Cyril thrust his hands skyward with an authority any tragedian invoking a thunderstorm would envy. "He has not named us yet, but he will name us soon."

Edwin extracted a handkerchief from his breast pocket and dabbed the moisture from his forehead. "We've been extraordinarily careful with our paper trail, dear brother," he said. "There is at least a grain of hope that the mongrel dogs of ethics oversight won't trace him back to us. Think of all the clever shell companies we established with Fitzgerald, in Legal."

Cyril stopped mid-pace and lowered his hands to a prayerful position. "Ah, dear old Fitzgerald. He was delicious, rest his conniving soul."

"Indeed, my dear. As Mother always said, it's best to eat the evidence."

Gloom lifted while they shared a prolonged snigger.

"Yes, Mother always knew best," Cyril said, dabbing his eyes with a handkerchief identical to Edwin's. "Which brings me to the matter of Ms. Patricia C. Leo. I am sorry to say that, through her close affiliation with Congressman Fotakis, I no longer have the confidence I felt when we first hired her."

A flicker of disagreement sparked in Edwin. "Are you sure,

brother? She's been a force of nature in R and D since her first day on the job. Three times the efficiency and effectiveness of our late, lamented Mr. Perkins." Besides, Ms. Leo was too lean to qualify for their usual method of employee termination.

"There may be merit in what you say," Cyril said grudgingly, "but she'll be ever so useful in resolving our current difficulty. Fotakis is enamored with her. Perhaps Ms. Leo needs to meet with life-threatening danger. Kidnapping, for example, would make the proper dramatic statement. What do you think our purchased friend would give in exchange for her safety—sealed lips, perhaps?"

Edwin tapped his bulbous fingertips together, considering. "Abduction," he said. "Tomorrow night, under the full moon, would be ideal."

WeDNeSDay, April 1, 2026

Cleo walked briskly in the deepening dark. Her rendezvous with Special Agent Garcia had run late. She'd missed her return bus connection and caught the next one available, its closest stop over a mile from home, near East Fossil headquarters. Already it was past 9pm. She pushed aside the discomfort of being in that neighborhood, all but abandoned after business hours, and focused her thoughts on the R and D proposal she needed to review one more time before she went to bed.

Garcia was unhappy with her. During Cleo's D.C. trip, armed with instructions to seduce Pan and thus get him to talk about his financial arrangement with the Easts, Cleo had methodically cleared their suite at the Sofitel of FBI video and audio devices, suspicious they'd want blackmail materials if the information they sought wasn't forthcoming. Cleo had played her innocence to the hilt when Garcia questioned her about this. Garcia pointed out she wasn't born yesterday. More and more, Cleo felt sick to her stomach.

Pan, in contrast, thrived on undercover work and improvised scheming. He'd been absolutely brilliant before the Office of Congressional Ethics, as anyone who followed the publicly available transcripts could see, alternately charming them and taking the Fifth. Cleo, herself, could hardly wait to get back to the normalcy and predictability of whatever desk or lab job awaited her when she returned to Olympus, Inc.

The full moon, rising, threw shadows of leafing trees onto the sidewalk. Still a long way to go. Something about the tree shadows shifted her senses to high alert. She turned on her heel and strode in the direction of Green World Juice Works. Better to find safety and, from there, figure out how to get home. The striped awning came in view. Sparse security lights left the shop interior dim but both Michael Guy and Kari, the juicer, had assured her an Olympus, Inc., agent would be there 24/7.

"Oof." Someone grabbed her around the midsection from behind, knocking the wind out of her. A cloth bag slipped over her head.

Think.

Cleo spun 180 degrees and raised her arm straight up, rapidly lowering the heel of her hand in the plausible vicinity of her attacker's nose. She connected with something that yielded a satisfying yelp. Victory evaporated as the sides of the bag rolled down past her waist. A rope zipped around the outside, lashing her arms to her sides under the cloth.

"Valiantly done, Ms. Leo." The shrill voice with a mild wheeze was unmistakably that of an East. "I'm afraid you gave poor Cyril a bit of a shiner, but no matter, we've got you now."

She sensed their ponderous masses flanking her, rubbery paws grabbing her elbows and propelling her forward.

"Don't be afraid, Ms. Leo, we do not intend to harm you. But we would like to have a friendly chat with your paramour, Congressman Fotakis. We have his number on our speed dial. As soon as we get you settled perhaps you'd be so kind as to call him and see if he can spare us a word?"

Washington, D.C., USA

The full moon shone down on the postcard perfect features of Washington, D.C., iconic configurations of marble glowing in the unseasonably warm April night. Pan surveyed it all from the comfort of an Adirondack chaise lounge, craft beer in hand, another day of being a charismatic political villain tucked joyfully under his belt. What amused him the most: the number of women wanting to sleep with him increased in direct proportion to the number of calls for him to resign. Pendarvus Fotakis was the man America loved to hate.

He tipped his bottle to the moon. "Cheers."

The sublime moment was cut short by his chirping cell phone. Pan sighed. Probably another well-preserved middle-aged socialite angling for an amorous rendezvous. Work, work, work.

The screen showed a Midland number.

A rush of foreboding hit when he picked up.

"Fotakis here."

"Pen?"

Cleo's anxious voice pulled him to the edge of his chair.

"Patricia? What's wrong? Where are you?"

"Someone wants to talk to you," she said in a rush.

"Congressman Fotakis." The sickening wheeze of one of his two foremost patrons wobbled across the relays. "My brother and I are none too pleased with your behavior. As a precaution against disgracing your-self further, we've insisted Ms. Leo stay with us as our honored guest."

Sweat slicked Pan's palms. "What do you want, East?"

"Call off whatever incrimination game you intend to play, Congressman Fotakis, and Ms. Leo will remain perfectly safe."

The connection died.

Pan hit the pre-programmed button to Olympus, Inc., Department of Diplomacy. Nearly 8am in the City of Mount Olympus. With luck—

"Chief speaking." Athena.

Green letters flashed on Pan's screen: secured connection complete.

"Chief, this is Goatherd. We're in play."

An owl hooted in the background. "At ease, Tim," Athena mut-tered. "Goatherd, how is the tribe?"

In encoded language Pan briefed her about the hostage call.

"The herdsman will be sent," Athena responded. Michael Guy would be sent to assess the situation and, hopefully, break Cleo free. Three beeps sounded. "The horn is sounded. Out."

In or Near Midland, Texas, USA

Cleo Petra, left alone, studied her surroundings. Solidly built walls of stone. One barred window near the top showed pale stars, too faint to identify as constellations given the full moon.

Her eyes adjusted to the dungeon, the atmosphere laden with chilled air and the odor of damp earth. A crude wooden cot with a straw tick mattress. No blanket, no source of heat or light. Plastic buckets sat in opposite corners, one filled with water, the other empty. All the comforts of home.

Think.

If she saw the moon descending, then the window faced west. The bag over her head had prevented her from seeing where the East brothers had taken her. She'd tried to follow the directional changes and estimate the elapsed time, a technique she'd read about during her brief stint at the training facility. Being assaulted, bagged and turned around several times in both directions before the brothers had loaded her into the vehicle—lushly padded bench seat and the scent of leather interior —had disoriented her. She'd listened for telltale sounds. The hum of a factory? Music spilling into the streets from a club? Subtle changes from coming and going through pools of light, faintly discernable through the tight-woven cloth of the bag, eventually gave way to darkness. They'd left the city; beyond that, she had not a clue.

Cleo stretched on the cot. Straw dust tickled her nose. They'd taken her shoulder bag, of course. All they'd find were the issued pieces of fake I.D., a lipstick, a packet of tissues. The key to her condo. She'd hidden her cell phone there. The secured line to Olympus, Inc., was password protected, but...

Backup. Pan would call Olympus, Inc., headquarters. Michael Guy would be alerted. Wouldn't he?

Cleo curled into the fetal position to collect her body's warmth, exhausted in spite of adrenaline overload, and drifted into a fitful sleep. When she awoke, moonlight slanted through the window, casting shadows of the bars on the flagstone floor. Out of a sleepy haze her ears strained toward a sound. Metal hinges, heavy ones, swinging. Her eyes landed on the door to her cell, solid planks with a grate inserted near the top. The hinge sound came through there, also the dragging fall of huge unhuman feet. Something lighter sliding over stone. Shoes on flagstones?

"Mr. Guy," shrilled a voice, "Cyril and I are so very disappointed in you."

"We kindly overlooked the yoga and the bleached stripe in your hair," the other East said, "but creeping around our home in the dead of night, Mr. Guy? I'm afraid that can't be excused."

A nearby door thundered shut. The dual heavy treads retreated.

"Edwin, my dear, these humans are too much to bear. I simply must get some rest before we dispatch them."

"Too true, brother. And I confess to being famished but simply don't have the vim for a cookout."

Cyril yawned. "Later, my dear. Later."

SUNDAY, APRIL 5, 2026

"Come now, Ms. Leo, you haven't touched today's cream puffs."

Edwin's words wheedled through the door grate. Near a low opening at the bottom of the door a silver platter laden with chocolate-iced pastries languished.

"I couldn't possibly eat another bite, Mr. East," she replied amicably, though the discomfort of dungeon life made her want to scream at him. When the brothers had returned to interrogate them the day after they were kidnapped they'd remarked to each other that their captives were unappealingly bony.

"Keeping Fotakis quiet and discovering the root of Mr. Guy's escapade is one thing, Edwin, but the rest of it is barely worth the trouble," Cyril had observed.

That's when the intense feeding began. Waffles for lunch. Double-decker burgers with fries for dinner. Banana splits in between. With nothing else to eat, Cleo had eaten some of it to keep going and dumped the rest of it into what had been the empty bucket. If all the sugar and fat hadn't killed her appetite, the compounded stench in her cell would have done it instead.

She'd made contact with Michael, first by pressing loud whispers through the grate and then, after a brief discussion, through knocking in Morse Code on their cell doors.

Don't eat more than u have to
Don't worry
Way out
Thinking

Escape seemed impossible. They'd both tried loosening stones in the walls, digging up the floor, pulling themselves up the mortar joints in the walls to shout out the barred windows, without success. A sort of matron was let in each day to replenish the water bucket and trade the brimming relief buckets for empty ones, but she was always accompanied by the Easts, making escape or even bribery impossible.

Michael, Heaven and Earth bless him, hadn't cracked. Fortunately for him the Easts' idea of torture was spending ten minutes under a sunlamp or being denied dessert. If they had to, she and Michael could hold out indefinitely. But their mission would stall indefinitely, too. The Earth would continue to founder under a carbon-loaded atmosphere, endangered species would continue to go extinct, with humans and the immortals who served them part of the death spiral.

Way out

An idea, probably the offspring of boredom and too many carbs, but...

S O S knocked Cleo

Just us

Likely, but the world and its unseen forces had surprised Cleo more than once. Like the amazing confluence of events that had brought David and his father together after two millennia of separation.

Maybe not

Cleo knocked and knocked and knocked the code.

You do she knocked when her knuckles were swollen and raw. No reply. She counted to one hundred and tried it again.

"Oh all right," Michael grumbled through his grate.

Three dots; three dashes; three dots.

MONDAY, APRIL 6, 2026

Somewhere in Iowa, USA

It happened so fast. Mother had summoned Persephone to her behind-the-scenes castle in the heart of corn country for the Okanagan Valley debriefing. Though Demeter had sounded cross when they'd spoken—who wouldn't be after the early cherry harvest debacle—she hadn't said anything about imprisonment!

At least the tower Persephone was confined to had fairytale charm. The stone walls were lined with the official state stone, geodes, which sparkled merrily when sunbeams peeped through the arrow slits. The tower was furnished with a curtained four-poster bed, the mattress plump, the mountain of pillows soft. Delicious food and drink (though no alcohol on account of the baby) slid through a low notch carved into the foot-thick timbered door. If she wanted anything—books, instruments, art supplies—all she had to do was ask. A long velvet pull with a tassel on the end hung from the conical ceiling.

Mother was furiously busy, of course, blessing the planting of hundreds of thousands of acres in the American Midwest. She'd reluctantly hired Pomona, her Roman counterpart, to pick up Persephone's duties in North America until the baby arrived. Pomona was competent, of course, but Mother had a thing about the Roman gods because mortals tended to confuse them with the Greeks. Plus, she'd had to pay a hefty recruiting bonus to get someone capable on such short notice.

Through an east-facing arrow slit Persephone squinted out on a glorious spring morning. Her own restless spirit and the baby stirred within. She should be gliding barefoot through orchards and vineyards, nurturing the trees and vines, the strawberry plants and raspberry canes with her supernatural love and abundance. But she was too abundant now, and would force every growing cycle to rapid completion if she cried or coughed or sneezed. Maybe her glance alone would cause the reaction? Demeter refused to even test it after the disaster in the Pacific Northwest.

Actions and consequences. The bill had decidedly arrived for her glorious weekend with Frey. Many immortals committed adultery. Outside of tantrums and the occasional thunderstorm (thunder gods, in spite of their own promiscuity, really lost it when they found out they'd been cuckolded), nothing much happened. Why was she singled out for punishment? Would her new power of super-fertility fade after the baby was born, or would she be classified disabled for her life's work, severed from her very identity?

If she couldn't work with crops anymore, would she be condemned to spend every minute of every day in the Underworld, for all eternity? Would she even be permitted to leave Hades' stony hematite castle for fear she'd cause the whole place to be overgrown by the faded flowers of Asphodel or the orchards of Elysium?

Persephone buried her tear-streaked face in her hands. One wild weekend and she was doomed! It was so unfair.

She wiped her hands on her toga. Something the color of corn silk arrested her downcast eyes. Hair. A section of her hair had abruptly grown down to the floor. How had that—

Oh.

Too amazed to yield more tears but confident there were many in her future, Persephone resolved to experiment with her liquid grief the next time she was thus blessed.

Elysium, the Underworld

Freya watched, riveted. Persephone had done it on her own, had transferred the potency of her tears to her hair to create a means of escape! With luck, she'd soon be on her way to—where? Escaping house arrest was one thing, but remaining safely hidden from Demeter and Hades until the baby arrived was another.

The Norse goddess drew back from the pond and looked inward, focused on the task of telekinetically urging Persephone to seek a reliable protector, someone who could think and act quickly in a crisis. Not Frey, certainly not Frey. Someone solid, and strong, who loved Persephone like no other.

TUESDAY, APRIL 7, 2026

Near Baja, California, USA

Pablo, strapped to Poseidon's chest, dozed in his sling, weary from five-plus days of crossing the Pacific. They could have been here long ago if they'd traveled alone, but the Old Ones topped out at 70 knots per hour and needed rest periods, too.

Poseidon angled up and broke the surface.

"Land ho!" he shouted. "Baja, California. Haven't laid eyes on it in centuries. Would you look at that beach, it's crawling with mortals."

The God of the Sea slipped below the surface and gestured to the contingent of Old Ones that it was time to fly. Throqutp ordered the two dozen soldiers he'd brought with him into formation. Poseidon led the ascent, bursting from the water like an arrow. Craning his neck as far down as he could, Pablo looked back at a V of what resembled whales flying behind them. No one on the beach looked up, thank Zeus, lulled as they were by the mid-day heat, but fisherman bobbing along in pale-colored boats spotted them. They shouted and waved their arms wildly.

Poseidon flicked a hand toward the water. The arms dropped and the shouting stopped. "Not much for charms," he said, "but that one's useful. They'll think they dreamed it."

The old boys were much faster fliers than they were swimmers, but it was over sixteen hundred miles to Midland, a trip of three hours plus.

"What's our ETA?" Pablo said.

"Adjusting for the change in time zones, we'll arrive in Midland at approximately 6pm, Central Time. If no one shoots us down. I'd cloak but we'd lose our convoy."

Pablo hadn't considered the mortals might fire on them. No one could be killed, of course, but a huge blob of a guy falling from the sky might raise suspicion. During their stay in the Mariana Trench they'd heard the history of unwary Old Ones who'd been captured by Antarctic explorers and ended up on dissecting tables. That incident had made the Old Ones extremely cross.

The prospect of being shot down, plus fatigue, made Pablo long for his grandma. He let loose an infant wail, something he'd suppressed for weeks under the weight of negotiations and preparation.

Aaaaaaph!

~ * ~

Poseidon wanted to cry, too, but Big-Gs couldn't afford that luxury. Throqutp still treated him as if he were Pablo's slave instead of his better, and the unwieldiness of his merry band of traveling companions grated on his sense of physical aesthetics. However, they were a needed source of muscle and were firmly convinced climate change had roots in some relatives of theirs, beings who could pass as humans. Children, Pablo had said, was the word Throqutp had used, selfish beings that were incapable of seeing the harm they caused.

Pablo quieted after eternity-soaked minutes of screaming. Poseidon's digital device vibrated on his wrist. Midland, Texas, appeared as a dot on the screen.

"Nearly there," he shouted. Their target was a business tower, home to a fossil fuel corporation that belonged to the selfish monsters who were destroying the world. The dot representing Midland dissipated to the edges of the screen. A new dot appeared at the rightmost edge: *East Fossil Fuels Corporation.*

Poseidon swerved toward the dot, intending to land on the solid-looking part of the roof that joined with a long ceiling of curved glass.

"Hey!" Pablo said. "You hear that?"

Poseidon screwed up his eardrums, not the best after millennia charging around under the pressure of the sea. He shook his head.

"Throqutp!" Pablo shouted back toward the Old Ones. "Can you hear it?"

A disturbance in the air. The leader of the Old Ones appeared in Poseidon's periphery and uttered some kind of goop he didn't understand.

"Yes," Pablo said. "Three short, three long, three short. That's what I heard, too."

With a grunt Throqutp surged ahead of Poseidon and veered east.

"But what about our mission?" Poseidon barked at Pablo.

"Hard to explain, but there's something immortal about the tapping," Pablo said. "These might be the beings we're looking for. Now follow that blob!"

City of Mount Olympus

Hermes hunched over his bench in the lab. The alarm he'd set on Poseidon's digital device had been going off for days but he barely noticed it now, he was so close to working out the final details of his Glorious Machine. So close! He'd stopped noticing how long he'd gone without sleep, was barely aware of the long stubble protruding from his cheeks and chin. Once the Machine was ready it wouldn't matter where P. B. or Poseidon or anybody was going, the world would be saved. The world would be saved thanks to him, to Hermes!

Outskirts of Midland, Texas, USA

Throqutp touched down on a spread of uniform green. Grass, he remembered, from a colonization attempt on the east coast of this continent a century ago. An exceptionally bright mortal had escaped telekinesis-induced enslavement and lured the Old One serving as expedition leader into a fish processing plant. The conclusion was an unhappy one.

The structure now rising before him was made of stone mined from the Pacific side of the North American continent, the overall shapes of the main house and its towers as familiar as his Mariana Trench home. The windows and doors were generously proportioned compared to what the mortals built for themselves, the puny things. Still, mortals made good slaves, and his more benighted kin persisted in using them as food. That's how this operation in Texas had started, he recalled. Two pipsqueaks, twins, sent out into what was then a wilderness to capture wild humans and raise them for market. The whiff of charred human flesh on the wind tickling the chimney caps spoke of a recent Feast of Man. Also, the live scent of Krehrapt, a runt branch of the Old Ones. It was documented that human genetics had entered the Krehrapt line eons ago. No surprise they could pass as such.

Throqutp dropped the formal diplomatic language of the Old Ones he used with Pablo for the vernacular to issue orders to Orthulp, his next-in-command.

"Scout the perimeter."

Orthulp counted off seven members of their party and set off with them, encircling the castle. Not a vast castle, but enough height and crenelated parapets to qualify. The rest of them took cover behind large pieces of vegetable statuary, pruned in the shapes of some animals or other, whether real or fictitious he did not know. The shiny man and the baby joined him behind a four-legged bush that was tall and broad with an obscenely long nose. The warrior baby had an expression of fierce concentration.

"Underground," the baby said, his eyes squinting with effort.

Throqutp sensed two separate heartbeats from hearts like Poseidon's.

~ * ~

Cleo's arms ached beyond comprehension; days filled with long shifts of tapping that Michael spelled her from with grumpy infrequency. Why hadn't Pan or someone from Athena's secret service tracked them down? She was exhausted—dirty, greasy, and, though she'd eaten sparingly, her jeans fit way too tight from the carb and fat diet. Someone was going to owe her big time when she got out of here.

If she got out of here.

Cleo slid down the door into a puddle and cried. The sky darkened beyond the bars. No. Something gray and solid blocked the high window. Foreign words outside. She must be hallucinating, she—

"Let me talk to them," barked a tired, angry voice. "They won't understand your gobbledygook."

For a moment her eyes were dazzled, what was left of the sun's rays refracting off a shiny surface. Someone on all fours with a baby strapped underneath peered through the bars.

"Are you all right in there?"

"Yes. Yes!" She scrambled to her feet. "There's another person in the dungeon next to mine. Please get us out."

The person crawled in the direction she'd pointed and was soon back.

"You're immortal. Both of you," her visitor said.

"That's right."

"But you, you've got a trace of gold corona. Who are you?"

"Tell me who you are, first," Cleo said reflexively.

The person, a man, gave an exasperated sigh. "This isn't the time to—I'm Poseidon."

That explained the sparkles but what about the baby?

"Now. Who are *you*?"

Cleo brushed back the tendrils of hair sticking to her face. "We met before, in Seattle. Sorry I didn't recognize you. I'm Cleo Petra, here on behalf of Olympus, Inc. And I'm…" After so many months of disconnection the desire for something familiar overcame her. "Peter Petra's my father. I'm your granddaughter, Poseidon."

MONDAY, APRIL 13, 2026

Somewhere in Iowa, USA

In one week Persephone cried enough tears to grow a braided rope long enough to make her break. One of the arrow slits, she'd noted, had weathered badly and was crumbling. With the table knife from the daily supper tray she'd dislodged enough geodes to make an opening wide enough to accommodate her rounding belly. And now...

With the extra weight of the baby she was certain getting airborne from the tower was not an option. At dusk Persephone snipped off her braid with embroidery scissors and tied one end around the bedpost. Down went the corn silk colored braid, glowing in the gathering gloom. The line bowed when it touched the ground.

Persephone sat on the sill, engineered herself around so her legs faced out and—how did the heroes in the storybooks do this? With a quick prayer to Heaven and Earth, she gripped the braid in both hands, summoned the power of her biceps and spun halfway around with enough control not to bash herself against the exterior stonework. Hand over hand, toes seeking holds where mortar dented in, she made her way down, down, down.

TUESDAY, APRIL 14, 2026

Northern California, USA

Cleo Petra reclined on a pile of cushions and gazed at the reflecting pond. Crizlapt, the medic traveling with the Old Ones, had examined her and Michael immediately after their rescue and pronounced them temporarily unfit for duty. The medic called in a favor from a monk he'd met during an herb gathering trip in the Himalayas half a century ago, who happened to have founded a spiritual order that specialized in treating those who'd been wrongfully imprisoned. The intended beneficiaries of these services were those incarcerated through flawed legal systems, but Crizlapt had been persuasive and secured two berths for the exhausted and abused immortals. Once the recovering operatives were settled at the retreat, Crizlapt returned to the Marianna Trench.

A few of the Old Ones, who'd learned basic invisibility cloaking from Poseidon, had stayed behind in Midland to ensure the Easts were brought to justice. With Cleo's assistance they'd set enough clues for Special Agent Garcia to track the Easts to their castle home. The FBI was currently investigating charges of human sacrifice and cannibalism. Michael had somehow procured and retained (no one asked how) the key to a safe deposit box containing proof of shell companies and other contracts in flagrant violation of federal regulations. He'd checked into a hotel to clean up and retrieved the documents for Agent Garcia before Crizlapt and Poseidon, with Pablo along for the ride, had taken their hands and flown them to the remote Buddhist compound.

Michael appeared on the other side of the reflecting pond. They nodded to each other.

"Any news?" she said.

He flopped back on another pile of cushions, looking every bit as weary as she felt. "Congressman Fotakis was released from custody on his own recognizance and instructed not to leave Washington, D.C."

"Hah! We'll see how long that lasts." It seemed a century since Pan had flown by her window on the plane from Athens to America.

"Doesn't really matter, now that the Easts will be indicted. The EPA has fifty field agents going over all of it with a fine-tooth comb. They'll put them away for a hundred years. Not that it matters to them."

"Or us." If she checked out okay medically, Cleo could leave tomorrow, free to return to the City of Mount Olympus. She'd booked the first Thursday morning flight out of San Francisco International Airport in anticipation. "What are you going to do, now that our mission is over?"

Michael laughed. Heaven and Earth, it was good to hear someone laugh. "Believe it or not, Legal wants me back at East Fossil to help with what everyone's pretty sure will be the corporate dismantling."

"You're going? You can't be serious."

He smiled serenely and shook his head. "Nope. Gonna stay here for a while and study yoga. *Really* study it beyond the designer mats and skin-tight suits. I'm ready to spend a few centuries as a monk. How about you? Any more spy work?"

"No thanks!" Now it was her turn to laugh. "I miss working at corporate. I left my dream job there, almost a year ago now to…" *Travel the world with David Bernstein.* "Lots of other things I miss in the city, too."

She and Michael had both worked with spiritual guides during their convalescence. The layers of intrigue Cleo had lived under for months were peeling away, the choked off spaces in her mind and heart tentatively opening. With time, her guide said, she would find a way forward.

Wednesday, april 15, 2026

City of Mount Olympus

The first thing Persephone did when she touched down was duck into a drug store and buy a pair of dark glasses. Not much of a disguise but maybe it would be enough, combined with her raggedly cut shoulder-length hair.

She scurried into an alley, pulled up the Olympus, Inc., directory on her digital device and scrolled to Heracles, Head of Security. She tapped the message icon. *It's Seph. Need help!*

The alley was shaded and chilly. She shivered in place, afraid of being spotted and reported to—who, exactly? Ares, the God of Agriculture? Mother? Maybe there was an APB out on her, a fugitive armed with the ability to make vegetation grow at a mind-numbing rate. Tears of stress and exhaustion spilled down her face. The crack in the pavement beneath her feet burst with dandelions.

No crying! It would be impossible to slip under the radar if she left a trail of vibrant flora in her wake. Persephone dabbed her cheeks with the hem of her toga. Tears twisted inside of her as she waited. And waited.

Ping.

Her bleary eyes focused on the screen.

Got your coordinates. Be there in 5.

Shit, she hadn't turned off tracking! Mother might already know where she was. Persephone pushed a button on the side of the device to disable the feature. In a few minutes a shadow passed over the sidewalk in front of her hiding place. Sandals slapped the pavement.

"In here," she squeaked.

The Hero of Mount Olympus was so broad his shoulders filled the width of the alley.

"Heaven and Earth, Seph," Heracles said, his eyes anchored on her rounded belly. "What have you got yourself into?"

~ * ~

After the initial shock of seeing Seph "in the family way" and calculating the chaos that could ensue if she was discovered AWOL,

Heracles quickly formed a plan.

"Give me your hand, Seph, and hold on tight. I need to apply an extra layer of security. Try not to be alarmed."

"Oh!" Her voice came out of thin air.

"Biggest of Big-G Cloaking. Not even Zeus will be able to see us," he assured her. It was one of his few perks as Olympus, Inc., Security Chief. "Step out to the sidewalk, there's a good girl, and now…"

Invisible, they rose into the air, on course for a cottage outside the city proper.

"Pan's away for a while, asked me to keep an eye on his place," Heracles shouted against the wind. "You like goats?"

"Uhm, okay, I guess," came the tentative voice alongside him. "Mostly I think of them in terms of crop damage."

"Not a problem where I'm taking you. It's all grazing land. Nice little place he has, very cozy, and the goatherd who runs things knows how to keep his mouth shut."

They passed by the Olympus, Inc., corporate tower.

"Fourth floor," Heracles said in the spirit of a tour guide. "That office on the corner belongs to Hermes. Haven't seen him in there for a while. Misses that baby of his is how they tell it at the water cooler. Official word is P. B.'s in Africa with his mom while she's running the microloan program for Elle's bunch, but the rumor is the tyke's been spirited off somewhere by Poseidon. All very mysterious."

"Monique must be worried sick," Persephone said, tears entering her voice. Natural for her to be emotional in her condition, and of course she'd met P. B. when he'd been taken to the Underworld as bait to trap The Power. That time, Persephone hadn't wanted to give him up.

They flew over the low border wall at the edge of the city, the remnant of fortifications Heracles had raised when chthonic monsters were a constant threat to the Olympians. He'd been a hero then, repelling them single-handed. He grinned, remembering his valiant attacks and nursing the cuts and bruises on a nice long holiday beside the Aegean Sea afterward.

"Just up ahead. Down we go."

He angled down to an expanse of lush green fields with a thatch-roofed cottage and a collection of outbuildings at the center.

"Mind your feet." He pulled up vertically and lowered them to the ground. At contact he thought the word to lift the cloaking. Seph's eyes spouted a flood of tears. She threw her arms around him and hugged him tight.

"Thank you, Clee, thanks so much."

Tears splashed the front of his toga and dripped to the ground. In seconds the grass around them sprang from goat-sheared nubbins to shoulder height.

"Don't cry, Seph," he said, marveling as the grass tips stretched overhead. "Don't want to make a jungle of the place. You're safe now."

"Sorry." She pulled back. "It's been so hard since Mother locked me in the tower."

He left that comment untouched. "Here, now, I have a few minutes to spare. Let me show you around and introduce you to Aja."

They pushed their way through the patch of towering grass and followed a tidy dirt path to the cottage, thatch roof glistening and the walls gleaming with a fresh coat of whitewash.

"Aja's taking good care of the place," he said as he pushed open the plank door. Sunlight spilled onto a jumble of dirty crockery and discarded togas. "Uh, on the outside, anyway. Pan's not much of a housekeeper."

Heaven and Earth, he hoped Persephone wouldn't start crying again. Who knew what might grow out of the dirt floor?

"It will…" she paused in the doorway, eyes wide. "It will give me something to do," she said with resolve. "I'm not used to having free time in the spring."

"Some nice spring housecleaning, just the thing to lift the spirits," he said to offer encouragement. "Let's take a quick look in the pantry." Heracles stepped over the discards to a corner of the one-room abode. There was a small open-hearth fireplace with a cast-iron pot suspended from a tripod, and a door, ajar, to the right. He opened the door far enough to make an inventory. "Some canned goods. Dolmades, those should be tasty, eh, Seph?" he said over his shoulder. "Olives. Good. Olive oil, rice, dried fava beans. Enough to get by for a day and Aja keeps some milk and cheese in the cold shed. Wine, of course—"

"Not for the baby." Seph had moved to his left and stood in front of the unlit fireplace. "I've always wanted to try cooking," she said. "Is it fun?"

She was such a timid person it was hard to remember she was a queen. Heaven and Earth, between that and her agricultural work she'd probably never done a day's housework in her life.

"Aja can show you the basics," he temporized. Most of what Hebe served at home was takeout, claiming most days that her migraines kept her out of the kitchen.

The goatherd wasn't in the long, low barn or any of the other outbuildings. "Probably with the herd," Heracles said. "I'll find him on my way out and let him know you're here."

Seph turned sad eyes on him. "Thank you, Clee, for helping me. I hope you'll visit sometime when I get the place tidied up."

She looked so small, if you discounted the belly, and vulnerable. "That'd be nice, Seph. You know how to find me if you need anything. And remember to keep tracking mode switched off on your digital. Unless you want to be found, that is."

~ * ~

After Clee flew away Persephone walked around the property, noting a musically flowing spring and an odd-looking orchard, apple trees with disproportionately high limbs and gouges in the trunks where the lower ones appeared to have been torn off.

"Goats," she said to herself, shaking her head. Not exactly the animals of an agricultural goddess's dreams but at least she had a safe haven.

The day had turned beautifully warm and the grass carpeting the farm smelled tender and sweet. She circled her hands on her belly. "A pretty place to be, little one," she said to the baby. It was the start of the fourth month according to the calendar. Persephone didn't know much about pregnancy but was certain her belly shouldn't be this big by now. Heaven and Earth, was she carrying twins? Oh, that would be wonderful!

Suddenly she was ravenous. While she sincerely planned on learning how to cook, now was not the time. Persephone gathered all three jars of Dolmades from the pantry and sat on a sunny bench in front of the cottage. The lid of the first jar twisted off easily. And the second. And the third. Oily, salty, spicily delicious down to the residue she licked off her fingers. A nap would be perfect, but the straw tick bed was covered with heaps of clothing and scrolls and plates varnished with the juices of meals long past.

Persephone rolled to her feet and ambled into the cottage. A willow basket, long and deep with two hand holds, was perfect for transporting Pan's discards out into the sun. There must be some sort of cleaning lore available on the internet? Water played a part in it, she knew, with clothing, at least. And some other component. She'd have to ask Aja when he returned. Heracles had shown her the goatherd's tiny and neatly kept shack next to the barn, a small room with a bed and a pitcher and basin on a stand. She'd learn all those washing and cleaning things by the time the baby—babies? —arrived. And then—

And then what? Her world, until now dictated by the seasons, her mother, and her husband, stretched before her unplanned. She'd run away from Hades and been banned from her career. Would her tears ever return to normal instead of spewing life from the earth like fertilizer on steroids? Pan would want his cottage back some day. If she liked it and learned how to manage without modern conveniences, like servants, would he consider leasing it to her and the babies?

Persephone set the basket down and returned to the cottage, stretched her arms high and yawned. She lowered herself to the bed. Musty straw crackled under her weight. Tomorrow, or someday soon, she'd stuff the frame with new grass and...

THURSDAY, APRIL 16, 2026

Athena stared across her desk at Ares. They'd run out of chit-chat. Hermes was late for their mandatory meeting regarding climate change secret ops. Even the war masks decorating the wall behind Ares looked impatient and bored.

"This is unacceptable," Athena said. She tapped Hermes' extension into her digital tablet. The call picked up in two rings.

"Hermes' office, Roderick Waller speaking."

Waller's voice was uniformly bright. In all her dealings with him, which had followed a geometric progression in recent months, he presented himself as an optimistic problem solver.

"Mr. Waller, this is Athena. Is he in?"

"Yes. Somewhere," Waller chirped. "He's probably in the lab. I'll transfer you. Have a wonderful day!"

"Thank you." She locked eyes with Ares. After a dozen rings, she signed off. "We'll start without him." And likely finish without him, too, if the past few weeks were a reliable indicator.

Ares sat up straight, rotated his shoulders a few times. He'd complained about stiffness, too much flying as he'd been in the field much more than usual, what with the weird absence of Persephone from overseeing her crops. That much was known through water cooler gossip. Per Veronica, the details were available on a need-to-know basis. It annoyed Athena to be out of the loop, as anything out of the ordinary could have diplomatic implications. She'd taken an unaccustomed number of deep, mindful breaths lately, telling herself there was a valid reason for this, and Veronica surely knew what she was doing.

"They'll be here to debrief tomorrow," Athena said. "Cleo's flying in today, commercial flight through Athens International."

"And Pan?" Ares asked.

The corners of Athena's mouth quirked. "He's planned a dramatic escape. After leaving ample evidence of foul play in his condo and office, he'll lose his mortal security detail on a stroll to the Washington Monument, where he'll duck out of sight, cloak, and fly home."

Ares laughed. "That boy's having way too much fun. I think he's found his niche at Olympus, Inc."

"I want him for future operations. Veronica's meeting with us tomorrow after we debrief with Cleo and Pan, to discuss how she'll adjust his responsibilities for herds and flocks. Not that he does much," she added under her breath. Everyone knew the herdsman Pan employed was the one who really did the work.

"What about Cleo?"

"She's brilliant, of course, performed well and reported everything we needed to complete the mission but…"

"More of a desk jockey?"

Athena chose her words carefully. "I think her strengths lie elsewhere. She's a capable operative but there are other positions she could hold that would make her an outstanding asset for Olympus, Inc."

Pan, on the other hand, had reported something of interest outside of the mission that might be worth pursuing.

"When Pan finished training and communications were restored he said he'd met one of us, an individual with a purple aura but there was a trace of pink underneath it, tight against the skin." Cleo, capable as she was, had either not observed this or had neglected to mention it. "Have you ever heard of such a thing?"

"I don't think so. What do you make of it?"

"I've turned Pan's intel over to Apollo for the biological perspective. Haven't heard back from him yet."

Behind her, Tim worked his feathers with his beak. Still no Hermes.

"That's all I have," Athena said, rising. "Thank you, Ares. See you tomorrow at ten."

FRIDAY, APRIL 17, 2026

Cleo reported to reception, Department of War and Diplomacy, and was shown by an athletic-looking young woman to a conference room. Artifacts of First Nation mortals—a mixture of weavings, beadwork and feathered weapons of war—graced the walls.

"This one is decorated with a North America theme," the young woman explained.

Four pedestals, one in each corner, were bedecked with single examples of basketry, pottery or sculpture. The materials varied. Grass, metal, earth, stone. Cleo drifted toward the model of a temple of stair-step design.

"The pedestals represent cultures from the north, south, east and west of North America," the receptionist said.

Cleo touched a fingertip to the model as if daring herself to touch a hot stove. The stone was identical to that used in the Easts' dungeons.

"Hello-o," someone called from the doorway.

"Oh!" The receptionist spun on her sandals. "Sorry, I should have been at the—"

"Never mind, young lady," Pan said, raising a flirtatious eyebrow. "I know my way around."

She scurried off, sparing Pan a backward look of admiration.

"Well, you cleaned up nicely," Cleo said. Pan wore a decent-looking business toga, slate gray and crisply pressed, a step above the loincloth he used to sport before he'd kicked alcohol abuse and become a hero. Her attire was less formal, last year's peach-colored number she'd excavated from her closet this morning. After ten months of almost continuous absence, her own condo felt like a hotel suite.

"The credit goes to the Mountain High Hotel. I, uh, got in later than anticipated, hit a couple of snags clearing D.C." He ran a hand through his dark curls and grinned. "I almost miss Pendarvus Fotakis and his can of foaming mousse."

Athena and Ares came in together, Tim perched on Athena's shoulder.

"Cleo, Pan, welcome back," Athena said, politely but without warmth. Her usual. "Please be seated."

A pitcher, sweating with condensation, and five water glasses sat in the middle of the round conference table. The four of them sat, talked about Cleo and Pan's flights home. In a few minutes conversation gave out to an awkward silence. Athena's lips parted to say something when Hermes shuffled through the door.

"Sorry I'm late," he said. The lower half of his face was covered with an uneven, gray-flecked beard and his hair, always on the casual side, looked oily. There was something about his eyes that made Cleo think of a light with a dimmer switch turned down to half.

Pan rose and extended a hand to his father. "It's good to see you, sir."

Cleo raised a hand and wiggled her fingers. "Hi, Hermes."

He didn't even look at her.

Athena set her digital pad to record. She asked Cleo and Pan a series of questions regarding the end of their mission and what steps they recommended moving forward.

"I think my part is done," Cleo said. "Poseidon can give you an update on the Easts. He and Pablo are keeping them in check with help from some of the Old Ones until the mortal authorities can place them under arrest. The details, as I understand them, are in the report I sent on Monday."

"Pablo? Who's Pablo?" Pan said.

"He's a baby. Said he'd changed his name. It used to be P. B."

Hermes looked up sharply.

"Why didn't anyone *tell* me about this?" he shouted, glaring at Athena. "You've blatantly endangered my son!"

"Security imperative," Athena said smoothly. "Monique doesn't know, either. She thinks he's still in the Marianna Trench, visiting family."

"He's just a baby!" Hermes raged. "He's—"

"He has the verbal and intellectual capabilities of a highly intelligent adult," Athena continued. "He needs to stay in the field to interpret for the Old Ones until the Easts are put away."

Hermes sprang from his chair. "This is bullshit!" He stalked toward the door.

"We're in a war against climate change, Hermes. All of us. You know that better than anyone."

He spun around, the look on his face poisonous.

"You can't blame this all on me! Everybody, even you, Athena, is part of the problem."

"And that's why we're all working on it now—"

"I'm done being the world's punching bag." Tears streamed down his cheeks. "I quit!"

He bolted out the door, Pan after him. Though her heart wrenched for her former boss, Cleo stayed put.

"Heaven and Earth," Athena swore. She took a deep breath. "There is one more thing I'd like to ask you, Cleo, before you go. You mentioned auras quite a few times in your reports, the Easts and our agent Mr. Guy, for example. Did you also happen to notice an unusual aura during your time in training?"

~ * ~

Heracles ascended the green marble stairs of Olympus Rest on Friday afternoon. Routine physical examination with Apollo was the order he'd been given by Immortal Resources.

He reported to Apollo's private office suite which had its own examining room. The door was open, a soothing melody played on a lute wafting through the entry. Recorded, Heracles realized. Apollo sat behind his desk, studying the screen of a desktop device.

"Ah, there you are." Apollo stood and extended a hand. Firm grip he had, though not as strong as Heracles who vigilantly guarded himself against crushing the hands of his friends. "Always a pleasure, Heracles. Please, have a seat. We'll do the preliminary screening here if you have no objection?"

The questions were the usual: frequency of drinking alcohol (special occasions only) and smoking (never), unexplained fluctuations in weight or mood (none), changes in living arrangements (regrettably, none, as Hebe was consistently on a tear about something or other). Any new health issues or concerns? None.

When the questionnaire was complete Apollo pointed to a room to the left of his desk. "We'll get your vitals in the examining room."

The extra-large blood pressure cuff was inflated and deflated (high normal range); reflexes tested with a hammer (normal); stethoscope pressed to heart and lungs, front and back (normal and clear). Apollo scrolled down the in-room digital pad that displayed Heracles' health history.

"It's been two years since your last full blood panel, all results in the excellent to normal range. Given your age and overall health I think we can let that slide one more year."

Just as well, as Heracles was not fond of needles.

Apollo's eyes tracked the outline of Heracles' head and shoulders. "You've been immortal for how long now?"

"Two millennia and a bit."

"Your vitals and overall health fit a true immortal profile, but your mortal aura persists. No reason it shouldn't, I suppose, but I'd like to understand the science behind it."

Heracles shifted on the edge of the examining table. Seemed an odd topic of conversation, made him feel as if the God of Medicine was pondering the possibility of dissecting him. Apollo's penetrating gaze softened.

"Questions?"

"No."

"We'll call it good, then. Nearly quitting time. I'll transmit your results to Immortal Resources with the batch next week." Apollo followed Heracles to the office door. "See you at the next family event," he said.

Heracles had one foot in the hallway when he heard a tapping. He glanced back into the office. Apollo was already engaged with his desktop device, eyes riveted to the screen, fingers flying on the keypad.

SATURDAY, APRIL 18, 2026

Pan circled his country cottage, weary not only from months of operative work and the long flight home but from hours of dealing with Hermes.

Heaven and Earth, it had been a nightmare! Chasing him down the stairs, five flights to his fourth-floor office where he'd disappeared entirely, discovered later in the Digital Devices and Robotics lab where Hermes had cloaked himself and hidden under a table.

There was an initial bout of kicking and wailing. Pan held Hermes tightly in his arms until the tantrum subsided. Hermes then babbled excitedly about his magnificent climate change reversal machine. The scribbles on a stack of legal pads he guardedly showed Pan were nothing but that, doodles of thickly inked clouds being fired upon by cannons.

And the negotiating! Tartarus, it was the hardest thing he'd ever done, persuading this incoherent god—someone he'd admired all his life and whose approval he'd only recently garnered—into going with him in the chariot waiting out front to Olympus Rest. He'd left Hermes under Apollo's care, sedated in a hospital room with twenty-four-hour monitoring. A breakdown, Apollo had assessed. Hermes needed rest, first and foremost, before treatment options could be determined.

All Pan longed for now was his one-room cottage and the bleating of goats to lull him into hours of uninterrupted sleep.

He landed out front at the perfect golden moment of sunset, pushed open the door knowing he would find a rank and disheveled mess but it was his rank and disheveled mess, damn it. The room smelled …fresh. His senses must be out of whack from exhaustion.

Pan staggered toward his straw tick bed. A pale golden pillow he didn't recognize was at the head, blankets rumpled in a heap in the middle. The heap rolled onto its back.

"What the—"

The pillow screamed. "Get out of here, immediately! You masher!! You fiend!!"

"Heaven and Earth, get out of my bed!" he shouted in return.

The figure rose. Dying daylight revealed the outline of a woman. A pregnant woman.

SUNDAY, APRIL 19, 2026

To reengage with all that had happened in his absence, Pan, seated on the bench in front of his cottage, slumped over his digital device, scrolling through the City of Mount Olympus chat board. The rumor mill was churning at warp speed.

Flash! Hermes committed to Olympus Rest due to a nervous breakdown; prognosis unknown. Mid-eternity crisis suspected as the underlying cause.

Flash! David Bernstein spotted, absent his right index finger. Suspicion centered on Zeus, known to resent Young Bernstein as the offspring of Hera's one known affair.

Flash! Woman squatter apprehended in Pan's rural cottage. Suspect resembles Persephone, reported on the lam for reasons unspecified. And, by the way, she's pregnant.

How this last one made the chat board so quickly Pan had no idea. He'd barely had time to assimilate the situation himself—how she got there, why she was there. The first action he'd taken, after the initial moments of anger and outrage, was to send a priority message to Heracles.

Home from mission. What in Heaven and Earth is going on here?

Heracles soon landed in front of the cottage, where Pan and Persephone stood in the dark.

"Well?" Pan said, without further greeting.

"Sorry. I'm sorry," the big guy said. "She took me by surprise. Didn't think you'd be back so soon."

Heracles looked from Pan to Persephone.

"Let's look at this with clear, calm minds," Heracles said, pointing to the bench in front of the cottage. "You too, Pan."

Heracles mediated their discussion. Persephone gave a full account of her hyper-fertility experiences in the field and being held captive by Demeter.

"My own mother!" she wailed. Tears spilled all the way to the ground, a screen of grass growing with lightning speed where they landed.

Pan looked at Heracles.

"Hormones," Heracles mouthed. As the father of three, Heracles would know.

"Okay, let me recap," Pan said. Heaven and Earth he was weary. "Seph, here, got in the family way at the climate change conference. Her tears, as we've just seen, act as a super-strength fertilizer, which makes her a clear and present danger in her agricultural work. She climbed down from a tower Demeter locked her in and came back to Mount Olympus. She called on you for help, Heracles, and here she is."

"Uh, yeah, that about sums it up," Heracles said.

"And I cleaned your filthy cottage," Persephone added. "At least you could say thank you."

Heracles nodded to Pan.

"Thank you."

Heracles begged off as soon as he could, citing it was date night with Hebe. Had Heracles somehow spilled the night's events to Hebe? However it had happened, word traveled so fast Hades had sent Pan a typo-filled text shortly after Heracles left them. The gist: he was on his way from the Underworld to deal with his wife.

"I refuse to see him," Persephone said, and locked herself in the cottage.

Bone tired, Pan lay down on the bench. He awoke to a thump. His eyes blinked open to two broad, sandaled feet.

"I'll deal with you later," Hades snarled at Pan. He tried to force the cottage door, but the bolt held tight. "Open up!" he bellowed, pounding the planks with both fists. "I've had it with you, woman! If you can't hold a job you can work at home and I can fire the maid."

"I'm not going back!" Persephone shouted with equal vigor. "I hate all the darkness and the penny pinching and—and you!"

"You can't leave your husband!"

"Oh no? Just watch me. Mother divorced a bigger god than you, Hades!"

Pan crept away from the marital fireworks to sleep in the barn with the goats.

MONDAY, APRIL 20, 2026

David Bernstein was cautiously optimistic. He'd received a message from Cleo over the weekend. She said she wanted to see him once she had a couple of days to adjust to life on Mount Olympus. They agreed on 8am, Monday, breakfast at his place (she'd bring fruit and pastries) before his 10am seminar.

He got up early, took extra care shaving as his missing finger made the process clumsy, and tidied his studio apartment. Two clean plates, two clean forks, two glasses of water on the tiny table where they'd sometimes shared meals.

Cleo's familiar knock hit the door a few minutes early.

"Hi."

"Hi."

She looked beautiful, of course. She always looked beautiful, but her choice of mini-toga was a somber dove gray, conservatively draped. So much for the image of the red sequined dress seared into his brain.

He stepped aside to let her in. Cleo quickly arranged the contents of the brown paper bag she carried on the plates, a croissant for her, two of his favorite chocolate chip muffins for him, and a bunch of grapes for each. Their knees touched under the table when they sat. Cleo eased back, breaking the contact. Her gorgeous eyes were guarded.

"Thanks," she said.

He smiled uncomfortably. "For what?"

"For seeing me. It's been a while. We didn't exactly…"

"Yeah." The way he'd treated her the day they'd left Seattle washed through him with shame. "I, uh, I was wrong about that."

She looked at him a long time. "Okay. What happened to your finger?"

"Long story. I'll tell you in a bit. Let's eat."

He wolfed down the first muffin. Cleo only picked some flakes off her croissant.

"David, there's something I have to tell you."

Tartarus. After months in relationship limbo she was going to make a clean break from him. He waited for the bad news.

"It's about Saul."

She told me about Saul at the training camp, that Pan had seen him, too, and asked her about his aura.

"Athena asked me about it at the debriefing on Friday," she said. "I hadn't reported it, didn't think it was safe for some reason. But Pan mentioned it and I think they want him to do a follow-up investigation."

David's stomach churned. "That doesn't sound good."

"Can you warn him somehow?" she said.

"Not sure," he said. "I'm kind of being watched."

His turn to tell about Lucia, the spell book, time traveling, his daughter, the blood sacrifice he'd needed to return to the present, that he'd only been released from quarantine days ago.

"Heaven and Earth." Tears brimmed in Cleo's eyes. "How did we get into this mess?"

He reached across the table for her hand.

TUESDAY, APRIL 28, 2026

Tuesday morning a grave matter landed before Veronica Zeta, CEO of Olympus, Inc. It came to her in a secured email from the Director of Immortal Resources marked CONFIDENTIAL. An unidentified employee had come directly to the IR director after overhearing a whispered conversation in the restroom about a mortal being made immortal by one of the Twelve Great Olympians. The email stated this was not a recirculation about the case of Heracles (which was common knowledge but considered in poor taste to talk about).

Veronica inhaled sharply. Ever the cool head in a crisis, she gave her executive assistant, Alexandra, the rest of the day off, and sent out twelve CONFIDENTIAL emails marked URGENT, requesting appointments with each of the Big Twelve. Zeus, Hera, Athena, Apollo, Poseidon, Ares, Artemis, Demeter, Aphrodite, Dionysus, Hermes and Hephaestus. Hermes, she realized with regret, was still under treatment at Olympus Rest. Four of them bounced back with out-of-office replies as they were engaged in the mortal world. Ares and Athena were the first interviewees. Both expressed shock but claimed no knowledge of the matter.

Hera's appointment came third.

Veronica read Hera the item of concern as stated in the Director of IR's email. Had she, herself, heard the rumor?

"The rumor? No."

Did she, herself, have knowledge of one of the Twelve having committed this offense?

The lines in Hera's forehead were deep with tension but her lips quirked.

"At least one."

Mother, always cunning in business and personal matters when any wiggle room was available. Veronica braced herself for the question she hadn't asked the other two.

"Mother, was it you?"

Many expressions succeeded each other on Hera's face. Anger. Defiance. Fear.

"Yes."

Piece by piece, Veronica mined details from Hera's hostile responses.

Her first reaction was shock, followed by rage.

"You have to understand, Ronnie, it was a different world for women back then. I was only trying to save myself, and David. Zeus was not the man he is these days. He was all pride and no judgment. His vanity was insuperable and his anger—he would have killed David, or tried to, and done everything in his power to degrade me. Making that *person*," she said the word with disgust, "making him immortal seemed a reasonable price to pay for his silence."

"Oh, Mother." Her heart broke for Hera. Misogyny was far from dead on Mount Olympus. Zeus' long line of bastard children were well known, some of them represented among the Twelve Great Olympians.

Still, the fact remained: Hera had broken one of Zeus' Great Laws, and for purely personal reasons. Veronica had a nuts and bolts intellect that respected rules and the order they were intended to maintain. There was precedent, of course, in acquitting the accused from this particular act in the case of Heracles. The application of such case law would certainly be argued by the defense.

"Hera, Goddess of Marriage, it is my duty to inform you that—"

"Heaven and Earth, Ronnie!" Hera sprang from her chair. "I've known the law since before you were a glimmer in Zeus' eye!"

Duty-bound, Veronica persisted in the required litany, Hera's proud, beautiful head held high throughout.

As CEO of Olympus, Inc., Veronica Zeta was now required to present the charges to the Twelve Great Olympians, minus one. At least her official duties ended there. Hera could arrange for her own defense counsel or have one appointed by the court. A judge would be elected from the eleven Greats; the rest would serve as the jury. Until the trial date and time were set, Hera would be released on her own recognizance but restricted to the City of Mount Olympus.

Veronica came around from behind her desk and reached out to Hera.

"Mother, I'm so truly sorry."

The two most powerful women in the Greek Pantheon embraced and wept.

SATURDAY, MAY 2, 2026

Valencia, Spain

It was a casually tended churchyard, the grass sheared by the convent's flock of sheep that also kept it fertilized. Short, oblong monuments marched uniformly down the lines of graves. Burials were laid out in chronological order, making it easy to find Sister Leo Maria, 1918 to 2007.

Easy to find in the sense of locating, but in the heart…

Cleo touched David's shoulder.

"You okay?"

He nodded, fighting down the sob that heaved in his chest. His daughter, Amàlia. He'd only seen her twice as a baby, through a window, had never held her in his arms. A long mortal life he'd helped create and he'd shared none of it.

David knelt and set the bouquet of white roses he carried below the stone. Cleo's shadow moved quietly away. Time and space alone with his child.

How to picture a life he'd never witnessed? It was as lost to him as his own.

Cleo's shadow was longer when she returned. Slowly he rose and silently said goodbye to Amàlia. They headed down the path, unpaved dirt just as it had been in 1918, toward the city.

"Hungry?" Cleo said.

He felt hollow from head to toe. "Starving."

Special clearance through Athens U, Olympus Rest and Olympus, Inc., Security, had been required to make this trip. Their return flight left early Sunday morning, Cleo due to begin her interim role as Director of Digital Devices and Robotics, David to return to his studies and prepare for the trial, set for Friday, May 8.

The turning point in indicting Hera had started with Apollo. He'd noted the signature of a mortal made immortal from a routine medical exam of Heracles. It was all in the aura and, as far as anyone knew or would say, only two beings possessed the pink and purple variety. Pan had tracked Saul through his work for the CIA and Saul, like David, had been called as a material witness.

They stopped at an eatery run by a husband and wife, four tables, total, the menu solid with stews and bread. David and Cleo shared a stone jar of raw local wine as they ate. She raised her glass.

"To Sister Leo Maria. Cheers."

To Amàlia. "Cheers."

After months of doubt and separation, the bond of friendship was weaving between them again. And when one had eternity…David hoped one day there'd be love again, too.

ABOUT The AUThOR

S. D. Matley lives in southwest Washington State. She writes, reads (sometimes to her tiger tabby companion Hoosegow), tap dances, and is a living history presenter (love that research!). In her past life she's been an actress, an accountant and a cowboy singer. In her future life— who knows? *Crisis in Big-G City* is the fourth volume in her contemporary fantasy/mythology series featuring the Greek pantheon.

For coming adventures, visit her website http://susandmatley.com

More Books by S.D. Matley from WolfSinger Publications

Small-g City

Seattle is on the brink of disaster, but nobody knows it! Nobody except Ralph, a "small-g" god from Olympus, Inc.

Ralph suffers from extreme job burn-out, and no wonder—his job is to reinforce Seattle's notorious raised highway, the Alaskan Way Viaduct, by disbursing his molecules throughout the unstable and hazardous structure.

But Ralph's molecules are feeling the pull of reconstitution. Will he survive one more agonizing rush hour without resuming his human-oid form and emerging from the viaduct, sending thousands of commuters to their deaths? And what about the familiar shadow hovering over him? If Zeus (Olympus, Inc. CEO and the Biggest of Big-G Gods) is spying on him, all Tartarus is sure to break loose!

Big-G City

Veronica Zeta, youngest child of Zeus and Hera, is at last CEO of the immortal owned and operated corporation, Olympus, Inc. The biggest project on her agenda is creating world peace, but first she must depose her bloodthirsty brother Ares, God of War. To do so, she must deploy a supernatural force called The Power, which can demand a terrible price.

Zeus, former CEO and Ex-Lord of the Universe, struggles with identity issues after his retirement. The bright spot in his life is baby-sitting his toddler granddaughter, but his marriage with Hera is foundering and he longs for someone to confide in.

Hera's new campaign, a mortal lifestyle series of books and seminars called Marvelous Marriage, is a huge success. The face of this project, small-g goddess Candy Smith, has become a media celebrity. Hera, Goddess of Marriage, revels in the market share she's stealing from the "adult" industries owned by her rival, Aphrodite.

But Aphrodite, Goddess of Love, is ready to fight back! Employing a photo-shopped tabloid cover photo and a box of enchanted chocolates, she disrupts the personal life of Candy Smith and goads Hera into executing her own sabotage plan.

The lives of these Olympians collide when Veronica succeeds in deposing Ares, and pays for deploying a large dose of The Power with blindness, anguish and, possibly, death. But how can an immortal die? The answer lies in an old family secret, daringly unearthed by Zeus in the eleventh hour.

Beyond Big-G City

The year is 2025 and Hermes is on the Olympus, Inc., hot seat. He has two short years to halt climate change before the irretrievable tipping point is reached, an existential threat to mortals and immortals alike.

David Bernstein embarks on a quest to learn about his unnamed mortal father. Assisted by would-be girlfriend, Cleo Petra, David scours the Middle East for clues that lead him to Rome, Italy, and points beyond.

Jim Smith observes unsettling changes in Stella, his mental health client, and fears an evil force, The Power, has secretly escaped its prison to terrorize the City of Mount Olympus once more.

And what of Seattle? Clifford Essex leads a desperate race to solve the riddle of an unstable seawall, poised to crumble and take a major transit tunnel with it.

From Mount Olympus to the Underworld, from Petra, Jordan, to Seattle, Washington-much is afoot Beyond Big-G City!

More Books from
WolfSinger Publications

The Seven Exalted Orders
– Deby Fredericks

Arkanost has Seven Exalted Orders. No more, no less. When a magus goes renegade in a far-off province, the Mage Lords demand that something be done.

Ryamon is bitter and frustrated. He longs to be a Fire magus; as a Stone magus, he's miserable. If he can bring the rogue back, he has a chance—his last chance—to fulfill his dream.

It's a great plan—until he actually meets Valdira.

Tails from the Front Lines 2: The Thin Blue Line
– edited by Carol Hightshoe

Come meet some of the four-legged members of Law Enforcement who also serve and protect.

Here our authors will introduce you to the brave K9 officers who serve alongside their human partners. They are their eyes, ears, noses and sometimes when necessary they are their shield, protecting others.

Proceeds from this anthology will be donated to the El Paso County (Colorado) Sheriff's Office K9 program in memory of K9 Jinx who was killed in the line of duty on April 11, 2022.

Ring of Fire – edited by Dana Bell

Enter the Ring of Fire, as unpredictable as the land masses shaking a city and volcanoes erupting covering the landscape. Could there be other reasons for these events? Or could these rings be more than a geological location.

They may be dragons playing tricks
or magic portals opened to mysterious realms
or sacrificing the best work of a lifetime.
Perhaps a rescue during a forest fire
or an attempt to raise the dead
or even while attending a high school reunion.

Journeys are taken to far off lands, another world, and through caves, each with their own unique twist.

Each tale presents a new idea on what the Ring of Fire could be. It is more than what many have been led to believe. Pull up a chair and warm yourself by our fires—just don't let yourself get burned.

Coyote – Charles Combee

While camping in a remote canyon in Utah Jim accidently sees an ancient rite taking place with a coyote like creature presiding over it. Now this creature wants Jim dead.

Audrey and her family go hiking in Utah and are attacked by this creature. Audrey is the only survivor, but she is pulled into a strange world of darkness and glass. She is 'rescued' by Jim, but is still linked to the creature, whose hold on her will end in her death unless Jim can find a way to break that link.

In his dreams, or are they ancient memories, Jim begins to learn more about Coyote as well as the magics that previously bound him. But those dreams end without teaching him the full magics. Can he find a way to free Audrey and stop Coyote from once again terrorizing humankind?

Believing is Seeing – Joanna Michal Hoyt

What we believe shapes what we see. Sometimes the stories we tell free us. Sometimes they trap us.

Some people see things their neighbors can't or won't see. Are they inspired? Delusional? Who decides?

As the faithful people of her village cry out for their god's help in disaster, a young peasant woman faces the terrifying possibility that she may be that god.

A time-traveling Jewish refugee visits 21st-century churches and confronts almost unrecognizable versions of himself.

Three troubled people make the dangerous visit to The Library where the maddening stories lodged inside them can be removed—on certain demanding conditions.

Having been warned away from the vacant lot which is said to house a portal to Hell, the new girl in town naturally goes to investigate.

Early in the grid collapse—or apocalypse?—a Christian lesbian farm couple paint "WELCOME" on their barn and await visitors.

An old man in the Terran diaspora enlists in a crusade to save humanity and belatedly wonders if he's on the wrong side.

Step inside these stories and see what you believe—but don't believe everything you see.

Out of the Darkness – edited by Carol Hightshoe

Mental Health issues have long been stigmatized, with those facing them pushed into the shadows, often unable to deal with the darkness they find themselves trapped in.

In this collection, stories explore many types of darkness—Suicidal Ideation, Death from Suicide, Survivor's Guilt, PTSD, Chronic Pain, Chronic Illness, Depression, Death of a Loved One, Secrets, Bullying, and other forms of darkness are explored. Some related to mental health issues and some not, but all of them offer very human perspectives. As in real life, some stories have happy endings and sadly others don't.

We offer these stories of darkness without judgement, but with hope and compassion. Some roads should never have to be traveled—but we understand that for many they are being traveled alone.

Proceeds from sales of Out of the Darkness will be donated to the American Foundation for Suicide Prevention—or more information on AFSP please visit their website at: afsp.org.

Never Cheat a Witch – edited by Carol Hightshoe

Magical curses. Arcane revenge. Being transformed into a frog. Things evil witches do to mere mortals who cross their path. But, what if there is more to the story...

Deals made with a witch are magically binding and can bring dire consequences to those who even think about breaking them.

Whether they are seeking revenge for wrongs done to them, helping others or simply trying to live their lives—it is NEVER wise to try and cheat a witch.

Open your spell book and join our authors as they relate tales of witches and mortals. From classic fantasy witches to modern day witches and even the legendary Baba Yaga. Good and Evil as well as every shade of gray in between.

And, yes—there is a prince who is turned into a frog.

Blood Bride – Belle Blukat

Dr. Bertram Hoel had ignored all women he'd met until being introduced to Cira Landon at his first Science Fiction convention. Knowing he should ignore the attraction, he still takes the dangerous step to begin a relationship, aware that by doing so he is placing her life in peril.

Cira Landon wrote tales of vampire lovers unaware the handsome scientist she'd just met actually was one. Drawn to him, she finds her life threatened by an old enemy who would do anything to exact his revenge, including kidnapping her and selling her on the black market for rare blood types.

With no other options, Dr. Hoel is forced to appeal to the Elders for assistance, hoping rescue does not come too late for Cira and knowing if she is found, there is but one ancient tradition that may save her life.

Return of the Black Witch – M.R. Williamson

One should not expect to slap the hand of an old crone and expect to walk away without at least a limp. The old witch Ethrel Ibenus is up to her tricks again and this time they've turned deadly. But where did her spirit go after Professor Martin shot her with his wee pistol?

Now, all are looking for the crone's familiar, Seleene. But the big timber wolf cannot be found. The search for the spirit of Ibenus now begins in earnest. Will Entwhistle and her Dwarves be able to help? Perhaps the Green Witch Pereen will be able to use a crystal derived from one of the Witch's own spells will do the trick. Fearing failure, Entwhistle improvises a plan 'C', the use of a mythical creature once thought to be long dead.

Time Capsules – edited by Carol Hightshoe

Time Capsules—history and mystery—a gift or a message from the past to the future.

Messages that can easily be misunderstood.

What were the reasons for passing along a pair of pink, fuzzy handcuffs?

A glass vial containing a perfect dandelion puff?

A Japanese Katana?

A red and blue scarf?

A wooden spoon?

What magic do these items contain? What stories do they tell?

From the past to the future. Mysteries and meanings abound within these pages, as well as reminders of the things people find precious. What will you find?

US/THEM – edited by Carol Hightshoe

US/THEM – THEM/US

Fear of the Other breeds hatred of the Other

They aren't like us—so they must be bad...inferior... dangerous...

Humans are by nature social animals, but we tend to bond with other humans with whom we have something in common: beliefs, experiences, likes and dislikes, etc.

With the expansion of humans across the planet, it seems that, even as our numbers grow, we find ways to whittle our groups into ever narrower, specialized, and exclusive blocks. We target the Other for the most minor differences and interpret everything from THEM as an insult or an attack.

Within these pages you will witness hatred, intolerance and fanaticism as well as love, understanding and acceptance. Most of all, I, and the authors, hope you discover stories that will cause you to pause and think before condemning someone as being THEM and not US.

Crunchy with Ketchup – edited by Carol Hightshoe

It has been said that one should never meddle in the affairs of dragons—for you are crunchy and taste good with ketchup.

Come enter the dragon's lair.

Take your chances with other would-be heroes and heroines who decide to face off against one of the biggest, baddest predators ever.

Witness a dragon civil war.

Hear the true story of the Battle of New Orleans.

Find out what it's like in the belly of a dragon.

Discover why cats can spell disaster when stealing a dragon's egg.

Meet a group of dragon riders who protect us from nuclear devastation.

Follow legends of modern dragons, only to find something very unexpected.

And more…

So enter in **BUT** tread carefully—remember you are crunchy and taste good with ketchup.

Crunchy with Chocolate - edited by Carol Hightshoe

It has been said that one should never meddle in the affairs of dragons—for you are crunchy and taste good with chocolate.

Come enter the dragon's lair and roll the dice. Within these pages you will still meet some of the biggest, baddest predators ever—but if you are lucky, you will also discover some that have a sweeter side.

Meet a dragon with a soft spot for hard luck cases and another who is a hopeless romantic.

Enjoy a musical battle between a dragon and the specter of one of the greatest guitarists to ever play.

Meet a dragon in trouble with other magical creatures because he enjoys hanging out with human children.

Join a mother and daughter and their teams of dragons on a dangerous cross-country race.

Reconnect with an imaginary friend—who is not so imaginary and escape the isolation of the pandemic.

And more…

So enter in **BUT** tread carefully—remember you are crunchy and taste good with chocolate.

Time Out – Jamie Mason

After the war, Chris's family fled to Earth. Chris grew up believing he was human. But his parents' unique cruelties soon awaken him to the truth: he and his family are Chronox, alien beings capable of time travel, now hidden among humans.

Dissatisfied with refugee life, Chris's father decides to break the Chronox pact and use time travel to gain dominion over their human hosts. Chris resists, sabotaging his father's efforts to create a working time machine for the military. In punishment, Chris is placed in the ultimate "time out" by being flung back and imprisoned within the pre-digital past of the 1960s. There he experiences a glimmer of acceptance among Laura, Theodore and Yogi Joe, whose friendship inspires him to awaken his repressed Chronox powers and return to the future to set things right.

The battlelines are drawn. On one side, Chris. On the other, an implacable alliance between time-traveling aliens and the U.S. military. A frightened, shattered boy who has never known love must begin a desperate race through time to stop a global genocide.

Bast's Chosen Ones and Other Stories – Dana Bell

Long ago in the land of the flooding Nile and sweeping sands, Bast created warriors called the Chosen Ones. They are her warriors. To them has been given the responsibility of protecting cats, whether on Earth or other worlds. Not always an easy task since often an ancient evil lurks, ready to pounce.

Not all felines walk in the goddess's domain. Some live in the far reaches of space, battling beside their humans or walk in lands long thought legend. Others tell their own version of human stories, walk as envoys of the creator, or appear as ghosts.

These cats walk where others dare not and do not prefer the comfort of cuddly lap warmers. Rather, they wish adventure, in present day, the past, or the far future.

And more – check out our books at
www.wolfsingerpubs.com